S.R. CLARK

Dangerously Safe

McDermott Empire Book One

First edition

Illustration by S.R. Clark
Editing by Dot The i Edit

This book was professionally typeset on Reedsy.
Find out more at reedsy.com

To all the women who want to be thrown up against a wall and be told what a good girl you are... this one's for you.

All the wonders you seek are within
yourself.

Thomas Browne

Preface

Welcome! I'm so glad you're here. Get ready for Harper and her guys as they juggle trying to run the Irish Mafia in New York City and dealing with psychotic family members. This is part one of a duet.

Warning

Content and trigger warnings include: kidnapping, murder, gun violence, explicit sex scenes, group sex scenes, mfmm, degradation, breath play, light bondage, and spanking.
If none of this is for you or if any of this triggers you, please do not continue. You're mental health matters.

PS: If you are related to me in any way, shape, or form, and have found your way here, please rethink your choices, and for the love of all that is holy, do not read this.
Thanks for buying it, though!

1

Ronan

"Fuck," I groan as I grab a fist full of the blond woman's hair on her knees in front of me. I don't know her name and don't need to. I grab the back of her head with my other hand and shove my dick further down her throat. She gags like she hasn't done this a thousand times before to a thousand different men. I know her type. "Fucking take it. Don't you stop." I fuck her face harder, not letting up.

I have the perfect arrangement with women, it's simple really: when I need a stress relief, they relieve the stress. I don't ask them for a relationship; they don't expect one. Telling everyone they know they got to sleep with Ronan Mc-Dermott is usually more than enough. There's no cuddling, no overnight stays, and no talking. Once I fuck their brains out, they simply pack up their shit and leave.

Just how I like it.

She swallows around the head of my dick. I feel my balls tighten and I'm just about to come in her mouth when my brother Cormac—or Mac as everyone calls him—slams the door open. He takes in the scene before him but chooses not to comment.

"Our parents are here."

Shit. The last thing I need is them breathing down my damn neck. When Dad handed over control of the "family business," I thought it meant that he would finally leave us the hell alone.

I was wrong.

If anything, he's been hovering more than ever, and it is starting to drive me certifiably fucking insane.

"What do they want?" I snap, not bothering to pull my dick out of her mouth. After all, it's nothing he hasn't seen before.

"How the hell am I supposed to know? They want to see all three of us in the den. Now." He stares at me deadpan without moving from his spot in the doorway.

"Fine. I'll be there in two minutes. Go get Finn." With a sigh, he gives the blond one last look and walks down the hall toward Finn's room.

Five minutes later, I walk into the den and the woman I just had my dick buried in walks past me and out the front door. I see my parents sitting on the couch and Mac standing and staring out the window with a glass of whiskey in his hand, doing everything in his power to avoid looking at our father. Finn sits anxiously in the armchair next to my parents.

No matter how old we are, Finn's panties get in a bunch whenever Mum and Dad are around. I know it stems from his desire to always stay on their good side, not wanting to become a castaway. When our parents took him in when he was eight, he became one of us. Now and forever. Finn never seems to understand that he is permanently part of this family, that we want him here, and that he doesn't always have to try so damn hard.

Already armed with an attitude, I sit in my usual chair opposite of Finn and wait to hear what I am sure will be a detestable request from my father.

"Who was that?" my mother smiles at me sweetly. Sometimes I don't understand how this incredible woman married the man beside her.

I smile back at her. "It was nobody, Mum. What brings you here today?"

"Oh, so formal. We can't just stop by to catch up with our children?"

Mac, Finn, and I all look at one another, knowing full and well that they both have an agenda. "Mum," Mac drones, hoping to get this show on the road. The less he's around our father, the better.

"I need you boys to take care of something," Dad finally pipes up.

"What do you need?" Finn asks. God, he's always so eager.

Mum sits back on the couch as my dad gets ready to explain. "Do you remember the Hayes', the couple that ran the bank?"

The bank is code for the bookstore, *Hayes' Bookstore*. We use it to hide all of the New York syndicate's money. We, of course, don't trust any bank to keep our shit safe, and keeping that kind of cash in anyone's home is just asking for a robbery and a bullet to the head. The amount of money that sits within the walls of that store is insane. Nobody outside this room knows what the bookstore is, and no one else takes money out or puts money in.

"Yeah, I remember them," Mac states as he stares out the window. "Cece has been running things since Aiden and

Freya died, right?"

"Murdered. They didn't just up and die. They were murdered," Dad snaps through gritted teeth, annoyed that Mac isn't showing him the respect he thinks he deserves by looking at him when he speaks.

"Sorry," Finn apologizes for Mac.

"Anyway," Dad continues, "Cece died of a stroke six months ago and her niece, Aiden and Freya's daughter, has been running things ever since."

We all stare at Dad, waiting for the other shoe to drop. "She has no idea what's hiding behind the walls in the back rooms and believes that she really is just running a bookstore."

"What?" I bite out.

"Aiden and Freya left Ireland shortly after we did and started working for us here. They both pledged their allegiance to me and swore they wanted nothing to do with Freya's dad, Declan, and changed their surname to Hayes to hide from him."

Declan Whelan. The literal bane of our existence. That motherfucker killed Finn's parents, killed Aiden and Freya, and he continue to mess with our shit. He's an asshole of epic proportions who doesn't deserve any of the respect he miraculously has.

"Their daughter, Harper, was thirteen when Aidan and Freya were killed. They never told her who her family was or what the two of them actually did. They wanted to protect her from this life as best they could. The less she knew as a child, the better. When they died, Cece took custody of her and ran the store for us. It was always Cece's plan to tell Harper everything one day, about the bookstore, her parents' murder, but then she died of a stroke and never got the chance."

Mac finally turns around from facing the window and glares at our dad. "How old is she now, twenty-four? Why the hell did Cece wait so long? She's an adult. It's not like she's a child."

"She's twenty-three," Dad states matter-of-factly, "and I think Cece was always scared of blowing up her life. She's already gone through enough." I can't help but roll my eyes at the fact that my father is sitting here acting like he genuinely cares about someone else's life besides his own.

Mac snorts while bringing his glass to his mouth. "Well, her mother is Declan Whelan's daughter, and her parents had an undercover identity and worked for the McDermotts. I think being involved with two major mob families earns her a right to know what the hell is going on."

Mac may act like a hard-ass, but he has a soft spot. He always wants the best for people. In this line of work, it will be his undoing.

Mum sits forward and looks at me. "She does, Cormac, and she's about to find out exactly who she is." Mac purses his lips at the use of his full name. He hates it but lets it slide with Mum. She's the only one allowed to call him that.

Dad follows suit and locks eyes with me. "Declan Whelan found out about Harper and is looking for her. She might not be my daughter, and she might not know any of us exist, but Aiden and Freya were loyal members of this syndicate, and we will look out for her."

"For her or your precious bank?" Mac snarls. Mac loves Finn and I. He'll always do whatever I ask of him, but he's always resented our father for everything he did to him growing up. I've tried to confront our dad countless times, but Mac has stopped me. He knows that Mum knows nothing about it, and it would kill her to know it all happened right under her nose, and she didn't do anything to stop it. Mac's heart wasn't made for this life, not like mine. Me, I love this shit.

"Don't you speak to me like that, Son," Dad snaps as he jumps out of his spot on the couch, "For once, can you just do as you're told?"

I don't miss how Mum cowers back in her seat on the couch as he raises his voice. "We need you three to go get her and bring her here. She needs to be kept here until we know Declan's plan. We don't know who he will send for her or if he will show up himself. She cannot go anywhere without your supervision."

"Absolutely fucking not. I am not a goddamn babysitter." I stand up and come face-to-face with my dad, the great Liam McDermott. I used to bend to his every will. He was larger than life. Now, he just needs to back the hell off and let Finn, Mac, and I do shit our way. "We have enough going on and don't need some girl walking around our apartment and taking up all our time."

Dad doesn't back down. "I don't care what you do or do not want. You will do this." His eyes level with mine. "Am I clear?"

"Consider it done," Finn interrupts, standing from his chair before I can argue further. I know he's trying to prevent a fight between Dad and me. It happens more often than any of us would care to admit.

I glance at Mac, who is back to staring out the window, gripping his now-empty glass so hard it could break. With a not-so-subtle roll of my eyes, I walk to the bar and pour myself a drink. "I'm going to bed, we can come up with a plan in the morning. We will have her here tomorrow night. Goodnight." I give Mum a soft smile before disappearing toward my room, whiskey in hand.

Great, just fucking great.

2

Harper

"Wow," I say to myself as I finish the last page of my most recent book. These are the kinds of endings I live for—happy ones. The type of ending where the girl gets the guy, makes her dreams come true, and discovers who she wants to be in this life. That's what I want. Dreaming of the life I could have is why I get so immersed in books. It doesn't hurt that the main characters in my favorite books have the most incredible, toe-curling sex. The kind of sex I've never had, nor could I imagine myself having. Maybe mediocre sex is all I'm meant for. I hope not.

Books have always been my escape. Before my parents died, they weren't around a lot. There were lots of late nights closing up the store and weekends away at book conferences. When they were gone, I would read and read until my eyes couldn't stay open anymore. I would dream of a life much more exciting than my own. My own happily ever after.

When they died in a car accident when I was thirteen, I was

left in the care of my dad's younger sister, Cece. I genuinely don't know where I would be today without her. She was my best friend.

Cece raised me as if I was her own child. She took over my parents' bookstore, so I would always have part of them, even after they were gone. It was always my dream to take it over one day. I just didn't realize that day would come so soon.

Since Cece's passing six months ago, my world has completely flipped upside down, yet it's stayed exactly the same. After her funeral, I sold her apartment, used the money on repairs this building desperately needed, and saved the rest for a rainy day. The rest of my time has been spent in the store. I wanted to learn everything I could as fast as possible to ensure it was successful. I would not let my parents or Cece down. I can't lose this, too.

I look at the clock hanging on the door: 7:45 PM. Time for me to do my final rounds.

I walk up and down the aisles, picking up books left on the floor and straightening out shelves so they look halfway organized. Once that's finished, I walk through the back rooms to make sure there isn't anyone left reading back here. This part of the store is my favorite. Cece said my dad built these three rooms after he and Mom bought the building. Each of the rooms looks the same. Dark-green walls with a large plum-colored velvet couch sit against the back wall with a dark-mahogany coffee table in the center and are lit only by an ornate table lamp on the end table next to the couch. Each room has its own mini fridge with water, juices, and a coffee machine with all the fixings.

Anyone can use these rooms, whether they buy a book from the store or bring one from home. They are welcome to hang out back here while getting lost inside the pages of a good book. I love it here. The three of us used to spend endless hours hanging out back here during shop hours. I remember Dad reading *The Velveteen Rabbit* while I would rest my head on Mom's lap. She would run her fingers through my curls until I fell asleep. When I remember them, I remember them here.

After standing in the doorway of room three a while longer, I switch off the lamp and head to the front to shut everything down and lock up.

After turning off the computer and throwing on a jacket, I round the front desk as I hear the bell above the door.

"Sorry, I already shut down the computers and I'm about to lock up." Before I can let whoever came in know that we open at ten tomorrow morning, I'm surrounded by three of the most beautiful men I have seen in my entire life.

Hayes' Bookstore is located in Greenwich Village, so all things considered, it's a relatively safe neighborhood. Crime isn't something I often concern myself with. Many people who live around here are more than well-off. Yet, something in their eyes tells me I must be on my toes. These are dangerous men.

The man in front of me is the tallest of the three, easily six-foot-five. His jet-black hair is long and wavy on top, fading toward his neck; a few strands fall across his forehead. He has piercing baby-blue eyes and dark stubble covering his perfectly sculpted jaw.

His broad build is covered in a perfectly tailored, expensive navy-blue suit, sans a tie and top button, and chocolate-brown shoes. He has an intricate tattoo crawling up from underneath his collar and up the side of his neck. When I look down, I see that the backs of his hands and fingers are also covered in tattoos. Several of his fingers are decorated in ornate silver rings, and a couple of silver bracelets stick out from underneath his dress shirt.

"Harper." He knows my name. "You need to come with us." I barely register his words as I make eye contact with the one on my right. Like the man before me, everything about him screams, "I shouldn't be messed with." These two must be related. They look too similar.

Unlike the one in the middle, he looks softer. Not in a physical sense, his body looks hard as stone, but in the way his emotions play across his face. He seems genuinely concerned about how I'm about to react.

His hair is dark like the first one but is longer and more unkempt, like he just ran his fingers through it. He's dressed far more casually than the other two men, wearing black jeans with holes on each knee, black biker boots, and a tight—you guessed it—black Henley shirt. His eyes are almost gray with flecks of blue. He's clean-shaven, making the thin silver hoop in his nose stand out even more. He stands a couple of inches shorter than what I'm assuming is his brother and isn't quite as broad.

Hold up, did they just say I need to come with them?

"Who are you? You need to leave," I finally manage to speak.

The first man glares at me, looking frustrated. "Don't worry about it. We can't talk about it here. Once you're safe in our apartment, we can explain everything."

Don't worry about it?! "What are you talking about? I am not going anywhere with the three of you. You need to leave, or I will call the police." As I reach for my purse to pull out my phone, a firm hand grips my left arm, and I am rendered utterly speechless at how his skin feels against mine. How can three men, who are clearly threatening, have this effect on me?

The third guy is, like, model-worthy perfection. He looks about the same height as the first one but more slender. His honey-blond hair is slicked back, out of the way of stunning caramel eyes. The beard that covers his face is well-groomed and beyond sexy. His black suit sits over a crisp white shirt and black tie. It doesn't look like there's a hair out of place, but when I look into his eyes, I can see the chaos brewing beneath his perfectly tailored exterior. "Don't call the police. We can assure you that won't be necessary."

For three people who are trying to get me to go with them, they aren't providing much information.

"Please, Harper, just do as we say," the one on my right softly says. His deep voice, paired with his faint Irish accent, soothes my frayed nerves.

Just do as we say.

They aren't leaving here without getting what they came for. *Me.*

I don't know if it's because I'm having a stroke or genuinely scared of what they might do if I say no, because, without another word, I take my hand out of my purse, step around the man in front of me and walk out the front door. As I turn around to lock the door, the biggest one pulls a key out of his suit pocket and locks it for me.

What the hell?

I'm definitely stroking out because I don't even question it. I simply turn on my heels and walk toward the black SUV that I'd be willing to bet my life savings on is theirs. Sure as shit, one of the men opens the back passenger side door, and

I climb in.

"What the hell, Harp," I mutter under my breath.

3

Finn

Shit. I can already tell that Harper will be a severe problem for me. I knew the second I saw her when we walked through that door.

That's the cheesiest shit I have ever thought in my life.

Ronan drives us back to the apartment while Mac sits quietly in the front seat. I know he's worried about whether or not Harper is freaking out. Of course, I'm in the back seat sitting next to her. I should have called shotgun. My dick can't handle being this close to her. Harper's staring out the window, hands in her lap, silently picking at her fingernails and chewing her lip. God, I'd like to bite that lip.

Chill the hell out, Finn.

I can't seem to pull my eyes away from her. I'm not even being subtle about it. Her thick and unruly cocoa-brown hair falls past her shoulders and reaches what I'm sure are her perfect breasts. She has her black-rimmed reading glasses pulled into her hair, giving me an unobstructed view of her face. *That beautiful face.* She has the greenest eyes I have ever seen in my life, like the color of the rarest emerald, and the bridge of her nose and cheeks are the perfect shade of pink, covered in a light dusting of freckles.

She's not the type of woman we are usually drawn toward—fake, plastic, and dumb enough not to ask too many questions. No, Harper has curves in all of the right places. Her curvy frame looks like something I want to sink my teeth into. My eyes gaze over her long legs, tucked into a pair of skintight jeans with holes in all the right places. She has a pair of boots with a small heel that makes her legs look like absolute fucking perfection. Just looking at her sitting in this car makes my cock strain against my zipper.

Not fucking good.

We were completely prepared to drag Harper out of the bookstore, kicking and screaming, but much to our surprise, she left without much of an argument and climbed right into the car. I don't know if it's because she is naïve and unaware of all the dangers of the world or if she has a more adventurous side than meets the eye. Something tells me it's a bit of both.

Ronan pulls into the parking garage of our building and drives to the lowest level. When Liam and Emma bought this apartment they also bought out a whole level of the parking garage and had a security gate installed. No one is allowed down here but us and those we approve of in advance.

Once Ronan parks the car, Mac climbs out and opens Harper's door, holding out his hand. "Come on, Harper."

"Where are we?"

Ronan answers without looking at her, "Our apartment."

"Why am I here?"

"Jesus, would you stop asking questions and get the hell

upstairs? We will explain everything once we're inside," Ronan snaps.

With Mac's hand still stretched toward Harper, she reluctantly grabs it and climbs out of the car. The four of us load into the elevator as Ronan swipes his keycard, allowing the elevator to take us to the penthouse. Much like the car ride here, the elevator is plagued with silence.

I'm standing directly behind her and find myself bending forward slightly to smell her hair. I don't have to bend far, though, as she's easily five-foot-ten. I inhale her vanilla and caramel shampoo. *Of course, she smells delicious.*

Finally, the ding of the elevator lets me know we've reached the penthouse, and I snap out of it.

The door opens and Ronan immediately storms toward the direction of the bar because he's an asshole, and Mac gives her a sympathetic look before following his brother. Last man standing, I guess. I gesture at her to follow me. "Come on Harper. I'll show you around and then we can talk about what's going on."

She looks at me deadpan.

I sigh and run my hand across my beard. "Harper. Come on."

She still isn't moving. I see it in her eyes; the shock of three men coming into her place of employment and practically abducting her is finally setting in. I don't want to have to grab her and drag her out of the elevator. It's just going to frighten her more. Not only that, but I don't know if I can handle touching her … at least not yet. After another minute, she finally exits the elevator and follows me down the hallway.

Our apartment is large. I wouldn't even classify it as an apartment. It's bigger than most homes and takes up the whole top floor of this building. There are floor-to-ceiling windows all the way around. It's a bachelor pad if I've ever seen one. The walls in the main living area are painted a deep gray that extends over the ceiling. A sizable caramel-brown leather couch sits in the den, two black suede armchairs on either side, and a huge plasma screen TV hangs above the fireplace. The place is almost entirely void of personal touches but has a fully stocked bar, of course.

I show Harper around the main living space as she silently follows behind. I'm not entirely sure she's listening to anything I'm saying.

I lead her down the hallway past our bedrooms and push open the door to the guest room at the end. Mac was in here all afternoon, ensuring it had everything she might need.

"This is where you'll be staying," I tell her as she stands in the hallway. Instead of walking through the door, she takes a step backward.

"I'm staying here?"

That finally got her attention. "Yes, Harper." I don't offer any more information, and she has no other questions. Realizing she isn't going to walk into the room, I motion for her to follow me back out to the living room.

Ronan and Mac sit in the armchairs, each with a glass of whiskey in hand, leaving me to sit on the couch next to her, again. Her cheeks are still flushed, whether from being hot or in shock, I'm not sure. I look at her. "Do you want to take your jacket off? You look warm."

"Oh, um, sure." As she peels her jacket off, her shirt lifts slightly, and I can see the pale skin across her stomach. I can't help but picture what that would feel like underneath my hands.

Stop it, Finn.

I grab her jacket and drape it over the arm of the couch. Ronan clears his throat. "Harper, do you know who we are? Do you know why we're here?"

She looks at the three of us like we're the dumbest bunch she's ever met. "No, I don't have a single clue who the hell any of you are. If you don't tell me what's going on in the next five minutes, I'm grabbing my shit, and I'm walking out that door," she says abruptly, the bravado she had in the bookstore back in her voice. Glad to know she knows how to stand up for herself. We're used to people, women especially, being afraid of us. This is a nice change of pace.

Not sure Ronan would agree, though.

4

Harper

Why am I not running from here, kicking and screaming? Why am I not asking more questions? Why am I not scared of them? What the hell is wrong with me?

What could be worse than what I have already gone through? Without warning, my parents died the same day, and my aunt had a stroke right in front of me. I have lost everyone important in my life. I have no more family and no friends—I am alone. If I go out, at least it will be at the hands of three of the most beautiful men I have ever seen.

Sure, they came in and took me in the night, but something in my gut was screaming at me that even though they are dangerous, I should trust them.

I finally snap out of my internal dialogue when one of them asks, "Harper, do you know who we are? Do you know why we're here?" I may not be afraid, but I don't have the patience for this shit. Either they tell me what's going on, or I'm leaving.

I have my own life to get back to, as bleak and boring as it may be. "No, I don't have a single clue who the hell any of you are. If you don't tell me what's going on in the next five minutes, I'm grabbing my shit and walking out that door."

The largest one glares at me. "You're not going anywhere." I can feel his icy-blue eyes peering into my soul. His accent is the same as the other two, just faint enough to notice it's there, but it does nothing to calm my nerves. His voice is rough and harsh. I assume it's from years of yelling at people like a dick.

"That's Ronan. He's an asshole," says the one sitting in the opposite chair, resting his elbows on his knees and staring into his empty glass between his hands. He finally looks up and offers me a genuine smile. "I'm Cormac. Everyone calls me Mac, and that"—he smirks, pointing his thumb at the one next to me—"is Finn. We aren't going to hurt you. Our job is to keep you safe, but we have a lot we need to cover. Okay?"

"Alright," I whisper.

Mac looks at Ronan. "Was that so hard? Why don't you try not being a dick."

Ronan rolls his eyes before directing his attention back to me. "Have you heard of the McDermott's?"

Shit.

Have I heard of them? Duh. Everyone in the city knows who the McDermott's are—the *Irish mafia.* Maybe if I play dumb, they'll divulge more information than I already know. I shake my head.

He sits up proud as a peacock. "Well, you're looking at the guy's charge."

Double shit.

"Our parents 'retired,'" he says in air quotes, "three years ago, and we've been running things ever since."

"What does that have to do with me?" I glance over at Finn sitting next to me, his suit jacket and tie are off, and he's leaning back in his seat. I gaze down his arms, and his white shirt is now rolled up to his elbows. His forearms are covered in tattoos but stop just at his wrists, carefully placed to not show past his dress shirts.

I feel a rush of heat between my thighs. Is there anything hotter than a man with his sleeves rolled?

Focus, Harp.

Ronan continues, "Your parents, Freya and Aidan." I nod even though he clearly isn't asking me a question. "Yeah, their real name isn't Hayes." My eyes go wide, and I can feel a bead of sweat drip down the back of my neck. "Your dad's last name is McGrath, and your mom's maiden name is Whelan." As he says the name, Whelan, I notice Finn tense up next to me.

"What are you talking about?"

"Aidan worked for our family. He has worked for us for as long as we can remember. Dad considered him part of the family. He was a loyal member of the New York Syndicate. He met your mom, Freya, in Ireland. She's a Whelan. Do you know what that means?"

I stare at him, trying to process all the information he's giving me.

"The Whelan Syndicate are our rivals. They're run by an evil bastard. I mean, we aren't angels, but that bastard takes it to another level." Finn abruptly stands, walks to the other side of the room, and begins pacing.

"Ronan," Mac snaps. "Move on."

"Anyway, from what we know, it was your classic forbidden

lovers' situation. Your mom fell in love with your dad. But, because your dad worked for my family, your grandfather, Declan, forbid it." Am I in a movie? What is even happening? "Declan repeatedly threatened them both, and your mother had finally had enough. Declan said if she betrayed her family, he would kill her. Point blank. End of discussion."

"Aidan confided in my dad, and they made a plan. Freya and Aidan moved to New York, changed their last name, and covered every track they could think of. Freya Whelan and Aidan McGrath ceased to exist. They bought the bookstore and had you."

I'm having trouble breathing. I can feel the impending panic attack rapidly approaching. Mac must notice. "Harper, do you need something to drink?" Before I can even nod my head, he's on his feet. "Stay right there, I'll get it." Once he returns from the kitchen, he takes Finn's seat next to me, hands me a glass of water, and puts his hand on my knee.

The minute his fingers touch the skin through the hole in my jeans, I begin breathing heavily for a whole different reason. His gray eyes meet mine, and I force myself to look away. He is captivating.

I look back at Ronan, and he's just sitting there like he hasn't dropped a bomb on my life.

"There's more," he says with an annoying little smirk. Yeah, he's not going to be my favorite.

"More?"

"The bookstore isn't just a bookstore. The back rooms have fake walls, and we store all our family's cash there. We use a key to come and go after hours to deposit and withdraw cash. Your parents ran the bookstore as a front for our family. How do you think they afforded that swanky townhouse in

Greenwich you grew up in?"

"And, before you ask, Cece knew all about it." Tears begin to well in my eyes as I realize the three people I loved most in this world lied to me my whole life. My sanctuary, my safe place, my parents' legacy to me—it's all a lie.

"Harper," Mac says with a sigh, "they were trying to keep you safe. The less you knew, the safer you were. If Declan Whelan finds you, he will kill you; he doesn't tolerate betrayal. Your parents' car accident wasn't an accident. He found them somehow. He sent one of his men to the States. They cut the breaks on their car."

The last ounce of restraint I had disappears, and tears stream down my cheeks. "He killed his daughter?"

"Yes!" Finn barks across the room, causing me to jump. "Fucking cunt. He and his goons can rot in hell."

Ronan takes another long drink of his whiskey. "Cece was supposed to tell you everything in time, but she must have been scared, too. She probably didn't want to fuck up your life even more. Then, she died and never got the chance."

"So what, you brought me here to make sure I keep up this lie? Or what? You'll kill me? What if I don't want to do it? What if I just leave? What if—"

"Harper . . ." The way Mac says my name does something to me. I instantly feel calmer. He moves his hand from my knee and wipes a tear from my cheek. "Sweetheart, you need to relax. We aren't here to hurt you. We want to protect you, but you need to breathe." He continues to run the pad of his thumb across my cheek.

After a few minutes, I finally get my breathing under control, and Ronan continues. "Declan didn't know you existed. When he murdered Freya and Aidan, he thought that was that. Somehow he found out about you. Word is he's coming for you."

"Well, that sounds ominous." I halfheartedly chuckle.

A small smile tugs at Ronan's lips. "Yeah, I'd say so. At the request of our dad, we brought you here to keep you safe." Just like that, his smile is gone. "Until we find out when and who is coming for you, you'll stay here. We are officially your live-in babysitters."

"Ronan, can you not act like a complete dick about it." Finn finally takes a seat in the armchair. "Liam and Emma want her safe, so that's what she will be."

Why didn't he call them Mom and Dad?

"We have more important things going on. But, I guess if it keeps the bank running"—his eyes find mine—"then I'll make due. Just stay out of our way, and don't leave the apartment without our say-so."

With that, he stands up and walks down the hallway. Storytime is over? Yeah, he's my least favorite—such an attitude.

Finn stands up from his chair, grabs his suit jacket and tie, gently draping them over his forearm, and looks down at me. "I know this was a lot of information at once. We can talk more in the morning. Any questions you have, we'll answer." He smiles. "Well, maybe not Ronan but Mac and I will." He turns on his heels and heads into the room at the front of the hall.

Questions. Of course, I have questions. You just told me my parents are members of the mob, I have an evil grandfather who killed his own daughter, and my favorite place on earth— my safe place—is a stash house for the Irish Mafia. Shit, more tears. Mac stands up and holds out his hand. "Come on. Let's go to your room." I look up at him with a pinched expression. I know damn well he isn't trying to make a move on me.

But would I mind? I'm not so sure.

"I'll *take* you to your room, and then I'll go to mine," he corrects, even though it sounds as if he's not sure that's what he wants to do.

I grab his hand and stand toe to toe with him. He leans down and whispers in my ear, "You're safe, Harper Hayes. I promise."

Safe.

After everything they just told me, I'm unsure of so many things, but I seem to be sure of one thing: with these three, that's exactly what I am—*Safe.*

5

Mac

I can't let it go. The image of what Harper's perfect, naked body would look like underneath mine hasn't left my brain since I left her alone hours ago. It's nearly 3:00 AM, and I can't rest.

Against my better judgment, I walked Harper to her room, wanting to keep my eyes on her as long as possible. Instead of stopping at the door and letting her explore the guest room for herself, I followed her inside.

I watched as she ran her fingers along the white satin bedspread, and I instantly imagined the noises I could get her to make while sprawled out over the sheets. My breath hitched when her eyes went wide as she spotted the soaking tub in the bathroom.

What I would do to see her flawless skin in that damn tub covered in bubbles.

I've been with my fair share of women. I'm fully aware of the effect I have on them. Something about a tattoo-covered mafia man screams, "Come, fuck me." And to be honest, I'm not complaining.

I love a quick lay as much as the next guy, but it has never really done it for me. I've always wanted something *more.* That being said, in our line of work, a long-term relationship isn't really in the cards.

However, there's something about Harper. Everything about her screams absolute and utter perfection. Her innocence and how she seems utterly oblivious to the evil that has surrounded her for her entire life. Not to mention I don't think I could have dreamt up a more beautiful woman if I tried. The way her body curves in all of the right places, her unruly curls, and her forest green eyes I could get lost in.

My cock immediately stirs under the sheets as I imagine Harper on her knees in front of me, looking up at me with those eyes, a fistful of hair in my hand, and those perfect lips wrapped around my … *fuck.* I need to get a fucking grip.

Unable to take it anymore, I walk into my bathroom and turn the shower on. After standing under the stream for what seems like an hour, I manage to relax enough to the point where I feel like I'll be able to sleep. Except when I crawl into bed, the only thing I see every time I close my eyes is the face of the woman down the hall.

* * *

I open my eyes to see the morning sun peeking through my shades. Fully aware I only slept three hours, I force myself to get out of bed. I can't sleep in. I need to see her. I know she'll have questions, and I want to be the one to answer them. I throw on a pair of gray sweatpants and make my way out to the kitchen. When I reach the end of the hallway, I find Harper wide awake—as suspected—rummaging around the kitchen. I'm sure she hardly slept, if at all. I know I wouldn't have if I were her.

She's wearing only an oversized T-shirt, barely reaching past the curve of her deliciously thick ass. Good to know she isn't overly shy about her body. I ensured her room had plenty of those and several sleep sets before we brought her here, not knowing what she preferred to sleep in. I just didn't count on her being so tall.

I stand at the end of the hallway for a few minutes, just watching. I know she hasn't spotted me yet, and I can't seem to make my feet move. She. Is. Captivating.

Harper opens a cupboard next to the stove and seems to find what she's looking for. As she reaches up to grab the coffee grounds, I notice the bottom of her ass poking out from underneath her shirt. *Fuck. Me.*

Once she manages to figure out the coffee machine, she walks around the kitchen island and sits on one of the stools.

Here goes nothing. I clear my throat and move toward her. "Good morning. Couldn't sleep?"

Her sleepy eyes meet mine but widen once she notices I don't have a shirt on. She eyes my chest briefly before forcing them back up to my face. "No. Can you blame me?"

"Honestly, I'm a little surprised you're still here."

"Trust me, I thought about it. But then I thought … why?" She shrugs her shoulders. "You guys didn't lock me in my room like some princess in a tower; for some reason, I feel safe here."

Safe. That one word brings a smile to my face. It isn't very often that we get to make people feel safe, me especially. "I'm glad you feel safe here."

"Hmmm." Her soft smile knocks me square in the chest. "Something tells me you aren't as bad as you make yourself out to be."

Oh, how wrong you are, Princess.

Before I can stop myself, I'm behind her, leaning down with my mouth an inch away from her ear. "Let's get a few things straight." I hear her take a deep breath. "One: you are most definitely a princess. Two: we are not good men. We won't hesitate to kill anyone who tries to get what's ours." I stand up straight, walk around the island, pull out two mugs, and fill them with coffee. I hand her a cup and she finally lets go of the breath she's been holding in.

Without looking up from her cup, she says so softly I hardly hear her, "What's the third thing?"

Reaching across the counter, I cup her chin in my hand, forcing her eyes to meet mine. "You, Princess, are ours."

With that, I walk back toward my room to prepare for what I'm sure will be the longest day of my life.

6

Harper

What just happened? Did he just say that to me? I must have been entranced by that deliciously tattooed chest or how his breath felt against my neck because there's no way I heard him correctly.

Princess.

Ours.

It's been ten minutes, and I haven't moved an inch, let alone drank my now lukewarm coffee, yet somehow I'm sweating. How am I theirs? I don't even know them, but they seem to know me.

The wetness between my legs tells me I *want* to be theirs—or maybe just Mac's. Nope. Definitely *theirs.* I felt it last night in the bookstore, then again in the elevator, and when we sat in the living room while they told me how my entire life was a sham.

Why do I find the three of them so irresistible? No. Nope. Not happening, Harper. Get a grip.

I need to find out more about my family. My real family. I need to know who Declan is sending for me. These men can help me. The sooner this is taken care of, the sooner I can return to my life.

My life includes a bookstore that is a front for the Irish mafia.

My life has no one in it but myself.

My life is nothing but disappointment and loneliness. I spend my days reading and imagining a life I can never have. Is the life I thought I had worth going back to?

* * *

When I finally snap out of it and finish my much-needed, albeit cold, cup of coffee, I spin around on my stool and look at the apartment around me. Every single thing in here screams *men.*

The walls are dark, the furniture is dark, the kitchen is dark, and even the lighting is a moody yellow instead of bright white. The dark-mahogany beams that spread the length of the ceiling nicely match the fully stocked bar in the corner of the den.

The only brightly colored room I've seen is mine. It looks nothing like the rest of the apartment and has me wondering if they decorated it just for me. That would be silly, right?

Its cream-colored walls surround a large cast iron bed frame. It's the most enormous bed I've ever slept on by a long shot. The white satin sheets felt like heaven against my skin. Several small plants are scattered throughout the room, and black picture frames housed black-and-white photos of different beaches. While the space is beautiful and incredibly relaxing, it almost feels fake. It feels like what they *thought* I would enjoy. Not that I can blame them. They don't know me.

There aren't any family photos in the rest of the apartment except two small images hanging on the side of the fridge. It's an older-looking woman. She isn't old enough to be a grandparent, so I assume that's their mom. She has long, gorgeous black hair with piercing blue eyes, the color of the deepest ocean blue. Her smile is a mile wide and between two perfectly placed dimples. I see where Ronan and Mac get their good looks from. I wonder why Finn doesn't look anything like them. Maybe he's adopted?

The other photo is of a younger couple in front of a cafe downtown. The man has perfect dirty blond hair, while hers is a stunning shade of gold, the kind women pay hundreds of dollars for. They're laughing at each other over the brim of their mugs. They look so in love. I make a mental note to find out more information about him later. I have to be careful not to ask too many questions. They say they're here to protect me.

Curiosity did kill the cat ... or so they say.

After a while, nobody else comes out to join me, so I make my way back to my room to shower. I usually shower before bed, but all I wanted to do last night was curl up under the covers—sleep or no sleep.

Walking past the room closest to mine, I hear a strange noise. I should walk away; it's none of my business. But, my curiosity trumps my common sense, like always.

The door is slightly open, and I peek through the crack.

My brain takes a second to catch up to my eyes, and I finally piece together what I'm seeing. Through the bedroom, I see directly into the open bathroom and find Ronan in the shower. I'm sure he wasn't expecting his snooping house guest to be staring at him.

Jokes on him.

My jaw goes slack as I scan his body. It's just … he's just … wow. Mac's upper body is covered in tattoos, but it's nothing compared to Ronan's. There is something so dark yet inviting about the artwork that covers their skin. Ink covers his arms and torso from his fingertips to his neck. The entirety of one leg is filled with an intricate design, and it seems as if he has only just started with the other one.

His hand lands on the steamy glass of the shower door, and a low noise escapes his lips. Just now, I notice his other hand is firmly wrapped around his dick. It's easily the biggest one I've seen in my life. I mean, I only have a few to compare it to but still. *What that would feel like.*

Ronan strokes himself eagerly from root to tip, and I can feel the warmth stirring inside me.

As he begins pumping faster, I find myself firmly planted against the door frame. I should walk away. I should let him finish in privacy … but I can't. I want to see the face he makes as he finds his release.

Before I can argue with myself any longer, his eyes snap open and meet mine. Instead of stopping, he begins to move even faster. His mouth hangs open as his gaze holds mine across the room. The entire scene makes my pussy throb, and I pinch my thighs together to relieve the pressure. I'm dying to slide my hand down my wet panties, but I stay still.

His eyes still locked with mine, Ronan's face curls as he

comes all over the glass with a roar.

He stands up straight and removes his hand from the glass. With that, my breath comes out in a quick exhale, and I realize what just happened. I just watched Ronan masturbate. *Oh. My. God.* I back away from the door and make a mad dash to my room.

I close my door *all the way* and lock it. I don't want him storming in here. He's going to be so pissed off. He specifically told me to stay out of his way.

"That was so stupid, Harp," I snap at myself.

But he *saw* me, and he *didn't* stop. If anything, it only got him more excited.

Ahh! What the hell am I supposed to do now?!

7

Harper

An hour later, after a *cold* shower, I can't take it anymore. I don't want to leave this room and run into Ronan, but I have questions. I wasn't afraid last night, and I sure as shit will not start being afraid of them now.

I pull on the outfit I came here in, take a deep breath, and open my door. I hear the three of them talking in the kitchen. Mac is sitting on the stool he found me on this morning, Finn in the spot next to him, and Ronan leans against the counter on the other side of the kitchen.

My god, do they look delicious.

Finn looks as put together as last night, sporting a navy-blue suit with a black shirt and shoes. He isn't wearing a tie today and has the top button of his shirt undone. I can see part of a phrase tattooed across his chest.

I wonder what it says?

I quickly look Mac up and down. He's changed from

his gray sweatpants and is dressed far more casually than Finn. He's barefoot and wearing light-wash jeans that look like they hug his thighs in all the right places. Much to my disappointment, he has a shirt on now. His slate-gray Henley has the sleeves rolled up, and I can see the artwork I got a show of this morning.

I couldn't tell you exactly what the hell Ronan is wearing because I'm afraid to look at him. Honestly, I'm scared to even be near him. I know they said I'd be safe here, but that was before he caught me spying on him masturbating in the shower not more than an hour ago.

Did he tell Finn and Mac?

God, they've killed people. I know it. What are they going to do to me?

I sit on the edge of the third stool along the island, ready to jump up at a moment's notice, but I'm not going anywhere until they make me. I have questions, and they have answers. Finn speaks first, "Good morning, Harper. How are you this morning?"

"Umm, I'm alright. Thank you." I can see Mac smiling on the other side of Finn.

A low chuckle sounds from the other side of the kitchen. The three of us look at Ronan.

"What?" Asks Mac.

"Oh, nothing, just thought of something funny."

God, he's a dick. I'm assuming that means he hasn't said a word.

Now that I'm looking at him, I can confirm he looks just as delectable as the two men next to me. His curly black hair matches his perfectly tailored dress pants, and his white dress shirt is open at the top with the sleeves rolled up to his elbows.

He has to be the sexiest mafia boss I've ever seen.

Okay, he's the only one, but that's beside the point.

One of them must have run out and got doughnuts while I was in the shower because two dozen of them sit in boxes in front of me, and Ronan is holding a chocolate-glazed one in his hands. I can see the delicious-looking chocolate coating the tips of his fingers. The same fingers I saw wrapped around his cock.

I wish I could walk over there and lick that chocolate right off.

What is happening to me? I adjust myself in my chair as Finn abruptly states, "So, what are your questions? We know you must have some."

"Yes, umm . . ." I begin fidgeting with the hem of my shirt. "How long do I have to stay here?"

"Until we say you can leave." Ronan looks at me deadpan.

Wow, so helpful. Not. "Okay, well, what about the bookstore? I have to go to work." He continues to stare at me, but now it's more of a "Are you stupid?" look. "I know the actual store must not be important to you, but it is to me. Plus, don't you need your precious bank?" I snap with an attitude.

Ronan pushes himself off the counter across the kitchen and stalks toward me. He stops at the end of the island next to me and grips the edge of it so tight his knuckles turn white.

Here it goes; he's about to chew my ass for this morning. Now I've gone and given him an attitude. Nice knowing you, world. I'll miss you when I'm gone.

Instead, he simply says, "We don't need you at the bank. We all have keys, remember? We can come and go whenever we please. You've never seen us there before, have you?"

I don't say anything because I know he's right. I've never

seen a single one of them come or go. So instead, I just sit there and look at him. "Exactly." He stands up straight and looks at Liam and Mac.

"I don't have time for this shit. I have other things to take care of. You two can explain this to her. Make sure she doesn't leave the apartment." With that, he walks to the other side of the apartment and into what I assume is his office.

Mac continues to sit there and smirk at me. Okay, now I'm starting to get annoyed. Someone better explain the plan to me. Right. Now. I feel my cheeks flush. "He didn't answer my question. What am I supposed to do about the bookstore? It's an actual business; I'm the owner and only employee. It's my parent's legacy, and I'm not losing it, too. No matter how fake it was." Tears begin forming in my eyes again. *Damn it, Harper. Don't cry. You're supposed to be annoyed.*

Mac's smile fades as he looks at me. "Princess." Finn looks at him inquisitively but doesn't say anything. I'm sure he's wondering why Mac just called me that. "It isn't safe for you at the store. If Declan figured out you exist, it won't take long for him to figure out you still work at the bookstore. There's no security there. Anyone can walk in." I know he's right. "You're parents and Cece spent years building that store and making sure the secrets hidden in the back room stayed secrets. We can't jeopardize it."

And there it is. They care more about their money than they do me. Then again, why wouldn't they? They don't even know me.

Nobody knows me. I'm entirely alone. I better get used to it.

Finn looks at me empathetically and stands. "For now, it will have to stay closed. We will have men looking after the store 24/7. Nobody will mess with it. As far as money is concerned, we will take care of all of the bills and make up for the difference in revenue, and *you* will not have to spend a dime while you are here."

"How long will that be exactly?" I say with a shaky breath, feeling defeated that the place I care about most is being ripped out from under me.

"We hope not long. But we have to figure out what Whelan's plan is. Until then, stay put." His tone instantly goes sharp. "I will be out most of the day, but Mac will return in a few hours."

"Then I'm all yours." Mac looks at me with a sly smirk on his face.

They gather their things and shoot me one last look before entering the elevator. Before the door slides closed, Mac speaks, "Ronan is in his office if you need anything. Behave, Princess."

Behave, Princess.

The way those two words roll off of his lips causes a shiver to run straight up my spine.

8

Ronan

I hear Mac mutter, "Behave, Princess," through my office door before the elevator closes. Great, now I'm stuck with her until one of them comes back.

I know I've said it twenty times already, but I really don't have time for this shit. I need to prepare for a delivery at the docks tonight. The last thing I need is to lose focus. We've had some low-lives trying to move in on us. Somehow, they keep getting their hands on our delivery information, and I can't seem to find the leak. When I do, though, I won't hesitate to make them wish they were never fucking born.

On top of that, I can't stop thinking about this morning in the shower. I didn't tell Mac or Finn what happened. For some reason, I wanted to keep that to myself.

I knew I should have stopped when I saw her staring at me through the glass. I should have climbed out of the shower and put her in her place. But as soon as I saw those forest-green eyes staring into mine, I couldn't help myself.

She was the reason I was jerking off in the shower anyway.

But those curves. I can just imagine what she would look like spread out on my desk. The way my fingers would bruise her hips as I slammed into her. The way those thighs would feel squeezing my face.

Fucking, fuck. Fuck.

I don't have the patience for her. She's beyond naive and belongs nowhere near this world. And I certainly don't have the patience for needing to jerk off over my new roommate like a horny fucking teenager.

There must have been a ringing in her ear because the next thing I know, I hear a knock at the door. I quickly pull the chair closer to my desk so she can't see my impossibly hard dick pushing against my zipper.

"What?" I snap.

She pushes the door open just a crack. "Can I come in for a minute?"

"What do you need, Harper? Mac will be back soon, and I don't have time to keep explaining things to you." God, I'm such an asshole.

"If I'm such a burden, why did you even bring me here?" she asks as she pushes the door open all the way and stalks toward my desk. She isn't sitting, just standing in front of me, hands on her thick hips, trying to intimidate me.

Good luck, Baby. Bigger men than you have tried and failed.

I grind my molars before I speak. "Because my parents asked me to."

She parts her lips ever so slightly and takes a deep breath. My eyes lower, and I watch her chest move up and down with her breath. I feel my dick twitch in my pants. I lean forward and rest my forearms against my desk. "Is there something else you wanted to talk about, Harper?"

"I … I'm … I'm sorry about this morning. I didn't mean to. I just heard a noise and wanted to make sure nobody was getting hurt."

"I was most definitely not getting hurt," I reply with a smug-ass smile.

Her cheeks and chest immediately flush. "Obviously not. But I shouldn't have stood there. So, I apologize."

"Why did you? Stand there, that is. Did you like what you saw?" *Because I sure as shit did.*

She doesn't answer. She just stares at me with those big green eyes. See, naive. She can't even handle this conversation. After a minute, I sigh and lean back in my chair, annoyed. "If that's all, Harper, I have work to do."

She spins around and walks toward the office door. I turn back toward my laptop and see her stop out of the corner of my eye. "Actually, I'm going to go back to my apartment before Mac gets back. I need to get clothes and some of my things if you three are going to continue to hold me hostage." There's that attitude again.

"The fuck you are. You will stay in this apartment unless one of us is with you, and I don't have time to take you back there right now. Mac can go with you when he gets back."

"I don't need one of you to go with me. I'm just going back to my apartment. I'll be in and out and back here to annoy you before you even notice I'm gone. I doubt Whelan even knows where I live. If he did, he would have come for me already."

"Harper," I snap as I stand up from my desk. She now has a front-row seat to my straining erection. *Why won't it go the hell away?* "You will *not* leave this apartment. You *will* stay here for as long as I say. And you *will* do as you are told." I round the desk and walk toward her as she cowers against the wall next to the door.

"Do not test my patience, Baby. You won't like the consequences."

I watch her resolve harden and force myself to hold back a smile as she stands taller in front of me. It would be a sight to behold if she wasn't so damn infuriating. "You are not in charge of me. I am a grown woman and can take care of myself. You're lucky I'm even staying in this damn apartment!"

Before I know it, I'm standing so close I can feel her tits against my chest. I wrap my hand around her throat and push her back against the wall. I bend down so my lips brush her ear. "You think just because you saw me come, you can talk to me however you want? You can do whatever you want? News flash, Baby"—I push my hips against her, leaving not an inch of space between us—"you are *ours* now." Slowly, I move my mouth to the front of her face. I'm grazing her lips with mine, and I can feel her breathing stop. I tighten my grip around her throat. "Which means I will not hesitate to punish you for disobeying me."

Harper's eyes close, and she lets out the breath she was holding. I genuinely can't tell if she's more scared or turned on. I hope, for both our sakes, she's afraid of me.

She should be.

Slowly, she opens her eyes and looks up at me. Our lips are still slightly touching but not kissing. I know she can feel my hard cock pushing against her stomach, but she doesn't acknowledge it. Instead, she whispers, "Is that all?"

Is that all? Is that fucking all? No, that's not all. Not even close.

For some reason I cannot understand, all I want to do is pick her up and bend her over my desk. I want to fuck her so hard that she screams my name. I want her to know who's in charge.

But I can't.

The last thing I need is to be screwing a girl I live with, especially a girl my dad asked us to keep safe. I am the exact opposite of safe. Plus, something shady is going on with him. Never in my life have I known him to want to protect anyone. Let alone go to these lengths. I know he has an ulterior motive, and I will figure it out. He may be my dad, but I don't fucking trust him.

So, I lower my hand and take a few steps back instead of doing what I want. "That's all, Harper."

She side-steps out the door, and I slam it closed behind her. Sitting back in my chair, I notice my dick is still hard. Painfully hard.

9

Harper

I storm out of Ronan's office toward my room. My skin feels like it's on fire. "Who the hell does he think he is?" I shout as I slam my door closed. I flop down on my bed and stare up at the ceiling, willing myself to calm down.

There that word was again, *ours.*

Mac said it to me this morning, and it elicited the same response when Ronan said it.

"I can't be theirs. I'm safer when I'm no one's. When I'm alone," I whisper.

For the life of me, I can't figure out why I'm so attracted to the three of them. Sure, maybe it's the tattoos. Or the muscles. Or the designer suits. Or the hair I'd like to run my fingers through. Or the perfectly luscious lips I'd love to bite. Or the . . .

Well, I guess I do know why.

The way Ronan felt against me was practically heaven. I felt his cock against me. His *hard* cock, at that. I know what that cock looks like. I saw it first-hand this morning, and it took every ounce of self-restraint not to reach down and grab it.

It's been so, so long.

The way his hand felt around my throat, his lips against my ear, then my neck. It was simply sinful. I didn't want any of it to end. Did I turn him on? Or was he just trying to threaten me?

I know which one I hope it was. I wanted him. I wanted him *badly*. I want *them ... bad.*

But they are so damn annoying. I am not their property. I can do whatever the hell I want. I have survived, albeit barely, this long without them. I'm not asking to run away to the other side of the world. I just want to go to my apartment and get my shit.

You know what. "Screw this." I stand up. I quietly open my door and peer down the hallway. I can see Ronan's office door, and it's still closed.

I tiptoe toward the elevator and hit the button. You don't need the key card to leave, but I will need it to get up. Oh well, I'll cross that bridge when I get to it. Easier to ask for forgiveness than permission.

* * *

Once I return to my apartment in Greenwich Village, I quickly shower, change my clothes, and start packing a few bags to bring back with me.

My apartment certainly isn't anything to write home about.

I bought it a few years ago with money left for me by my parents. I wanted something I could call my own. It's small, but it's mine.

The entire thing is an open-concept studio. The walls are painted a deep navy blue with dark-wood floors. Rugs in different shades of red are scattered throughout, and plants and books rest in every nook and cranny. Random tchotchkes and pictures of my parents and Cece fill my shelves. Reminders of the family I once had.

My apartment is dark and moody and lived in. Basically the exact opposite of the guest room they have me in.

I walk over to my bed and pull two large duffle bags from beneath it. One for clothes and one for books and pictures. If I'm going to stay there, I want to be comfortable.

I start rummaging through my dresser as fast as I can and fill one bag with my usual attire: jeans, graphic tees, and sweaters. I don't even bother grabbing anything nice to wear. I obviously won't be going anywhere.

I run around the apartment, pick out my favorite books and some of my most cherished pictures, and stuff them in the remaining duffle. After quickly watering all my plants, I grab my jacket and bags and lock the front door.

After climbing down four flights of stairs, I push open the front door of the building and run straight into the back of a tall figure.

"Oops, so sorry about that!"

The man turns around, and I immediately take a step back. His appearance is jarring. He's dressed in black from head to toe. His black hair is cut short and does nothing to hide the evil glimmer in his eye.

"Oh, that's alright, Harper."

Did he just say my name?

Giving him the benefit of the doubt, I ask, "I'm sorry, have we met before?"

A wicked grin spreads across his face. "No, we haven't, but I know all about you."

I feel my pulse quicken. This isn't like when the guys showed up at the bookstore last night. Deep in my bones, I know I should be afraid of this man. I need to get out of here. "You must have me confused with someone else. I have to get going." I quickly turn and walk down the street and around the block to catch a cab to get back to the guys' apartment.

The man quickly falls in step behind me and tightly grabs my arm.

I shouldn't have left. I shouldn't have left.

"Where do you think you're going? I've been waiting for you," he hisses.

"I don't know who you are, but I really need to get going. My boyfriend is waiting for me." Smart, Harp, let him know you have a boyfriend. Someone who will be missing you. Someone he should be afraid of.

"No … I don't think you do. Let's go. Don't cause a scene." The grin falls from his face, but the evil glimmer in his eyes remains.

I shouldn't have left.

This man isn't Declan, he's far too young, but I know he's here because of him. Who else would be after me?

I need to run. I need to make a scene. I don't know what this man plans on doing with me, but I know it can't be good. Declan killed his daughter, after all. I'm sure he'll show me no mercy.

I can't let him take me.

I rip my arm out of his grip, and just as I'm about to scream, a tattooed hand wraps around the man's throat. There's only one person I know with hands like that. Shit.

Ronan.

Before I know it, the man is on the ground with Ronan's gun pressed against the center of his forehead. I look around, ensuring nobody is watching, only to realize I accidentally turned onto a dead-end street while trying to escape.

Well, that was stupid of you, Harp. Where were you planning on going after this?

The only people I see are two equally large men coming up behind Ronan. I haven't known them long, but I immediately recognize Mac and Finn stalking toward me. They look furious.

Ronan still has his gun pressed to the man's forehead as Mac comes toe-to-toe with me. "What the hell are you doing out of the apartment? We told you not to leave." The flirtatious man from this morning is long gone.

Finn puts a hand on his shoulder before I can open my mouth to defend myself. "Mac, get her back to our place. Take our car. I'll stay with Ronan and take care of this piece of shit."

Mac takes a deep breath, and his shoulders relax slightly. I still can't get myself to move. I disobeyed them, and they don't exactly seem like rational men.

"Harper!" Ronan barks from the ground. "Just do as you're told and go with Mac."

"Okay..." I whisper.

Finn hands Mac his keys, dragging me toward two black SUVs parked outside my apartment building.

They knew where I lived.

Mac shoves me into the passenger seat and throws my bags in the back before speeding off, not even giving Ronan and Finn a second look.

I can feel myself shaking in my seat. I needed to explain to Mac what I was doing. I can't bring myself to look at him, so I stare at my hands in my lap as I mutter quietly, "Ronan said I couldn't leave, but I just needed a few of my things. I was in and out. I didn't know anyone knew where I lived. I didn't think—"

"Exactly! You didn't think!" Mac cuts me off. I finally look at him. His hands are gripping the steering wheel so tight his knuckles are white. He's clenching his jaw hard enough it looks like he might crack a tooth. Everything about his posture says he's furious, like he's fighting the urge to explode, but when I look at his face, I sense something else entirely.

Worry.

"He could have killed you right then and there, Harper. Or worse" He lets out a shaky breath. "He could have taken you to God-knows-where, and we would have never found you. You're lucky we knew where you lived."

"Maybe you should have let him. Then I wouldn't be your problem anymore," I bite back defensively. I don't need them yelling at me like I'm a child. I'm smart enough to recognize the danger I just put myself in. Then again, I guess I shouldn't have left in the first place. I should have listened, but I'm certainly not about to admit that I was wrong and they were right.

He whips his head in my direction. "Don't you dare say that. Don't you fucking dare! You *are* my problem. You are *our* problem."

I don't say anything. I'm not even sure I'm capable of

forming words at this point.

The rest of the drive back to their apartment is filled with so much tension someone could cut through it with a knife.

I messed up. And we're only two days in.

10

Mac

What the hell was she thinking? That guy could have killed her. We were almost too late. All I can think about on the way home is what could have happened to her.

Why didn't she just listen?

How did they figure out where she lived? Her address is scrubbed from every database possible. They had to have been following her.

Shit.

I want to scream at her. I want to pull this car over and make her understand how bad that could have been. But I don't. I need to keep my temper in check. She's going to get it bad enough when Ronan gets home. She doesn't need to hear it from me. She feels guilty enough already.

I look over to find Harper cowering in the passenger seat, and I sense that she's afraid of me. I hate it. I don't want her to be scared of me.

I want to be a safe place for her.

I pull my black Land Rover into the parking garage and grab her bags from the back seat. There better be priceless heirlooms in here, considering she risked her life for them.

Harper doesn't wait for me to open her door and follows me into the elevator, and I set the bags down in front of me as the door closes. I look over and notice she's shaking. I reach out to put my hand on the small of her back and she flinches. It's like a dagger to my chest. I put my hand on her back and sigh, "Princess, please don't be afraid of me. I'm not going to do anything to you. I'm just upset."

"But Ronan," she whimpers, "he must be furious with me. He specifically told me not to leave, and I did it anyway. I just wanted my things." I watch a tear roll down her cheek. "Is he—Is he going to hurt me?"

I gently grab her jaw, making her face me. "He's not going to hurt you, but he is going to be pissed, and he's definitely going to yell."

She doesn't respond for a moment, then brings her eyes up to meet mine. "Is he going to kill that man?"

There's no point in lying to her. "Yes. However, we need to get some information out of him first." Goosebumps dance up her neck. I'm sure her imagination is running wild. She needs to understand that *she* may not need to be afraid of us, but everyone else should be. I take a step closer to her. I want to make her feel better. With her eyes still staring at mine, I bring my opposite hand up to tuck a lock of hair behind her ear and place it on the other side of her face.

"I'm just glad you're safe, Princess."

"Thank you for coming for me."

"We will always come for you," I say with certainty. I'm not sure if I mean it because she's a job our father tasked us with or because of something entirely different.

Unexpectedly, the air in the elevator changes. Harper's breath quickens as I tighten my grip on her face, almost afraid to let her go.

There's something about the way I feel when I touch her. The electricity between us is undeniable, and I haven't even kissed her... yet.

I wonder if she can feel it too?

She must because her eyes close like she is waiting to see what I do next.

I take another step toward her so she's pressed up against me, my hands still holding her sweet face.

Sweet face. Who am I?

I bring my forehead to hers, and a breath escapes her lips. I find myself staring at her full pink lips. I would do just about anything to hear my name escape those lips. Ah, fuck it. I can't take it anymore; my lips are crashing into hers.

The kiss starts soft. The stiffness of her body lets me know she wasn't quite ready for it. I tilt my head to the opposite side to better capture her mouth with mine. Finally, she raises her hands from her side and rests them on my chest. A shiver runs through me at the feel of her hands on my body. Her lips start to part slightly, and that's all the invitation I need.

I push my tongue into her mouth to deepen our kiss. Her tongue dances with mine, and I honestly think I've died and gone to heaven for a second. A kiss should *not* feel this good. One of my hands slides down from her face to the small of her back, and I pull her body tighter against me.

A small whimper escapes Harper's lips as she runs one hand up the back of my head and grabs my hair. I moan in appreciation and nip her bottom lip in my teeth.

Jesus, she tastes better than I could have imagined.

I'm about to pick her up so she can wrap her legs around me when the elevator pings and opens on our floor, breaking whatever trance we were just in. We quickly pull our lips apart and stare at one another. Breathless.

Wow.

11

Harper

"Wow." It's the only word I manage to find in my vocabulary.

Looking like I read his mind, Mac just says, "Yeah."

Unsure of what to do next, I reach for one of my bags. "No, let me grab them for you." Mac seems just as flustered as I am. I follow behind him like a lost puppy. I'm no doe-eyed virgin, perks of having your cool aunt raise you during your formidable years. She was a very sex-positive person and taught me not to be ashamed of my sexuality but to embrace it. With that being said, my sexual experiences have been abysmal at best, leaving me to rely on myself and my battery-operated friends. However, try as I might, I don't know how to proceed right now.

I would love nothing more than to climb him like a tree, but is that smart? The last thing I need is to get involved with someone like him. His life is that of a criminal's. The last thing I need is someone who can be taken from me at the drop of a dime.

Plus, there's that little thing about having the hots for the other two men that live here as well.

"God, Harp," I mutter under my breath.

"What's that?" Mac asks as we make our way toward my bedroom.

"Oh, nothing. Just a tickle in my throat." *Smooth.*

Mac sets both of my duffels on my bed, and my eyes are drawn to the thin silver hoop in his nose. Normally, I'm not drawn toward men with facial piercings, but Mac makes it work. It *really* works. His stormy eyes meet mine, and I can tell he's thinking the same thing I am. Just throw me on that bed … please. Instead, he moves toward the door.

"I'm going to call Ronan and see if they've made any progress with that guy. Why don't you eat and have a drink before they get back. You're gonna need it." He wouldn't be wrong. I'm a little scared for Ronan to get back.

"Oh, alright." Is he really not going to make another move? *Damn.*

He spins on his heels and gently closes my door. A few seconds later, I hear his bedroom door open and shut.

I just made out with Mac McDermott and it was one of the hottest moments of my life, and not a single article of clothing even came off. How sad is that? The worst part is I can't even focus enough to relieve myself because any minute now, I'm going to get my ass chewed by the big bad wolf.

Great.

* * *

I'm lying in bed, scrolling through my phone, when I hear yelling. "Harper, get your ass out here." Ronan's home.

I *slowly* walk down the hall toward the den. "Where the hell is she, Mac?" Ronan glares at his brother, who's sitting relaxed in an armchair. Glass of whiskey in hand.

Before Mac can reply, Finn speaks up, "Ronan, you need to chill the hell out. She's afraid of you enough as it is."

"Good! She should be fucking scared of me. I specifically told her not to leave this damn apartment. I told her—"

I cut him off as I enter the room, "Jesus Christ, Ronan, I'm right here. Relax." I notice a slight smile slide over Mac and Finn's faces.

"Sit. Down. Now."

He's pissed. I can't say I blame him. Finn looks at me empathetically as I sit close to him, as far from Ronan as possible. Maybe if I sit close to him and Mac, they'll protect me from the wolf marching around the den. No one speaks a word. We're all waiting for Ronan to say whatever he needs to say.

Today was by far one of the stupidest things I've ever done in my life. I'm not sure why I did it, honestly. In the back of my mind, I knew it wasn't safe. I don't know much about this life, but I do know the people in it don't shy away from violence. If anything, it's welcomed and encouraged. I think, more than anything, I just wanted to push back against Ronan and his irritating attitude.

I can't help but admire his physique as he shrugs off his coat. Even when he looks murderous, he's painfully gorgeous. Rolling up the cuffs of his shirt, staring directly at me with those piercing blue eyes. They're darker now, as if his anger has cast a shadow over them. His gaze doesn't leave mine for a second and a chill runs down my spine. There's something between us. I can feel it. Although, I'm not quite sure what it is.

Annoyance, yes.

Rage, yes.

Disdain for one another, yes.

Passion… maybe.

Whatever it is, the chemistry is as undeniable as it is intense.

"What the fuck is wrong with you?"

Aaaaand he ruined it.

I am not the type of woman who lets a man—or men—push her around. And I'll be damned if I let Ronan back me into a corner.

Instead of curling up into a ball on the couch, like I want to after the last twenty-four hours, I straighten my shoulders and stand up from my spot next to Finn. I'll be damned if I let him tower over me like that. "What's wrong with me? What's wrong with you?" I can't help but silently admire the look of shock on his face. Like, he doesn't believe I'm standing up for myself. "I told you I wanted to run to my apartment *quickly* to get my things, and you completely dismissed me. I'm willing to live in your damn penthouse just like you asked, with three strange men I hardly know." I can hear my voice growing louder. "All I wanted was my things so I would be a little more comfortable. Instead of giving me one hour of your precious day, you sent me to my room like a damn child!" I can feel my nails digging into my palm as I clench my fists and force myself to take a deep breath. "Yes, I left when I shouldn't have and put myself in danger. For that, I'm sorry."

Closing the distance between us, I raise my hand and poke my finger in the center of his chest. "But I will *not* apologize for wanting the things that make me who I am when *you* have made me question who exactly that is!"

Holy shit. I can't believe I just did that.

Ronan's gaze sweeps across my face as his lips tighten. I watch his chest rise and fall as he takes a deep breath like he's trying not to strangle me with his bare hands.

Finn's voice cuts through the tension. "Harper, Angel… Come sit back down." His hand is outstretched toward mine.

I slowly return to my seat, tucked even closer to Finn than before.

Ronan calmly walks over to the bar and pours himself two fingers of whiskey. He gulps it down in one swallow and spins back to face me. With his blue eyes locked on mine, he taps the side of the glass a few times with one of his rings before sending the glass flying across the room, shattering it against the wall.

12

Finn

F uck. This isn't good.

I knew as soon as Ronan called and told us Harper was gone that he would go off the rails. He doesn't do particularly well with people disobeying his orders—never has.

When we pulled up to her apartment and saw her running around the corner with a strange man on her tail, I knew shit was about to hit the fucking fan. Ronan sprinted out of his car before Mac even put ours in park. As Mac and I rounded the corner, Ronan already had the man on the ground with the barrel of his gun pressed into his forehead.

The second my eyes found Harper, my lungs seized in my chest. The look on her face will haunt my nightmares. She was petrified.

I hate to think what would have happened if we had shown up just a minute later. She has no idea what her "family" is capable of… *but I do.* Declan Whelan ruined my life.

It's been less than forty-eight hours with her, and I can tell there's something about this woman. I just can't quite put my finger on it. I know Mac and Ronan feel it too.

The sound of glass shattering brings me back to the scene before me, and I notice Ronan is on the brink. The fact that he's this pissed off tells me he feels something for Harper, whether he likes it or not.

My hand grips Harper's thigh as I glare at him. "Ronan, that's enough. She gets it. She fucked up."

"Does she get it, Finn?" I notice a tremble in Harper's thigh. She may not act like it, but she's afraid of him. He takes two steps closer to us, and she immediately freezes. "Do you know what the sick fuck would have done to you?"

"Ronan…"

"No, Finn. She should know. She needs to understand who the hell she's dealing with. Maybe next time she will do as she's told."

I'm sure whatever Harper's imagining is terrible enough. She doesn't need to know that twisted asshole was planning to take her to an abandoned warehouse upstate. Ronan and I sent a couple of our guys up there after we not so politely asked him for some information. After Ronan beat him within an inch of his life, I put a bullet through his head and dropped him in the Hudson. This isn't our first fucking rodeo.

My stomach dropped when our men called to tell us they found the warehouse with nothing but a mattress, chains, and a bucket in the middle of the floor. Who knows how long he planned on keeping her there.

Declan hired him to kill Harper. But he took it upon himself to have some "fun" with her first. Bile rises in my throat at the thought of it. I wish I could bring him back to life just to kill him all over again. He deserved more than a quick bullet through the brain for what he was going to do to her. She doesn't need to know any of this right now. I will tell her about it later when she isn't already scared shitless. Before I can say something, Mac barks, "Ronan! That's enough. She fucking gets it. Leave it the hell alone."

Mac never argues with Ronan, *ever*. He's usually too busy battling his own demons to have the energy. Plus, he knows that Ronan is the boss. Mac and I both have our own roles, but we respect Ronan and his decisions.

Neither of us dares to dismiss him.

I know the only reason he's speaking up right now is to protect Harper.

Ronan must be just as surprised by Mac's outburst as I am. He doesn't respond. Instead, he glares at his brother with a furrowed brow before storming down the hall toward his room. Ronan has never been good at confrontation when he can't use violence as an outlet, and that's not an option right now. We don't hurt women and children.

Especially not Harper.

So instead of using his words to express his feelings, he runs. Mac and I are used to it by now. We're always around to pick up the pieces of Ronan's outbursts.

Mac crosses the room and starts literally picking up the pieces of Ronan's tantrum. I stay firmly planted on the couch next to Harper.

"I'm really sorry. I know I messed up," she whispers, staring down at her lap. I watch a tear fall from her face and land on her jeans.

I hate knowing she's so upset. There's a relentless urge

inside me to do anything I can to make it better.

I'm a fixer. That's what I do.

"Harper…" When she doesn't answer, I kneel on the ground in front of her and grasp her hands in mine. "Angel, you're safe. That's what matters." I squeeze her hands harder in mine. "Do you understand how dangerous this is now?"

Without looking up, she answers, "Yes."

"Then it's done. It's over with. Ronan and I took care of it, and he won't bother you again, but that doesn't mean Declan won't send someone else to find you." The thought of someone else coming for her sends ice through my veins. It's strange how protective we have all become of her in such a short amount of time. None of us have ever had so much as a single serious relationship, and all of a sudden, we're fascinated with the woman in front of us. "They know where you live now and probably have people following you. Promise me you won't leave without one of us again."

Finally, she raises her head. "I promise." I can tell there's something else she wants to say, so I don't move from my spot. "I'm sorry you had to kill that man because of me." I can't help the small chuckle that escapes my lips.

"Princess," Mac says while throwing the broken pieces of glass in the trash, "if you think that is the first man we have killed, you are sorrily mistaken." A smug grin spreads across his face. "And it won't be the last."

Her eyes comically widen. I grab her chin with my fingers and make her face me. "And make no mistake. We will kill anyone that tries to harm you. Happily."

13

Ronan

It's been a long time since I've been this pissed off. It isn't because I had to kill a man. I mean, what else is new? It isn't because she disobeyed me. Okay, maybe it's that a little bit. It's because we were one minute away from being too late.

We almost lost her.

We almost lost her, and I haven't even had her yet.

The second she left my office this afternoon, I knew I had crossed a line. I shouldn't have put my hands on her like that. Even though I wanted to do a hell of a lot more.

I wanted to pin her up against that wall and fuck every single ounce of attitude out of her. I wanted to feel her pussy squeeze the life out of my cock as I came inside her.

I wanted *more.*

But I can't. I know as soon as I step over that line with Harper, there will be no going back, and I don't do relationships. All I need is a good fuck. One where I don't have to worry about her feelings, remember her damn birthday, or try to explain the ins and outs of syndicate business. Harper would be the exact fucking opposite. I don't need that in my life. I have an empire to run. Things to accomplish.

Yet, when I saw her in the street with that fuckers hand wrapped around her arm, I saw red, and everything else went out the window.

I didn't care about tonight's shipment, I didn't care about disappointing my parents, and I definitely did not care whether or not she was relationship material. I just wanted to save her.

Then, I wanted to watch him suffer while I broke every bone in his body. The fucker was lucky it was the middle of the day, and we only had time to shoot him. I would have tortured him until he begged for death if I'd had it my way.

As Finn and I drove back to our apartment, I wasn't quite sure what I wanted to do with Harper when we got back. Kiss her with everything I had or scream at her. The first option was almost the one I chose. Then I remembered all of the reasons why that was a bad idea. Still, I can feel my self-control slipping every single time I look at her.

So, If I can't stop myself, I have to make her hate me. And I'm well on my fucking way too.

* * *

It's been three hours since I stormed out of the den like a child. I only left my room to go to my office to take care of some last-minute details before I meet my team for our delivery at the docks. This has to go perfectly. I can't have people thinking they can fuck with our product. We buy and sell just about every illegal thing you can think of. Everything except people. I mean, we're bad men, but we aren't fucking evil.

Just as I'm about to throw my coat on and head down to the docks for our delivery, Mac opens my door and sits in a chair in front of my desk.

"By all means… come in."

"I just wanted to see if you needed me tonight. I can come with you and Finn."

"No." I raise a hand at him. "I need you to stay here with Harper. After the shit she pulled this morning, I don't trust her here alone." Mac lets out a heavy sigh, and I know he's about to lay into me. "Spit it out."

"You need to ease up on her, man. Her world has been flipped upside down in the last two days, and she's just trying to make sense of it all. She knows she fucked up. Just drop it."

He's so irritating sometimes. Him and his bleeding fucking heart. "I'm not going to go easy on her, Mac. She needs to understand what kind of world she's living in," I explain, growing more and more irritated.

Standing from my chair, I lean forward and let my palms rest on the top of the desk. "And you, Brother, need to stop acting like you're some knight in fucking armor."

Knowing I won't back down from this argument, Mac stands and takes that as his cue to leave. "Call me if you guys need anything," he murmurs on his way out, not bothering to give me another glance.

I just need tonight to be over with. Once this shipment is in my hands, I can focus on more important matters, like why my dad is suddenly so interested in the curvy brunette in the other room.

14

Harper

It's late, and I'm ready for a hot shower and bed after today. Ronan and Finn left about an hour ago to do what I can only imagine is some super shady shit.

After I got my ass chewed like a child, it was actually kind of a nice night. Finn whipped up a delicious spaghetti dinner, and after we were finished eating, the three of us sat in the living room watching *The Office* reruns.

Every so often, I caught Mac staring at me across the room with those stormy-gray eyes. His soft stare made me melt on the spot.

Finn, on the other hand, was far less subtle. It was blatantly obvious he was keeping his eyes on me, but with an entirely different look on his face, like he was afraid I would disappear into thin air if he looked away.

I *liked* it. It made me feel… wanted.

A few hours later, I crawl into my entirely too big-for-one-person bed after the most delectable bath, and my eyes instantly feel heavy. But I can't fall asleep. My mind won't rest. It's probably due to the fact that I was almost kidnapped eight hours ago. I toss and turn for what feels like ages, growing more and more frustrated. I hear the faintest knock at the door. I know it's Mac. While the other two are out, he was tasked with babysitting me for the night.

"Come in."

"Hey, Princess. I just wanted to see if you needed anything before I went to bed."

The second I look at him, I want him in my bed. I want to feel *safe*. But I can't ask him for that. Can I?

No, I've known the man for only a few days. I certainly don't want him to think I'm some floozy by inviting him into my bed.

"Umm, no, I think I'm okay."

"Alright. Well, goodnight. I'll be just down the hall if you need anything."

Before he can take so much as a step, I say "Actually…"

Mac looks at me inquisitively. "Yeah?"

"Could you umm… I mean, you don't have to… but…" I can't quite seem to spit it out.

He takes two steps toward me. "What do you need, Princess?"

Princess.

That pet name warms my insides like the best cup of coffee during an east-coast snow storm.

"Could you–Could you lay with me? Just for a little while. I can't sleep, and it might help."

He pauses only for a moment before smiling. "Of course. I'll stay as long as you need."

He slides off his shoes and, to my happy surprise, his shirt.

As he stands before me in only his jeans, I have to stop myself from reaching out, crawling across the bed, and running my tongue over his perfectly chiseled abs.

The man is a walking wet dream.

Just as he's about to climb onto the bed, I lift the covers. "You can climb in if you want." Without a word, he slides under the covers and puts his hands behind his head.

I roll over to face him and forget how to breathe. He is beautiful.

You're really testing yourself tonight, Harp.

Every muscle looks like it was carved from stone by gods. Whereas Ronan has a mixture of random tattoos covering his body, Mac's look to be intricately designed Celtic designs. They really are works of art.

A slight stubble has covered his jaw since I met him, and all I can think about is how it would feel against my skin. I force my eyes closed to stop from staring. Through closed eyes, I whisper, "Thank you… for staying."

"Of course, get some rest."

After a while, I'm still not asleep. And am growing even more restless. Probably because all I want to do is jump Mac's bones.

He notices my constant fidgeting and a small laugh escapes his lips. "Come here, Princess."

I open my eyes, and he has an arm stretched out in my direction, the other one remaining tucked behind his head. Eagerly, maybe too much so, I scoot over and rest my head on his warm chest as he wraps his arm around me, his chest hair rubbing against my cheek. The second his arms wrap around me, I feel safer than I have since my parents died.

Mac moves his hand up and down my arm as if he's trying

to get me to relax.

His face presses against the top of my head as he takes a deep breath.

Did he just smell my hair?

Unsure of how to respond to the intimate gesture, I remain quiet and wiggle against him. Wanting my body to be as close to his as possible.

Mac brings his other hand from behind his head, rests it on his stomach, and begins tapping his abs with his fingers. I sense a hesitation in him that matches mine in every movement he makes. Both of us are afraid to do what we really want to. The electricity between us is overwhelming, and I know he feels it too. I want to do something about it.

Testing the waters, I drape my left leg across him and gently shift my hips against his. I'm wearing only an oversized T-shirt and a pair of cotton underwear, so there isn't much between us. His large hand moves from his stomach as he grips my thigh. Hard. With bated breath, he whispers against the top of my head, "Harper…"

I shift my hips again. "Mac…" He quickly rolls us over so I'm beneath him. His arms rest on either side of my head, and I can feel his *impressively* hard length against me through his jeans.

Oh my God.

"What are you doing to me? I shouldn't want you like this," he groans, his forehead pressed against mine.

I can't speak. Like, I literally can't form any words. Mac has stolen my ability to communicate, and he hasn't even kissed me yet.

One of his hands begins running through my hair and finally rests on the side of my throat as his lips gently brush mine. Not quite yet a kiss

With an uneven breath, his eyes search for mine in the darkness, whispering against my mouth, "What do you want, Princess?"

"You," I whisper.

His lips instantly meet mine with more intensity than I've ever experienced. This is different from our moment in the elevator. There was so much uneasiness at that moment that neither of us was sure what was happening was a good idea.

Now everything's different. The way he's devouring my mouth tells me he wants every second of this, that our bodies together are what he craves. And I couldn't agree more.

His tongue continues brushing against mine, and I melt against his touch. He moves his hand from my neck toward my hip, brushing the side of my breast as he goes. Once his fingers move beneath the bottom of my shirt, I tense.

I'm not exactly skinny. I've never been ashamed of my body and love every curve and dimple. Yet, every man I've been with seems to try and avoid them. Almost like the act of touching a single curve or roll would make their dick automatically deflate. So, instead of appreciating my *whole* body, they'd skip to the parts they deemed worthy.

Instead of removing his hand, he freezes. "Do you want me to stop?"

I shake my head. "No."

"Is this okay?"

Yes, yes, yes. A million times, yes.

"It's okay."

He leans forward and runs his tongue along the length of my jaw. A shiver runs through my body as he moves his mouth over that perfect spot on my neck, right next to my collarbone. Slowly, he moves his hand from where it was resting on my stomach to one of my already hard nipples. He growls deep in his throat.

He softly bites my neck while pinching my nipple, and I can feel myself growing wetter by the second. "God, Mac…"

He removes his hand from my shirt and sits back on his knees between my legs, breathing heavily. I worry I've done something wrong and can't help the look of disappointment that sweeps across my face.

What? No, that can't be it.

"What do you want, Princess?"

"I want you, Mac," I reply, slightly confused.

"You have me. I'm right here."

Damn it, no. *I want more. Is he going to make me spell it out for him?*

"Say it."

I see the look on his face, and I know exactly why he wants me to be so clear about what I want. He wants to make sure I feel safe. He wants to take care of me.

That's why I asked him to stay with me… wasn't it? Because I was afraid.

At this moment, I know there is something here. I'm not imagining it. If there wasn't, he wouldn't give a shit about what I want. This dangerous and beautiful man could have any woman he wants any day of the week, but right now, he wants me, and I want him, more than anyone I've wanted in my life.

Here goes nothing. "Fuck me, Mac… Please."

15

Mac

She needs to be mine. That kiss in the elevator was nothing compared to this. That moment was rushed and filled with tension from her escape attempt this morning. But this... this is perfect.

There isn't a doubt in my mind that she is what I want. She's what I need. Quickly jumping off the bed to take off my jeans, a thought occurs to me as my fingers reach for my zipper. "Shit, I'll be right back."

Her face drops. "Why?"

"Condom."

Before I can take a step, she sits up straight in bed, "Are you clean?"

My mouth drops open in shock because I know exactly what she's about to say, and I cannot fucking believe it. "Yeah, I'm clean. We get tested every six months."

I wince at the admission, knowing how that must sound, but she deserves the truth if she's willing to trust me with this.

"So am I, and I have an IUD. I trust you. Stay."

I don't know why the hell she would trust a man like me, but I'm all fucking for it. "Are you sure?"

"Yes, Mac… please."

She. Is. Perfect. There's no way this woman is real.

I practically rip my jeans off my body and throw them across the room where I left my shirt. I look over at Harper, who has shed her shirt and underwear and is throwing them in a pile on top of my clothes.

While she's just lying there waiting for me, I see all of her for the first time, and I feel like I can't fucking breathe. She's so beautiful.

Harper has curves in all of the right places, curves I want to sink my teeth into.

Adrenaline courses through me as I begin to think about everything I want to do to this woman. Every horribly dirty image runs through my brain, and every ounce of blood rushes straight to my painfully hard cock. I want to defile every square inch of her.

Everything about her draws me in. That makes sense, though, doesn't it? I am darkness, and Harper is a beautiful light in this world. Wherever there is light, darkness lurks around the corner. If I were a better man, I would push her away instead of snuffing out her light, but I'm not a good man, not entirely, anyway. I have to have her. I'm already fucking obsessed just looking at her.

She giggles. "No boxers, huh?"

"Nah, gotta let the boys breathe." I don't want to talk anymore. I climb back on top of her and fuse her lips with mine, stealing her chance to make a smart remark.

As I press my mouth over the spot on her neck that made her cry out minutes ago, her hands grab fistfuls of my hair. Pulling hard enough to cause just the right amount of pain.

I grab one of her legs and wrap it around me. I can feel my cock rubbing against her wet folds. Just grinding against her is enough to make me come on the spot. "More—Mac, more," she whines.

"Fuck, Princess." I need to make this last, but my control is slipping.

Slowly, I kiss and bite my way down toward her breasts, taking a nipple in my mouth. I begin lapping hungrily until it forms a tight bud against my tongue. Another small whimper slips past her lips as I gently bite down.

Every noise is like music to my ears.

Her hands, still gripping my hair, begin pushing my head toward the apex of her thighs. Knowing exactly what she wants, I don't waste another second.

Once my open mouth meets her sweet pussy her other leg wraps around me. I can feel her thighs clenching the sides of my face, and I swear, she could kill me right here, right now, and I would die a happy death.

I make sure I take my time, knowing I won't last but a few minutes once I'm deep inside her.

I begin fucking her with my tongue. "Yes, Mac," she gasps, "Don't stop. Please don't stop." I can feel her body tense beneath me. Her hands have moved from my hair and are now tightly clenching the sheets. She's close. I can feel it.

"Come for me, Princess."

"God, Mac. I'm gonna..." Before she can even finish her sentence, I suck vigorously on her clit and plunge two fingers deep inside her. Her back arches and an intense orgasm rips through her body while she calls out my name.

"Jesus Christ, you taste delicious when you come, Princess."

As she lays on the bed, letting the waves of her orgasm wash over her, I kiss the inside of her thighs before sitting back on my knees.

Before her body can fully come down from her orgasm, I grip her by the hips and pull her toward me until her pussy is right where I need it.

Grabbing the base of my cock, I gently slide into her, but only just an inch. Reaching down, I run my palm from her hip down her leg, still wrapped around me, and she looks up at me.

"Is this okay?" My repetitive need for her approval might be overkill, but I have to be sure. Harper needs to be cared for and protected, and I want to be the one to give that to her.

Hell, I think I'd give her anything.

Her gaze moves down my body until it finds my swollen cock, barely inside her. With wide eyes, she whispers eagerly, "Yes, just go slow. It's been a while."

"Don't worry, Princess. I'll go slow at first. But once I'm all the way in, I can't make any promises." She already feels too fucking good.

"Okay."

Tenderly, I sink inside her an inch at a time, rocking side-to-side as I go, allowing her to accommodate my size. "Shit, Princess. Your pussy is so fucking tight." A soft moan rises from her throat.

Once I'm balls deep inside her, I pause, giving her body a minute to get more comfortable. I'm gripping her legs so tight I'm sure there will be marks in the morning. But it's the only thing stopping me from coming. Wanting to help her relax, I reach forward and pinch one of her tight nipples between my fingers, and I feel her walls relax around me.

"I'm going to move now, okay?"

Without a word, she tightly grips my forearms and nods. With my cock still fully sheathed inside of her, I pinch her nipple tighter. Her eyes fly open and meet mine. "Say it, Harper." My tone is more serious now. I need to hear her say it. I don't want to risk anything with her.

"Yes—Fuck me—Now."

Those four words tip me over the edge. Still gripping her delicious thighs, I pull out of her. Before she has a chance to protest, I slam back into her. Any restraint I was showing just seconds ago is now gone. My entire body lights up with pleasure, seeing how her body reacts to mine.

I keep a steady rhythm as I watch her tits bounce up and down with each hard thrust. I'm going to come any second, but I need to feel her pussy tighten around me first.

I find her clit with my fingers and start rubbing it in fast circles. It only takes a few seconds before she stills, and her jaw drops open.

"Come with me, Princess. Give me one more. Now."

The second I feel her walls pulse around me, a wave of pleasure crashes into me so hard I can barely see straight. I bend over and bury my face into her neck as I shoot my cum deep inside her.

I've never had sex without a condom. I don't know what made me break one of my strictest rules for Harper, but I'm not sure I can ever go back. It feels too good. *She* feels too good.

After a few minutes, we both come down from our highs, and I notice I'm still inside her while her hands rub up and down my back.

I could stay here forever.

This isn't like me. I've only ever had quick fucks. It's just enough to scratch an itch without ever getting attached. Sure, I'm better than my brother. I bother learning their names and make sure they enjoy it as much as I do. I enjoy making people feel good, making them happy. I don't get to do that often.

Harper wiggles underneath me, and I take that as my cue to get up. I'm not exactly small. Climbing off, I grab the covers and lay right back down, draping them over us.

"You're still sleeping in here?" she asks in surprise.

Rolling over, I drape my arm over her hip and run my thumb across her skin. "Of course I am." I move closer until I can feel her breath against my chest. "That was amazing, Harper. I can't think of any place I'd rather be."

She nuzzles her face against my chest. "It was, Mac... amazing."

Not more than two minutes later, I feel her breathing relax, followed by the cutest snore I've ever heard. With one last kiss to the top of her head, I find myself drifting off into the deepest sleep I've had in months.

16

Harper

Ughhh. Rolling over to check my phone for the time, I find it's barely 6:00 AM. There's a delicious soreness between my thighs from last night, and my mouth feels as dry as the Sahara.

I need water… *now.*

Mac's still sleeping soundly next to me. He stayed all night, cuddled up tightly behind me. I can't believe last night happened. I'm not the kind of woman who sleeps with a man she just met. Let alone a dangerous mobster who is practically keeping me prisoner in his swanky penthouse.

Yes, Mac may be dangerous to everyone else, but he isn't to me. I can already tell I can count on him. I can count on him to protect me. I can count on him to give me what I need. I can count on him to make my body feel things I never thought possible. I mean, he gave me not just one but two of the most intense orgasms I've ever experienced in my life.

While all of that may be true, I can't help but question my

sanity. Is it smart to feel what I feel for him?

For *them*?

Everyone I've ever truly cared about has left me. No, they didn't just leave me… they died. They're gone. *Forever.*

I should be helping them stop whoever Declan, *my grandfather,* is sending for me, and I shouldn't be sleeping with them. And I definitely shouldn't be watching them masturbate in the shower.

God, what is my life?

Needing a second to think, I gently sneak out of bed, careful not to wake Mac. I grab a shirt off of the pile of our shed clothes from last night and make my way toward the kitchen for the glass of water I desperately need. I nearly jump out of my skin when Finn chuckles across the room.

I spin around to find him sitting in the den, cloaked in darkness and sipping a glass of whiskey. He looks like some sort of bond villain. He's wearing the same clothes as he was last night, and judging by the bags under his eyes and his messy hair, I can tell he hasn't gone to bed.

"What's so funny?"

"Nothing…" he says through a devilish grin. "Just nice to see Mac made his move."

How does he know? It dawns on me, and I look down. *Crap.* I grabbed Mac's shirt off the floor, not mine.

Play it cool, Harp.

"What do you mean?"

"He's been dying to get his hands on you from the second we walked into the bookstore. Honestly, I'm surprised it took him so long."

Finn must be drunk. He's not usually this blunt, let alone this talkative. His usual put-together persona isn't anywhere to be found, and mischievousness has taken its place.

"Well, it's none of your business."

Grinning, he brings his glass to his deliciously full lips for another drink. "Whatever you say, Angel."

"What time did you two get back?" I ask, hand propped on my hip.

"About an hour ago. We had an issue at the docks. Had to go to Liam's after to explain what happened. Let's just say he's not pleased."

I don't know much about Finn, but from what I've already observed, he likes to be in control. Both of himself and the world around him. He feels the need to please everyone. I want to know why.

"What happened?"

"Nothing. You don't need to worry about it," he says, exasperatingly running his hand over his face.

I step around the kitchen island and ask again, more firmly this time. "Finn, what happened?"

My firm tone makes him rise from the chair with a sigh. "Some assholes heard about the delivery. They stole half of it before we even got there."

"What was it?" My curiosity has officially peaked.

"Drugs… mostly." I don't know why I'm the least bit surprised, yet, I am. Maybe because I've never gotten so much as a parking ticket, and here I am, shacking up with criminals. "Ronan freaked the fuck out and nearly beat one of the dock workers to death trying to find out who it was."

"Well, did you?"

"No. Hence the many drinks I've had." Finn seems to carry the weight of the world on his shoulders, and I can tell he hates disappointing people. Or maybe he just hates disappointing the McDermotts. "We just need to figure out how they knew when and where… and soon. Otherwise, Liam might actually kill Ronan."

My eyes widen over his last sentence. Finn swallows down the last of his whiskey. "Relax, Harper. I'm kidding… mostly." Setting down his glass on the bar, he walks over to me until he's standing so close I can feel his breath on my face. "But if I were you, I'd stay clear of Ronan today."

"No worries there. He doesn't want me anywhere near him anyway."

"Oh, I wouldn't be so sure about that, Angel."

He can't be serious. Ronan hates me. Not wanting to discuss Ronan when I'm in such a good mood, I decide now is as good a time as any to ask Finn about something that's been nagging at me. "How do you know them? The McDermotts', that is. You obviously aren't related to Ronan and Mac. You look nothing like them."

He scratches at his bear, looking like I just made him wildly uncomfortable. "How do you know I'm not adopted?"

"You don't call Emma and Liam 'Mom and Dad,' and you walk around here like you're not sure you belong. Like you're afraid even to touch anything."

"Well, aren't you observant?"

"That's not an answer to my question."

He lets out a heavy sigh. "My last name is Donovan. Liam and Emma took me in when I was eight after my parents died. They're the closest thing to family I have left."

And there it is. His constant desire to do what everyone asks of him. To not let anyone down. He's afraid that if he messes up, he'll be cast aside.

I don't ask how he lost them. If he wanted me to know, he'd

tell me. Instead, I say the only thing I think might ease his pain at this moment because I know what it's like to lose both of your parents. It's a hole that can never be filled. No matter how many years go by or how many new memories you make. "I see them in you," I say softly. His eyes immediately dart to the picture on the fridge.

I can tell he doesn't want to discuss this anymore, so I don't push further. Instead, I wrap my arms around him, comforting him. If only for a moment.

When I move to let go of him, he only holds me tighter and buries his face in my neck. The longer we stay in each other's arms, the more rapid Finn's breath becomes. This hug is quickly turning into something else entirely.

His hands move from the small of my back to the backs of my thighs, and I'm suddenly being lifted off the ground and onto the counter behind me. I place my palm in the center of his chest as he steps between my legs, not completely sure what is happening. "Finn, we shouldn't." Mac is still lying in my bed.

"Why? Because you fucked Mac." The crudeness of his tone takes me by surprise. "You think we haven't shared women before?"

What?

Finn slides one hand up the back of my head so he's gripping a handful of my hair. "Oh, Angel. The things we could show you."

I can't deny that I crave all three of them. The way heat builds inside of me at the mere sight of them is something I can't deny. But never did I ever think about having more than one of them.

That they could all be mine.

Without warning, I can only think about being with him. I don't care that Mac was inside me just a few hours ago. Something about his wanton behavior at this moment is drawing me in. He's uncontrolled. Dangerous. *Free.*

It's an entirely different side of him. One I want to know. Intimately.

Well, if I'm going to be stuck here and torn away from my life, I might as well make it worth it.

Go all in, Harp.

"So, show me."

His honey-colored eyes are instantly clouded in darkness. Like I just flipped a switch inside of him, and the quiet and collected man everyone knows is gone.

Finn's grip on my hair tightens as I zero in on his gaze. A smug grin creeps over his lips as he releases my hair and moves his hand to the center of my chest. "Lie back. Now."

A command. No asking for permission. No, "please." The feeling in the air is the exact opposite of my night with Mac, and at this moment, with Finn, it's exactly what I want, what I *crave.*

Obeying his command, I let him push me back onto the kitchen island.

"Knees up."

Crimson shades my cheeks as I realize he's about to have an all-access pass. I didn't even put on underwear. I was just getting water, for Christ's sake. After a moment of hesitation, Finn repeats, more sternly this time, "Harper. Knees. Up."

I bring my knees up and firmly plant my feet on the edge of the counter, fully aware that he can see every square inch of my pussy.

Finn grips both of my thighs and spreads my legs as far as

they can go. "No panties? You were just going to walk around here teasing me with this sweet pussy?"

"I... I didn't know you would be out here." Is he really trying to have a conversation with me right now? His face is so close I can feel his breath against the wetness between my thighs.

"Well, I was. And now this pussy is *mine*." Before I can ask what he means, his grip on my thighs tightens. "Don't make a sound, Angel. Do you understand?"

The roughness of his voice sounds nothing like it did minutes ago. Finn is in control. I don't dare argue. "Yes, I understand."

Guilt floods me. Mac is still sleeping in my room. What kind of woman sleeps with two men less than eight hours apart? Let alone two men that live with one another. Two men who are practically brothers.

The second Finn's mouth brushes the inside of my thigh, any guilt I felt fades away. His head stays between my thighs as he peppers them with kisses.

"Mac may have had sex with you."

Kiss.

"Whispered sweet nothings in your ear."

Kiss.

"Took it nice and slow."

Kiss.

"But me, Angel..."

Bite.

"I'm going to fuck this pussy so hard you won't be able to walk for three days."

Bite.

All of the air whooshes out of my lungs after the second hard bite. I can feel my core growing wetter as each delicious word spills out of his mouth. No man has ever spoken to me like this before. I'm so wet I'm sure I'm dripping onto the counter.

I can't believe these words are coming out of Finn's mouth.That underneath his cool, amenable, and composed exterior, there's this forceful and oh-so-dirty man.

"Yes," I whisper. Giving him consent to do whatever he wants with me. I don't think there's anything I wouldn't do for him at this moment.

His head pops up from between my legs. "You misunderstand me, Harper. I wasn't asking for your permission. And what did I say about making a sound."

"Ow!" I shriek as a third bite sends a wave of pain through my body. That one is definitely going to leave a mark. Before I can sit up in protest, Finn sinks two fingers deep inside me, and my head falls back against the counter.

"You're so fucking wet already, Angel."

He begins moving his fingers in and out of me at an agonizingly slow pace. I try to thrust my hips toward his hand to gain some friction. He adds a third finger inside of me and presses his thumb against my clit. I clench my walls around his fingers, trying to pull him in deeper as his hand picks up speed. Just as I'm about to let out a moan, I remember I'm not to make any noise. I move my hand over my mouth to muffle any sound that might slip out.

Keeping his fingers inside me, Finn replaces his thumb with his mouth and sucks on my clit, *hard.*

Suddenly, it's all too much. My hand over my mouth, his fingers moving in and out of me, his beard rubbing against my thighs, his talented mouth against my aching clit. The familiar feeling of orgasm arises at the base of my toes and makes its way up my legs to my core. Slow and unrelenting.

As I'm about to crash around him, Finn quickly removes his fingers and snaps, "No."

"What?" I sit up straight. Did I break his rules? I could have sworn I was quiet. "I didn't make a noise," I whine, practically begging for him to give me the orgasm that was just within my reach.

Reaching up, he tightly grasps my throat with his hand and growls, "If you're going to come, you're going to come around my cock."

Finn slides his hands under my ass, picks me back up off the counter, and places me on the ground. My body feels cooler at the loss of him. His every touch feels like lightning against my skin. Wanting him to take my shirt off, I raise my arms. Instead, he fists the collar of the shirt with both hands and rips it down the middle.

Oh.

My.

God.

"I'm sure Mac won't mind," he quips snarkily.

I'm standing bare-ass naked in the kitchen while Finn studies my body, fully clothed. The power dynamic between us is clear as day. I have a burning desire to reach for him and tear his clothes off, run my hands over every inch of muscle, and kneel in front of him and take him in my mouth. But, I refrain. Not wanting to move until he gives me further instructions.

He's in control.

I watch Finn run his tongue along his bottom lip, and that one action has me clenching my thighs to relieve the pressure building inside of me.

If he doesn't make me come soon, I might actually die.

"Turn around and bend over."

Hell yeah.

I spin around and face the kitchen island. Slowly, I fold over until my chest rests against the countertop, my nipples now painfully hard against the cold granite. Finn tracks his hand up the inside of my leg before he runs a finger through my folds. I swear I'm so wet I can feel it dripping down my thighs.

A pinch to my clit causes a whimper to slip past my lips. I can't take it anymore.

"Finn… please… I can't—I…"

Thankfully, he doesn't punish me for speaking. "Don't you worry, Angel. I'm going to give you exactly what you need."

My breath stills as I hear him undo his belt buckle, followed by the sound of a zipper.

"Are you on something?"

It takes a second for my brain to catch up before I realize what he's talking about. "Yes, I have an IUD," I say breathlessly with my face against the counter.

"Good. I don't want anything between that tight cunt and my cock."

I quite literally go weak in the knees. If I wasn't draped over the island, I would collapsed.

Without any warning or preparation, Finn slams into me. I'm hit with such a sense of fullness, unlike anything I've ever experienced. I didn't get a chance to see it, but I can tell his cock is huge. I'm not sure how he will even be able to move inside of me.

There can't possibly be more room.

"That's it. Take all of my cock like a good girl."

Good girl. His praise is the final nail in my coffin. There's no turning back now.

"Better hold on," he snarls as he grabs a fist full of my hair and wraps it around his hand.

Finn pulls out and slams back into me with so much power my hips slam into the edge of the counter. "Finn!"

I'm not sure if my scream is one of pain or pleasure. Either way, I don't care. He doesn't stop, and I don't ask him to.

Out of the corner of my eye, I see a shirtless figure standing against the wall at the mouth of the hallway.

Mac.

My whole body goes rigid, afraid of what his reaction will be. Finn said he wouldn't care, but who am I to take his word for it?

Finn continues pounding into me at an unrelenting rate, his grip on my hair tightening as he notices Mac across the room. "Don't think I'm stopping on his account."

"But…"

"I promise, Angel, he wants to watch me fuck you. Don't you, Mac?"

I glance at Mac as he shoves off the wall and stalks toward us, doing nothing to hide his massive erection. Finn slows his thrusts, almost like he's giving Mac time to walk over.

This cannot be happening.

Mac rounds the opposite side of the island. As he rests his forearms against the countertop, he smiles from ear to ear. "Well, good morning, Princess."

I should be mortified, but I'm not. Mac standing across from us, watching, only makes this entire dirty and depraved scene sexier. Instead of shying away, which is what me of just a few days ago would have done, I reach back and squeeze

Finn's thigh urging him to keep going.

Remember, Harp, you're all in.

"Heard you two out here having a good time, so I thought I'd join."

"Sorry about that," Finn converses as if he's not still *inside me.* "I told her to be quiet, but obviously she didn't listen."

"We can punish her for that later."

Huh?

"Pussy feels good, doesn't it, Finn?"

These men cannot be real.

"Fucking perfect."

"And you, Princess… How's Finn's cock feel inside of you?"

I can't answer that. Can I?

Bottomed out inside of me, Finn stills and tugs at my hair. "Answer him."

Screw it.

"Good," I mutter.

A sharp slap stings my ass cheek as Finn snarls, "What was that?"

"It feels good… so good."

He slightly loosens his grip on my hair. "Good girl."

I finally manage to let my gaze meet Mac's. A look of pure passion burns in his eyes. He stands up straight, and I gasp as I realize he has his pants pulled down and is firmly gripping his rock-hard cock.

This is it. I really might die from being so turned on.

Finn begins slamming into me again, and I close my eyes as I feel him reach a spot inside of me I didn't even know was there. "Open your eyes, Harper," Mac demands with a heavy breath.

I snap my lids open and lock eyes with him as he lazily

strokes his cock while Finn brings me closer to my impending orgasm from behind. "Yes, Mac! Yes!"

Another sharp slap hits me square on the ass. "When I'm inside of you, you're only screaming my name. Do you understand me?"

There's too much going on. Mac's name slipped out before I could even think twice. "Yes. Finn… Please." A tear rolls down my cheek, it all feels too good.

A deep growl draws my attention back toward Mac. His head tilted back as his jaw muscles tighten, a thin layer of sweat coats his tattooed chest. After two final strokes, Mac comes into his hand with such force I worry he might pass out. Finally, he picks his head up. "Come for us, Princess… come on his cock."

It's my undoing.

My orgasm crashes into me like a freight train. I shudder around Finn, my walls squeezing him tighter and tighter, my screams filling the apartment. "Finn!"

"Fuck!" he hisses as he fills me with his release.

I'm not entirely sure what just happened or why I feel so blissfully happy with it, but I know two things for sure.

One… I want that to happen over and over and *over again*.

Two… *I'm so screwed.*

17

Finn

It's been a week since my morning with Harper and Mac, and I can't get enough of her.

I let my guard slip that morning. It was a shit-ass night. Between the shipment getting stolen, not knowing who the hell took it, Ronan's absolute fucking freak out at the docks, and Liam's very obvious disappointment in us, I needed a drink. Or three.

I'm not a drinker. Sure, I sip on a glass of whiskey now and again, but I never get drunk. When you get drunk, inhibitions are lowered, lines are crossed, and mistakes get made. I don't make mistakes.

I rarely sleep with women. Let me rephrase that; I don't need to sleep with women. Actually, let me rephrase *that; I* have better things to do with my time than getting lost in pussy. Don't get me wrong. I'm no virgin. I've had my fair share of experiences with women. But I'm not like Ronan and Mac. I can't just fuck someone to scratch that preverbal itch and move on. Whenever I try, whether I have her to myself or I'm sharing with Ronan and Mac, it never quite satisfies me. I need to connect with the woman I'm with to lower my inhibitions and be who I really am, and not many women can handle who that is. Trust me, I've tried.

As fucking annoying and cheesy as that is, it's the truth. I'm sure if you psychoanalyzed me, it would stem from my parents being murdered when I was eight and having no real family left, me wanting to fill that void in my life with any emotional connection I can… *blah blah fuckin' blah.*

Since I need that connection to enjoy sex, I don't even take the risk. Because if I develop that bond with a woman, she becomes special, and I lose control. If she becomes special and I lose control, she can be taken from me. And if another person is taken away from me, I might not make it. But… *Harper.* After just three days with that woman, all I could think about was sinking into her, controlling her, wrapping my hand around her throat, and turning that pretty ass red. Seeing her walk out of her room wearing Mac's shirt, knowing he had her, and knowing they slept together, sent me over the edge. Not because I was jealous but because I wanted to feel her *too.* After what her family did to mine, I should fucking know better, but I couldn't help myself. I wanted to have a part of her. Contrary to every one of my instincts, I wanted to connect with her.

I'm not sure whether it was seeing her ass peek out the bottom of Mac's shirt when she reached for a glass, how she pried information out of me with ease, or the three glasses of whiskey I had. But I am sure that the woman in front of me is just what the three of us need… Ronan included.

"What are you reading over there?" I'm sitting on her

bed, staring at her while she's reading like some damn fool. Mac had the chaise delivered to our penthouse yesterday, so Harper would have somewhere to relax while she reads. It's a deep green velvet color reminiscent of the walls in the bookstore. We can tell she's homesick even if she won't admit it out loud.

After her jailbreak last week, she hasn't even hinted at wanting to leave. I'm not sure if that's in fear of who lies in the shadows or because of what Ronan might do if she asks to leave again.

He's not known for his patience.

"One of my favorites." She smiles back at me. She looks absolutely adorable, nestled on the chaise, the sun beaming in from the window beside her. Her curly hair is piled on top of her head, her black glasses are perched on her head, wearing one of Mac's obnoxiously large shirts, and she has a blanket draped over her bare legs. I couldn't paint a more perfect picture if I tried.

Fucking hell. I'm not entirely sure where the Finn of a week ago went, but he isn't here anymore.

"What's it about?"

"Oh, you know, just stuff."

"Stuff? Could you be any less specific?"

"Actually, yes, I could… don't tempt me." I love when she sasses back. She needs to learn not to let the world walk all over her. It's a cruel fucking world, after all.

"Angel," I say, standing up from my spot on the bed, "I'm not asking for shits and giggles… I want to know. I want to know what puts that cute-ass smile on your face."

Cute-ass smile… Holy fuck, Finn.

"It's a romance book." She pauses with flushed cheeks.

"With some spicy scenes mixed in."

"Spicy?"

"Yeah, you know… *spicy*," she says as she curls up her nose and smirks.

"Oh, so you're reading porn?" I'm leaning over her now, hands resting against the back of the chaise on either side of her head.

"It's not porn!"

"Well, let me see it then."

"Yeah, not happening."

I drop my head so my forehead almost touches hers. "And why not?"

"Because I don't need you getting any ideas. You and Mac are plenty dirty already."

"Ha, I knew it… It's porn."

"Oh, shut up." She grins, shoving her book between the cushion.

"But trust me when I say this, Angel. You haven't even seen dirty yet." I move my mouth so she can feel my lips against her ear as I whisper, "The things we could do to you don't even compare to what you read in those books of yours."

She swallows hard, and I curl my lips to hide my grin. "I guess I'll just have to find out for myself then, won't I?"

I bite at her earlobe, grab her by the hips, and hoist her into the air.

"And where do you think you're taking me?"

"I'm about to show you how dirty I can be?" She giggles as I throw her onto the bed and climb over her. I love how I feel when I'm with her. I've walked through my entire life feeling like a dark cloud follows me everywhere I go. But when I'm around her, it feels as if it's lifted. She makes me feel like I can be free to be whoever I want to be, and I want to show her who that is. I just have to find the right time.

I'm not sure what comes over me, but I suddenly feel the need to ask, "Is that what you want?"

"Is what?"

"A happily ever after…"

A moment of contemplation crosses her face before she answers, "Yeah, I think so." She searches my face for a reaction, but I remain still, hovering above her. "I've read about them my entire life. I used the stories of other people's happily ever afters to escape from my own sad and boring life."

A feeling of guilt settles in my stomach. Not because I wouldn't *want* to be the person who wants to give it to her, but because I'm not sure I can. That *we* can.

Over the past week, Mac and I have spent virtually every minute possible with Harper. The three of us haven't been together since that morning in the kitchen, but she seems to be more than okay with splitting her time between the two of us. I'm sure multiple orgasms a day helps. And what's more, I don't mind sharing her with Mac. Actually, I really fucking like it.

I just wish Ronan would pull his head out of his ass and admit he wants her too. We can all tell he's been avoiding us the past week. He's never home, and when he is, he hides out in his office or bedroom, acting as pissed off as ever. I know he has a lot going on, being the head of the McDermott syndicate and all, but Harper is exactly what he needs. I try to stay out of it, though. This is something he needs to figure out on his own. If anyone pushes him, he'll push back tenfold.

"I want that for you."

"I want that for you too, Finn."

"I'm not entirely sure that's in the cards for someone like me, Angel."

Her hands slide up to cup the sides of my face. "It is. When you're ready for it."

When I'm ready for it, hell, I will never be *ready* for it, let alone be ready for it with Harper.

I know I will eventually have to tell her how our families are connected, but I can't bring myself to do it yet. She may be related to the Declan by blood, but that doesn't make her a Whelan. She is Harper Hayes, an angel that walks this earth, and as soon as I tell her the truth, the guilt will consume her. She won't look at me the same, and I don't know if I can handle that fucking look.

Ronan and Mac won't say anything. They know it's my story to tell, but I can't keep it a secret forever.

"Hey," she whispers, pulling me out of my thoughts. "Where'd you go just now?"

"Nowhere. I was just thinking about something."

"About what?"

"Just that… Mac and I want to take you out tonight."

Smooth, Finn. Ronan's not going to like that one.

"Really? I thought Ronan said I couldn't leave the apartment?"

You can't.

"You'll be with both of us, Angel. We will keep you safe." I climb off of her and stand at the edge of the bed. Reaching my hand out, I sit her up in front of me. "We'll go to our club. There's plenty of security there. Do you like dancing?"

"You're club?" She looks genuinely surprised that we would own something so fun.

"Yes, our club, Angel. It's one of the few operations we run legally, and it gives us a place to conduct meetings and let off steam."

"Will… will Ronan come with us?"

I tuck a strand of curls behind her ear. "I'm not sure. I know he's busy with everything going on. He's trying to track down whoever stole our shipment." I decide not to mention that he's also trying to figure out why his dad wants us to keep Harper here.

I've known Liam McDermott for a long time, and he isn't the type of person to protect someone, especially a Whelan, out of the kindness of his heart.

Harper breaks eye contact with me and looks at her lap. I know she's hurt that Ronan is doing everything he can to avoid her. The two of them may fight like cats and dogs, but it would take a complete moron not to notice the chemistry between them. I grab her chin and bring her eyes to mine. "Hey, don't worry about him. He'll come around eventually. Let's go out and have some fun, okay?"

"Okay, but I don't have anything to wear."

"Don't worry. I'll have a dress and shoes sent over for you within the hour. Why don't you draw a bath and take your time getting ready? Mac and I will meet you by the elevator at nine."

I lean over and give her a quick kiss before leaving her room and closing the door behind me. I walk down the hall and knock at Mac's door.

"What's up?"

Pushing the door open, I sigh deeply. "You and I are taking Harper to Kings tonight."

"What? Why? Ronan said she wasn't supposed to leave the apartment."

"She's not."

"So, why are we taking her there then?" As Ronan's second in command, I can tell he's hesitant about disobeying a direct order from his older brother.

I run my hands through my hair and lean against the door frame before taking a deep breath. "She was reading this book, and I asked her what it was about. She said it was about a happily ever after. Then like a fucking moron, I asked if she wanted a happily ever after. She said yes, because why wouldn't she? Then I said she deserved one. She said I did too. And because I'm a masochistic asshole, I started internally spiraling about the fact that she's Declan Whelan's granddaughter, and I haven't told her what he did to me. Because if I tell her, she's going to feel guilty, and I don't want her to feel guilty. I also don't want her to look at me with those big green eyes like I'm broken. I hate when people look at me like that. Not to mention that I haven't slept with a woman in I don't even know how long. And I especially haven't slept with the same woman more than once. I can tell that I'm starting to feel something for her, and it's only been a goddamn week. I don't know if I can handle having feelings for someone. Especially if that someone is Harper Whelan... Hayes. She noticed that I was thinking about something, so instead of telling her the truth, I panicked and told her we were taking her to Kings."

Mac's eyes widen when I finally take a deep breath. "Ummm... Okay, that was a lot." A smirk pulls at his lips.

"Dude, this isn't fucking funny. I don't know what's happening to me."

"You're right. Totally not funny." He hides his laugh with a cough as he strides over to me. "I just don't think I've ever heard you say that much at once."

"Exactly my fucking point."

"It's not that difficult to figure out, man. You like Harper. I like Harper. We both know Ronan likes her, regardless of him acting like the biggest asshole on the planet. So, let's have some fun and try not to think about it too much." He puts a hand on my shoulder. "Okay?"

I feel my shoulders relax. "Yeah, okay. You're right."

"Let's go talk to Ronan about tonight. He'll get over it. If we're taking her to Kings, there will be plenty of our security. Nothing will happen."

"I know. I just know he's going to be pissed off."

"He's always pissed off. Don't worry about it."

"Hey, do you know if he's heard anything about the shipment or figured out what's going on with Liam?"

"Not that I've heard. But he hasn't talked to me much this week. I'm sure it has something to do with the fact that I've had my face buried between Harper's legs." Mac's head falls back as he lets out a laugh.

"You're such an asshole."

"Yeah, I know, but he deserves it. Come on." He spins me around to walk out of his room, "Let's go talk to the boss man."

"Alright. I just gotta have a dress for Harper brought up."

"Fuck yes. Make sure it shows off her ass. That might just be my favorite thing on earth."

Now it's me who lets out a laugh. "You don't gotta tell me twice."

18

Ronan

"Nope. No. No fucking way." Finn and Mac are standing in front of me, giving me their stupid puppy dog eyes, and I'm not having it. I don't care if I'm always the bad guy. Enough is going on between our shit being stolen, figuring out what's going on with my dad, and having to walk around with a constant fucking hard-on because of the woman down the hall. Now, these two morons want to take her to our nightclub, knowing that there is someone out there who is quite literally trying to kill her.

I know the three of them have been sleeping together. It's why I've been avoiding them. And honestly, I don't care… much. I can see the effect she has on the two of them.

Over the last week, I've seen the rigid edges of Finn's body relax. He's always so worried about pleasing everyone and making sure everything is perfect all the time; it's nice to see him let go and relax. And Mac, all he wants is somebody to care for. All he's ever wanted is to have a woman he can worship and dote on. He's never allowed himself that. He knows what being part of this life means, and he would never want to put someone he cares for through that shit. But I can see that being with Harper fills a hole inside him.

I'm not jealous of the relationship the three of them are forming. Hell, I don't even care that she's sleeping with both of them. More than anything, I think I just want what they have. I see how happy she makes them and how happy they make her. If I could give her that, too, I would.

But I can't.

I have too much responsibility. As the leader of our empire, the amount of shit I have to do in a single day makes my fucking head spin. And Harper, she's the definition of distraction. If I let myself cross the line that Mac and Finn have, she'll make me soft. She will be a weakness that our enemies can use against me.

I *cannot* have a weakness.

My brother cocks his head, and I just know he's getting ready to irritate the shit out of me. As if this conversation hasn't already accomplished that task. "Ronan, it's not that big of a fucking deal. I won't be parading her around the streets of New York. She will be in *with* Finn and me, and at least a half dozen of our men are securing that building every night."

"We will make sure each of them knows exactly what she looks like. There's no way she would get out of there without them noticing," Finn adds. I can tell he's uncomfortable with this conversation. Very rarely does he do anything without my say-so. I know he's doing this only to make Harper happy.

Mac slumps down in one of the chairs. "Come on, man. She hasn't left this penthouse in a fucking week. We practically stole her life out from underneath her. She doesn't go to her apartment, she hasn't been back to the bookstore, and she doesn't see any of her friends. Shit, we don't know if she even has any. She deserves a few hours of fun."

I lean back in my chair, trying to get my temper under control, as I notice Finn taking a seat next to my brother. "You don't think I fucking know that. But we still have no idea who Declan is sending after her or what his plan is. And I definitely have no idea what Dad is up to yet. It's driving me fucking crazy." I can feel my nails digging into the arms of my leather desk chair. "I'm also not sure I trust her enough not to run away."

"We will keep an eye on her the whole time," answers Finn.

I love my best friend. As far as I'm concerned, he's just as much my brother as Mac. Which means, I know when he's distracted, and right now, with Harper, he's distracted. "It's not your eyes I'm worried about. You two need to think with your fucking heads. And I'm talking about the head between your damn ears, not the ones in your pants."

"You're one to talk," Mac huffs. "You've been moping around this damn place all week. And it sure as shit isn't over our shipment issues. Stuff like that has happened before. It's never affected you this much." He's not wrong. "Which means you have your panties in a fucking wad over that woman down the hall."

He's lucky he's my fucking brother or I would have already punched him across the face.

"So why don't you use *your* head and get it out of *your* ass. Just admit you want her. You know it. She knows it. Hell, even Finn and I know it. Yet, you're the only one that cares."

I don't even bother denying it. These two know me better

than anyone. It's useless lying to them. "It doesn't matter. I'm not good for her. Plus, she has you two. She doesn't need me. And as soon as we figure out what Declan's plan is, she can return to the life she was living before."

Mac leans forward, resting his elbows on his knees. "For someone as smart as you are, you're so damn dense sometimes. She may not need you, she may not need any of us when this is over, but she wants you, Ronan."

I look over at Finn. "He's right, man, she does."

"Why don't you come with us tonight? You'll be able to keep an eye on her, and know she's safe. Plus, Finn got her the sexiest fucking dress you've ever seen."

It doesn't even pay to waste my breath anymore. I know the two of them will protect her, and Kings is one of the safest clubs in the city. Security won't let anything happen to her. If they do, I'll put a bullet in their fucking brains.

But I can't go. I can't put myself in that position.

"No. I have some things I need to take care of." They know I'm lying. "You guys go. But you will *not* let her out of your sight. You *will* send me updates. And you *will* go straight there and back. No extra stops."

Mac stands and salutes me like a smart-ass. Brother or not, I really might punch him. "Yes, sir."

Finn rises. "Nothing will happen to her, Ronan. We'll keep her safe."

"You fucking better." They definitely know I'm full of shit now. If I didn't care about her, I wouldn't be so worried.

They spin on their heels and practically skip out of my office in excitement. I wish Harper would have come in here and talked to me herself, but I know that's wishful thinking. She's been avoiding me as much as I have her. It's why I find what the guys are telling me so hard to believe. If she genuinely wanted me, wouldn't she want to be around me? No, because you act like a world-class dick every time she's in the same room as you.

Fuck, I hate that I'm even thinking about this shit. I have to focus. If I'm being honest, the stolen shipment is the least of my worries. Some of my men are already on it. I have them tracking our rivals in the area to rule them out, and I've taken care of the piece of shit dock workers who let that whole thing happen. My dad's on my ass about it, but he can fuck off. All I can think about is figuring out Declan's plan for Harper. Even more so, what my dad's plan is for Harper.

I don't buy that he sent Harper here for her protection. Sure, we knew of the Hayes family growing up, but we were never that close. My parents helped Aidan and Freya scrub their identities and turned them into the Hayes'. Running the bookstore for us was their payment.

Declan Whelan has been doubling down since I took over three years ago. Word is spreading that I'm not the sadistic and ruthless asshole my father was, and he seems to think he can take over our turf in America. With the way my dad is always up my ass, I'd say he agrees.

Part of me wonders if the Declan's men are the ones who stole that shipment. That they're trying to make it look like we're weak. *Like I'm weak.* I won't stand for it. Because if Declan Whelan starts stepping in on our turf all the way from Ireland, who says it will stop there? Other syndicates will get word, and before we know it, we won't have control of shit.

Or at least that's what Dad repeatedly tells me.

I respect my old man for what he's created, but it ends there. He's a ruthless man. There isn't much he wouldn't do to get ahead. My gut is screaming at me, and I have a feeling I know precisely why Harper is here.

I really hope I'm fucking wrong.

Because if I'm right, I have absolutely no clue what I'm going to do.

I don't know if I could do it.

I don't know if I could let her go.

She's sunshine in our sea of darkness. The light she brings into our home is unlike anything I've ever seen before. The three of us battle our demons every single day; whether she notices it or not, she helps put those demons at bay. I'm not a loving person by nature, shit I'm the exact opposite, but this woman deserves everything good in life. Even if I can't be the one to give that to her, the good man I am deep down is telling me that I want to help her get it.

I spin back toward my computer to finish a few things before the three leave for the night. Once they're gone, I know I won't be able to focus on anything else besides her. I run my hands through my hair, trying to refocus on the task at hand.

Protecting Harper.

19

Harper

"Holy shit," I whisper to myself, standing in front of the mirror. I don't often put too much effort into my appearance. I'm usually far more comfortable in jeans and a graphic T-shirt, but right now, I look hot.

I don't know how he did it in just a few hours, but Finn found the perfect dress. The black sequin dress stops just below my ass and leaves little to the imagination, hugging every curve. The cowl neckline dips low between my breasts and is held up by two thin straps that tie behind my neck, while the back sits at the base of my spine. It's not something I would have picked for myself in a million years, but I have to admit, I've never felt better.

Finn paired the dress with a pair of strappy black studded Louboutin heels that are just edgy enough to pull the look together.

I walk back into my bathroom and put the finishing touches on my makeup. I decided to let the dress and shoes do the talking and kept my hair and makeup simple, nothing but some concealer, bronzer, nude lipstick, mascara, and the perfect winged eyeliner, which may or may not have taken six tries.

If you know you know.

I pulled my unruly curls into a bun on the top of my head while leaving a few pieces around my face.

After giving myself one last once over, I gather the courage to find the guys. I have never been this excited to go clubbing. For just a few hours, I want to forget about everything else. I know it's not exactly safe for me to go out right now, but I'll be with Finn and Mac. I know they'll protect me. I want to go out and dance. I want to have some drinks. I want *fun.*

Something my life has always seemed to lack.

As I emerge from the hall, I find Finn and Mac standing at the elevator.

My. God.

I can honestly say I have never seen two better-looking men in all of my life. They haven't even touched me yet, and I can say with one hundred percent certainty my panties are already wet.

Finn's dressed in his usual suit, but there's a lightness about him tonight. His black suit isn't paired with a tie tonight, and the top two buttons of his white dress shirt are undone. His hair isn't slicked back like it usually is. Instead, it's pushed to the side, a few strands falling ever so slightly across his forehead. I like this Finn.

Mac's dressed in a black fitted polo that is stretched perfectly tight around his chest and biceps. He's paired his shirt with cuffed black dress pants and shoes, and a matte black watch sits on his wrist, drawing attention to his hands. There's something about men's hands… I swear it's like pornography. I've never seen him look so put together. He's usually the most casual of the three, dressing in jeans or sweatpants, but not tonight. Tonight he looks like an absolute smoke show.

As I stand there admiring them in all their glory, Mac does a double take in my direction. He stands there, eyes locked with mine for a few seconds before he hits Finn in the arm.

Finn's eyes follow Mac's. I stand there momentarily, loving how their gaze feels like fire on my skin as they look me up and down. I let out a breath I didn't realize I was holding and walk toward them.

"Harper…" Mac runs his hand down his face. "You look… fuck… you look fucking gorgeous."

"You think so?" I can feel my cheeks blushing as I do a quick spin.

He grabs me by the wrist and pulls me into him. I immediately feel his erection pressing into my stomach. "Oh, I know so." He slants his mouth over mine, and I don't hesitate to open my mouth, letting him taste me for just a moment before Finn moves next to him.

He doesn't pull me from Mac's arms. Instead, he reaches down and grabs a handful of my backside before he puts his mouth to my ear and whispers, "We better leave this apartment now, or we'll never make it."

"Why?" I ask, momentarily confused.

He grips me harder, neither of them moving an inch. "Because I'm about five seconds away from throwing that sweet ass over my shoulder and tying you to my bed so Mac and I can fuck you until the sun comes up." Finn practically growls in my ear.

"Oh…"

"Yeah. Oh."

He's probably right, we need to leave. I really want to go to the club, but I'm beyond turned on hearing him talk like that, feeling them both pressed against me.

"Come on, Princess." Mac gives me one last quick kiss before we climb into the elevator and make our way to the car waiting out front.

* * *

The car ride over to Kings was absolute torture, in the best way possible, I mean.

If one of them rubbed their hand up my thigh, the other kissed and bit at my neck and shoulder. Neither of them would relieve the pressure between my legs, and by the time we pulled up in front of the club, I climbed out of the car, practically dripping, while these two assholes followed behind, grins as evident as their erections.

Now, I'm sitting in a private booth at the back of the club while Mac grabs us our next round of drinks, and Finn checks in with the security guards. I know Finn is telling them to keep a close eye and not let anyone else near me. There is someone out there who is trying to kill me, after all.

That should be enough to make me want to hole up in the apartment, but I can't help it. I want this night out with Finn and Mac—more than I want to be safe. But I am safe. They won't let anything happen to me.

A few more minutes pass, and one of my favorite songs,

"Needed Me" by Rihanna, starts playing throughout the club. Mac isn't back yet and I can still see Finn talking to some of the security guards. I'm getting antsy, and I really want to dance.

Sliding out of the booth, I make my way to an empty spot on the dance floor and begin moving my hips to the beat of the music. I may be a bookworm who doesn't go out much, but I know how to shake what my mamma gave me.

As the song blasts through the speakers, I relax and get lost in the music, thinking about nothing but how the music makes me feel and how happy I am to be here, having fun. The music changes to something slower, and I'm about to head back to the booth when I feel an arm snake around my waist. Finally, one of them found me.

I turn around to see which one of them it is, only to see a man I don't recognize. I step out of his embrace and offer him an apologetic smile. "I'm here with someone."

A sly smile spreads across the man's face, and he steps toward me, grabbing my forearm. "Come on, sweetheart. Just dance to one song with me, and I promise I can make you forget who you came here with."

I can say without a shadow of a doubt I have no interest in this man whatsoever. His black hair is slicked back and coated in so much gel that it doesn't look like it would move if I took a leaf blower to it. His chest hair sticks out of his V-neck and is tangled in his gold chain.

This is why I never go out. Men are the worst.

"No, I'm fine. Thank you." I remove any semblance of a smile from my face, hoping he gets it—no such luck.

He pulls me tight against his front, and I can feel his hot breath against my face. "But you are so fuckin' hot. I promise

I'll show you a good time."

I plant my hands against the man's chest, this time shoving him away. "I said no, and I meant it… *No.*"

He tightens his grip. "People don't tell me no, sweetheart. Now turn around and back that ass up, or I'll…" The sleazy man can't finish his sentence before a hand grabs him by the collar and slams him to the ground.

Great. Now I made the bouncers cause a scene.

It's not one of the bouncers, though. It's Finn. He has the man pinned to the ground while Mac rears his fist back and slams it into the guy's nose, instantly splitting the bridge. "You don't get to fucking touch her!" The rage in Mac's voice is unlike anything I've ever heard. Blood begins pouring out of the douchebag's nose, but Finn doesn't let him go, and Mac doesn't stop punching.

I don't move. I just stand there. Watching the two of them beat the hell out of this guy. Frozen in place. Not out of fear but in awe. The way their muscles ripple underneath their suits, the pure rage coursing through them because someone touched what was theirs… *me.*

I notice the man is no longer fighting back and has gone limp. Alright, this has gone on long enough. The guy doesn't need to die over it.

"Mac!" I shout over the music. "I think that's enough." He doesn't stop. Neither of them acknowledges me. I step closer. "Finn, I think you got him!"

Still nothing.

Mac pulls his fist back for another punch, and I grab his arm. His head spins toward me so fast I'm sure he pulled a muscle. He's looking at me, but it's almost like he doesn't see me, like he's looking right through me. Blinded by rage.

I cup his face in my hands. "Mac, I'm okay. That's enough."

His face changes almost instantly, and I know he finally heard me. He stands in front of me as Finn lets go of the man's shirt. He roars at the security guard beside us, "Get this fucking asshole out of here."

The guard grabs the guy by the front of his shirt and pulls him up to his feet, his eyes opening ever so slightly. Finn gets in his face before the guard can pull him away. "The only reason you aren't dying tonight is because of her. If I ever see you again… If you ever come near her again, I will not fucking hesitate to rip your spine out of your fucking asshole and shove it down your fucking throat."

Without another word to the guy, Finn takes a couple of steps toward me, fire burning in his eyes. He grabs my hand and drags me through the crowd with Mac hot on our tails down a hallway in the back of the club and into what looks to be their office. Mac slams the door closed before he comes to stand next to Finn in front of me. Both of them look like they're about to boil over with rage.

I should have stayed in the booth. I should have waited.

Shit, Harper. Can't you just do as you're told? Ronan's words from earlier pound through my head. My eyes well up in frustration. I don't want them to be upset with me. I wanted to have a fun night. I ruined it. I feel a tear roll down my cheek as I look up at the two of them standing there. Breathing heavy. Not speaking.

"I'm sorry. I–I didn't mean to."

They're pissed that I caused a scene. That I didn't behave. They're going to realize I'm not worth the trouble. They're going to leave me.

Just like everyone else.

20

Finn

"What?" I'm still firmly planted in my spot next to Mac, fucking stunned and trying to simmer the rage that's boiling inside me. Why in the hell is she apologizing?

"Princess, why are you apologizing?" Mac keeps his voice low, trying not to startle her.

"I–I should have stayed in the booth and waited for you guys. I just wanted to dance. I wasn't trying to draw attention, but then that guy…" Tears spill down her cheek, and she sucks in another harsh breath. "I thought I could handle him, but he wouldn't let go… and then… then you guys showed up… and… I'm sorry I made you do that."

Harper has her arms wrapped around her middle, now looking at the ground like she's trying to make herself as small as possible.

Seeing her like this is something I wasn't prepared for. I want to move mountains to take her pain away, to stop her from being upset. Seeing tears stream down her face, knowing I could have prevented them, fills my body with a wrath I've never experienced before. I'm clenching my fists at my sides, willing myself to get a grip. I need to be calm. She needs to understand that we're not upset with her. The only person I'm upset with is that asshole sitting outside on the curb, who is lucky enough to still be breathing.

Mac moves toward Harper to comfort her. He's always been better at that. He reaches up to cup her face and brushes a tear away with his thumb. "You have nothing to apologize for. Yes, I wish you would have stayed in the booth and waited for us, but"—Harper raises her eyes to meet Mac's—"just because you were dancing alone doesn't give anyone permission to put their hands on you."

"Ever," I snarl from behind Mac.

Harper's gaze meets mine. "You are ours. Fucking *ours*, Harper. Anyone who puts their hands on you will be lucky to walk away with them still intact."

Her mouth drops open as if she's shocked we would be capable of something so violent. Most people think Ronan has the worst temper out of us. And really, I don't blame them. His hard-ass exterior and short temper do nothing to convince them otherwise. But Mac and I, we're the ones you should fear.

If Mac comes for you, you'll wish you were dead. His rage has no limits, and he will do anything to get his point across. It's how he was trained. But me? You won't have time to wish you were dead. You already will be. My anger is something I keep under careful lock and key all day long. So, when it does boil over, it's an explosion of epic proportions. That fucking asshole sitting outside should be thanking god for Harper.

Because *she* is the only reason I didn't drag him behind the club after Mac was done with him and snap his fucking neck. But no, just two words from her, "That's enough," was all it took to get Mac and me to stop in our tracks.

"I don't want you to have to do that for me… It's not worth it," she whispers.

Now it's me who steps toward her. I need to be touching her. I go behind her and rest my hands on her waist, leaving her sandwiched between Mac and me.

"Angel, I want to make one thing crystal fucking clear." Possessiveness causes my grip on her to tighten. "We will keep you safe. No matter what. I would give my life to keep you safe. Every fucking time. *That* is how much you are worth."

"Do you understand?" Mac asks.

She doesn't answer him.

"Answer him, Harper. Do you understand?"

Nothing, I know she doesn't believe us. She doesn't think she's worth it, that she's worth our protection. She's putting up a wall, trying to push us away before we get too close. Because if we're close, we can leave her; if we leave her, she'll be alone.

I know what that feels like. And if I have anything to do with it, she will never be alone.

The last fifteen minutes, combined with the broke look on her face and my need to make it all better, are enough to tip me over the edge.

I can't take it anymore.

She may think we have her in our lives because we have to. That once the threat is gone, she'll be able to leave.

No. She needs to understand what I feel. What Mac feels.

And, as soon as he grows a pair, what Ronan feels. She's *not* fucking leaving. I already know she's too important.

I shoot Mac a look over her shoulder; without a word, he knows exactly what I'm thinking. He bends over and lifts her off the ground. On instinct, she wraps her legs around Mac's waist. Gently, he sets her on the black leather couch against the wall.

His nature with women is to be gentle because that's who he is at his very core.

Not me.

In the bedroom, I'm in control. I like it fucking rough, and I want a woman to do exactly as I say. Most would argue it's a complete one-eighty from who I am outside the bedroom.

A people pleaser who does as he's *told.*

It's part of the reason I've mostly avoided women all these years. I've never found one who can handle the whiplash that is my sexual appetite.

I know Mac's instinct is to be soft with Harper, but right now, I'm not so sure that's what she needs. She needs someone to make her understand what she does to us. She needs to know how she makes us lose control. I know Mac's up for the challenge. I've seen him do it before. Taking a step forward, I grab Harper's hand and stand her up.

"Turn around, Harper." She hesitates, barely mustering the courage to look me in the eye. I've been going easy on her the last week, not fully unleashing my demons. I don't want to scare her away, but with Mac here, I know he won't let me get too far. He won't let me hurt her.

I firmly grab her jaw. "Harper. Turn. Around. Now." Her eyes instantly widen. She knows I mean business. She turns around, and I gather the bottom of her dress in my hands and lift it up over her head, grazing my fingertips along her skin as I go. I hear Mac taking his shirt off behind me.

I begin biting at the skin along Harper's shoulders, causing a shiver to run through her body. "I'm going to mark every fucking inch of this beautiful body. Everyone will know who you belong to."

Slowly, I lower myself, biting down her spine as I go until my lips meet the lace of her underwear. I run my fingers between her legs over the fabric. "God, Angel. These are soaked. Did we do this to you?"

Once again, she doesn't answer. I bite her ass hard. She yelps and tries to turn around, but not before I grab her hips, keeping her facing the couch. "Here's how this is going to go, Angel. If Mac and I ask you a question, you answer, or you'll be punished. Do you understand me?"

Nothing.

I bite her again, harder this time. "Answer me, Harper. Now."

"Yes. Yes, I understand."

"Good." I hear her breath quicken. "Who made you wet? Was it that fucking asshole on the dance floor?"

"No! I swear!"

I knew it wasn't, but I wanted to hear her say it. "Then who?"

"You, Finn."

"And?"

"And Mac. God, you two always make me so wet."

Mac groans deep in his chest. I know he's just waiting to get his hands on her.

"Good girl." I hear her whimper at my words. I've noticed it before. I think our girl has a hell of a praise kink. She couldn't be more perfect. I'd love nothing more than to tell her what a good fucking girl she is over and over again.

I grip the sides of her underwear and slide them down her leg, inhaling her arousal as I go. Harper lifts her shoe, waiting for me to undo the straps. I tisk, "Oh no, Angel. Those stay on. I've been dying to fuck you in those heels since I picked them out for you." A sound between a moan and a whine escapes her lips. "What about you, Mac? Don't you think the shoes should stay on?"

"Fuck yeah, I do."

"Turn around," I say as I rise to my feet. "Look at me, Harper." Finally, her beautiful green eyes are open wide and staring at me. Right into my fucking soul. "That's it. You're about to understand exactly what you do to us. That from here on out, the three of us are the only ones that matter."

Immediately there's a bit of sadness in her eyes. I know she wants Ronan. I know it hurts her that he is doing everything possible to avoid her. But I understand why he's doing it. He's scared. I also know that he's walking the razor's edge. He's right on the brink of giving in to his urges. She just needs to hold on. In the meantime, I fully intend to cherish not having to share her with one more person. I grip her chin between my thumb and forefinger. "Hey, he will come around. I promise."

The sound of Mac's belt cuts through the room. Her eyes immediately shoot over my shoulder. Judging by the look on her face, I'd be willing to bet his dick is out.

Taking her hand in mine, I move it to the erection that's currently trying to bust open my zipper. I could come just from feeling her touch through my fucking pants. "Do you feel that? That's what you do to me." I glance over my shoulder at Mac, who does indeed have his shirt off. His pants are pulled down just below his cock, and he's stroking himself. "You see Mac? What you do to him?"

She nods. "Remember the rules, Angel. You answer me when I ask you a question."

Breathlessly, she answers, "Yes."

"Exactly. We've barely even begun yet, Angel, and I'm ready to fucking burst. *You* do that to us." I squeeze her hand over my erection so she grips me harder.

"Go to him, now." She steps around me and moves toward Mac. I need a damn second to compose myself. I'm about to blow, and I'm nowhere near done with her.

Sliding my suit jacket off, I turn around to sit on the couch and watch as Mac picks her up again, his dick still hanging out of his pants. I unbutton my shirt and notice I've already broken into a sweat.

Jesus Christ, Finn.

Mac whispers something in her ear, and I watch as she reaches up to the bun on top of her head and pulls out her ponytail, letting her delicious curls cascade down her back. Smart man. I love her curls. I love them even more when they're wrapped around my fist.

"We will always come for you, Princess. Wherever you are, whatever happens, we will be there." I can tell he means it as both a threat and a promise. He's in just as deep as I am.

Mac begins kissing Harper with such fierceness I'm sure he's bruising her sweet lips. The harder he kisses her, the louder her moans get. I unbutton my pants and pull my cock out, giving it a few good strokes. I need her fucking lips on me. Now.

"Bring her over here."

A sly grin slides across Mac's face, like he knows what I'm thinking. He walks her over and sets her on her feet in front of me. "On your knees, Angel. I want to feel your pretty lips around my cock." We've never done this before. I honestly haven't even thought about it. Over the last week, I've done nothing but make her feel good. And I've done it happily. But seeing her with Mac, knowing that she's ours, it's making me fucking feral. She drops to her knees and rests her hands on my thighs. "Once you're done sucking my cock we're going to fuck you. Okay?"

Her eyes grow wide. "We?"

A chuckle escapes my lips. "Yes, we."

"But... but how?"

Mac leans down and puts his lips to her ear. "Finn is going to fill that sweet pussy with his cock. And me..." I feel her nails digging into my thighs. "That ass is all mine, Princess."

"I can't. No. That won't—" I don't let her finish her sentence.

"You can, and it will, Angel. Don't worry. We have you. We won't hurt you. Okay?"

It takes her a few seconds, but she answers, "Okay."

"Do you trust us?" Mac asks.

"Yes. I do."

"Good, now suck Finn's dick like a good girl."

21

Harper

Not giving myself a chance to bail, I grab the base of Finn's dick and take him in my mouth. Immediately his hands find their way to my hair, gripping me tight enough to send a wave of pain down my spine but not enough to make me stop.

I lick the tip a few times, tasting the beads of cum that starts dripping out.

"Fuck, Harper. Your mouth feels so good, Angel."

His praise spurs me on. I've never done this to either of them. If I'm being honest, I've only given a man a blow job a handful of times, so I'm by no means an expert. That's probably why I try to avoid them if possible. I don't want to be disappointing. But, I want to pleasure Finn. I want to make him feel good.

Everything he said to me, how he made me feel, was just… well… *shit.*

I don't even have words for it.

Feeling brave, I give the head of his dick one last lick and take him in my mouth as far as I can go, stopping before he hits my gag reflex.

"Oh no, Angel. I know you can go further than that." Finn thrusts his hips forward, making his dick hit the back of my throat. I gag slightly and can feel tears roll down my cheek. He doesn't move, though. I'm about to pull off, but then I hear him. "It's okay, Angel. Your mouth was made for me. Relax your throat and breathe through your nose for me." His voice immediately pushes away any self-doubt. I do as he says and begin bobbing back and forth, sucking hard as I go. Finn starts thrusting rhythmically into my mouth, picking a pace that's just right for him. I brace my hands against his thighs as he begins to fuck my mouth. He's in control.

I can hear Mac moaning in the background, getting more turned on by the second. "Touch yourself, Princess."

He doesn't have to ask me twice. I move one hand down to my clit and start rubbing small circles. I moan around Finn's dick, loving how my fingers feel between my legs while he's in my mouth.

"Harper, I don't want to come in your mouth. Moan like that again, and I'm done for." I do it again, just to see if he's serious. His hands, still in my hair, rip my head off his dick, and he grabs me by the throat. "What did I just say?"

"Not to," I answer with a devious grin.

He smirks and lets go, and I turn around to give Mac the same treatment, but he holds his hand out and stops me. "But…" I mutter, confused.

"If you put your mouth on my cock then there's no chance of me fucking that sweet ass of yours. So, spin that pretty face back around"—he moves his finger in a circle—"and sit that pussy on Finn's cock."

I'm trembling with anticipation. Never in my wildest dreams would I have imagined two men inside me at once. I should be scared. But I'm not. I want it more than I've ever wanted anything.

I turn around to find Finn leaning back against the couch as far as he can go, and he hooks his finger at me in a "come hither" motion. Doing as I'm told, I straddle his lap and wait until he tells me what to do next.

Finn reaches between my legs and grabs the base of his cock, lining it up with my entrance. "Sit." I throw my head back, pleasure coursing through my body as Finn fills me. I will never get tired of the way he feels inside of me. "So beautiful," Finn says as he twists a strand of my hair through his fingers.

I swear a switch flips inside me just then. I'm not entirely sure what happens, but I feel something shift within me. Whether it's a good thing or not is up in the air.

"Hey," Finn snaps, bringing me back to the present, "focus on me, Angel. Nothing outside of this room matters. Focus on how we make you feel."

"Easier said than done."

He keeps moving inside of me. Slowly. The pace is agonizing. I can feel the orgasm building, but it's not enough to get me there. "Finn, please… I need… I need more." His finger finds my clit, and he pinches. "Ahhh!"

"Oh, don't worry, you're about to get *way* more. Mac, I think our girl is ready. She's practically dripping."

Mac's strong hand grabs my shoulder while he runs the opposite down my spine. "Lean forward for me, Princess." With Finn still deep inside me, I lean forward and rest my face against his shoulder.

"Stay still. When Mac is all the way inside, you can move. Okay?" I can't speak. I can't breathe. The anticipation might kill me. Suddenly a sharp smack hits my ass. "Harper," he snaps. Oh shit. I didn't answer him.

"I won't move." Lifting my hips, Finn pulls himself out of me, and not more than a second later, Mac slams into me. I'm more than wet enough, so he fills me without resistance.

"We don't have any lube in here, so this will have to do."

This is happening. Mac is going to fuck my ass.

"Tell me, Princess. Has anyone ever had you here?" His thumb gently presses inside the tight hole.

"No." I can't see him, but I know a satisfied smile has spread across his face.

Finn whispers in my ear, "And no one else ever will. This pussy, this ass, every fucking square inch of you, it's *ours.*"

After just a few strokes, Mac pulls out of me, and Finn pulls my hips back down onto him. "Stay still, Angel."

"I'm nervous," I blurt out. I don't know what prompted me to say it, but I am. I've never done anything like this.

"Don't be nervous," Mac says as he continuously runs his fingertips up and down my back. "We won't do anything to hurt you." He leans forward so his mouth is on the opposite side of my face as Finn's and presses a soft kiss to my cheek. Slowly, and I mean *slowly,* Mac pushes the head of his cock inside me.

"Holy shit."

Finn chuckles. The smart-ass actually chuckles. "It must be intense, man. She never swears."

"I can't help it. How is there going to be enough room?"

"Trust me, Princess. There's enough room. It will burn

for a second, but once that passes and I'm all the way in, I promise it'll feel so fucking good."

I've never felt anything like this. I feel undeniably full. I love it.

Mac pushes inside me a few more inches, and I feel the burning. "Ahhh…"

"I'm halfway, Princess. Almost there. Relax for me. Let me in."

Jesus, only halfway.

"Just do it."

"I don't want to hurt you."

"Mac!" I snap. I want pleasure. But right now, all I feel is pain. "I'm okay. Just do it."

Mac slams the rest of the way inside me with a loud groan. "You are so fucking tight, Harper. I've never felt anything so good in my life." Mac's grip on my shoulder tightens, and I can tell he's trying to control himself. He pulls out of me until just the tip of his cock is inside me and slams home again. We all stay still for a few seconds, all three of us breathing heavily. Then I notice it. It doesn't hurt anymore. It feels… good.

So damn good.

They must feel me relax because Finn slowly begins to move. Small shallow thrusts. "You ready?"

"Yessss… so ready."

Mac and Finn begin thrusting in and out of me. When one goes in, the other goes out, creating the perfect rhythm. And once they can tell I've fully adjusted, they pick up the pace and begin thrusting into me with unbridled passion.

"Oh my god, oh my god, oh my god." I chant over and over again, willing myself to hold out as long as possible. I don't ever want this to end. Finn grabs my jaw and makes me face him, his lips meet mine, and we sink into a deep kiss. All the while, Mac reaches around and pinches one of my nipples hard.

"Who do you belong to, Princess?"

I rip my lips from Finn's. "You."

"And?"

"Ahh! God… Finn!"

"And?"

I don't answer right away. I know what he wants me to say, but Ronan and I haven't crossed that line yet. I'm not sure if he even wants to. Mac's hand lands hard against my ass. A warning. "And?"

"Ronan! I belong to all of you."

"That's fucking right. You belong to us. Nobody will ever touch you again."

"Yes… yes!" Overcome with emotion, tears fall down my cheeks.

Still gripping my jaw, Finn snarls, "Come. Come for us, Angel. Now." His lips crash into mine again, swallowing every sound I make.

It's all too much. Finn slamming into my pussy. The way Mac feels inside a place nobody else has ever been. Finn's lips on mine. Mac pinching my nipples to the point of pain. I can't take it anymore; an orgasm, unlike any other, crashes into me. White spots fill my vision. "Yes, Mac! God, Finn!" Every muscle in my body tightens as I climb higher and higher. It feels like one orgasm comes after another, never-ending.

I know we're never going to be the same after this. I know *I'm* never going to be the same.

Mac follows. He bottoms out inside of me and bites down on my shoulder, filling me with his release. He pulls out, and

Finn begins fucking me into oblivion.

"See what you do to us, Angel? You are fucking worth it. This cunt is worth it. That ass is worth it. That sweet heart of yours, fucking worth it."

I can't answer him, too lost in his words and the look on his face. He means it. He really means it.

I'm worth it.

"Fuck!" Finn screams as he bottoms out inside of me. His jaw clenches so hard I'm afraid he might crack his teeth. Then I feel it. I feel him come harder than he ever has with me before.

I did that to him. To them. Me.

"You did so good, Angel." Finn gently kisses my forehead, and pride fills my chest.

I rest my head on his shoulder a moment longer, dripping in sweat, before climbing off his lap. I want to stay here forever, but I know we have to get back out there. Mac's already working on putting his shirt back on as I walk past him toward the box of tissues sitting on the desk. He stops me and grips my chin. "No, ma'am."

"What do you mean? I'm a mess."

"I want every man in this club to know you've been fucked. That *we* fucked you. I want them to fucking smell it on you."

My cheeks instantly blush. "Well… alright then. Can I at least put my panties back on?"

"Nope," Finn answers behind me.

"What do you mean no?!"

"We want to watch our cum drip down those delicious legs."

Mac's already stuffing my panties into his pants pocket.

Smart-asses.

"Plus, we're leaving anyway. No use in putting them back

on," Mac adds.

"Why are we leaving? We haven't even danced?"

"I know, Princess. We can come back another night. Soon." He looks at me sympathetically. He knew I was excited to get out of the apartment. "But we need to take care of something first?"

"What?"

"I'm sick of my brother being a goddamn pain in the ass. You're going to go back to the apartment and fix him."

"And how am I going to do that?" I ask as I put my dress back on.

"Please," Finn quips. "Between seeing you in that dress, you're freshly fucked hair, the hickeys all over you, and the sight of cum dripping down your legs… he doesn't stand a chance. You just need to push him."

"Oh, great. I just have to crack through the stone wall that is Ronan McDermott. Perfect." They press their lips together, trying not to laugh at my heavy sarcasm.

Mac lowers his head and kisses my forehead. "Oh, relax, Princess. You just might give him a run for his money."

22

Ronan

Those assholes have had Harper at the club for over an hour now, and not once have they texted or called me to check-in. They're lucky I have access to the security cameras. They seem to be behaving for now.

I stare at my computer screen and watch Harper sitting in the booth while Mac is at the bar getting drinks. She isn't even doing anything, yet I can't bring myself to look away. Mac was right about the dress Finn bought her. She is fucking stunning. Not a single other woman in Kings holds a candle to her.

I'm both annoyed and in awe of how she looks tonight. I couldn't bring myself to say goodbye to them before they left. As soon as I saw her, I knew I would change my mind and want to join them. I need to keep my distance. But that sure as shit didn't stop me from obsessively staring at her through Kings' security cameras.

Every man's eyes were on her the second she walked

through the doors. Meanwhile, I resisted the urge to gouge out the eyes of anyone who looked at her. Her creamy skin was the perfect contrast to that goddamn dress. It clung to her every curve and left little to the imagination while the club lights reflected off every sparkle. What I would give to run my fingers through her unruly curls and pull them out of the bun on top of her head. And *fuck me,* those heels. Her already long legs seemed to go on for miles in those heels. I have got to give Finn credit. He did good. *Too damn good.*

I don't think Harper realizes how beautiful she is. How sexy she is. She commands all the attention in the room by just *existing.*

Mac's still at the bar getting drinks when I notice Harper slide out of their booth and make her way toward the dance floor. I instantly tense, not wanting her to go anywhere alone. "No, Baby. Wait for the guys," I whisper to myself, willing her to hear me across town.

Harper finds an empty spot on the dance floor and begins swaying her hips to the beat of the music. "Fuuuuck," I sigh, wiping a hand down my face as I feel myself getting hard. I could watch this all fucking day.

"Focus, Ronan," I snap.

Neither Mac nor Finn seems to have noticed that she left the booth, and she's starting to grab the attention of some men around her. I grab my phone to call Mac and Finn, hoping one of them will answer, but both of their phones ring out.

"I'm really going to kill the two of them."

Fisting my hands, I continue watching Harper through the security cameras. Another minute passes, and the song must change because everyone starts moving their bodies slower while simultaneously getting close to their partners.

Shit.

It's only a matter of time before—

I don't even have a chance to finish my thought before it comes to fruition. Some sleazy-looking motherfucker wraps his arm around Harper's waist. "Fuck!" Slamming my fist onto my desk, I stand up from my chair. That's it. I can't sit here anymore.

"Fuck this." I'm not going to sit behind a goddamn computer and watch this shit happen when I could be there, protecting her. I need to get to the club. I don't wait to see what happens. Grabbing my suit jacket off the back of the chair, I move toward the elevator, willing the rage that's boiling inside me not to explode once I see Harper. She makes me so fucking mad it's hard to even look at her sometimes. At the same time, I only want to hold her in my arms where she's safe—two sides of the same damn coin.

I'm about to push the button for the elevator when it dings and opens in front of me.

"Hello, Son."

I blink in confusion. He only shows up here if he needs something. This should be good.

"Dad."

"We need to talk." I don't have time for this. I need to get to Harper.

"Actually, can it wait? I have something I need to take care of. It's—"

"Now," he snaps as he interrupts me. "Whatever it is needs to wait."

Fuck.

Fuck, fuck, *fuck.*

I need to know what that asshole is doing to her. Did she

push him away? Did Mac and Finn come back and find her? Is he hurting her?

That last thought is enough to make me break out in a sweat. But I can't leave. I can't go back to my computer. Because what dear old dad wants, he gets. Whether I like it or not. "Alright. Ummm, come on in," I mumble, pissed off with him already.

Dad slides past me and makes his way toward the bar, where I know he's about to pour himself a double. If he's pouring himself a drink, I know this conversation is bound to piss me right the hell off. What else is new?

I turn to follow him but pause. Looking up at the ceiling, I whisper, "Harper, you better be okay."

* * *

My whole body is so tense I can practically feel my muscles growing sorer by the second. Then again, that seems to be my constant state of being these days. I'm just sitting here, waiting for him to drop whatever bomb he came here to deliver, and I still have no damn clue what's going on at Kings with Harper.

I haven't felt my phone vibrate in my pocket, which means Mac or Finn *still* haven't checked in with me. Like I fucking instructed them too. I can't handle not knowing what's going on. The lack of control is eating away at me.

The three of them are going to get the ass-chewing of a lifetime when they get back.

I continue to spiral as Dad just sits there, staring at me,

swirling the glass of whiskey in his hand. The constant noise of the ice rattling in the tumbler grates my nerves. "Jesus Christ, Dad. What is so important?"

He brings the amber liquid to his lips and polishes off the glass. *Oh great.*

With a dramatic sigh, he leans forward and sets the crystal glass on the coffee table. He rests his elbows on his thighs and asks, "How are things going with Harper? I notice she isn't here."

I fucking knew it. Of course, this is about Harper. I make a mental note not to give him too much information. I want to keep a few cards close to my chest. "They've been fine. She's out with Mac and Finn."

"Out?"

"Out." I continue to meet his stare, deadpan.

"And where exactly is 'out'?"

"They're at Kings." *This should be good.*

"You're joking, right?"

"Nope." I pop the "p" to get some attitude across. His face turns red with anger almost instantly.

"What the hell are they doing at Kings?!" He's sitting up straight now, and I know it's only a matter of time before he explodes.

"She was going stir-crazy in the apartment and wanted to go out. It's the safest place we could think to take her." I neglect to tell him that it was Finn's idea and that no one has checked in since they left. That's for me to worry about, not him.

A few seconds pass, and, *as predicted*, he explodes out of his chair. "What the fuck is wrong with you?! How are you supposed to keep an eye on her if you let her go gallivanting all over the goddamn city?!"

I remain seated on the couch. "She's fine. Mac and Finn are with her, and Kings is crawling with security, who knows exactly who she is and what she looks like. She won't be able to leave without anyone besides the guys." Before they left, I called in some extra security at the club.

"I should have known not to trust you with this. I should have taken care of it myself," he seethes, pacing around the den like a fucking crazy person.

Wait. *Taken care of it.* Taken care of what? I want to know the answer, so I continue to push. "What the hell is your problem? Either you trust me to take care of things, or you don't. She's just a girl. I'm pretty sure we're more than capable of—"

"She's not just a girl!" There it is. I can always count on his temper to get the better of him. "I swear to God, Ronan. If anything happens to her, then it's over. We won't be able to…" He stops mid-sentence, and a look of instant regret spreads across his face as if he's said something he didn't want to have said.

Unease crawls up my back. "We won't be able t— what?"

He doesn't answer, and rage consumes me. My temper is finally getting the best of me. I am my father's son, after all. I won't deal with the secrets, not when it comes to Harper. "Dad! Answer the fucking question." I stand and curl my hands into fists at my sides as I take a couple of steps closer to him. "We won't be able to… what?" I bite out the last word.

"It has to be done."

Fuck. "What does?"

"We came to an agreement… a truce, if you will. You have enough to worry about. You can barely handle the responsibilities I've given you as it is." I ignore yet another comment about my inability to lead because I already know exactly where this is going, but I want to hear him say the fucking words. "So, I took it upon myself to deal with the problem across the pond and gave our friend Declan a call."

A slow smile spreads across his face, and for the first time in my life, I lunge forward and put my hands on him. "Tell me you didn't," I say with my hands gripping the front of his shirt.

"Oh, but I did."

I move to push him against the wall behind him, and I hear a low chuckle escape his lips. *He's fucking laughing.*

"I asked him what it would take for him to leave us alone. His answer was simple… Harper."

"Why? She is of no threat to him."

"She's no immediate threat, no. However, she's the next in line to run their syndicate, being Freya's daughter and all. He's worried that if she's left in charge, she will dismantle everything he's built, and he's probably not wrong."

No, he's probably not. But wait. "Then why the hell did you bring her here? Why are you having us protect her?"

"He put a hit out on her. He doesn't want his men to know he would kill his own granddaughter. Hell, they don't know he killed Freya and Aidan. If he's willing to do that to family, imagine what he would do to anyone else."

I grip his shirt harder. "That still doesn't explain why she's here!"

"Are you fucking daft, boy?! Where did she work? What did her whole life revolve around?"

It dawns on me. "The bank."

"Yeah, the fucking bank. Do you think I wanted Declan

Whelan to find out where she worked, where she spent *all* of her time? Do you think I wanted him to find out what was in the walls of *Hayes' Bookstore*?"

I release his shirt and step back. "You're trading her like cattle for…*for money?*"

"You bet your ass I am. Not only to keep our money safe but to collect the enormous payout he's shelling out for her. I honestly had no idea he was even looking for her anymore, not until I contacted him. I knew he killed her parents, but I thought his vendetta stopped there. But he's never been able to find her. Aiden and Freya covered her tracks well. Her life was a complete mystery to him until just a few weeks ago. As soon as he said her name, I knew she was the answer to our problems. I convinced him to call off the hit and have her brought to Ireland instead. That way, he could ensure she was taken care of in whatever way he saw fit. We don't need more of his hired help crawling around the city than necessary. Harper just needs to lay low here until all the arrangements are made."

"But what about the guy who tried to take her the day after we brought her here? The guy at her apartment?"

"Some asshole who never got the memo that the hit was called off."

"What's he going to do with her?"

"If I had to guess, he's either going to force her to get with the fucking program or—"

"He'll kill her." I can feel my heart beating faster in my chest.

"I'm assuming it will be the latter of the two."

"What is wrong with you?!"

He stares back at me like I have two heads. Like I'm a complete moron for not understanding why he would do this.

"We don't do this kind of shit. We don't sell *people*. That's not who we are. And we sure as shit don't send innocent women away to be murdered!"

"Oh, don't start acting all high and fucking mighty on me now, Ronan."

I can't believe this… I really can't. For as long as I've been involved with the shady side of our family business, there have been two sure and steady rules. We don't buy and sell people, and we don't hurt innocent women and children. Point blank. End of discussion. My father's need for power and greed has gotten so bad that he's willing to break both rules in one fell swoop.

I spin on my heels and walk to the other side of the room. I need to get some space between the two of us before I do something I'm going to regret. *Like murdering him.*

The sheer rage and fierce sense of protectiveness racing through my veins is a complete surprise to me. I've never felt like this before. But I can't ignore it.

It's *Harper.*

Sure, I haven't let things get out of hand between her and me, but that doesn't mean I feel nothing for her.

Hell, I feel the exact opposite of nothing.

She's what Mac needs.

She's what Finn needs.

She's what *I* need.

She. Is. Everything.

In the short time she's been in this apartment with us, she's brought out the best in each of us. Okay, yes, I've been a pain in the ass lately, but that's only because it is taking every single ounce of restraint in my body to deny what I really want, and what I want is her. And the fact that I'm left wanting another human being beyond just sex is alarming, that I feel something when I see her walk into a room, or that her voice is like music to my ears, or that the sweet smell of vanilla and caramel can now make my dick hard or that for the first time in a long time… her presence makes this place feel like a home.

"So what? Do you just want me to store her away until you're ready to ship her off? Are we sinking ourselves to that level?" I wonder if he notices the slight shake in my voice.

"Yes."

"What the hell happened to you?"

"Don't fucking start with me, son," he enunciates that last word. As if to remind me that whether or not I'm in charge, he is still my superior. "This is Declan Whelan. With one simple handoff, we can be rid of him and his entire syndicate. We wouldn't even have to get our hands dirty."

He straightens his shirt and walks toward the elevator, signaling he is done with this conversation and doesn't want to hear anything else I have to say. Once he hits the button on the wall, he looks over his shoulder. "I expect you to do what's best for the empire I've created… for our family. You will do as I say, Ronan." The door opens, and he steps inside. "I'll let you know when we have a plan in place for her." The doors close, and just like that… conversation over.

"Fuck!" I continue to release a loud string of expletives into the apartment.

What the hell am I supposed to fucking do now. If I don't follow his orders, if I interfere in any way, it will mean that not only will Declan come at us hard, but Dad will know exactly who was involved in fucking him over. Because he left her with us. She's our responsibility.

She's our *responsibility.*

She. Is. Ours.

That's it. That's all there is to it.

But what the hell do we do? How do we protect her? How do we keep her safe?

I don't know who my dad has become. When I looked into his eyes tonight, I didn't see my dad. I saw Liam McDermott, the great mafia boss. When I was younger, I thought those two men were separate. I thought my dad was a good person. An honorable man. One who lived by a particular set of rules, by a code. I thought the mafia boss was just who he was when he went to work. Maybe that was naive of me. Perhaps that was just because I was a child. Or maybe it was because he was good at hiding who he truly was. Now, I realize those two men are one in the same.

Regardless, three things have become true.

One. We can't trust him, especially not with Harper.

I wonder how much my mom knows. I make a mental note to figure that out later.

Two. I will *not* be like him. I will be better. Just because we are criminals does not mean we are evil men. Sure, we do bad things. But that doesn't mean we can't do them with honor and a little bit of fucking integrity. I will run this empire better than he ever did.

Three. Harper is mine. She is ours. There's no going backward. And there's certainly no letting her get shipped off to the fucking Declan Whelan. Over my dead body will I let them take her. I will protect her and keep her safe no matter the cost. I will give that gorgeous woman whatever she wants in this world. I'm done second-guessing. I'm done fucking doubting. I'm done pretending that I don't want her. And I'm sure as hell done acting like she doesn't exist. Because she does exist, she's quickly becoming the center of my universe.

I need to talk to Mac and Finn.

"Shit!" I suddenly remember what was happening at the club. I run into my office and pull up the security feed to Kings.

I don't see them anywhere. They're gone. I pull out my phone and call both the guys again. No answer.

"I swear to fucking God…"

Time stands still. All I can do is sit here and wait. Wait until the three of them walk through that door and explain what the hell is going on.

She is never going anywhere without me ever again.

The sudden intrusive thought is like a shock to my system. The idea of wanting someone, not just someone, this woman, around all the time is new to me. But for the first time in my life, I want it. I want her. Now we just have to figure out how to keep her.

I'm unsure how much time passes when I hear her laugh float through the apartment. And just like that, the sound of her voice causes my whole body to relax.

I move to stand in the doorway of my office. When I take in the sight of the three of them, I am immediately tense right the fuck back up. "What in the hell is wrong with the three of you?"

23

Mac

"Oh shit. Now we're really in trouble." Finn, Harper, and I are rooted in place in front of Ronan's office. I'm not ashamed to admit that Finn and I are hiding our giant bodies behind her five-foot-ten frame. He won't hit her, but he sure as fuck will deck the two of us.

Finn chuckles next to me. "Dad's mad, guys."

I can't see her face, but I know Harper is trying not to smile.

I know why he's pissed. If I had to guess, he kept an eye on us through Kings' security cameras and saw what happened on the dance floor. Then, the three of us got so sidetracked in the office that none of us checked in with him the entire time we were gone. Which he explicitly told us to do. I also am fully aware of how the three of us look. My knuckles are covered in blood from punching that asshole in the face, Finn has blood on his shirt, and all of our clothes are disheveled from the fight and the mind-blowing sex afterward.

The icing on the cake is Harper. He might not have seen it,

we don't keep cameras in our offices, but I know he can tell what happened once we pulled her into that room. Everything about her gorgeous body screams, "I just got my brains fucked out." She no longer has a styled bun on top of her head, and her unruly curls fall down her back. Her cheeks are still flushed, and her lipstick has all but disappeared. And those hickeys… God, just looking at those marks covering her creamy skin makes my cock stir in my pants.

Her panties are still in my pocket, and it's taking everything in my power not to slip my hand underneath that dress and touch her pussy again. I'm like an addict who can't get enough. I *need* another hit.

Shit. I can feel myself starting to get hard. I peel my eyes away from Harper and move them to Ronan's red face. If he sees me get a boner right now, his fist will meet my face.

"You assholes think this is fucking funny?" he seethes.

None of us respond for a moment, so I take one for the team. I'm his brother, so he's least likely to kill me. Right? "Well, you see—"

He holds a hand up, signaling that I shut the hell up. "No. I don't want to fucking hear it. Not from you two. I'll talk to you dickheads later." He looks between me and Finn, then to Harper. "You"—he points at her, then throws his finger over his shoulder—"let's go. Now." He spins around and walks back into his office.

Harper's whole body tenses, and I know she's nervous. I share a look with Finn, sending him an unspoken message. I think our girl could use some encouragement.

Finn leans forward and whispers into her ear, "You got this, Angel."

My lips meet her other ear. "You really wanna fuck with

him?" She nods. "He has a weak spot. I've seen it a hundred times." I lower my lips just below her ear and brush them against her neck when I whisper, "It's right"—*kiss*—"here." A shudder rolls through her body. I know she loves that shit too. "You do that, Princess, and he'll be putty in your hands."

I gently smack her on the ass urging her toward the door. She makes it about halfway before she stops. Her shoulders rise as she takes a deep breath, and I watch as she stands up straight, sets her shoulders back, and raises her chin. Steeling herself for whatever is about to happen.

That's my girl.

I smile as she walks through the door and closes it behind her.

"He's so fucked it's not even funny," Finn laughs as he makes his way toward the bar. As he pours us each a drink, I catch a glimpse of my bloodied hands. I'm not squeamish by any means; I've tortured and killed more men than I can count. Even though I'm a bit smaller than Ronan and Finn, I'm usually the muscle. People tend to underestimate my violent tendencies just because I come off more relaxed, but that's where they're wrong.

Ronan has always been the brains behind the operation, making plans and executing them by whatever means necessary. We all lean on him to make the tough decisions nobody else wants to make. And he makes them with no remorse. It's what has made him a great leader. We both respect the hell out of him.

Finn observes everything and everyone. He's constantly watching what's going around him. He's got a natural gift for reading people's body language and assessing a situation as it's happening in front of him. I've never seen anything like it. That's why, more often than not, we let him do all of the interrogating. He can instantly tell whether someone is lying or telling us the truth. If they're not… well, he knows how to pull the truth out of them. Interrogation helps Finn tap into his anger without losing control. His rage is always sitting just below the surface. Not that anyone would ever know.

Then there's me—the muscle. I'm quick on my feet and damn strong too. I spend hours in the gym making sure I'm in the best shape that I can be to protect those I need to. My weapons skills are top-notch, and I'm not ashamed to brag that there isn't a better shot or fighter around. My days often end with blood on my hands, but something about tonight is hitting me differently.

I flex my fists in front of me, zoning in on my crimson-stained hands. This man touched her. He could have hurt her. He wanted to take what was ours. After Finn pointed them out across the club and I saw that asshole touching her, I saw red. Before I knew what was happening, Finn was holding him down, and I was pounding his face into the floor. I couldn't hear anything, couldn't see anything. I just kept hitting him. I was so full of anger. All I could do to fix it was hurt him over and over again. The world ceased to exist until I knew he was taken care of. But when Harper grabbed my arm, and I looked into her sweet face, everything that was spiraling inside me slowed down.

She wanted me to stop, so I did. That's it. She wanted it, so I gave it to her, no questions asked.

"Hey, Mac." Finn is eyeing me hesitantly, holding out a glass. "You good?"

I take the drink from his hands and throw it back. "Yeah. It's just…"

"I know, man. I know."

"I don't know what's happening to me. I have never felt this way in my entire life." I scrub my hand down my face, trying to think of a way to word what I want to say to Finn. "What I feel for her… I feel it deep in my bones. She's it, man." Finn doesn't respond. He just looks at me, waiting for me to continue. "But that's crazy, right? We've known her for all of five fucking minutes, and the only reason she's here is because my dad wants her to be. There's no way I should be feeling what I'm feeling." Finn downs the rest of his drink and puts his hand on my shoulder.

"There is a reason, Mac. You just said it… she's *it*. I don't know why or how this happened. But it did, and she's here. Now, all we can do is hold on to her with everything we have and pray that she wants to stay."

"What about Ronan?"

He smiles. "Don't worry about Ronan. You know how he is. It's going to take him time to let someone in. But I would be willing to bet my right arm that whatever is happening in that room"—he points behind me—"is just what they both need."

"But do you think she would want this, though? I mean long term."

"Want what? All three of us?"

Being involved with someone in the mafia is no small task, let alone being involved with three someones. It's dangerous, and you have a constant target on your back. I wouldn't fault her for leaving the second this is over.

"Yeah."

"If she didn't, she would have told us already. She's stronger than we give her credit for. I know that much for sure. Do you… want this?"

I know what he's asking. Am I really okay with sharing her with the two of them long-term? I know the answer before I even have time to blink. "Yeah, man, I am. Harper deserves everything in this life. If the three of us can give that to her, then that's what I want."

Finn smiles. "I couldn't agree more, Brother." He squeezes my shoulder and walks to his room, calling behind him, "I'm going to bed. This night was fucking exhausting, and I need to get some rest before our ass-chewing tomorrow. See you in the morning, man." I can't help but laugh.

I look at Ronan's closed office door and notice I don't hear any yelling. Hell, I don't hear anything. I step toward the door and stop myself. The two of them need this time together. If I go in there, Ronan is just going to shut down. He needs to let her in.

I fish her panties from my pocket as I go to my room. After running the lace through my fingers I stuff them under my pillow.

24

Harper

Waves of disappointment, anger, and frustration roll inside of me. I have been sitting in this god-forsaken office for the last fifteen minutes in total silence. I thought, for sure, when Ronan saw us when he demanded that I follow him in here, that the two of us would finally have it out. But nope.

He just sat me down on the couch and has been working away on his computer ever since.

With each second that passes, I grow more and more irritable. Why the hell does he want me in here if he is just going to ignore me?

I had an amazing, no, incredible, night with Mac and Finn. After the little tussle on the dance floor, the three of us shared something incredible. We connected in a way I never would or could have imagined.

Finn continues to surprise me at every turn. His need to be in control turns me into a puddle every freaking time. He

150

looks at me with those delicious brown eyes, full of fire and determination, and I know there's so much more to him than meets the eye. I see how he walks around here, and interacts with everyone else, barely holding himself together, teetering that knife's edge. Afraid of disappointing everyone around him. Sex seems to be when he feels like he can take back all of the control. He gets off on giving orders and having them followed. I will gladly follow him wherever he leads me.

And, Mac. Sweet, sweet, Mac. From the second I saw him, I knew he would take care of me. That there is a constant internal struggle happening behind the mask he wears. To others, he comes across as a moody, introspective asshole. But they don't know that he is as fierce as they come. His willingness to put others first and care for them how they need to be cared for, no matter what it costs him, makes him one of the strongest men I have ever met. He really does treat me like a princess, and I fucking love it.

And that's another thing. Why am I all of a sudden swearing like a goddamn sailor?

Ugh! See what I mean?!

A few weeks with these men and I have already turned into a sex-craved degenerate.

Dull Harper is no more.

And here I am, sitting in Ronan's office, where I intended to engage in further debauchery, but now all he's doing is managing to piss me the hell off, as per usual.

Maybe he forgot I was here. He hardly pays any attention to me as it is. I clear my throat, hopefully reminding him that I am literally sitting right across from him.

He still doesn't look up.

Okay, so maybe he's deaf all of a sudden. With a little more force, I cough again.

Nothing.

You know what, I don't need this. I have two men down the hall who would love to spend time with me. I'm not going to subject myself to his broodiness any further. Dramatically I slap my palms on the tops of my thighs and move to stand from the couch. "Well, this has been loads of fun, but I'm leaving." I make my way toward his office door, once again leaving this room feeling defeated.

"Sit down," he grits out behind me.

I don't stop. *Sit down.* Who the hell does he think he is?!

My hand reaches for the knob of the door. "Harper! I said, sit. Down. Now." His tone tells me I shouldn't argue. Reluctantly, I sit back on the couch. I sit up straight and look him dead in the eye. I'm not going to let him think I'm afraid of him. Because I'm not.

Right?

No. I'm not.

I am not scared of Ronan McDermott.

Ronan McDermott does not scare me.

Good pep talk, Harp.

Ronan turns in his chair to face me head-on. I continue to stare. With a heavy sigh, he leans forward, resting his forearms on his desk, and laces his fingers together like this is some sort of business meeting. He's so fucking irritating.

I realize that I haven't taken a good look at him in a few days. He looks tired. Like there is more going on behind the scenes than he leads on, like he is quite literally carrying the weight of the world on his shoulders and can't manage to shed even a pound. As much as he grates on my every single nerve, I don't want that for him. I want him to feel lighter, to feel whole. I relax my shoulders, forcing my body language not to look so guarded. "What, Ronan?"

"You tell me, *Harper*."

And, I'm back to wanting to throttle him. As much as I want to help him help himself, a girl can only take so much. "Honestly, I don't know. You're the one who called me in here. You're the one who has been sitting in here for the last fifteen minutes ignoring me. You're the one who is pretending like I don't exist." I feel my voice getting louder and a sudden sting behind my eyes. I will myself not cry in front of him. "You're the one who can't seem to stand the sight of me. And you know what, Ronan? I'm fucking sick of it!" *Okay, wow, Harp.* "You will not have me sit here while you scold me for having a fun night out. I felt free tonight for the first time since Cece died, hell, for the first time since my parents died. I let myself have fun, damned the consequences. And I don't need you spoiling it with your temper tantrum because I didn't behave how you wanted me to!"

If he's shocked by my outburst he doesn't show it. In fact, he looks even more pissed off than he did before we walked in here. Probably wondering where I got the nerve to speak to him like that. King of the Irish Mafia and all. But I'm not done. I'm not backing down, and I just thought of the perfect way to drive my point home.

He doesn't scare me. He doesn't intimidate me. And he sure as hell doesn't have the right to judge me. I may be in this apartment because I need to be, but that doesn't give him the right to treat me like he has been.

No. I came here tonight with a purpose, and I'll be damned if I don't get underneath his skin one way or the other.

I stand from my spot and make my way around the desk

toward him. His eyes track my every move like a lion stalking its prey. Except for once in my life, I'm not the prey… he is. Once I reach his chair, I hinge at the waist, place my hands on each armrest and spin the chair so he's facing me. With my face an inch from his, I can practically hear him grinding his molars. I lower my lips to the spot just below his ear, the one I love and the one Mac told me is his weakness too. My lips are featherlight against his skin, and I whisper, "Fuck. You. Ronan."

In the span of five seconds, several things happen at once. Ronan grabs my hips, lifts me off the ground, and slams me onto his desk. Before I have time to process, he wraps his tattooed hand around my throat, and I feel the metal of his rings against my skin. He pushes me down so my back is flat against the wood. His massive six-foot-five frame towers above me. The baby-blue color of his eyes is nowhere to be found; in their place, the color of the deepest sea. The longer I look into them, the more I see the storm brewing inside him. His perfectly hardened composure is slipping. I can see his chest's rapid rise and fall, the tick in his jaw. The longer he holds me, the more turned-on I become.

Finally, I got to him. Show me what you've got, Ronan.

I don't move. I don't speak. I don't look away. I'm afraid any sudden movements will scare the wild animal in front of me. I don't want him to run. I want him to give himself to me. I know he's been holding himself back. He thinks he's not good for me, that he's too dangerous. Maybe he is. I don't care anymore. I want him to own me. I want him to ravage me. I want him to let go.

Ronan lowers his face, hand still gripping my neck, his lips brushing against mine as he speaks. "We will talk about your actions later. But right now…" he takes a deep breath and closes his eyes. I worry he will stand up and walk away for a moment, but then he opens them, and my breath seizes in my chest. The way he looks at me is enough to burst me into flames. "I can't fucking take it anymore, Harper."

"Take what?"

"You being here. I thought I could stay away. Hell, I need to stay away. Things are going on that you should have nothing to do with." His opposite hand slides up my calf until he grips just above my knee and wraps one of my legs around him. "But you're just too… too… too fucking perfect. I can't stay away."

This is it. I broke him.

"So don't."

He takes another deep breath through his nose and moves his mouth to my ear, "I can fucking smell them on you, Baby." He moves his hand up my thigh toward the hem of my dress. I'm practically shaking with anticipation. His hand burns my skin in its wake, and the way he calls me "Baby" in that deep gravelly voice makes me wet on the spot.

"Let's get one thing straight right fucking now. If this happens"—he gently bites my earlobe—"you will be mine. You'll be mine to protect. Mine to keep safe. Mine to please. Mine to fuck. *Mine.*" His hold on my neck tightens now to the point of pain. But I don't ask him to stop.

"But Mac and Finn…"

"Are yours." His eyes snap back to mine. "Mac and Finn are yours, and you are theirs. But you will also be mine. You are part of us now, and you aren't going anywhere. Do you understand me, Baby?"

"Yes, Ronan."

"Shit. I love hearing my name come from those lips."

I know he's not lying. I can feel his erection pushing against my thigh. I love knowing that I drive this man crazy. A man who is so rarely affected by others. So, I sit up straight so I'm face-to-face with him and whisper, "Ronan." I watch him suck in a deep breath.

"Now, tell me, Baby. You want me to make you come? Right here on my desk?"

Sweet Jesus... I'm done for. Dead. Deceased. Right here. Done.
"Yes."

"You want me to fuck this pussy while their cum is still leaking out of you?"

I feel my eyes go as wide as saucers.

"I told you, I can smell them on you. Don't act like you didn't do this on purpose." His lips turn up in a tight smile. "Why do you think I sat you on the couch for fifteen minutes? I was trying to regain some damn composure. Knowing that they fucked you, knowing that if I move my hand, I won't find any panties under this dress..." *What, is he a mind reader?* Ronan chuckles, knowing I've been busted. "I was trying to stop myself. But I can't, Baby."

"So, don't stop. Take me."

"Stay it again."

"Take me, Ronan." I'm practically breathless now. "Ruin me."

I know that's what he needed to hear. He needs to know that this won't be a mistake, that he will be so, so good to me. That I'll be good to him. Whatever else happens after this, we will figure it out together. All of us.

Just like that, I watch him unravel right before my eyes. "Fuck."

Ronan

T"Take me, Ronan. Ruin me."

I should not be doing this. The four of us have some serious shit to figure out. But I can't think about any of that right now. My only thought is that I need her, and I need her *now.*

Tonight, this exceptionally beautiful woman who has consumed my every thought since we grabbed her in the night will finally understand what it means to belong to *me.*

"Fuck." The thought alone is enough to send me over the edge.

I quickly pull her dress over her head and throw it across the room. Hands threaded into her hair, I kiss her as if my life depends on it, stroking her tongue with mine, savoring every taste. Her body relaxes against mine, willing and ready for whatever is about to happen between us. "Shit, if your lips taste this fucking good, I can't wait to taste this pussy." A small whimper escapes her lips before I drop my head and kiss my way down her neck.

I notice small purple spots across her chest and let out a small laugh against her skin. Her hands grab my face, and I tilt my head to look right at her. A smile plays across her face. "I see you guys had some fun while you were out." I knew what had happened between them as soon as they entered the apartment. It was all over their faces. I'm not an idiot. But I like getting her riled up. It's quickly becoming one of my favorite pastimes.

"Yeah, well, they were teaching me a lesson." She beams confidently, not showing a hint of remorse or embarrassment. *I fucking love it.*

"What was the lesson?" My lips find her soft skin again, nipping my way toward her perfectly pink nipples.

"That I'm yours," she whispers breathlessly.

"And?" I close my mouth around one bud and suck hard.

"*Oh, God...* I'm not going anywhere."

"And?" I make my way across to give her other breast the same attention.

"You're all... You're all *mine.*" The way that sounds coming out of her lips is music to my fucking ears. I bite down on her nipple and release it with a pop.

Grinning like a fucking Cheshire cat, I look up at her. "And did you learn your lesson, Baby?"

"Ummm... I'm not sure." She's teasing me now. "I might need you to send the point home."

"I think I can manage." Placing my palm on the center of her chest, I lay her on the desk. I make my way down her stomach, trying to kiss every square inch as I go. I want to memorize her body. Every freckle, every stretch mark, every. Fucking. Inch.

"You have no idea, Harper." I place another kiss on her stomach. "How much I've been dying to taste you."

She sucks in a deep breath, waiting for my next move. "All I've thought about is what you would taste like on my tongue." Moving to the side, I pace another kiss on one hip bone, followed by a sharp bite, and I hear her hiss.

"If they get to mark you, then so do I." I move across her body and do the same to the opposite hip. Leaning back, I look at my handiwork, pleased with the purple marks already forming. I lean back down and place a deep kiss on the center of her pussy. A groan builds deep in my throat as I inhale her scent. Harper pushes her hips toward my face, trying to seek more friction.

"Ronan... please..."

Fuck. The way she moans my name.

"Please, what, Baby?"

She lifts her thighs and rests them on my shoulders, silently telling me what she wants. It's not enough. I want to hear the words come out of her pretty little mouth. "Words, Harper. Do you want me to eat this pussy like it's my last fucking meal?"

"Yes," she whines, and I arch a brow. "Yes, please."

"That's my girl."

"*Shit,*" she moans. "I love when you guys talk to me like that."

"Like what?" My mouth is hovering right above her clit. But I want to take ten seconds to confirm a hunch before I dive in.

"When you... when you call me your 'Good Girl.'" She rakes her hand through my hair, and I can't stop the shiver it sends down my spine.

"You like to be praised, Baby?" I've seen the way she is with Mac and Finn. She lights up when they tell her how beautiful she is, or the pride that swells in her chest when they tell her she did something right. Don't get me wrong, she loves to stand her ground and push back, but I know she secretly gets off on doing as she's told. Harper wants to know how valued she is, how treasured. She feels in control when she knows she's pleasing those around her. I think it's safe to assume that our girl has a pretty strong submissive side. Honestly, it couldn't be any more perfect because she just so happens to be living with three very dominant men. "You like hearing what a pretty pussy you have?"

"God, Yes."

"Good, because I can't wait to devour it." My lips find her clit, and I suck it into my mouth, her hips instantly thrusting into my face.

"*Oh, fuck.*" Hearing her curse, letting herself go, scratches an itch in my brain. I want to see her unhinged.

My tongue darts out as I begin licking through her folds, savoring her taste. "You taste so fucking delicious, Baby."

"Mhmmmm…" I look up to find her eyes closed.

That won't fucking do.

I bite at her clit, and her eyes snap open. "Eyes on me, Baby. You look at me when I make you come."

I resume taking long strokes, tasting every inch of her. I can't help the groans that fall out of my mouth as I go. My hands wrap around her thighs and pull her to the edge of the desk, trying to get her as close to me as possible. I can't get enough. Now that I've tasted her, it will *never* be enough.

After a few minutes of listening to her moans and sighs, I find the perfect rhythm. Her thighs begin squeezing my head, and I know she's right there. I use my tongue to flick her clit at a rapid pace. Every few seconds sucking it into my mouth. Once her back begins lifting off the desk, I plunge two fingers deep inside her pussy.

"Oh… Ronan. Don't stop. Don't stop. Don't stop." Her chant is like a fucking prayer. I curl my fingers and find her G-spot with ease. *Fuck, Ronan.*

"That's it. You're doing so good. You're so fucking tight, Harper. So fucking perfect."

I reach up with my other hand and pinch her nipple between my fingers. "Scream my name, Baby. Scream my name when you come for me."

My words send her into freefall. I can feel her pussy tighten around my fingers. So much so that I can't even fucking move them. The thought of her sweet cunt clenching around my dick causes me to groan against her, the sound getting lost between her legs. I lap up every ounce of her as she comes down from her orgasm, never letting up. I want another one.

"Ronan, it's too much. I can't."

"You'll come when I tell you to, Baby," I say as I stand back over her. Curling my fingers inside her, I aggressively rub against that magic spot. She begins clawing at my back so hard I'm sure she's drawing blood.

I will wear those fucking scars with pride.

She tightens around my fingers again. "I knew you could do it. Come for me. Now."

"Ronan!" she screams, and I mean really screams. I look up at her. Eyes still locked on mine. The look on her face is euphoric.

Once I can, I slowly pull my fingers from her pussy and, with my face hovering above hers, I slide my fingers into my mouth and lick up every drop of her release. "You are so fucking delicious."

She slides her hands from my shoulders, down my arms, to my wrists. She pushes the hand in my mouth back toward her pussy with a cocky little grin. I can't believe the words that come out of her mouth. "Show me."

I pause for a second, completely stunned. I quickly recover and slide two fingers back inside of her. She moans at the intrusion. Pulling them back out, with her hand still around my wrist, I bring them to her lips. She opens just wide enough for me to slide them in. She begins running her tongue around them, and I quickly realize what she's doing because now all I can picture is her doing this to my dick.

Smart girl.

"That's it, Baby. Suck harder."

Like the good girl she is, she does as I say and sucks my fingers to the back of her throat. I thread my opposite hand through her hair and jerk her head off the desk. She moans at the forcefulness of my movements, and I watch her eyes roll to the back of her head. She hasn't seen anything yet. If I didn't know any better, I'd swear she was about to come for a third time from just sucking on my fucking fingers.

"Eyes, Harper. Open them. I won't tell you again."

Her beautiful green eyes meet mine, and I know I'm fucking done for. I haven't even been inside her yet and know there's no turning back. Ever.

I pull my fingers out of her mouth. Using the hand behind her head, I lift her so she's sitting upright. With the hand that was just in her mouth, I grip her hip tight, loving how she feels against my palms. Her soft porcelain skin is a stark contrast against my tattooed hands. "I fucking love these curves. You are so damn beautiful. It's literally hard to look at you sometimes." She scoffs at my remark, and I can tell she thinks I'm joking. "You don't believe me?"

Looking down at her lap, she says, "I know I'm pretty, but I wouldn't go that far. I'm sure you all have had better… and skinnier women than me. I'm just… just average."

Anger courses through me. Not at her, but at anyone who hasn't made it crystal fucking clear that she is an angel walking this earth. Average? *Fuck that.* I pull at her hair so her eyes meet mine again. "Listen to me right now. You are fucking perfect. These curves are perfect." I slide my hand up to grab a breast. "These tits are perfect." My hand slides up further to cup the side of her face. "This beautiful face… fucking perfect. I don't want you ever to think any less of yourself than what you are. And what you are, Harper—" I use her name so she knows I'm serious—"Is perfect. Do you understand me? I never want to hear you talk like that again."

"Okay," she says softly.

"I hear you talk about yourself that way again, and I'll take you over my knee." Harper's mouth pops open in shock, and I can see it in her eyes. She likes the idea of me punishing her. *Good to know.*

"You like that idea? Me spanking your ass until it's raw?" I can practically feel it. My palm stings just thinking about it.

"Yes," she breathes out.

She's like a fucking dream come true, I swear.

She releases a small nervous giggle, and I can't stop my smile. "You should do that more."

"Do what, Baby?"

"Smile… it looks good on you."

"Thank you." She doesn't know that I'm not sure anyone

else besides those living in this apartment can do that. "Now, let's go."

I pick her up off the desk, and she wraps her legs around me.

"What? Go where?"

"My room. I want to fuck you until the sun comes up, and I'm not doing that in my office." I can feel her wetness soaking through my shirt. I can't get to my room fast enough.

"Ronan! I don't have any clothes on."

I throw my head back and let out a deep laugh. "Nothing anyone in this house hasn't seen before."

She slaps my back as I walk toward my room. "Asshole! Can we go back to not talking to each other?"

"Not a chance, Baby. Not a fucking chance."

26

Harper

Ronan busts through his bedroom door and throws me on the bed. A deep chuckle forms in his chest, and I can't help but smile. I've never seen him look so happy. I don't know if it has all to do with me, but the romantic in me hopes it does.

I won't worry about that now, though. Now, I can only pay attention to the man towering above me. He's nothing like the man I've seen storming around the last few weeks. He's practically exuding sex appeal and dominance.

"Do you have any idea how fucking stunning you look right now, Baby?"

See, that's what I'm talking about. Never in a million years would I have imagined hearing that come out of Ronan McDermott's mouth. This unexpected side of him is one I never thought I would see. I'm so here for it. I can't think of anything to say, so I just smile at him, waiting for his instructions. I want him to dominate my ass.

Well, not literally.

Maybe later?

"On your knees for me." He commands from the foot of the bed as he slowly unbuttons his shirt. I sit up on my knees and shuffle toward the end of the bed. I sit back on my heels, eager for what I know he will tell me to do. I want my mouth on him. *Bad.*

Ronan pulls his shirt off his shoulders and lets it drop to the floor. My jaw drops open as I stare at his delicious body. Sure, I saw him in all of his glory the morning I watched him in the shower, but this is the first time I've seen him up close. He stands in front of me, shirtless and in his black dress pants, chest heaving, black hair messy from my hands, letting me get my fill. He. Is. Beautiful. The dark ink that covers his body does little to hide the amount of muscle he has. His body is big and smooth and hard. He's all man. Every muscle is perfectly defined. I want to run my tongue over his entire body. I *crave* him.

When my gaze finally makes its way back up his body, I see his baby blues staring back at me, hooded and filled with lust. "You done staring at me yet?"

I feel the blush spread across my face. "Probably not, no."

"Well, since you're sitting there… why don't you go ahead and take it out, Baby."

I move my hands to unbutton his suit pants and slide them down over his hips. He steps out of them and removes his socks, left standing in front of me in only a pair of black briefs, leaving nothing to the imagination. I can see his massive erection pushing against the black fabric. I'm going to feel this tomorrow.

"I'm waiting, Harper."

I reach down the front of his briefs and fist his cock at the base. I move my palm up his shaft and swipe a bead of precum gathered at the head.

"Fuck, Baby," he hisses. I pull my hand out and slide his briefs the rest of the way down, gaining full access to the rest of him. I rake my hands over his muscular thighs up to his abs. I don't miss the goosebumps on his skin as I trail my fingertips over him, memorizing every dip and divot. I look up at him, waiting for his instructions as he slides both hands into my hair. He pulls my head toward his cock and rubs the head of it against my lips.

"Have a taste. Show me what that little mouth of yours can do."

I open my mouth, lick him from base to tip, and instantly feel him throb against my tongue. I pull his cock into my mouth and take him as deep as I can go, which isn't all of the way because, let's face it… his dick is massive. As I come back up, I taste another bead of precum. I sweep my tongue across the head, loving the taste of him.

"That's it, Baby." Ronan lets out a deep moan. I continue sucking him leisurely, waiting for him to take control. I know he's holding back; he has more to give me. He wants to control me. Dominate me.

And I want him to.

I give the head of his cock one last lick before pulling off and looking up at him. "What do you want, Ronan?"

He looks puzzled at my question, like this is the first time any woman has asked him what he wants. I run my hand over his abs up to his pecs, letting my nails lightly graze his skin on the way. "Ronan. Tell me what you want from me."

"You said you wanted me to ruin you…" It wasn't a question,

simply a reminder of what I said. But I don't need him to remind me because that's exactly what I want. I want him to take it from me. I want him to take anything he needs from my body and use me for his pleasure. Whatever he does to me will have me screaming his name. I might not know much about him, but I do know that even though Ronan McDermott is a man who appears hard as stone, he'd never force me to do something I didn't want to do.

"Yes," I reply.

"I don't think you know what that means, Baby." His eyes are darker than I've ever seen, as if everything he wants to do to me is running through his mind in rapid succession. There's a beast inside of him that is waiting to be unleashed. I want it. I want to see and experience every side of Ronan McDermott and whatever he has to give me.

"I want to."

"It's a lot for some women to handle."

"Please. I just hooked up with three dangerous mafia men in one night. I think I can handle plenty," I sass, trying to lighten the mood. He's still trying to decide how he wants to proceed. "Ronan, I know you won't hurt me. If you do something I don't like, I'll tell you, and you'll stop. I trust you."

I see him thinking through what I just said, weighing all his options. "Pick a word."

"What?"

"Pick a word, Harper. If I do something you don't like or it's too much and you want to stop, you say the word. Not 'stop' or 'no'…because I won't. Once I'm inside of you, I won't stop. So, pick. A. Word."

I say the first word that comes to my mind, "Bubbles." He

tries to hide the smile that tugs at his lips before he nods.

"Bubbles it is. You say it if anything becomes too much." I know I won't say it. I want to take whatever this dangerous man has to offer me. "Harper." He lifts my chin with his finger. "Say you understand."

"I understand."

"Say that you know I won't hurt you."

I swallow heavily. "I know you won't hurt me." And that's the truth. I know he won't.

"What do you say if you want to stop?"

"*Bubbles.*" I'm practically breathless with anticipation.

"That's my girl."

His entire demeanor changes in an instant. His eyes are no longer filled with longing but with unbridled passion. His strong jaw tightened in anticipation. With a deep breath, he grabs me under the arms and throws me backward onto the bed. It's just a reminder of how strong and massive this man is. At five-foot-ten, I've never been someone men can throw around, but these men sure as shit don't have an issue with it. Ronan gets onto the bed and crawls to me on all fours, cock still standing proudly at attention between his legs.

Fuck, that's hot.

"Are you going to lie here and be a good girl?"

"Yes." I am. I'll be so good for him.

"Good. I'm finally going to fuck this tight pussy of yours, and you'll take all of it. Won't you?"

"Yes, I will."

Ronan mirrors my movements from earlier and runs one tattooed hand up my stomach and over my chest. His strong hand moves past my breast and firmly grips my neck yet again.

I let out a small giggle.

"What's so funny, Baby?"

"Just thinking about all the hand necklaces I've been getting lately," I sass.

"Get used to it, Baby. Because we own your ass." I know he means that both figuratively and literally. "You better get all those giggles out now. You won't even be able to breathe once I'm inside you."

"Oh, you think so, huh? Because—" I don't have a chance to finish what I'm about to say because Ronan's lips crash into mine.

"Enough. You don't talk anymore unless I ask you a question or you're screaming my fucking name. When you are in here, you do as you're told. Do you understand me?"

"Yes, sir."

"*Fuck*," he mumbles as he shakes his head. He leans down for one more quick kiss. "Turn around. Hands and knees."

"Yes, sir."

I do as he says, quickly positioning myself in front of him. He runs a hand up my inner thigh until his fingertips meet my pussy. He hisses. "Fuck, look at this pussy. Dripping wet and ready for me. Greedy girl."

Yes, I'm greedy. So, so greedy.

Ronan moves his opposite hand up to my hair and wraps my unruly curls around his wrist, pulling my head back tight enough that I can't move. He removes his hand from between my legs. I can feel him notch the head of his cock at my entrance. "I know Mac and Finn didn't wear a condom, and I'll be damned if I don't get to come inside of this cunt too. I'm clean." He obviously knows I am. Pulling my hair tighter, he growls, "Tell me you want it, Baby. Tell me how needy you are for my cock."

"I want it so bad, Ronan," I reply without shame. "Fuck me, *please*."

Ronan slams his massive cock inside of me. Not giving me any chance to adjust to his size. "Ahhh! Ronan."

"That's it, Baby."

Pulling at my hair, I sit up straight, my back against his front. He slides his hand from my hair to the front of my neck. Holding me in place, he begins thrusting into me. The sounds of his thighs slapping against mine fill the room. "You are so fucking tight. This pussy was made for me."

A wanton moan is my only response. He didn't ask me a question, and I don't want to break his rules. I couldn't speak even if my life depended on it. Ronan's thrusts are so hard I swear I can feel his dick in my throat. He shifts his pelvis slightly, and my legs give out when he brushes against that magic spot inside me. "There it is. You going to come for me, Baby?"

He keeps going at an unrelenting pace. Sliding in and out of me harder than I've ever been fucked before. Squeezing my neck harder, Ronan leans down and bites my earlobe. "I asked you a fucking question. Answer me."

"Yes!" I honestly don't know the question, but that answer is "Yes" to whatever he wants.

"I want to feel you squeeze cock, Baby."

I can feel beads of sweat forming against our skin. Both from how hard he's fucking me and how hard I'm being fucked. His hand is still tightly gripping my throat, restricting blood flow ever so slightly. The edges of my vision begin to blur. His opposite hand moves around me, and he pinches my clit.

"Fuck!" I scream out. He releases my clit, but only for a second, and does it again. My orgasm explodes out of nowhere. I grab his forearm with both hands, trying to find purchase on anything I can. I ride out wave after wave of my orgasm in pure bliss. Ronan doesn't let me come down. He continues pounding into me as hard as he can. His fingers begin moving roughly against the tight bud. The hand around my throat squeezes tighter, and I know that if he doesn't let go soon, I'm going to black out. But I don't want him to stop. I don't say the word. I want it. I want everything he can give me.

I feel another orgasm start to build at the base of my spine. Or maybe it's still the same one... I'm not really sure. But it's not abrupt like the one before. I can feel it slowly building. So slow it's almost unbearable. I'm almost afraid of what it'll feel like.

"Ronan..." I plead.

Ronan begins to slow his pace but slams into me even harder than before. His long smooth strokes continue to bring me closer to the edge but not over it.

"You're doing so good, Baby. You take my cock like a fucking queen. Another."

"Ronan..."

"Do as you're told. You can do it, Baby." He enunciates each word with a thrust inside of me. "Give. Me. One. More."

The lack of blood supply to my brain is causing just enough fuzziness that everything he's doing to me feels heightened as if each touch is an earthquake wreaking havoc on my body. Ronan's lips meet my shoulder, biting me hard enough that I'm sure he broke skin. But I don't feel pain. All it does is shoot a shot of pleasure straight to my core. My climax peaks, and I begin shaking and writhing against him. "Yes! Ronan… Fuck! Yes!"

I'm clenching so hard around him that it's a miracle he can still move inside me. His thrusts become erratic until he stills.

"Yesssss, Harper," he hisses against my shoulder as he comes deep inside me. The moans from his mouth are enough to draw out my earth-shattering orgasm. The only thing holding me upright is his hand around my neck. After a few moments, he releases his hold on my neck, and I feel all the blood rush back into my brain. He lightly cups my jaw and turns my face back toward him, lips meeting mine in a deep kiss. We languidly brush our tongues against one another, and I notice the metallic taste of blood against his tongue.

Breaking from our kiss, I look at my shoulder out of the corner of my eye. Sure enough, he bit me hard enough to make me bleed. "Ronan! What are you, a fucking vampire?!"

Still inside me, he lets out a deep belly laugh, and I smile back at him despite myself.

I really do love that sound. I wish I could bottle it up for a rainy day.

Ronan slowly slides out of me, and I fall against the mattress, letting my muscles relax for just a minute. "Matches the hand print around your neck well. Don't worry, Baby. I'll clean you up."

He climbs off the bed, and after a few seconds of rummaging around cabinets to find something, he pads back into the room. He begins wiping his bite mark with antiseptic and finishes by rubbing an antibiotic cream over it, a stark contrast from how he acted just moments ago. After he grabs a wet rag and wipes in between my legs, he plants a soft kiss plants on my shoulder before walking back to the bathroom to put everything away.

Once Ronan makes his way back to the bed, he lays next to me and drapes a blanket over our naked bodies.

"Why don't we just crawl under the covers?" I murmur into the mattress, too strung out to even lift my head.

He chuckles. "I'm not done with you yet, Baby. Get some rest, and then I'm taking you again."

Ronan kisses the crown of my head and drapes his arm over my torso. I roll to my side and spoon against him. The last thing I remember before drifting off to sleep is the feeling of him softly rubbing the pad of his thumb across my skin.

It isn't long before I wake up with his face between my legs.

27

Harper

Morning comes all too soon. Rolling over, I notice the spot next to me is cold. Ronan must have gotten up a while ago. I hear a murmur of voices coming from the kitchen, along with the clattering of pans against the stovetop. The guys must be out there making breakfast.

I move to my back and stare at the ceiling, taking in everything that happened in the last twenty-four hours. The goofiest smile spreads across my face. I can't believe this is happening to me. *Me! Harper freaking Hayes.* My sex life has been abysmal at best. I've had some small flings, had fun nights with men I've never seen again, and brought myself to orgasm more times than I can count. But never, and I mean *never,* has anything felt like it has with the three men sitting outside that door.

The way it feels when their bodies are touching mine is everything. They make me feel cherished in every way. When they look into my eyes, it's like I'm their whole world. I haven't felt like someone's world since my parents died. I didn't realize how much I'd missed it. They've made me want things I could never have even dreamt of.

I always hoped that one day I'd meet my Prince Charming, my true love. That there would be a hero who would swoop in and turn my shitstorm of a life into something worth living. Call me unrealistic if you must, but that's what happens when you spend your life reading one romance novel after another. But, three men... *three!* Is that something I can handle? Is that something I want? Shockingly enough, I don't necessarily care that I'm sleeping with all three of them. What does worry me is what this means for us, long term.

I don't want to be some random girl they pass around from room to room while they kill time. That's not who I am. I'm someone who goes all in. If I am going to risk getting my heart broken, I want it to be worth it. And that's another thing, I have had my heart shattered in my short life more times than a person should. I've lost everyone close to me time and again. So, is entering a relationship with not one but three men worth it? Because if they break my heart, I'll feel it threefold.

I know these men aren't my Prince Charming... my *heroes.* They're villains. They do bad things every day. They take what they want, no matter the consequences. I think that's what is drawing me in. My entire life, I've done what was expected of me. I was so grateful when Cece took me in after my parents died. I didn't want to do anything to make her regret her decision, so I followed every rule and expectation laid out for me. And when Cece died, I jumped right into her life without question. It's what I wanted. Or at least, what I thought I wanted.

In just a few short weeks, Ronan, Mac, and Finn have made me question exactly what that is. What do I want?

Do I want to be the type of person who continues to sit around and wait for life to happen to her? *No. No, I don't think I do.*

I want to make my own decisions. I want to have control of my future. Could those three stupidly gorgeous and dangerous men help me find the courage to do that? If they're willing to fight for me, I should be ready to fight for myself.

Shit.

Everything comes crashing back in an instant. I haven't been home in weeks. I have no idea what state the bookstore is in, *my* bookstore. I'm still practically being held hostage in this obnoxiously fancy apartment. And, *oh yeah,* I have an evil grandfather. The fact that I literally haven't thought about all of it in twenty-four hours goes to show how good the dick is. They might have actually fucked my brains out.

Don't judge.

Begrudgingly, I pull myself out of bed and rummage through Ronan's closet. I find an oversized T-shirt and slip it over my head. After I've found a spare toothbrush in the bathroom, I brush my teeth, throw my curls up in a messy bun, and run some cold water over my face. I take a second to catalog the marks across my body. Between Finn and Mac giving me hickeys across my chest, Ronan's bite mark on my shoulder, and the bruise on my neck from his hand, I look like a hot mess. It was so worth it.

I give myself a little pep talk in the mirror before leaving the solitude of Ronan's bathroom. Obviously, Mac and Finn know what Ronan and I have been doing all night. They had to have heard us; neither of us was exactly quiet. I spent the entire night screaming Ronan's name. Whenever I would doze off to sleep, he would wake me up for another round. He couldn't get enough, and neither could I. I run my finger across my bottom lip, swollen from kissing, and continue to stare at myself in the mirror. *Fuck it.* After one last deep breath, I open the door, walk down the hallway, and find them in the kitchen.

I stop in my tracks while I drink in the *sexy-as-sin* men in front of me.

Ronan is sitting at the kitchen island, back turned to me, talking to Finn, barefoot and in nothing but a pair of sweatpants. His dark curls disheveled from me running my fingers through them all night. I can see scratch marks up the length of his shoulder blades. Heat rushes through me knowing I put those there, and he's not ashamed to show them off.

Finn stands on the end side of the island, forearms resting against the countertop in a pair of sweatpants much like Ronan's. I watch Finn lift his muscular arm and run his fingers through his sandy blond hair, pushing it out of his face. The stubble he was sporting last night at the club has grown and is now covering his jawline. I clench my legs together, thinking about how his beard felt between my legs.

To my right, Mac is standing in front of the stove in stone-washed ripped jeans and, *you guessed it,* no damn shirt. The button of his jeans is undone, and I see a path of dark hair that runs from his belly button, disappearing into the denim. I can tell from here that he doesn't have any briefs on, as usual. I have never seen a man look sexier while cooking pancakes.

This is all a fever dream. It has to be. No way I'm this lucky.

Finn must see me out of the corner of his eye because he does a double take at me standing across the room in Ronan's shirt. I watch him eye me up from my toes, pausing momentarily at my neck, to the top of my head. Before I can worry whether or not he's upset about last night, my eyes meet his, and his face softens. He's staring at me with such fondness I could melt into a puddle on the floor. Ronan follows Finn's gaze and peeks at me over his shoulder. I'm still stuck in my spot, staring at the three of them. I mean, seriously, I'm ready to throw the pancakes in the trash and eat them for breakfast.

Talk about a well-balanced meal.

Ronan stands from his chair and walks across the kitchen toward me. "Morning, Baby," he says as he reaches for me. With one hand on my ass, he pulls me flush against him, cupping my cheek with the opposite hand, kissing me like he hasn't seen me in months, as if we didn't spend all night wrapped up in one another.

"Mmmmm. Morning," I reply, reluctantly pulling my lips away from his. "How long have you guys been awake?"

"Only an hour. I wanted to let you get some rest." The corners of his lips lift, knowing good and well he's the reason I'm so tired. *And sore.*

I place my hands against his chest, noticing how his muscles tighten beneath my touch. I lean forward and place another quick kiss against his lips. "Thank you."

"Don't get me wrong, I love seeing you naked. But seeing you like this, messy bun and in nothing but my T-shirt, our marks covering your skin, it's a close second." I practically feel my cheeks blushing. "You look beautiful, Baby."

I love all the praise they give me. I'm just not used to it.

Sometimes it catches me so off guard I genuinely don't know what to say.

With a soft pat against my ass cheek, Ronan ushers me toward the kitchen. "Come on, Mac's making us all breakfast."

I hesitantly follow Ronan to the kitchen and sit beside him. I don't know what to do or how any of this should work. I mean, do I kiss all of them good morning? Would that weird them all out? Finn must sense my uneasiness. Rounding the island, he sits on the opposite side of me and spins my chair toward him. He leans forward and places a firm kiss against my lips. "Morning, Angel."

"Good morning," I reply before he slides a full coffee cup in front of me.

With his hand firmly squeezing my thigh, I face the counter and grip the mug with both hands. I'm about to ask Mac to grab the creamer from the fridge when I feel him come up behind me. He leans down and kisses my neck just below my ear, right where I love. I take a second to savor the scent of him. Even the way he smells is warm, like cedarwood and ginger. I want to wrap myself up in it. "How are you feeling this morning, Princess? Heard you two had a fun night."

My head snaps toward Ronan, and the three of them let out a laugh. I should have known they were sitting out here talking about me all morning. "Relax, Princess. He didn't say anything. But my room is right next door, and we all know you're not very quiet."

I drop my head into my hands. I shouldn't be embarrassed that they heard us together, but I can't quite shake the feeling. Finn squeezes my leg, and I peek at him between my fingers. "Angel, don't you feel ashamed for even a second. We will never make you feel bad for taking what you want or doing what feels good. I promise the three of us are good."

I take a deep breath and sit up straight in my chair. Mac reaches around and pours a splash of creamer into my mug. I peek back over my shoulder and smile at him. I didn't even have to ask for it. He just knew. That action alone makes my heart burst.

I'm such a goner.

Mac's lips meet my neck again, and whispers low enough so I'm the only one who can hear him. "I'm so good with it, I laid in bed all night stroking my dick to the sound of my brother fucking you. Glad I kept those panties of yours."

I inhale a sharp breath and hear Ronan chuckle into his coffee mug as he looks away, pretending he didn't just hear that. *Smart-ass.*

Placing a quick kiss on the top of my head, he rounds the island and makes his way back to the stove to pour another round of pancakes onto the griddle. "You okay there, Baby? Your cheeks are looking a little red."

Finn pipes up before I can answer, "Who knew all we had to do to get Ronan to act like less of an asshole was get him laid."

Mac tips his head back and roars a laugh. "He didn't need just anyone. He needed that one." He spins around and points his spatula at me. "That pussy of hers is practically magic."

Finn reaches around me and pats Ronan on the shoulder, "Glad you finally pulled your head out of your ass, man. We were getting ready to murder you."

Ronan shrugs Finn's hand off his shoulder. "Shut the hell up. You three are going to be such a pain in my ass."

I love the banter between them. Since I've been here, constant tension has lingered in the air due to Ronan avoiding us and everything else happening. This is a nice change of pace. So, instead of scolding them for talking about my so-called "magic pussy" at breakfast, I let it slide. "It's only going to keep getting worse. You said it yourself, you're addicted now." I wink at him around the brim of my mug.

Ronan grips my jaw and spins my face toward his. I'm met with his steely-blue gaze. "You better watch that mouth of yours. But, you're damn right I am, Baby."

"Awe, aren't you two just the cutest," Mac says as he continues to poke fun at his brother. Ronan picks up a strawberry from a bowl on the counter and whips it at the back of Mac's head.

The entire exchange makes me feel something I never expected to feel here. A calmness washes over me. I never thought I would feel complete, I've lost too much in my life to be whole. For the first time in a long time, it feels like there might be more out there for me than imagining a life like the one I read in books. A life that's not filled with loneliness and "what ifs" but is filled with belonging and adventure. I've always felt like I was floating from one day to the next, drifting between feeling too settled and not settled at all. But right now, with them, despite the circumstances that brought me here, I feel like this is where I'm supposed to be. I feel like I'm home.

28

Finn

Once I finish my breakfast, I make quick work of the dishes and clean up the kitchen. All the while listening to Mac, Ronan, and Harper make light-hearted conversation. I can't wipe the stupid grin off my face, and she didn't even spend last night with me, for fuck's sake. In all of the years we've lived here, I don't think this apartment has ever felt as bright as it does this morning.

And it's all thanks to *her*.

I mindlessly move through the motions of putting everything away where it belongs. When the three of them are finished eating, I clear their plates and load them into the dishwasher before pouring myself another much-needed cup of coffee. I didn't even have the energy to throw on a suit this morning, which is saying a lot coming from me. Not only did I lay awake most of the night listening to Ronan and Harper fuck each other's brains out, but Ronan proceeded to burst into my room at the ass-crack of dawn. I wanted to throw a pillow at his smug face when he told me to meet him and Mac in the kitchen, but I knew it must have been something important if it was worth him leaving a naked Harper in his room.

Once Mac and I strolled into the kitchen, Ronan filled us in on Liam's impromptu visit while we were at Kings. As Ronan explained everything, I watched his relaxed demeanor slowly slip away, and his usual state of rage took its place. That is until he saw Harper again.

Every time I looked at Mac, I could tell he was biting his tongue, trying not to scream, "I fucking knew it!" Mac has never wanted this life. Liam realized quickly that Mac was a force to be reckoned with. Mac is faster and stronger than the rest of us, and Liam knew it. It's why he trained him to be the kind of killer he is. However, sometimes I wonder if it was only to teach Mac a lesson. It was clear that he often despised Mac's nurturing and caring nature. Liam saw it as Mac's biggest weakness.

"Don't be so fucking soft, Cormac." I heard Liam bark at him on more than one occasion. Which is why, as years passed, Liam pushed and pushed Mac until he became the man he is. One our enemies fear. He hates his father for forcing him to be someone he doesn't want to be, someone he despises.

I've had a more challenging time straightening out my feelings for Liam. I know he's not a good person. Hell, none of us are. But the older I've gotten, the more I've realized just how much Liam McDermott lacks even the smallest conscience. His only goal is to get ahead and take out anyone who steps in his way.

Anyone... even Harper.

The thought of him hurting her makes my blood boil. Yet,

I still can't shake the feeling that I must obey him. I owe him. *Don't I?*

He and Emma saved my life when I had nothing. When that fucking family took mine away from me, the McDermotts stepped up and took me in as one of their own and made me part of their family. They love me just like they love Mac and Ronan. Emma reminds me time and again that I'm not just some orphan they took in. I'm their son. I'll be forever indebted to them. I can't disappoint any of them. *Right?* I can't seem to make sense of any of it.

This is why Ronan looked directly at me when we asked what we should do. And why my only response was to stare back at him with a puzzled look on my face like some fucking moron.

Ronan knew how I was going to feel about all of this. My best friend can read me like a book. He knew I'd be conflicted. Not because I don't care that Harper is in danger, hell, knowing Liam doesn't care about her safety is enough to make me want to lock him in a room and make him wish he was never born, but because they know I'll second guess everything. I'll hesitate.

As good as I am at reading other people's thoughts, I can't seem to get mine in check. None of it is rational. My feelings for Harper are complicated enough, and this is just making it worse. She still doesn't know what her grandfather did to me. I'm still not ready to tell her. I'm not ready for the way she'll look at me. She'll pity Finn, and I don't want to be pitied.

After a quick discussion filled with hushed yelling, the three of us decided, much to Ronan's disappointment, to sit down with Harper and tell her what's going on with Liam and Declan. I know Ronan wants to protect her by keeping her as far away from all of this as possible, but this life is dangerous enough as it is. The last thing she needs is not to understand what she's up against. Once she knows what's happening, the four of us will come up with a plan together.

$$* * *$$

Harper sits on the couch next to me, Ronan in the armchair closest to me, while Mac paces in front of the window, unable to sit still.

I notice Harper fidgeting with the hem of Ronan's shirt she's still wearing. She's nervous. While glancing at her fingers, I can't help but become acutely aware of the fact that the shirt barely hits her mid-thigh. I zone in on the creamy white skin of her delicious legs, remembering how they feel wrapped around my face. Just like that, I feel all my blood rush straight to my cock. I shift in my seat and tear my eyes away from her body, willing myself not to get a hard-on.

Now is not the time, Finn.

Unable to sit still anymore, Harper finally breaks the silence. "Okay, guys, what's going on? You're really stressing me out. I thought we were having a nice morning. What happened in the ten minutes between breakfast and now?"

The three of us exchange glances, silently trying to figure out which one of us will be the one to tell her. Harper lets out a frustrated sigh. "Whatever brotherly telepathy shit the three of you are doing… knock it off. Use your words."

Ronan curls his lips in, fighting to hide his smile. Mac stops pacing and sits in the armchair closest to Harper. He reaches out, firmly gripping her exposed thigh. "Princess. You know we'd do anything to keep you safe, right?"

She quickly glances at Ronan and me before meeting Mac's worried stare. A crease forms between her brows before she hesitantly replies, "Yes…"

He lets out a heavy sigh. "Okay, good. Remember that when you hear what we're about to tell you."

She quickly looks at Ronan, who's staring directly at Mac, silently pleading for him to explain. Mac and I both know Ronan's temper is hanging on by a thread, a thread that has only been made thinner by the fact that she's about to become even more involved in our life. But we all agreed that this was for the best. Mac drops his chin, agreeing to Ronan's request.

Harper must notice the apprehensiveness on Ronan's face. She tries to stand from the couch and move toward him. I reach my hand out and clamp down on the thigh opposite the one Mac is still holding, keeping her in her spot. We know him well enough to know he won't want to be touched right now. "Guys, you're starting to scare me. What's happening?"

"Just listen to what Mac has to say, Angel." I begin stroking the inside of her thigh with my thumb. I glance over, and Mac is mindlessly doing the same. I'm not sure whether we're trying to calm ourselves, her, or both.

Taking a deep breath, Mac begins to explain. "While we were at Kings last night, our dad came here to speak with Ronan."

"Okay… About what? Oh no. Is it something bad? Did he find out what happened at the club? Is he pissed you guys took me out? I'm so sorry! I'll tell him it was my fault. I'll—"

"Harper," Ronan bites, his hands clutching the armrests of his chair. "Don't interrupt. Let Mac finish what he has to say." I instantly see a look of hurt flash across Harper's face, disappointed that the Ronan I know she experienced last night and this morning at breakfast is gone. I understand where she's coming from. Harper must have whiplash from dealing with all of our multiple personalities. But I also know that Ronan is doing everything he can to keep his temper at bay. Ronan has always had the privilege of being able to say what he wants to anyone without worrying about the consequences. He's not used to factoring in someone else's feelings, let alone someone as special as Harper.

"It has nothing to do with the club, Princess. And we won't tell you again." She stiffens at the seriousness of Mac's tone, one he rarely uses on her. "That man putting his hands on you was not your fault. We won't talk about it again. That scum isn't worth your time or energy. Do you understand?" I notice Ronan tense even further at the mention of what happened at the club. If he's not careful, he's going to puncture the leather of his chair with his fingernails.

He laid into the two of us this morning before he told us about Liam. Mac and I know we fucked up. We shouldn't have left her alone. When Ronan asked why the asshole wasn't dead, Mac simply said, "Because she asked us to stop." Surprisingly, Ronan didn't argue. After we told him how guilty she felt and how upset she was, he promised he wouldn't bring it up again. After all, there are more important things going on.

"Yes," she weakly replies.

Mac's face softens. "Good. But you're right about one thing. He did come here to talk to Ronan about you."

I watch Harper's face carefully as Mac goes over Liam and Declan's deal with one another. Each minute that passes, I watch her build up one wall after another. Of all the people I've been able to read over the years, I don't have the slightest clue what's going on in that gorgeous head of hers. I can only imagine what she's thinking. All I can do is brace for impact as we wait for her reaction.

Once Mac is finished laying everything out on the table, the three of us wait. We wait to see her reaction. We wait for questions I know she has. We wait for her to cry, scream, or do anything really. Minutes go by, but it feels like hours. Silence fills the room as we stare at Harper. *My Angel.* But there's nothing. I look at Mac and Ronan, and I can tell by the look on their faces that they're just as confused and worried as I am. Never have I seen her be so... so still.

A single tear rolls down Harper's cheek. Before I can wipe it away, she abruptly stands and walks to her room without so much as a word, not even a glance. The soft click of her door closing feels like a bomb going off. I think I would have rather she screamed at all of us and slammed her door. Anything would have been better than this.

"Fucking hell." Ronan slides his hand down his face and leans back in his chair. "So much for coming up with a plan today."

"Now what?" I ask Ronan out of habit.

Mac and I sit on the edge of our seats, waiting for Ronan to assess the situation. Except we're all well out of our depth here. None of us know what to do, but it doesn't stop us from waiting for his instruction anyway.

Ronan nervously taps at his lips a few times before he takes a deep breath. "Go," he reluctantly tells Mac. "She needs you. You'll be able to take care of her best right now."

Without a word, Mac nods and rises from his chair. Once

he makes his way to the end of the hall, we hear him knock twice, followed by the opening and closing of Harper's door. While her door is open, we hear the soft muffles of her cry. It's like a dagger straight to my heart. Judging by the look on Ronan's face, he feels the same.

I wish I could be the one to comfort her. To hold her and tell her that everything is going to be okay. I'm sure Ronan does too. But he's right. That's not something we can provide her, at least not yet. Mac can.

And I think for this to work, for *us* to work, that's what we need. We need to understand what each of us can give her. We each need to overcome our own battles. Because if we don't, Harper, our light, will be snuffed out. She'll be sent into the darkness. Before, we were all living in the shadows. I didn't know it, but we were barely existing. Like we've been walking through life dealing with the fallout of other people's decisions rather than making our own. Now that she's here, now that she's brought her light with her, it feels possible to chase away our demons and create our own paths.

Just like that, I've decided. Right here and now. No matter our past, no matter my past, I will do everything in my power to protect her and never hear her cry ever again. That's what she deserves. She deserves everything. And we can be the ones to give it to her, if she'll let us.

29

Harper

This cannot be happening. There is no way that this is happening. Nope. No fucking way. Not happening.

But it is Harp. It is happening.

As I sit on the end of my bed, my chin trembles, and much like when I was sitting on the couch, I feel a singular tear roll down my cheek. I quickly swipe it away, willing another one not to fall. If I let the damn break now, I'm not sure how to stop it. But what else am I supposed to do? I can't get my body to do anything. I couldn't even look them in the eye before I catatonically walked in here.

Has it all been a lie?

The question slams into the forefront of my brain before I can stop it.

My gut told me something from the moment I laid eyes on them. It told me I was safe, that I could trust them. I've never had that feeling before, such an instinctual draw toward someone. So, even though they were cloaked in danger, I went willingly. I leaned into my instincts headfirst and trusted them. Sure, there have been moments over the past few weeks where I've doubted and questioned their motives, especially Ronan's. Lord knows I've argued with him. But I think that's because, for the first time in my life, they pushed me—him the most. They've been challenging me at every turn. Showing me a world I never thought possible for a wallflower like myself.

I know there's more to their life that they're not telling me. They belong to the mafia, after all. No, not *belong*. They *run* the mafia. I'm not naive enough to know what that all entails. I know that there are secrets they have to keep, and I've been okay with that. I haven't pushed. I haven't prodded. I took their word that they were doing everything they could to keep me safe and would share things with me when they felt like I was ready to hear them, even if it meant uprooting my entire life. Because deep in my bones, I felt it… *safe.*

You know, in all of the dark romance novels you read, the ones where the woman gets taken? Where she argues and pushes back at her captors at every turn? Where, after fight after fight after fight, she realizes she loves and trusts him? Where enemies finally become lovers? That *is not* how I felt. I knew that they would alter the course of my life forever. Maybe that's why I was so willing to get in the car that day.

But now, I can't help but wonder if it's all been a lie.

It can't be. The things they've done to me. The things they've said. The looks on their faces. That can't all have been a lie. *Right?*

There's no way they knew about this. *Right?*

But Liam is their father. He is the one who told them to bring me here. So he had to have told them the plan. *Right?!*

I can't make sense of any of it. My brain is going a mile a minute, and I can feel my breathing growing more rapid, the all too familiar feeling of a panic attack working its way through my body.

I've been sitting here, replaying every moment of the past few weeks, for what feels like hours, but I know it's only been a minute or two.

The light sound of tapping on the door pulls me from my thoughts. I don't know if I'm ready to face them, to hear the answer to the questions that are causing panic to tear through me. I press my hand to the center of my chest as I feel it tighten. After a few seconds of silence, the door slowly opens, and I see Mac. His face covered in remorse. And, with one look at that man's sweet face, a sob slips past my lips. The damn breaks, and tears stream down my cheeks. Without hesitation, Mac steps into my room, closes the door, and kneels on the floor in front of me.

"Come here, Princess." His strong arms pull me onto his lap as I sob. I sit, straddling him on the floor. He has one arm around my waist and the other holding the back of my head. I continue to cry into his shoulder when I suddenly feel like I can't breathe. I sit up straight, tears still falling, gripping my throat, trying to get myself to breathe. It's not working. My eyes widen as I try to suck in a full breath. I can't. Everything feels like it's crashing around me all at once. I can't.

I can't breathe.

I lock eyes with Mac, gasping for air. He must recognize what's happening to me. Still holding me on his lap, he cups the side of my face with one hand and removes my hand from my throat with the other. "Princess, you need to breathe."

I shake my head. My breathing is becoming more and more

rapid as the panic continues to take over my body. Laying his hand over mine, he places them on the center of his chest.

"Princess…" I still don't answer. I can't do *anything*.

"Harper." The use of my name brings my panicked eyes back to his.

"Breathe. Breathe with me." He takes a deep breath, and I feel it against the palm of my hand. I repeat his motion and suck in a shaky breath. Mac breathes out slowly as his thumb ghosts over my cheekbone, trying to center me with every touch.

I exhale.

"Again." I match my breath to his as he deeply inhales. With my eyes still locked on his, we exhale.

"That's it, Princess. You're doing so good. Keep going."

Mac and I continue to breathe. I meet every rise and fall of my hand on his chest until I realize what felt like a vice around my throat has disappeared. I'm breathing normally.

I can breathe.

Mac senses it too. Only when relief washes over his face do I notice how panicked he was, but he didn't show it. He kept his panic locked up because he knew that's what I needed. He kept me safe.

Safe.

Instantly, every doubt I had racing through my mind just a few minutes ago is gone. You can't fake this.

They didn't know.

Mac releases my hand and cups the other side of my face. "*Mo grá*… you scared me."

I don't miss the nickname, but now's no time to ask. Instead, I savor how his accent sounds as it rolls off his lips. I reach up and grab both of his wrists. We both cling to one another as if it will help ground us. "I know. I'm sorry."

"Don't be sorry. Don't ever apologize for feeling the way you feel." I can practically feel my heart bursting. Leave it to Mac to tell me exactly what I need to hear. To care for my heart in a way I know only he can. "Are you okay?" Worry is still etched across his face.

"I'm okay. I... I just—"

"Panicked," he says to me. "I know how it feels. I've been there." I look at him in surprise. "Don't be so shocked, Princess. This is not an easy life. And for someone who feels as deeply as I do, it's easy to feel out of control."

I lean forward and rest my forehead against his. Every so often, I feel a stray tear fall from my eyes, but Mac quickly wipes them away.

"But you don't need to panic, Princess. We have you. You know that, right? You know we will keep you safe. Even from *them*."

The word "them" is filled with so much venom. I hate that his father is now part of that word.

"He's your dad, Mac."

"I don't give a fuck who he is. He's not getting to you. End of discussion." The ferocity in his statement lets me know how serious he is. My chin begins to tremble once more as I grip his wrists harder. "I know it's hard, Princess, but you need to trust me. I won't let anyone hurt you. Neither will they."

"I do. I do trust you." My reply is instant. "But, Mac... what are we going to do?"

"We will figure that out. The four of us. Together."

"Promise you won't let them take me?"

"I promise, *Mo grá*."

Exhaustion suddenly washes over me. It's not even noon, and I already feel like I've been awake for days. My entire body starts to sag in Mac's hold. As usual, he knows exactly what I need.

"We can come up with a plan later. Why don't you get some rest for a few hours." He kisses my forehead before standing with me in his arms. He walks over to the side of the bed to fold back the covers using one hand. He softly lays me down and pulls the blankets back over my body. Just as he's about to turn around to walk away, I reach out and grab his hand.

"Will you stay with me?

"You don't even have to ask, Princess. Let me just tell Finn and Ronan that you're going to rest for a while. I'll be right back."

I feel my eyelids getting heavy as soon as Mac leaves the room. I hear the muffled sound of them speaking in the den as I try to relax. It's only when I feel Mac climb into bed and pull me to him, when his arms wrap around me tight enough to steal the air from my lungs, that I feel safe enough to fall asleep.

30

Mac

It's rare that I'm ever thankful for my emotions. I know I feel more than most. It's who I am. However, why I am this way remains a mystery to everyone, including me. Especially considering the man who raised me feels nothing. My best guess is my saint of a mother rubbed off on me.

While I may not be sorry for it, I wouldn't say I'm thankful. My strong moral compass has made me endure more in this life than I should. It's made my father turn me into the killer I am, hoping I would turn it all off. But I didn't. I couldn't. Yes, I've done his bidding. I've gotten my hands bloody to protect my family, but that doesn't mean I haven't felt every second. Every drop of blood spilled, every act of violence, every life taken crashes through my body like waves slowly chipping away at stone. I feel it all as if it were happening to me. Ronan and Finn worry it will be my downfall. They may be right. But I refuse to turn it off. As soon as I stop feeling, I'll be no better than him. I refuse to walk through this life as the monster he tried to turn me into.

But today… Today I've never been more relieved to be who I am. It's why Ronan sent me in here. He knew I could give Harper something neither of them could, and I did. I comforted her.

Me.

I never get to use my "weakness," as Liam calls it, as a strength. I'm only ever allowed to bring out weaknesses in others. Not today. Today, I was able to help Harper, and I'm beyond relieved because what I just witnessed shook me to my very core. I never want to see her like that again.

As I lay here, staring at the ceiling, with a head full of curls draped across my chest, Harper's warm breath against my skin, I can't help but remember all of the times I've felt that way. All of the times panic has riddled my body. All the times that my father has made me feel like the walls were closing in around me. Which is why I'm not at all surprised. I'm not surprised that he's trying to pull something like this. I've seen him for who he is since I was a boy. Someone who will take whatever he needs to make himself stronger. Whether it's stealing his own son's way of being or plucking an innocent woman from her life. He just takes.

He's tried to mask it from the world by doing things like taking in Finn all those years ago or "retiring" from the game to live a more relaxed life. It's all bullshit, and I'm done.

I refuse to let him destroy another person. I refuse to let him destroy Harper.

My phone dings on the nightstand next to me. I see a text message from Finn in our group chat.

Finn: Just ordered us all dinner from the Thai restaurant down the street.

Hell yeah. I'm fucking starving, but I haven't had the heart to wake her. She's been sleeping soundly against me for hours. I know she needs it. We've given Harper the afternoon to rest after we pulled the rug out from under her yet again, but now we need to figure out some sort of plan.

I set my phone down and begin playing with the ends of her chocolate brown curls, trying to savor this quiet moment with her curled up next to me just a little longer.

Taking a few extra seconds, I look down and memorize how her body's draped over mine. She fits against me perfectly, like her body was made to be entangled with mine. Still dressed in only Ronan's shirt, I run my hand over the creamy skin of her exposed thigh. It feels like silk against my rough hands. She doesn't flinch at my touch, but I watch a trail of goosebumps form across her leg. Unable to help myself, I firmly squeeze the top of her thigh just below her ass. I love that she's curvy enough that I can truly get a handful of her in my grip. She nuzzles into me, further, the inside of her thigh rubbing right up against my now half-hard dick. I squeeze her leg a little harder, and she lets out the softest moan into my chest, but I know she's not awake. It's just her body responding to mine like it's on autopilot.

The idea that she is already so in tune with my touch sends a jolt straight to my groin, and now I'm fully straining against the zipper of my jeans.

Fuck it.

I release my hold on Harper and quickly grab my phone.

Me: How long until food is here?

Finn: Why? She still sleeping?

Ronan: She's been sleeping for hours. Is she okay?

Me: She's fine. She just needed to rest. You didn't answer my question. How long until the food gets here?

Finn: Should be here in 20.

Me: Perfect.

Ronan: Fucking hell. At least keep it down. I'm trying to get some work done.

I chuckle, knowing Ronan is just on the other side of the wall, and he's going to hear everything I'm about to do to my Princess.

Me: Not likely. I had to listen to you two all night. Payback is a bitch, brother.

Me: Plus, better get used to it. She's not going anywhere.

Ronan: Damn right, she's not.

Finn: Agreed.

Me: We'll be out in 20.

I move to put my phone back down as Harper runs her

hand across my stomach, and I swear to fucking god, I stop breathing.

I quickly amend my last text.

Me: Better make it 30.

I practically throw my phone across the room. *I can always buy a new one.*

Gently, I roll us over so Harper is lying on her back beneath me, my legs straddling her hips. She still barely even stirs. "Harper, Princess…" I whisper as I stroke my hand down her cheek. Finally, her eyelids begin to flutter. "Finn ordered us dinner, it'll be here soon," I say a little louder this time.

Comically, her eyes fly open at the mention of food, and I can't help the smile that takes over my face. She takes a few seconds, her sleepy eyes adjusting to the orange glow of her bedroom as the sun begins to set over the city.

"It's dinner already? I've been asleep that long?"

I nod, unable to speak, as I look down at her memorizing every inch of her adorable face. Her long, dark lashes hang over the most beautiful set of green eyes I swear I've ever seen. A few tiny freckles dance across her nose and cheeks, only adding to the glow of her pale skin in the orange light. And that hair. Those delicious fucking curls lay unruly beneath her, spread out across her pillow. I never thought I'd say this, but her hair alone makes me fucking hard. I don't know what it is. Probably the fact that the women that throw themselves at the three of us never look anything like Harper, with their perfectly styled hair, rail-thin bodies, and expensive designer clothes. They're all the fucking same. Not Harper. Her voluminous curls and eyes that could ravish your damn soul speak to the wild nature she keeps tucked away.

Just looking at her is enough to drive me absolutely wild.

But the sadness that took over her face in the living room this morning is still there. I mean, why wouldn't it be? I want to take away her pain, if only for a few minutes.

"You should have woken me up. I didn't need to sleep all day." I swipe away a stray curl from her forehead.

"Yes, you did," I say firmly, leaving no room for argument. "Come on, let's shower, and then we'll eat."

I lean down to kiss her quickly before climbing off and holding my hand out. She grabs it without a second thought. The simple action makes my chest tighten. Leading her into her bathroom, I reach into the shower and turn it on before picking her up and setting her down on the vanity. She gasps at the cold marble meeting the backs of her thighs. Rifling through her drawers, I find a silk scrunchie and pull her hair into a bun on top of her head.

"I'm not even going to ask how you know how to do that so well." A sassy smirk pulls at her lips.

I tip my head back and laugh. "Probably for the best." I tap both her elbows. "Arms up."

Doing as she's told, she lifts her arms above her head, and I pull her shirt off, leaving her in only a pair of panties. As the steam from the shower fills the room, I step back and begin to slide off my jeans, all while taking in her sexy as sin body. An unexplained look of panic takes over her face. "What's wrong?"

"You're showering with me?"

"Princess, laying in bed with you all afternoon and not being inside of you was practically torture. You're delusional if you think I'm passing up this opportunity."

"But—but I haven't showered since yesterday."

Suddenly it dawns on me why she's so hesitant to let me shower with her. Moving forward with my plan, I slide my jeans off—no boxers because they're the fucking worst—not missing the way her eyes immediately find my hard dick. Stepping back in between her legs, I plant my palms on her knees. Her lips open slightly at my touch. "You think I don't want to ravage you just because you smell like him?"

Slowly, I slide one hand up her leg until the tips of my fingers meet the wet fabric covering her pussy. Her tongue runs along her bottom lip as my fingers brush against her. "You think I don't want to taste you just because my brother's cum soaked these panties?" I slide the fabric to the side and run two fingers through her wet folds. Whether it's from her or Ronan's cum, I don't give a fuck. Call me depraved. I don't care.

"You think that just because he fucked you all night while I had to listen, I don't want to be inside you?" I shove my fingers inside of her. She slams her hands against my pecs at the intrusion and squeezes.

"No," she says breathlessly.

"No is right."

I pull my fingers out, and she moans at the loss. Not taking the time to slide them down her legs I rip her panties clean off and throw them on the floor. I slide my hands underneath her ass and lift her off the counter. Her legs wrap around me, and I feel her wetness against my stomach.

Turning around, I walk across the bathroom, step into the walk-in shower, and slam her against the wall, not bothering to close the shower door behind me.

I'll clean the mess up later.

I'm not usually this savage, especially not with Harper. But the last twenty-four hours and having her draped over me all afternoon has done something to me. A man can only take so much.

She shrieks as her back meets the cold wall, and her legs instinctually wrap around me tighter. I reach up and adjust the shower head to hit the wall behind her, warming up her and the tile. I don't need it. I already feel like I'm on fucking fire.

I firmly hold her against the wall with one arm underneath her ass and place my other hand on the wall next to her head.

"Mac. No."

I stop everything and lock eyes with her. "No?" I begin to internally panic. Did I do something wrong? I don't want her to think I'm forcing her to do something she doesn't want to do. *Ever.*

She shakes her head. As if she's reading my thoughts, she quickly reassures me, cupping my face in her hands, "I mean… I want to, I really do. But not like this… I'm too heavy. You can't hold me here like this."

I can't help it. I laugh.

Harper slaps my chest. "It's not funny! I don't want you to drop me!"

"Harper, Princess…" I hold her gaze so she knows how serious I am when I say this. "First of all, I would never hurt you. If I thought I couldn't hold you, I would never have even put you in this position." Her eyes dart from mine, and look at the water swirling down the drain. I move my hand from the wall and grip her chin, forcing her to look back at me. "Second of all, you are not too heavy. I lift heavier than you as a warm-up."

"But—"

I cut her off. "But, nothing. Whatever you weigh, it doesn't matter. Because the way you look and your curves"— I thrust my erection against her ass—"are sexy as fuck. You are absolutely perfect. Anyone that has made you feel less than is insane. And if they couldn't lift you, they weren't man enough for you."

"And your man enough?" She raises a brow.

"Oh, I'm more than man enough, Princess." I hike her a little higher up the wall with one arm to further prove my point. "I'm going to be so deep inside you, make you feel so good, that no matter who's cum is leaking out of this perfect pussy… Ronan's, Finn's, or mine, you'll never forget that you belong to me."

Her eyes glaze over, burning with desire. I can tell she's shocked by my words. I don't usually talk like this. I'm more of an actions speak louder than words guy, but I wanted to get my point across. I want her to understand how much I want her. How much I burn for her. We will make her feel so good about herself that she never questions her beauty or worth ever again. Not only that, but I know she gets off on it when we talk to her this way. I've seen it with Finn. And, based on previous experiences with my brother and women, I know she heard it from Ronan. If this is what she needs, what she likes, then it's what I'll do. Fuck, I think I'd do just about anything for her. Before I let my urges take over and fuck her into oblivion, I take a moment to give her back some control over the situation.

"How do you want this, Princess?" I ask as I look into those big green eyes

"Take me, Mac."

"Oh, I'm going to take you, Princess. There's no doubt about that. I need you to tell me how you want this." She tilts her head in confusion, so I clarify. "Because I want to ravage this body… ravage you. But if you need slow and gentle, I can give you that. I just need you to tell me. Hard or soft, Princess?"

Without a second thought, she answers, "Hard, Mac. Make me forget it all."

Suddenly, I know exactly what she needs. Her need for me burns as hot as mine does for her. Right now, in this shower, the two of us need our bodies to take over. We need the outside world to cease to exist. The only thing that matters is the way we crave one another. Without any foreplay, I reach down, grab the base of my cock with one hand, and line the tip up at her entrance. Her entire body tenses in anticipation. I gently push forward so just the head sits inside of her.

"Shit, Princess. You feel so good." She wiggles her hips against the wall, trying to slide herself further onto my cock. I tighten my hold, keeping her still for just a moment. "Tell me, Princess. Tell me how bad you want it."

"So bad," she whines.

"You can do better than that." I push my hips forward ever so slightly, eyes still locked on her gorgeous face. Her nails rake down my back, sending a shiver through my body.

"Mac, please. Move. Fuck me."

I slam my hips forward so I'm fully seated inside of her. Harper's breath catches, and I take a second to appreciate how her body looks pressed against the shower wall; how water droplets decorate her skin. I begin pounding into her with short, quick thrusts, hitting her G-spot perfectly. In no time at all, her walls start to tighten around me. "That's it,

Princess. You like when we're like this? When you've got us so fucked up, we become fucking feral?"

I continue driving into her, not letting up for even a second. Giving her no time to think about anything besides here and now. "Yes, Mac. Don't stop. Don't stop."

"I'll never stop. I would live buried inside you if I could. This pussy was made for me." I move one hand to her clit and start rubbing it in fast circles. "So tight. So wet. So fucking perfect," I groan out.

"You're perfect, Mac. So perfect." My breath immediately catches in my throat. I don't think she realizes what those words mean to me. As someone who has spent his entire life being forced to change who he is, I have never thought of myself as perfect. Not by a long shot. Knowing that she feels that, that she wouldn't change anything about me, does something to me. Something that I've never felt before.

Sensing I'm stuck in my thoughts, Harper pulls me back to the present, cupping the side of my face with one hand. Her eyes quickly search mine, making sure I'm okay. I slam my lips into hers, earning a groan from her when my tongue brushes up against hers. Harper's legs tighten around my waist, and I know she's almost there.

She tears her mouth from mine. "Mac," she moans.

Shit. *I love hearing her moan my name.*

I pinch her clit, and it's enough to send her over the edge. Her pussy clamps down on my dick, squeezing it like a vice. "Yes, Princess. Come for me. Milk my cock."

Not wanting to be done yet, I rub her clit in fast circles. "Yes! Mac, yes!"

Her legs begin to tremble as she rides out wave after wave. She buries her head into my neck and bites down. The pain from her mouth does me in. I thrust hard into her twice before stilling deep inside her. With her pussy still clamped around my dick, I come with a groan. "Princess."

Harper keeps her face pressed into my neck as she comes down for her orgasm. The aftershocks cause her pussy to spasm around me every few seconds. If we didn't have shit to do, it would be enough for me to go for round two.

After a few minutes, she lifts her head and gives me the sweetest smile. She brushes a stray strand of hair away from my forehead. I haven't gotten a haircut since before we met, and it's starting to get a little longer than I'd like.

"Thank you," she whispers.

"You don't need to thank me. If there's ever a time when it gets too much, I want you to come to me. I'll take care of you. I'll make you feel good. Whatever you need, however you need it. Okay?"

"Okay." Her sweet smile pulls at my chest, only intensifying the feeling from earlier.

"Can you stand?"

She lets out a giggle. "I think so."

I slowly lower her feet to the floor but keep a firm grip on her until I'm sure she has her balance. The last thing I need is for her to slip in the shower and crack her head open. Once I'm sure she's okay, I reach up, readjust the shower head, and turn up the temperature a little. I take my time washing her body, cataloging every inch. Every mole. Every stretch mark. Every stray freckle. Every time I see her perfect body I make sure to take it all in. I can't get enough. Looking at her sets my soul on fire, and I'll never know which time will be the last. If I have anything to do with it, I'll have a thousand more moments with her just like this one.

After washing one another, we step out of the shower, and I wrap her in a fresh towel. I give her a few minutes alone in the bathroom while I run to my room and grab a pair of sweatpants and another shirt for Harper. When I return to her room, I set the shirt on the bed and sit on the chaise I got for her. After a few minutes she walks out of the bathroom, hair still in a bun on top of her head, skin glistening from covering her body in her favorite lotion. I don't think I'll ever be able to smell vanilla or caramel again without getting hard.

"I have my own shirts, you know." She smiles as she slips my shirt over her head and pulls on the pair of panties I set next to it.

"I know, but seeing your woman walk around your shirt is the dream." I'm pretty sure every man on the planet would agree with me.

She strolls over to where I'm sitting, and I can't help but stare at the sway of her hips on her way over. With the way my dick pays attention, you wouldn't think I just fucked her senseless. "So I'm your woman, huh?"

Standing from the chaise, I wrap one hand around her waist and pull her tight against me once she's in front of me. She laughs and shakes her head when she feels my erection against her stomach. "You really have no refractory period, do you?"

I lean down so my lips hover just above hers. "Yes, you are, and no, I don't." I give her a quick kiss on the lips, forcing myself not to get distracted again. "Come on. Let's go get some dinner and talk to Ronan and Finn." She looks at me hesitantly, and I run my thumb along the small of her back where I'm still holding her against me. "It'll be alright. We will figure out a plan. We will keep you safe. I promise." I know without a shadow of a doubt, I have never wanted to keep a promise more in my entire life. Her face relaxes at my words. "But first food. Because I'm so fucking hungry I might whither away and die."

She tips her head back and lets out a laugh. I want to make her laugh like that over and over again. "Come on, drama king, let's go."

31

Finn

It's just after eight when our takeout arrives. Ronan went downstairs to get it at the front door, as nobody else is allowed on this floor, and I busy myself with getting out plates and drinks. Mac and Harper have been holed up in her room for most of the day, and I miss her after only a few hours. I know she needed the rest, though. Between our evening at the club, her night with Ronan, and everything we dropped on her after breakfast, I'm not the least bit surprised that she could sleep the day away. I wish I could have held her all day. I wish I could have been the one to comfort her. But I don't know how to do that, at least not as well as Mac does. He's what she needed.

I mean, how am I supposed to help other people with their emotions when I do everything I can to keep mine at bay?

A problem for another day, I suppose.

I'm just about to send Mac another text in our group chat to let him know dinner is here when I hear Harper's laugh float down the hallway. Like magic, I instantly feel all of the muscles in my body relax. To know that she can still smile after everything she's been through, that *we* can make her smile, is like a balm to my cracked soul.

Harper's eyes meet mine as she emerges from the hallway. Mac gently kisses her on the crown of her head before he gives her a light pat on the ass, and she makes her way over to me. She wraps her arms around my waist, and I lean down so my lips hover above hers. I brush a stray curl off of her forehead to get an unobstructed view of her gorgeous green eyes and those adorable freckles. "How you feeling, Angel?"

"I'm okay."

I raise a brow at her, and she lightly sighs before relaxing her shoulders as if pretending to put on a strong face. Except she doesn't need to. I know better than anyone what it feels like to mask your emotions in fear of losing control, and I don't ever want her to do that around me. I want to be her safe space. A person she can go to with whatever she's feeling.

"I'll be okay… eventually. But I am feeling better."

"You sure?"

"Yes. I know we'll figure something out. I have you guys to keep me safe. Right?"

I smile and lightly kiss her lips. "Always," I whisper.

I faintly hear Mac setting the table when the elevator door opens, and the smell of Thai food immediately fills the apartment. Right on cue, I hear Harper's stomach growl. A blush sweeps across her cheeks as Ronan comes to stand behind her with the food. Uncaring that I'm still holding her in my arms, he bends and kisses her cheek.

"Hey, Baby."

She turns her head to smile up at him. "Hey." This time,

he kisses her on the mouth, and I hear her stomach rumble again. Ronan smiles against their kiss.

"Hungry?" he asks.

"Starving."

He winks at her, letting her know he's asking her about an entirely different kind of hunger, and makes his way toward the table where Mac is now sitting.

"Come on, let's get you some food, Angel."

* * *

"Damn, that was good," I groan as I sit back in my chair at the table, beyond full.

"Mhmmm." Harper nods her head in agreement.

"You should know," laughs Mac. "You ate helpings of just about everything. I don't ever think I've seen a woman eat that much so fast." Harper quickly averts her eyes to her lap. Mac instantly notices and grabs her leg under the table from his spot next to her. "Hey, look at me."

She listens and brings her head up to look at him. "I didn't mean anything by it, Princess. Don't be embarrassed. I'm impressed, actually."

She pulls a half-smile, but I can tell it's forced. So does Mac. He leans in to speak, his lips touching her ear. "As a matter of fact, you and I just had this conversation in the shower." He's talking to her just loud enough that Ronan and I can still hear him from where we're sitting across the table. No doubt ensuring that we're all on the same page with this conversation because I know what just went through her mind. Most of the time, she seems pretty confident in the skin she's in. Then there are times like this when I watch the self-doubt creep in. I wish she could see herself the way we do. It's like she was made for us, and I want to devour her every second of every day. If she doesn't believe me, all she has to do is look at my dick every time she walks into a room.

"If I catch you saying anything bad about yourself, I'll take you over my knee," Mac snarls. Harper sucks in a breath, likely both turned on and surprised by Mac's remark. Spanking isn't usually his thing. That's more mine and Ronan's lane. I know it's because he inflicts so much violence on others daily. He worries he won't be able to control himself if he explores that side of himself sexually. But something tells me Harper could help him. She could take whatever he gave her.

She looks at Ronan and me across the table. "Don't look at us, Baby. Finn and I are with Mac on this one." I nod my head in agreement.

"But I didn't even say anything."

"No, you didn't, but we all knew exactly what you were thinking, Angel. There will be none of that here."

Mac grabs her chin between his thumb and forefinger. "You are fucking gorgeous. End of story."

"In fact, if we didn't have so much stuff to discuss, I would lay you out on this table and eat that sweet pussy for dessert." My cock hardens at the idea of her spread out on this table. I watch her chest rise and fall with each breath, likely imagining the scene Ronan described. I look between the three of them and can tell we're all thinking the same thing. If we don't get a grip, we will forgo our much-needed discussion all together and fuck her right here on this table. There's time for that later. Right now, we need to focus. I clear my throat, and three sets of eyes immediately snap to mine, breaking everyone from their spell.

"As much as we would all like to spread Harper out on the table right now, we have more important matters to tend to."

A faint smile spreads across Ronan's face before he nods. "Finn's right."

"Spoilsports," Mac pouts as he sits up straight in his chair, keeping his hand on Harper's thigh.

"Finn and I were talking while you two were resting, and we think we came up with a halfway decent plan."

"Well, half of a halfway decent plan, that is," I correct him.

I quickly glance at Mac, ensuring he's not annoyed that we discussed this without him. When I do, there isn't a hint of frustration in his expression, more curiosity in what we've come up with. He knows that, like him, we will do what we must to keep her safe.

"Right." Ronan sighs deeply before he shifts in his seat and stares at Harper. His expression is fierce, letting her know he is serious about what he is about to tell her. "From here on out, you won't go anywhere without one of us with you. There will be extra security posted at the door downstairs and two guards assigned specifically to you when the three of us can't all be with you. They won't follow you around the apartment, but they will be posted at the elevator at all times and do sweeps throughout the apartment."

"You guys, that's too much. I don't need all of that protection. I'm sure everyone else has better things to do with their time."

Ronan leans forward, interlocking his fingers on the table-top, leveling Harper with a glare that would make any man fall to their knees. Not my Angel. She doesn't move a muscle, silently challenging him as always. She can try all she wants, though. I know Ronan won't cave on this, and I completely agree with him for once. Judging by the look on his face, so does Mac.

"It's not too fucking much. There is no such thing as too much when it comes to protecting you. There is not a damn thing that is more important than keeping you safe. The guards will be here in a few minutes to meet you, and from here on out, the *best* thing they can do with their time is keep you safe. I will not bend on this, Harper. For once, you will do as I say."

Arms crossed, Harper stares him down. I swear, sometimes she argues with him just to argue. The tension in the room is thick, and I wonder how long it will be before one of them gives in. For just a second, Harper lets her gaze slide over to me. I give her a silent warning, begging her to give us this. To allow us to protect her. I see her posture relax in understanding before she meets Ronan's stare again, but I know she isn't going to be the one to speak first. Not where Ronan is concerned.

It feels like minutes more pass by when Ronan's soft voice cuts through the silence, "Baby…" His voice is laced with desperation. "Give us this, please."

Harper slowly uncrosses her arms. "Okay."

Ronan reaches across the table and grabs her hand, and squeezes. "Good girl."

The fact that Ronan McDermott just pleaded with another human being speaks volumes to Harper's hold on him. He bends for no one. But for Harper, he would break.

Harper softly smiles back at him, but it doesn't reach her

ears like usual. I know she's unhappy about being under a microscope, but I am thankful she is willing to give us this. Ronan releases her hand and continues reviewing what he and I discussed while Mac and Harper listen in—occasionally nodding in agreement.

When Ronan and I began discussing earlier, I pointed out that our biggest problem was that Declan Whelan called off the hit on Harper. If it were as simple as wanting her dead, we could easily fake her death and keep her hidden from his watchful eye. However, that's not the case anymore. Since Liam got involved, Declan now wants her hand-delivered to Ireland so he can deal with her however he pleases. This means we not only have to find a way to deal with Delcan but Liam McDermott as well.

If I had it my way, I would fly to Ireland myself and slit the neck of that hellish man and everyone that follows him, but I know that can't be done. I would never even make it off the damn plane. We have to get Declan to come to us.

Ronan and I figured that if we were to eliminate Declan, we could kill two birds with one stone. If Declan were dead, his syndicate would be no threat to us. Our shipments would stop getting tampered with, and he would never know about the bookstore. We have it on good authority that those below him in his ranks have no interest in our business here in the States. Why would they? Our dealings are of no threat to theirs. The only reason he's fucked with us for so long is because of Liam and Emma.

The war between the McDermotts and the Whelans has gone on for decades. The battle runs as deep as the Montagues and the Capulets. However, besides Harper, Delcan is the last living Whelan. Once he's gone, the syndicate will be handed over to his second in command, Patrick O'Connell. Whom we've heard is unhappy with how his boss has handled things over the past few years. We don't know what has been happening within their syndicate and don't care. We just need to be sure they would leave us alone if Declan were gone.

A couple of hours ago, Ronan sent a message to a few of our contacts in Ireland that he's hoping to speak with Patrick. With any luck, Patrick will get the message without Declan finding out and will be willing to talk to us. We need to find out where his head is at.

The entire time Ronan is explaining all of this, I keep my eyes on Harper, mesmerized at the way she is handling all of this. I can tell by the look on her face she is truly listening to everything Ronan is saying to her. Taking in every bit of information she can instead of shying away from it. Once Ronan is done speaking, the three of us pause, waiting for any questions she may have.

"So, when you mean take care of Declan, you mean…"

"Kill him," I say point blank. Next to Harper, I have reason to want that son of a bitch dead more than anyone. He murdered my parents, just like he did hers, without remorse.

"Okay." She sits up straighter in her chair and pushes her shoulders back. "So, how do we get to him then? He's got to be well-protected. Not only that, he's all the way in Ireland. There's no way you guys can get into the country without him knowing, so we would have to get him here somehow. Right?"

She looks between us as we sit and stare at her. Pride swells in my chest. I said she would be helping us kill a man, not just any man, her grandfather, and she didn't even flinch. Harper understands what needs to be done, that some people don't deserve to walk the face of this earth. She understands that Declan Whelan has caused enough damage to her and everyone around him. Harper's ready to do what needs to be done. Like a true fucking queen. Mac grins like a cheesy bastard beside her, and I hear Ronan huff out a heavy breath. Likely just as stunned as I am.

"That's one of the reasons we want to speak to Patrick and gauge his reaction. If he despises Declan as much as we've heard, he may be able to help us get him into New York," Ronan explains.

Harper taps her lips with her fingers. "Two more questions."

"Shoot, Princess."

"One. If Declan is gone, doesn't that mean I would take over his syndicate? I'm the next in line, or whatever."

"No, Baby. You would only take over if you wanted to. Any sane person knows it would be useless and disappointing to force someone to take over a business if they have no interest in it. Do you want to?"

"No. I want to stay here."

All three of us share a quick glance at one another, too afraid to ask exactly where *here* is. Here in New York or here with us? We hope we know the answer.

"Exactly. What's your other question, Baby?"

"Ummm… what about… what about your dad?"

"That's where we seem to be a little bit stuck. One would hope that if Declan is out of the picture, he would stop caring about you. After all, the only reason he is trying to hand you to Declan is to get him to stop fucking us over and keep him away from the bookstore."

"Don't forget about the reward," Mac adds.

"How could I fucking forget. The man is acting like he

doesn't have enough goddamn money as it is." I swear there's more tension in Ronan and Mac's bodies from talking about their father than I have ever seen.

"We can solve the Declan problem, but that won't stop him, Ronan. You know I'm right." Mac's anger rises, and I see the vein pulsing in his neck. He moves his hand from Harper's leg for the first time since we've sat down and balls his hands into fists on the table. "He thinks we're making some sort of mockery of him just because we're not running things the way he would have. The only reason he stepped down is because people started doubting him because of his age. People started whispering behind their backs. He thought he was going to be able to control us. When he found out he couldn't, he started pulling this kind of shit."

Mac's breathing is heavy, growing more and more agitated.

"I know, Brother. I'm as done with him as you are." Mac seems to relax slightly. "But what do we do? Kill him? Mum would never forgive us."

Mac rubs a hand down his face. "I don't fucking know, man, but I can't keep doing this with him. I can't keep letting him try to break us. Because one of these days, I think... I think he just might." It's a strange admission coming from Mac. From someone who has been trained to be nothing other than unbreakable. To be the one who breaks others. To be a killer.

I know neither one of them knows what to do. I know they're at a loss. Quite frankly, so am I. Liam and Emma took me in. They gave me a life. So, how can I bring myself to take theirs? We sit and stare at each other, at a loss for words. Finally, Harper speaks, and her sweet voice fills the room. "We don't have to figure that much out right now. Okay? We have a start with Declan. Hopefully, taking care of him will get your dad off your backs for a little while until we can figure something else out."

We. She said *we.* Maybe she wants to stay with us, not just in New York.

She reaches out and grabs one of Mac's tightly closed fists. Instantly, he opens his hand and intertwines his fingers with hers. Ronan follows Harper's lead and puts his on his brother's forearm. I do the same to Harper.

We all sit there like that for a while, offering our silent support to one another. Letting each other know that none of us are going anywhere. Because these are my brothers, they might not be by blood, but they are family in every other way that matters, and I would die before I let anything destroy them. And Harper, she's my... well, I think she's my *person.* I would do anything for her.

Suddenly, a thought hits me like a freight train, stealing my breath away for a moment. I reach up with my opposite hand and rub the phrase I got tattooed on my chest after my parents died. The one that currently feels like a giant weight on my chest.

Teaghlach.

32

Harper

It's just after eight o'clock, and I'm in the back reading rooms, stocking the coffee bar while Cece closes up the front.

As always, once I'm done in the last room, I take a moment to sit on the giant purple sofa and close my eyes. This is always my favorite part of the day. The store is quiet, the smell of old and new books floats through the air, and I have a smile on my face knowing that I spent the day helping others discover new and exciting worlds. It's when I feel closest to them—my parents.

So, every day I sit on this couch, close my eyes, and remember them. Or at least I try to. Every day it gets harder and harder to picture them in my mind. I wasn't super young when they died, I was thirteen, but the memories of those earlier years are fading. It's getting harder to remember the sweet sound of Mom's laugh or how she always smelled like cherries. I can barely remember how Dad's scruff felt against my cheek when he kissed me good morning or how his face lit up when I caught him staring at Mom across the kitchen. The memories get further and further away as

I get older and are replaced by newer and less happy ones. But that doesn't stop me from trying.

Cece's voice relieves the tightness in my chest as I hear the only living relative I have left singing "I Got Sunshine" like she does every day. It's become the soundtrack to my daydreams.

Then, a loud thud drags me from my walk down memory lane, and I notice the singing has stopped. I flip off the ornate lamp tucked in the corner and walk down the hallway toward the front of the store, noting that the familiar tune is no longer floating through the air.

"Cece?"

There's no answer. A sinking feeling fills my gut as I call out her name again, "Cece?!"

As I emerge from the hall and look around the front of the store, I don't see her head floating above any of the bookshelves. She's tall, standing taller than me at almost six feet, with a head of bright red curls, much like Dad's. That gene skipped me, but I have my mom's chocolate-brown hair, which is still incredibly curly.

My eyes dart around the room faster, frantically looking for my missing aunt. I don't see her anywhere. I walk toward the front door, noticing that it's still locked.

Okay, so nobody took her. Where the hell did she go, and what was that noise?

Suddenly, I hear a faint noise coming from behind the checkout counter. A cold sweat breaks down my back, terrified to see whatever is behind it, but I have to move.

Move, Harper!

Running, I run around the counter to find Cece lying on the ground gasping for breath. I drop to my knees next to her. "Cece! What happened? Oh my god! Cece!" I'm practically screaming in her face.

I can't lose the only family I have left. I can't.

"Cece, please! Hold on, okay? I'm calling an ambulance."

I reach for my phone in my back pocket, only to find it missing. Shit! I must have left it in the back room.

"Cece, I'm going to get my phone. I'll be right back." I know she can't hear me. I'm afraid to leave her, but I have no choice. I don't know what's going on, but I do know that she'll have no chance if I don't call an ambulance.

Faster than I have ever moved in my life, I run to the back room and grab my phone from the couch, where it must have slid out of my pocket. I dial 9-1-1 on my way back to Cece. Dropping down again beside her, I prop her head onto my lap. Once I connect to an operator, I give her all the necessary information, and she lets me know an ambulance is coming.

Once nothing is left for me to do but hold her, tears stream down my face. "Cece, hold on. They're coming, okay?" I watch as one of my tears falls from my chin and lands on her cheek. She doesn't even flinch. Then, I notice her breathing has slowed, her body barely even trying anymore.

Her green eyes stare up into mine, filling with unshed tears. She blinks every few seconds like she's trying to stop herself from crying. Even now, she's trying to be strong for me.

Cece lifts one hand and cups my cheek as a sob racks through me. "Please, Cece. Please. *They're on their way. Don't leave me." I hold her tighter in my arms as if that will prevent her from leaving this earth, from leaving me all alone.*

Her thumb lightly swipes away a tear on my cheek as she takes a slow, ragged breath. "My... sweet... girl."

Her hand softly falls from my face to my lap. I watch a single tear roll down her cheek as the last bit of light drains from her eyes.

No, no, no, no. No!

"You can't leave me all alone. Cece, please. Please don't leave me all alone. I can't do this without you," I beg her as I hold her body in my arms. *I know she can't hear me anymore. She's gone.*

Dead.

The last person I loved in this world, the last person that loved me, is gone. I. Am. Alone.

It's then that I hear the faint sound of sirens approaching. Moments later, I hear frantic pounding on the locked front door, but I can't move from my spot to let the paramedics in. I can't.

The sound of glass breaking doesn't even draw my gaze from Cece. I can't look away. I can't.

A paramedic rushes to me and drops his bag beside me. I can faintly feel him trying to move my body away from Cece's, but I won't go. I can't. "Ma'am. You have to move. Let us help her."

I can't look at them. I can't answer them. I can't move. I can't.

"Ma'am... Can you move for us?"

"Ma'am."

"Harper." *Wait. How does he know my name?*

"Harper!" *I begin to panic as the man starts shaking me. Trying to pull me away.*

"Harper!"

I sit up in bed, covered in sweat, frantically checking my surroundings. It takes me a second to recognize where I am, but I breathe a sigh of relief when I do.

Bringing my knees up to my chest, I set my elbows on them and hold my face in my hands. "You're not at the bookstore, Harp. Cece isn't here. You're okay," I mumble to myself.

I feel a large hand slide up my bare back and jump. "Fuck... It's just me, Angel."

Angel. Finn.

I take a deep breath and lean into his warm touch instead of away from it. "You're okay. Everything is okay." His deep voice calms my racing heart.

Finn doesn't say anything else. He continues running his hand up and down my back, not even caring that I'm covered in sweat. Once I finally get my breathing under control, I lay back down against my pillow and turn to face him. He threads his fingers through my hair and strokes my hairline with his thumb. I stare into his beautiful brown eyes and notice the wrinkle between his eyebrows. His face filled with concern. But he doesn't ask me any questions. He just continues to stroke my hair silently, waiting until I'm ready to explain to him what happened.

Honestly, though, I'm not even sure what that was about. I haven't had many nightmares in my life. Sure, my life has been traumatizing but not in the "It'll haunt your nightmares" type of way. I don't remember my parents dying. I remember my life before and my life after but not them actually dying. I wasn't in the car that day, and I was only thirteen. My memories from that time in my life have already started to fade.

And when Cece died… I guess I don't know why that never haunted my dreams. Yes, I was there. Yes, I experienced her death firsthand, but it never really affected me that way. Maybe because she died of natural causes. Maybe because I chose to block it all out.

I don't know. I really need to go to therapy.

But that dream… that was what nightmares were made of. I never want to relive that day again, and that made it feel all too real.

I'm sure it has everything to do with what has been

happening, all of the threats hanging over my head. It's been a few days since we all sat down at the table and came up with a sort of plan, but nothing new has developed, and I'm getting antsy. Even though I haven't left the apartment, I feel like someone is always watching me. Someone is always watching me; Logan and Tanner are my two new shadows. They're the guards that Ronan hired to watch over me. But it feels like something else besides them, a truly unwanted presence. It makes my skin crawl, and I constantly feel on edge.

But why dream about Cece's death?

Finn stares at me, and I can tell he wants to help. He wants to fix it like he always does. I'm not sure if there's anything to be fixed, honestly. It was just a bad dream.

Right?

I open my mouth to explain what happened, but no sound comes out. Tears fill my eyes. I don't want to live through that nightmare a third time. I shake my head and bury my face into his chest as he pulls me closer, letting my tears soak his skin. The scent of him, all crisp and clean, like how it smells right after it rains, brings me comfort, and after a few minutes, I notice the tears have stopped. He pulls my face away just enough to look down at me before shuffling out of bed.

I look up at him, confused and disappointed by the spot he's left. Before I can ask him where he's going, he holds out a hand and smiles at me. It's a rare smile, only reserved for a few. He may not be related to Ronan by blood, but if one thing shows they're brothers at heart, it's how serious they are all the time. I don't mind, though. I like that their smiles are only for me.

I reach out and grab his hand, and he pulls me off the bed. I wrap my arms around his neck as he grabs my waist. "Where are we going?" I look down at the both of us, a little concerned. Neither of us has any clothes on, as none of them let me sleep in any. They say they like to feel my skin up against theirs. I don't disagree.

Finn leans down and places a quick kiss on my lips. "To shower."

"Right now?" I look at the clock beside my bed. "It's two in the morning."

He brushes the ever-stubborn stray curl from my forehead as he looks down at me, "It'll help you feel better."

"Okay." I smile up at him. As I spin to walk toward the bathroom, he lightly smacks my ass.

"Plus, all that sweating made you stinky."

I whirl around to face him. "Hey!" I sound offended, but I can only smile as he hits me with a panty-dropping wink.

It would be if I were wearing panties.

"Go turn the shower on, Angel. I'll be there in a few minutes."

I walk into the bathroom with a smile on my face, momentarily forgetting the nightmare that woke me in the first place.

Once the shower is turned on and warm, I stand under the spray and let the water run down my face, willing it to wash away the bad memories. But the longer I stand, the more obvious it becomes that they're not going anywhere.

* * *

Once Finn got into the shower, he took his time bathing me. His delicious fingers scrubbed my scalp and worked conditioner into my ends, lathering every square inch of me with a sudsy loofah. Honestly, I don't think I've ever had a more relaxing experience. Something about him holding me against him while he scrubbed me, washed away most of the anxiety I felt when I woke up. Not once during the whole shower did he pressure me to explain to him what happened. He just let me enjoy the moment, being there with him.

Now that I'm calm and not entirely on edge, I feel ready to explain it. As much as I want to know each of them, I want them to know me and my past. Cece, and how she died, is part of that. Once we get out of the shower, Finn silently dries my hair and wraps me in a fluffy white towel before tying his own around his waist. I move toward the vanity to pull my comb out of one of the drawers as he grabs my wrist. "Let me."

He pulls the comb from its designated drawer and gently detangles the ends of my hair before working through the rest of my unruly curls. Standing in front of him, my back to his chest, I can't help but stare at the picture in front of me in the mirror. The way he gently brushes my hair after taking such good care of me in the shower is enough to bring tears to my eyes. Then it hits me. He has no idea what happened or why I was so upset, so this is what he's doing to try to fix it.

I can't help but admire the man in the mirror who is now raking my multitude of products through my hair. He really is gorgeous. He's the most classically handsome of the three. The blond hair that he usually keeps so perfectly styled is now disheveled and looks a few shades darker from being wet.

And his beard. *God, that beard.* I could spend all day running my fingers through it.

How did I get so lucky to have this sweet, misunderstood man, and Ronan and Mac as well?

I constantly feel like my life is spinning out of control, like I'm walking on unsteady ground, just waiting for the earth to split open and swallow me whole. But the three of them make me feel steady. They make me feel grounded. After knowing me for such a short time, they are so sure that they'd do anything for me. They would *kill* for me.

Shit, now I really am going to cry.

Finn must notice a tear roll down my cheek. He wipes the product left on his hands on his towel and grabs me by the shoulders, spinning me to face him. He slides his hands up and cups my face in his hands. "Talk to me, Angel. Tell me what's going on."

I suck in a shaky breath. "It was just a bad dream."

"Okay. A bad dream about what? You seemed terrified when I woke you up."

"I dreamt about the night that Cece died. I replayed the whole thing all over again. It was so real, Finn. I felt like I was holding her in my arms. I felt so helpless. So weak." Tears are now streaming down my face. I rarely allow myself to think about it, willing myself to keep moving forward and not focus on the bad things that have happened. It's the only way I know how to survive.

"I know what it's like to lose the people you love. To have them taken from you. I know how fucking helpless it can make you feel. But I also know"—he lowers his forehead so it's resting against mine—"I know how strong you are. You have survived more in your life than anyone should have to go through. You're rising to the challenges life throws at you without backing down. I know it may feel like it, but you are anything but helpless and weak."

"I just feel like my entire life has been one big tornado spinning out of control, and I have no idea how to stop it, Finn. Everyone I have ever loved has up and died, and I've never been able to do anything to prevent it. I don't want to have made it through all of this just to have my life taken from me now. I have survived too much. I've already had enough taken from me. Haven't I?" I'm not sure where this is coming from, but I apparently need to let it out to someone. Obviously, my memories of Cece aren't entirely to blame for my sudden sense of panic. All my emotions and worries seem to have reached a boiling point, and the dream was just my mind's way of getting me to acknowledge them.

Not cool, brain. Not cool.

"Yes. Yes, you have. We've got you, Angel. We're here to help you and won't let anything bad happen. All of this will get figured out, and you will be able to live the life *you* want, the way you deserve. Okay?"

"Okay," I say as I let out a deep sigh.

Finn searches my eyes, trying to decipher whether I truly believe him. I'm honestly not sure if I do, not entirely, at least. I know the three of them can promise until they're blue in the face that they won't let anything happen to me, but I know that isn't realistic. They can't control everything, and if something or someone wants me bad enough, they will find me.

When he can't find the answers he's looking for in my eyes, he pulls me out of the bathroom, from my room, and toward his.

"Finn, what are you doing?"

"Going to my room, I have an idea."

I silently hold his hand as he drags me down the hallway. His room is at the opposite end of the hall than mine, and we have to walk past Mac and Ronan's to get to it. I expect them to be asleep with the doors closed considering it's almost three in the morning. Ronan's is shut tight, but as we approach Mac's, I notice it's not closed all of the way. Hopefully, my screaming didn't wake him up. Maybe I should peek my head in and let him know I'm okay. I try to wiggle my hand free of Finn's, but he's got a tight grip. I know he's not letting go, dead set on whatever idea he has cooking up in that brain of his.

As we pass Mac's door, I peek inside to find him sitting in bed watching TV. I'm about to say something when he smiles and winks one of those stormy gray eyes at me. He doesn't move from the spot on his bed, though. Giving me the alone time with Finn that we need.

Still wrapped in his towel, Finn shoves his door open and pulls me through it. Once I'm inside, he kicks it closed with his foot. Every time I'm in his room, I smile. If you didn't know any better, you wouldn't think anyone even sleeps here. The charcoal-gray duvet on his bed is pulled so tight it looks like you could bounce a quarter off it, and there isn't an article of clothing in sight. His solid black bed frame and dresser stand out against the stark white walls, and the light gray curtains framing each window are perfectly pleated. There are no personal effects in his room other than a small framed picture of his parents on his dresser. Honestly, I couldn't imagine a space that screamed "Finn" more than this one.

Behind me, I hear the distinct noise of a towel hitting the

ground. "Drop the towel, Angel."

33

Harper

Finn walks around to stand in front of me with a devious look. I untuck the cotton towel and let it fall to the floor, watching as Finn's eyes roam my body, appreciating every part of me, not just the toned and perfect parts, but the imperfect ones too. These men love my body for what it is. Flawed. However, I know they don't see it that way at all. They worship my curves and my cellulite. They trace my stretch marks with their tongues, and I am fucking here for it. Slowly but surely, they make me see my body for what it is. It's not *flawed* at all. My body is perfect. It's sexy and powerful. It's a body that makes three insanely powerful men fall to their knees.

Once his eyes reach my face, I see the fire that's always burning in his eyes, looking for something to reach out and destroy. To most, Finn looks like an absolute dream, but right now, he looks like a nightmare. I've never seen him look at me quite like this. It's so captivating it's terrifying. How he's looking at me strips me bare, and I know all of my deepest, darkest desires lie within his reach.

Wetness gathers between my legs as we linger by his door. I grow thirstier for him by the second, and he hasn't even touched me yet. "I think I know what you need, Angel."

"You do?" I ask breathlessly. Finn takes a step closer, now only an inch away from me.

"Yes. You need to let go. You need to trust that we have you. We will help you figure this all out." I suck in a shaky breath when he reaches out and gently brushes my cheek. I shiver at the contact. "I know it feels like you have no control like everything is falling apart around you, but that's not true, Angel."

My eyes begin to well up with tears.

No, Harp. Do not cry again.

"It's not?"

"You have all of the control, more than you realize. You control us. We will burn down the world for you. We will kill anyone who gets in our way. Nothing and no one will stop us from protecting you. *You. Own. Us.*" His words are so harsh and powerful, yet they seem to soothe the pain inside my chest.

"I want you to forget. Just for tonight. Forget about today, forget about what happens tomorrow, forget about every fucked up thing that's happened in your life. Let me take care of you the best way I know how. Let go, Harper. It's okay. Give me control. Then, when the night is done, I'll give it all back."

Taking half a step, he's tight against me now, cradling my face in his hands. His hips press against mine, and I feel every inch of him. Finn has a dangerous need, a hunger that festers inside of him. We've been dancing around this since I arrived here. Sure, he's shown me his controlling side here and there, but I always knew he needed more. "Let go, Angel. I'll make you feel so good."

"Yes." I close my eyes and lean into his hands, loving how his body feels against mine.

When I open my eyes, I see a different person before me. The Finn I knew from seconds ago has disappeared, and a new one stands in his place. Everything about his demeanor changes in an instant. He's a caged monster ready to be set free.

He's about to own my ass.

A full-body shiver runs through me from his stare. "Finn…" I can't help but moan out his name, and we haven't even started.

"Not anymore." I look at him in confusion. "If you're letting go and giving me control, I'm not Finn. For the rest of the night, in this room, that's not who I am."

I don't understand. I stare up at him, hoping he'll tell me what I'm supposed to say, but he doesn't say anything. Unmoving and silent, he just raises a brow at me. Waiting for my mind to catch up with whatever scenario he's trying to lay out for us. Then it hits me. I've read enough romance novels and watched enough porn to know what he needs from me. I open my mouth to respond, but I can't get the words to come out.

"Say it, Harper." The dominant tone in his voice gives me the little shove I need.

"Please, Daddy," I whimper.

For a second, I worry it wasn't the right thing to say. Maybe that wasn't what he wanted, and I've just ruined the whole mood. Then I see his eyes smolder, and I know I made the right choice. *Fuck.* Finn, my quiet control freak, has a Daddy kink. Daddy kink? Dom kink? Who the hell cares? He's the freakiest one of us all.

I should have seen that one coming. It's always the quiet ones.

Finn exhales a harsh breath and squeezes the sides of my face harder. "Again."

"Please, Daddy. Make me feel good." Releasing my face from his hold, Finn takes a giant step back, trying to regain his composure.

"Go lay on my bed on your back, arms above your head." I do as I'm told. Once I'm situated how he wants me, Finn walks along the side of the bed and removes the pillows, setting them neatly inside the trunk underneath one of the windows. I hear him rustling around above me. My heart stops when I look up to see what he's doing. Sitting low on the headboard are two gold rings screwed into the wood. Finn is busying himself by knotting a black rope onto each ring. Once done with those, he walks around and does the same with two rings at the foot of the bed. They were tucked beneath the mattress, so I had never noticed them. I know what's about to happen, and I can't help my chest's rapid rise and fall as he works around me. Finn notices me becoming uneasy, and he runs a hand up my leg, stopping once he reaches the apex of my thighs.

"Don't be nervous, Angel. I won't do anything you won't like." I believe him. Unlike when I'm with Ronan, I know I won't need any sort of safe word. Ronan gets lost in the moment, so focused on walking that line between pain and pleasure. He needs a way to ensure I'm not only feeling pain.

For us, that's perfect, but not with Finn. I know that whatever he's about to do, he will have thought it through meticulously. He will pay attention to every noise and movement my body makes, analyzing everything. Finn's about to dominate me in every way possible. My body is his.

"I know, Finn." He brings his hand down and slaps my pussy, causing me to cry out. As suddenly as the pain came, it's gone, leaving a shock of pleasure in its wake. I felt that slap all the way down to my damn toes.

"What did I say? Who am I?" He's practically growling.

"Daddy," I correct myself. "I know, Daddy."

"That's my girl. Don't make me tell you again." A devilish grin slides across his face, and my pussy anxiously clenches. Seeing Finn come undone is doing all sorts of things to me.

In a way, he's still as precise and controlled as ever. Yet, right now, he seems free. All of his inhibitions have gone out the window because, right now, with me, he gets to be exactly who he wants to be. Do exactly what he wants to do. He is in complete and total control. He stands at the end of the bed, naked with a body that looks like it was carved from stone, his blonde hair still tousled from our shower, tattoos perfectly placed up and down both of his arms and across his chest. A trail of dark blond hair runs from his belly button, down to his perfectly sculpted V, to his thick and ready cock. Right now, Finn looks like he holds power beyond measure, and in a way, he does. I am bound and entirely at his mercy. I honestly don't think he's ever looked sexier.

I know this night will be burned into my brain for the rest of my life.

"You look so beautiful like this, Angel. Spread open and ready to take my cock like a good little whore." There's a bit of apprehension on his face, waiting to see if I will react negatively to his words. Maybe the old Harper would have, but not now, not this Harper. All it does is make my core fill with heat. I wiggle a little, trying to bring my thighs together to relieve some of the pressure. It's no use. Finn has me tied tight.

Seeing the way that I squirm at his words, he continues. Dropping to his knees at the foot of the bed, he bends forward and slowly—*oh so slowly*—begins dragging his tongue up the inside of my leg, biting down every few inches. Once his mouth is about to reach the apex of my thighs, right where I want him to be, he drops back and starts at the other angle. I'm a mess by the time he makes his way up my second leg. "Fi... *Daddy*, please."

He lifts his mouth from my leg and looks up at me as he chuckles darkly. "You sound so pretty when you beg. I've barely even started yet, Angel."

Finn continues his leisurely torture up the rest of my body, kissing and biting at every inch of my skin, well, almost every inch. He's sure to avoid my pussy at all costs, getting as close as possible before pulling away. Once he makes his way up to my tight nipples, I can hardly take it anymore. I'm thrashing around on the bed, trying my hardest to move him to where I want him most, even though I know it's useless. Between him lying on top of me and the ropes tied tight to my limbs, I'm not going anywhere.

"Ahhh!" I scream when he tugs at one of my nipples with his teeth. I swear, I could come from this alone. I can't help the whimper that spills from my lips. Noticing I am near the edge, Finn removes his mouth from me. He pushes himself up, now hovering on all fours above me.

"You're doing so well, Angel. I want to hear you beg some more." His large hand grips my throat as he brings his face close to mine. "I want to hear you beg for my cock like the little slut you are. Only then will you get Daddy's cock."

I can't help it. I lift my hips off the bed, hoping to make contact with him. I see how hard he is for me, the tip of his cock glistening with his arousal. But he's hovering too high above me. I can't reach him.

"You like that, huh." It's not a question. He knows I do. "You want my cock? You want to be Daddy's good little girl?"

"Yessss."

"I know you do. Because that's what you always want. To be filled with our cocks. You want us to use you to fill all of your holes until you're dripping with our cum?" He leans down, takes my bottom lip between his teeth, and bites.

"Fuck! Yes!" I do, I really do. I should be mortified at his words, but I'm not, because he's right. I want them all to use me in every way imaginable. I want each of them to bring me more pleasure than I could have imagined.

"I fucking knew it. Maybe you're not our good girl after all. Maybe you're our bad, bad girl."

"I'll be anything you want me to be." That's the truth. Not even a hint of a lie.

"That's a dangerous thing to say, Angel." His hand squeezes tighter around my throat now. As spots begin to dance in my vision, Finn's mouth bites at my nipple again, and I can feel it in my toes.

"Yes, Finn!" He sits up and removes his hands from me.

"Now that's just a shame. I was about to let you come, but you had to go and break the rules."

Fuck.

"Maybe I should just leave you in here for a while, tied up to my bed with an aching pussy, until you learn how to beg properly."

He can't be serious, can he? I can't take this anymore. I really can't. If I don't get some relief from him soon, I might explode. I know I said I'd give him control, but this is almost too much.

"I–I'm sorry. Please." I'm not past begging. I'll give him what he wants. I'll beg for him and his delicious cock all day long. So long as he makes me come.

"That's a start, but not quite." He slaps my pussy again, harder this time. Pleasure pulses through my body, and it's unlike anything I've ever felt before. It's almost more than I can handle.

Tears spring up in my eyes. Not from sadness or pain but something else entirely. *Desire.* I don't think I've wanted anything in my entire life as much as I want him right now. I want him so deep inside me that I'll feel it in my soul. As a tear rolls down my cheek and onto the bed beneath me, I realize this is exactly what Finn was trying to accomplish. He wanted me to leave all my worries and doubts at the door and be here with him entirely. He wanted me to understand that the only thing that matters, right here and now, is the pleasure he can bring me. To let go and just *feel.* And fuck if that isn't exactly what I'm going to do.

He must see everything slide into place on my face because the side of his mouth curls, and his eyes beam with pride. "Go on, Angel. Try again. *Fucking beg for it.*"

"I want to come. Please. *Please* fuck me. Let me come."

Slap.

"Oh, that sounded so fucking pretty, but you can do better

than that. Try again." I'm afraid to open my mouth. I know if he slaps my pussy again, I'm a goner. I'm going to come, and this entire game will be over. He doesn't want me to come until he tells me, that much I know. He wants to control every last facet of this fantasy we're living in.

"Who am I, Harper? What's my fucking name? *Say it.*" The last words come out of his mouth deeper than I've ever heard. His brown eyes are so dark they're almost black. He looks like a man on the brink of madness. I know he needs this just as much as I do. I pick my head up ever so slightly off the mattress, trying to get closer to him in any way possible.

"Please, make me come. I'll be your good girl. Fuck me, *Daddy.*"

His nostrils flare, and I see his self-control slip if only just a little. Before I can take another breath, his lips crash into mine. He kisses me with bruising force. I part my lips to try to breathe, and he uses that as an invitation to taste me with his tongue. He begins fucking my mouth with his. If this is any indication of how hard he is about to fuck my pussy I *can't. Fucking. Wait.*

As quickly as his lips crashed into mine, he rips them away and makes his way back down my body. This time, not stopping once he reaches my sex.

His finger slides through my pussy. "Jesus fucking Christ, this pussy. So fucking wet." He sinks two fingers inside me and grins when I cry out. Finn pushes against my clit with his thumb and begins pumping his fingers inside me. I pull at the ropes above my head, desperate to run my fingers through his hair. "You don't get to fucking move." Stilling his fingers inside me, he reaches up with the opposite hand and squeezes the sides of my face. I feel my pussy clench around his fingers at the forcefulness of the action. "That's right, Angel. Once you come on my fingers and my face, I'm going to fuck this pussy with my cock, and you're going to lay there and take all of it. Aren't you?"

I squeeze around his fingers again and stare him dead in the eye. "Yes, Daddy."

"That's my girl."

He begins moving his fingers inside of me again. When he shoves a third finger inside me, I feel myself begin to fall. His fingers move quickly, hitting the perfect spot inside of me that only they seem to be able to find. *"Daddy."*

With one final slap to my clit my orgasm crashes into me. "That's right. Fucking come for me."

Without missing a beat, he withdraws his fingers and replaces them with that handsome fucking face. "My girl has the sweetest fucking pussy," he mumbles against me. His tongue laps up my cum as he shoves it inside my pussy.

"Oh, yes." One hand comes up and tightly pinches one of my nipples as he continues to tongue fuck me. I look down at his face between my legs to find him already looking at me. The look on his face does me in, and I scream out as he sucks my clit into his mouth. My head thrashes side-to-side, my body a quivering mess as I experience one of the most intense orgasms of my life.

I ride out my orgasm as he stays buried between my legs, drinking up every ounce of my release like it's the best thing he's ever tasted. As I come down from my high, I feel him give me a few languid passes with his tongue, ensuring he doesn't miss a single drop. He lifts his head, and I watch him drag his deliciously talented tongue across his lips. Spinning around on his knees, he crawls to the end of the bed and begins untying my ankles while I stare at his perfectly sculpted ass as he works. Once my ankles are free, I slide my feet up the bed, bending my legs, trying to work out the stiffness in my muscles. I get excited, hoping he will untie my hands, too, so I can touch him.

"Uh-uh. Your hands stay where they are. I just wanted to feel you wrap those thick-ass thighs around me when I fuck you." Finn crawls up the bed until his face reaches mine.

"You came like such a good girl. You're so fucking beautiful when you submit to me. But I'm not done with you yet." His lips meet mine, and I immediately open for him. Tasting my release on his tongue, I moan into his mouth. "You taste that, Angel? I could stay buried in that cunt forever and never get enough."

"Please..." I don't know what I'm begging for, just that I want more. More of him.

"Don't you worry, Angel. I'm going to fuck this pussy so hard you won't be able to scream anything besides my name. You'll have my cum leaking out of you all fucking day. Everyone will know who this pussy belongs to." I lift my head to meet his lips, but he backs away slightly, just out of my reach. Reaching between us, he grabs the base of his thick cock and lines it up at my center. I drop my head back to the mattress when I feel the head slide inside me.

"Say it, Angel. *Say my fucking name.*"

"Daddy." He slams deep inside of me in one quick thrust. I wrap my legs around him and hold on for dear life. I swear he's so deep I can feel him in my throat.

"Yes, Angel. Don't stop. Scream. Let them hear who owns this cunt."

Finn shifts his hips slightly as he wraps his arms underneath me, gripping my shoulders tightly. The new angle has him dragging the head of his cock against my G-spot over and over again. *"Oh, yes. Yes, Daddy. Don't stop. Don't stop. Don't stop, Daddy."* I'm screaming, and I know it. His thrusts become frantic. His hips slam against my thighs so hard it's almost painful.

Sweat begins to cover our skin as my walls tighten around him. "That's it," he snarls into my neck. "Come for me. Come on my cock, Harper." He thrusts inside me one, two, three more times, and I unravel beneath him.

"Yes, Daddy! Yes!" My legs wrap around him so tightly I'm slightly worried he can't breathe. The sounds that leave my mouth are unlike anything I have ever heard, but I can't find it in me to care. I continue to ride out wave after wave until I hear Finn moan, "fuuuck," and feel his release spill inside me.

I hear him whisper ever so faintly, almost like he doesn't mean to say it, but he can't stop the words, "You are everything. You're *my* everything."

We lay there for a few minutes before Finn lifts his head from my neck and lightly kisses the tip of my nose before slowly pulling out. I feel my cheeks redden as a rush of cum spills out. He dips his hand between my legs, wipes his fingers between my folds, and slides them into my pussy. "That stays right there where it belongs," he says as he shoves his cum inside me. I moan at the intrusion. Even after everything he did to me, I could go for another round at the feel of his fingers. Why was that so damn hot? Who am I kidding? Everything he does is hot. *Everything.*

Finn climbs off the bed and begins working at untying my wrists. Once they're free, I bring my arms down, wincing slightly at the stiffness in my shoulders. He grabs his pillows back out of the trunk and arranges them at the head of the bed. Once they're just right, he sits back against them, tapping the one next to him with his palm.

"Come here." I climb up the bed and curl up next to him. I look up at him and reach up to swipe a blond lock off of his forehead. He grabs my wrist and examines the faint red mark. "How do you feel?" *There's my Finn.* Always checking in. Ready to fix anything that needs fixing. But there is nothing here that needs to be fixed. Absolutely nothing. "That was amazing, Finn."

"Yeah?" he asks hesitantly.

"Yeah." The smile that spreads across his face warms my chest. "I don't ever think I've felt that… that…"

"Free?"

"Yeah. Free." He's right. Finn gave me exactly what I needed. He gave me a way to ground myself when I felt like I was spinning out. To be present and let go while getting to know a side of Finn that he keeps in the dark. If that's who he is in the dark, I want to live there with him. "Thank you for giving me exactly what I needed. You were amazing." I cup the side of his face lovingly.

He reaches up, places his hand over mine, and begins stroking the side of it with his thumb while planting a kiss on the crown of my head. "Always, Angel. *Always.*"

34

Ronan

It's just past six in the morning when I finish putting on my suit, and I'm fucking exhausted. The last thing I want to be doing right now is going to deal with this shit, but it has to be done. These assholes need to be dealt with.

I make my way out of my room toward Mac's to drag his ass out of bed. If his night was anything like mine, I'm sure he hardly got any more sleep than I did. Not that he ever sleeps much anyway. Unless he's with Harper. His room is even closer to Finn's than mine, and I had to spend half the goddamn night listening to her scream for him. I was hard as steel listening to the two of them. I fucked my fist twice to the sounds of her moans, and it did nothing to curb the hunger I felt for her. *Feel* for her still. I lightly knock on Mac's door, careful not to wake Finn and Harper. I know they only went to sleep a couple of hours ago. Little to my surprise, Mac opens the door a few seconds later, wearing nothing but an annoyed expression. He looks like shit.

"Couldn't sleep either?" I ask with a smirk.

He runs a hand through his messy hair. "Lack of sleep isn't my problem."

I step around him into his room as I laugh. "You heard them too, huh?"

"Of course, I fucking heard them, Ronan. I watched them go in there. If I had known he was going to go all Daddy Finn on her last night, I would have joined them!" My laugh grows louder as I watch his face turn red. "I don't think I've ever been this horny in my life," he sighs exasperatedly.

I hold my hand up to his face. "Okay, didn't need to know that."

"I have half a mind to walk next door and wake their asses up."

"Oh, don't be such a whiner. She needed it, and you know it. Plus, it was about time Finn showed her that side of himself." I could tell he's been holding on by a thread, only showing her bits and pieces of the real him. I don't know what happened last night that finally made the thread snap, but whatever it was, I'm grateful. Finn doesn't allow many people in, afraid that they will leave him and he'll wind up hurt. I suppose he's a lot like Harper in that way. Children who have had their families stolen from them and were left to feel all alone in this world. Finn rarely sleeps with women. It's just not who he is. It's not because he doesn't like to fuck, he probably needs it more than Mac and I, and that's exactly his problem. Finn wants to get lost in his partner. He wants to connect with them, mind, body, and soul. He could give two shits about a random hookup. It's just not who he is. Because of this, he does everything he can to avoid women altogether, to avoid any sort of relationship at all, really. Don't get me wrong,

Mac and I haven't had any serious relationships in the past either, but we definitely don't avoid women like the plague.

Finn doesn't need to worry about Harper. One, she's not going anywhere. The four of us are already in too deep. She has reached inside each of our souls and filled the cracks in only a way she knows how. For three men who are so dramatically different, she is perfect for each of us. I don't know how she does it or what we did to have the universe put her in our lives, but I won't let her go. *We won't.* And two, he has us. Me and Mac… his brothers. Finn won't ever be alone.

I hear Mac mumbling under his breath, only catching "I'm not a whiner" and "Finn and his fucking Daddy kink," and it pulls me from my train of thought, reminding me why I came here to wake his cranky ass up in the first place. "Stop complaining and put some fucking clothes on. I'm sick of looking at your dick. Meet me by the elevator in ten."

"I'm not putting clothes on, Ronan. I'm fucking exhausted, and I want to sleep. Go away."

"God, you're being a real bitch today." I watch him roll his eyes at me in annoyance. I love riling him up sometimes. That's what big brothers are for, right? "Fine. I guess you'll miss out on all of the fun."

"What could possibly be fun at 6:00 AM?"

"I put the word out about one of our shipments being delivered at the docks this morning. Fake, of course. I had some of our guys stake out early, and lo and behold, they found some rats trying to steal our shit."

I see the light flicker in his eyes. Usually, Mac hates having blood on his hands, but sometimes I know what my brother needs. As much as he hates to admit it, sometimes his soul needs the violence, to feel bones breaking under his fist, to hear the screams in his ears. If he doesn't let it out on them, it will eventually boil over until he explodes. He'll unleash the killer inside him and show no remorse, and he will never forgive himself if he hurts someone he loves. That's what our father turned him into, and I'll be damned if I let it destroy him.

"They have them?"

I shoot him a calculated grin. "They're holding three of them in the warehouse by the docks. Figured after last night you could stand to blow off a little steam." I see the clenching of his fists at his sides like his body is already gearing up to inflict pain on those who would dare to defy us, and I know I've got him.

"Should I go get Finn?" he asks.

"No, let them sleep. I called Logan and Tanner an hour ago, and they're already here to keep an eye out while we're gone. Plus, you and I haven't had some brotherly bonding in a while, and I'm itching to get my hands dirty."

Mac smirks back at me. "Give me ten."

I wait for my brother out in the hallway, and after only five minutes, Mac steps out of his room dressed in his usual black boots, jeans, and Henley. "Would it kill you to wear a suit?"

"You know that's not my style. One of us needs to be the cool one, and I know Harper likes it." At the mention of her name, I glance toward Finn's door. A sudden wave of anxiety crawls up my throat at the thought of leaving her. I know she'll be safe here with Finn, Logan, and Tanner, but that does nothing to calm the nervousness that is taking over me. Like he always does, Mac reads my mind instantly.

"Wanna go tell them goodbye quick?"

Thankful for his suggestion, I pat him on the shoulder. "Yeah."

We quietly slip into the room and find them sleeping peacefully on the bed. Finn wrapped around Harper's delicious body. They look so peaceful I almost hate to wake them. *Almost.*

We walk around to Harper's side of the bed, and I sweep my hand down her face. Seeing her dark eyelashes dusting over the freckles on her cheeks calms some of the anxiety coursing through me. She stirs at my touch, and after a few seconds, her eyes blink open to meet mine and Mac's. "Hey, Baby," I whisper.

"Mhmmm. Is everything okay? What time is it?" She moves to sit up in bed, but I stop her.

"Everything is fine. It's a little after six. Mac and I have to take care of a few things. Logan and Tanner are already here, but we will be back soon. We just wanted to say bye." She gives me a sleepy smile, and I swear my heart stops for a moment. She snuggles back into Finn, who is still dead to the world.

"Okay, have fun." I bend over to drop a featherlight kiss on her lips before stepping aside so Mac can get to her. He whispers something in her ear, causing her to give him a seductive giggle. He kisses her lips, cups her cheeks, and whispers, "Bye, Princess."

I watch as she settles back against her pillow, and I realize almost all the anxiety I felt minutes ago has disappeared— what this woman does to me.

Mac and I tiptoe out of her room and head toward the elevators. "Wipe that shit-eating grin off of your face."

"I'm just wondering where my brother went. I've never

seen you like this over a woman. Usually, it's me who has heart eyes." I can see his smart-ass smirk out of the corner of my eyes as we ride down to the parking garage.

"Yeah, well, she's not just any woman, is she?" Mac takes a deep breath next to me. It's not one of frustration or annoyance but one of deep understanding.

"No, Brother. No, she is not."

Once we reach the parking garage, I grab one of the keys off the rack and climb into my black Lamborghini Urus. "Let's deal with these assholes so we can get back to our girl."

Mac settles into the passenger seat as I let the car roar to life. "Well, aren't you the cutest?"

"Shut the fuck up, Cormac." I hear him laughing in my ear as I peel out onto the city streets.

* * *

We've been in this damn warehouse for over four fucking hours. None of these assholes will tell me what I want to know, and my patience is wearing thin. Two of them can't talk anymore as they lie in bloody heaps on the ground. Mac killed the first guy within the first fifteen minutes of our arrival. He beat him to a bloody pulp with his bare hands. The guy doesn't even have a face anymore, and Mac is covered in blood from head to toe. When it became clear that the two left weren't going to talk easily, I took the other one out. Choosing a far cleaner option than my little brother, but effective nonetheless. A bullet between the eyes did the trick.

I knew this third asshole would be hard to crack, but I didn't think it would take this goddamn long. The guy still hasn't said a word I care to hear. The only thing that has slipped past his lips are his insults and pleas to God.

There is no God here, not in this world.

I'm becoming more agitated the longer we're here and away from Harper and Finn. The calming effect she had on me hours ago is long gone. Mac steps away from the man chained to the ceiling as I admire his handiwork. The guy, whose name we now know is Max, looks like he's seen better days. He's hanging from the ceiling, naked, covered in his blood and piss.

Yeah, that one was pretty funny. I always love it when they're so terrified that they piss themselves. They might not speak, but it still shows me what I want to know. They fear us. Max did it right after we shot his little friend in the head. Mac has left no inch of him untouched. He's now missing most of his fingernails and a few of his toes. He has stab wounds covering his body, nowhere where near enough for him to bleed out, of course, that would be too easy. Mac ripped one of his ears clean off, which is always a fun party trick to watch, and I'd be willing to bet he has over twenty broken bones from Mac's fists.

The dude's a fucking mess, and I haven't even touched him yet.

I know I'm not as skilled as Finn is in reading people, but even I can tell Max knows something. He's not just a hired hand. If he were, he would have told us that by now in hopes we'd let him go, but he's given us nothing. Rolling up the sleeves of my white dress shirt, I make my way over toward Max. "You're gonna wish you would have talked up now, Maxy boy," Mac snickers behind me.

I step in front of Max, fear in his eyes. Not good enough. He won't give me what I need until he's given up. I don't know enough about him to threaten the ones he loves or destroy his life, but I do know one thing: I can take away the thing every man loves. I grip him by the jaw and force him to look me in the eyes. "Still don't have anything to tell me? Who's your boss? Who is telling you to steal our shipments? Just tell me, Max, and I can put an end to all of this right now."

"Fuck. You," he spits.

I let out a dramatic sigh. "Uh, uh, uh. Wrong answer, Max." Letting go of his face, I give him a light tap on the cheek before holding my hand over my head. Mac places his knife in my hand without me needing to say a word. In a split second, I grab Max's pathetic excuse for a dick in my hand and hold the knife to it with the other. I laugh at the fact that my knife is bigger than his dick.

"Tell me what I need to know, Max," I seethe. "And before you respond, just know that if the next words out of your mouth aren't what I want to hear, I will cut your dick off without a second thought." He looks at me, then down at his dick, my knife pressing against it just hard enough to draw a droplet of blood, and back up at me again. It's then I see it. *Hopelessness.* I've got him. I watch a tear roll down his cheek, and with a resigned sigh, he opens his mouth to speak.

"I was just supposed to fuck with your shipments, man. Me and my guys were just hired to steal your shit. They told us when and where. We stole the goods, delivered them to a dropoff point, and left. That's it."

"Where's the dropoff?"

"It was different every time. They would come and pick it up after we left and take it somewhere else."

"Who is they?" Mac snaps behind me.

"I don't know. I only ever talked to the boss on the phone."

I press the blade down a bit harder, and Max begins to shake in my hold. "You're not lying to me now, are you, Maxy?"

"No! No, man. I'm not lying! I swear! I've never met her in person or even seen what she looks like. I have no idea who she is! *Please!*"

He's full-on sobbing now, snot and tears mixing with the blood covering his face. *Wait.*

"She?"

"Yeah, man. It's some woman. She sounded older, though, and it was hard to understand her sometimes with her accent."

Fuck. Suddenly, it feels like there's a boulder sitting in my stomach. I'm almost afraid to ask my next question. "What kind of accent was it, Max?"

"It… it sounded like yours." He looks between Mac and me. "but a lot thicker."

Fuck, fuck, fuck! I quickly turn my head to look at Mac. Judging by the shocked look on his face, he's thinking the same thing that I am. If my assumptions are right, which they usually are, this just got so much fucking worse. Max's sad voice brings my attention back to him.

"That's all I know, I swear. You're going to let me go now, right? Please. I told you everything that I know." I release his dick from my hands, and a wave of relief washes over his face, but it's too little too late.

"Sorry, Maxy. We can't let you go. Have to send a message. But"—I give him a menacing grin—"At least you get to go out as a man." Max thrashes against his chains, trying to escape, but there's nowhere to go. I don't allow him to speak when he opens his mouth to plead for his life. I let the rage I'm feeling consume me, and in a split second, I plunge the blade of the large knife through his chin and into his brain, and watch as the life drains from his face.

Call me sick and twisted, but I usually feel some sense of relief after killing someone who's crossed me. But as Max's body relaxes in the chains, the familiar feeling doesn't wash over me. Instead, all I feel is panic, betrayal, and anger as the claws of desperation grip my chest in a vice over this new development.

I face my brother and see his expression mirrors mine as he asks, "Do you think it's true?"

"What reason would he have to lie? He thought we would let him go if he told the truth?"

"Fuck. I know… I just…"

"I know, Brother."

"None of this makes any sense, Ronan."

No, it fucking doesn't.

"Come on, let's go home. I'll call some of the guys to come and clean this up."

We're silent as I drive through the city streets toward the apartment. Surely wondering how in the hell we got here. It's been clear to us since we were old enough to know better that there are only a handful of people in this world that you can truly trust, and for men in our line of work, the circle is even smaller. We always knew our father was a bastard. He would do whatever he needed to be on top until the day he died. His latest actions have proved that he is exactly who we thought he was—a monster. But I never thought that we couldn't trust her. I thought she was ours to protect, and we were hers, no matter what. Looking over at my brother, I can see the hurt across his face clear as day. He doesn't want it to be true, and neither do I. None of this makes any fucking sense.

Mac's voice breaks the tension in the car. "I will gladly put a bullet through that asshole's brain. You were more of a father to me than he ever was. But..." He scrubs his face with his hands. I can feel his gray eyes scanning my face for answers, but I don't have any more than he does. "She's our mom, Ronan."

I take a deep breath and carefully think about my answer because I know what I have to say will hurt him, but he needs to hear it. "I know she is, Mac. But she might not be who we thought she was, and we need to prepare for that. I don't know what happened. Maybe Dad finally got in her head, or maybe she's been this way all along, and we loved her too much to see it, but whatever the case, it doesn't matter. I won't let anyone hurt my family. You and Finn are my family, and now so is Harper. I don't care if that someone is my parent or the damn Pope. *No one* will hurt the ones I love. I will kill anyone who tries." I quickly take my eyes off the road and level him with a stare that conveys everything at once. I'm his big brother, and I will protect him. As much as it may hurt, I will protect our family no matter what. "Do you hear me?"

"Yeah, I hear you."

"Right now, I don't have any more answers than you do. We're going to figure this all out. We always do."

Mac doesn't answer this time. A few minutes go by before he exhales a heavy breath, resigned to the fact that nothing can be done now, and I'm grateful for what he says next. My little brother always trying to lighten my mood. "I'm fucking starving. I don't know what sounds better, a burger or Harper's pussy. Either will do, honestly."

I tilt my head back against the seat and let out a deep laugh. Once I regain my composure, I answer, "Pussy, definitely."

"Mhmmmm, as much as I'd like it to be true, I don't think we can live off pussy alone. Although, she does taste fucking delicious."

"I could die of starvation with my face between her legs and still go out a happy man." Now it's him who lets out a roaring laugh.

"Who says we can't have both? Burger for lunch, Harper for dessert."

"Best idea you've had all day."

"We should probably stop at the Kings to shower and grab a change of clothes before we go home. Don't want to give our dessert a heart attack before we have a chance to eat it."

I wave my finger in his direction. "You're a smart man."

We ride the rest of the way home in silence.

35

Harper

Finn and I finally pulled ourselves out of bed a half hour ago. I'm rummaging around the kitchen, trying to find something to cook us all for lunch while Finn's cleaning up in the shower. He got deliciously dirty this morning after he made me ride his face.

Pulling open the fridge, I assess my options, finding everything I need to make some juicy burgers. They'll like that, right? I get to work setting everything out on the counter. I can't help but notice a set of eyes burning holes in the side of my head. I glance over to find Logan standing perfectly still next to the elevator while Tanner makes a lap through the apartment. I know it's their job to keep an eye on me, but the way Logan rakes his eyes over me makes my skin crawl. I tell myself it's just because I'm not used to being watched like this, but a dark glint in his eyes sets me on edge. I know I shouldn't worry, though. I'm never alone with him. Tanner is always with him, and the guys never leave me without one of them. I don't want to say anything to the guys about it, either. They have enough going on as it is, and the last thing they need to worry about is me being picky about the security guards they hired for me. I'm safe, and I know it. I need to stop being so paranoid.

Pushing my worried thoughts aside, I turn on some music and start with lunch. As I run through the mindless task of chopping tomatoes and onions and forming burger patties, I notice the pain in my cheeks. I don't think I've smiled this much since my parents died. This apartment that once felt like it would close in on me is starting to feel like a home. The men who live inside of it, who turned my world upside down, now own pieces of my soul. The girl I saw in the mirror all those weeks ago is nowhere to be found. Don't get me wrong, there are still pieces of me that aren't going anywhere, like my love for stories and fairytales, or the fact that I'd choose leggings and sweatshirts over a dress any day, or that I have a crippling addiction to coffee. But there are new parts of me that make the old shine a bit brighter. I don't feel I have to hide in the shadows or constantly hold my tongue. I've never felt as sexy in my skin as I do now, and I've unlocked a side of me I never expected. A side that holds her pleasure in the palm of her hand and isn't ashamed of it. A bolder side. Braver.

I knew that they would change my life that night at the bookstore. Deep down inside, I know I'm supposed to belong to them and them to me.

However, as peaceful as I feel, a constant state of panic still stirs deep within me. There are so many unknowns it's impossible not to let my mind wander. We have yet to hear from Ronan's contact in Ireland, which has prevented us from moving forward with any kind of plan regarding not only Declan but their father as well, and I'm still locked inside this apartment, unable to come and go as I please. I know the guys just want to keep me safe, but I can feel myself slowly crawling out of my skin. I miss my things, my favorite coffee shop, my books… the store. If all of that weren't bad enough, I can still feel it. Deep down in the depths of my soul where I keep the last part of me under lock and key. The part of me that allows me to give myself over to them. The part of me that feels love like I never have toward another. If I give them that last piece of me, if I hold it out and let them take it, they can crush me. It will destroy me if I lose them, like I've lost everyone else.

But, I could keep them just far enough away, there will still be enough of me left to put myself back together when they're gone. Despite how we all feel for one another, a relationship like this can't continue forever. *Right?* Someone will get sick of it. They'll tire of having to protect me, to worry about me constantly. They'll tire of having to share me with one another. Someone will get hurt. Someone will leave. And part of me knows that as selfish as it is, if I can't have all three of them, I want none of them. I don't want to think about these things. I want to live in the present with them, to soak up all the happiness I feel when I'm around them, but I can't stop thinking.

I'm in the middle of flipping the burgers when I feel a strong set of arms wrap around me. I was so lost in my thoughts I didn't even hear him walk in the kitchen. His clean smell envelopes me, instantly calming all of the thoughts I was just swimming in. Turning in his arms, I find Finn in a white V-neck, delectable ink-covered arms on display, and gray sweatpants. Very unlike him. "No suit today?"

"Hmmm…" He stares down at me, taking in the way I look in nothing but one of his button-ups. His hand works its way under the hem and tightly grips my waist. "I don't have any plans today except being here with you. Besides, you seem to have stolen my shirt."

I set the spatula on the counter behind me, run both my palms up his chest, over his shoulders, and wrap them around his neck. "Well, I didn't have any of my clothes in your room, and mine was *so* far away."

"Oh really?" Finn lowers his head so his lips rest gently on my ear.

"Yes, really."

"Because I think you just wore one of my shirts to torture me all day." He gently tugs the lobe of my ear between his teeth. "Do you even have any panties on?"

I tap my lips with my pointer finger as if I'm thinking hard about my answer. "You know. I must have forgotten."

"Fuck… Harper." Pulling me tightly against him, I feel his rapidly growing erection.

I'm feeling a little sassy toward him today after the torture he put me through last night. I use the word torture loosely because I really did love every delicious second of it. But that's beside the point. So, I smile coyly and pat him on the chest. "Now, now, Finn. Can't you see I'm busy? Don't want me burning these delicious burgers, do you?" I see a fire light in his eye at my brattiness. It only spurs me on. "Hands off. Go take a seat until lunch is ready." I watch as he tries to hold off the impossible smile that takes over his face, and what a beautiful smile it is. I'll never tire of seeing this side of Finn.

He gives me a firm slap on the ass before stepping away

from me, rounding the kitchen island, and climbing onto one of the stools. "Keep it up, Angel. I know you're just trying to get a rise out of me. It's in your best interest if you behave."

I must be a glutton for punishment for today. "Yes... *Daddy.*"

He points a firm finger at me. "Harper. Don't start something you can't finish." I tip my head back and let out a deep laugh.

They really are easy to rile up.

After a moment, I notice a familiar tattoo peeking out of the collar of his shirt. "Hey, I've been meaning to ask you." I wiggle a finger toward his chest. "What does that mean?"

Instantly his hand moves up to his chest and begins rubbing at the black ink. Almost like the reminder of the word is causing his pain. He closes his eyes and sits back in his chair. I almost immediately regret asking him. I could have looked it up, but I wanted him to explain it. Finn doesn't seem like the type of person who gets tattoos that don't mean anything. Finally, he lowers his hand and opens his eyes to look into mine. The ravenous look he had in his eyes only minutes ago has disappeared, and in its place is pain.

"It's a Gaelic word. *Teaghlach.*" The foreign word sounds beautiful coming out of his mouth, like when Mac calls me *Mo grá.* I don't ask him what it means. Instead, I wait for him to tell me when he's ready. Whatever it means obviously causes him pain.

A moment stretches between us, and I want to go to him, to hold him and let him know that I'm here, but I know that's not what he needs. Finn's love language isn't physical touch like Ronan's or words of affirmation like Mac's. No, Finn just needs me here, to be around when he needs me. He needs moments, no matter how small, to feel connected with the people he's around. So I don't move. I just wait. After a few minutes, he sits up straight in his chair, looking like he's trying to summon the courage to explain it to me. He looks at the burgers and then back at me. "Those about finished?"

"Ummm." I give them a quick once over and then turn off the flame. "Yeah, they're done."

"Why don't you go ahead and cover them. We'll eat when the guys get back. They should arrive shortly."

"Oh. Okay." I hesitantly go about plating and covering the burgers in foil before setting them inside the microwave to keep warm. I worry that's the end of a very short-lived conversation when Finn gently speaks, "Come over here, Angel." I walk around the island and move to pull out the chair next to him before he grabs my wrist, halting my movement. "What are you doing?"

"Uhhh… sitting?"

"Not there." He pats the counter in front of him. "Right here. I want to be able to look at you when I tell you this story."

My tall frame easily allows me to slide onto the counter in front of him. He rests his palms on the tops of my thigh and begins mindlessly rubbing one of his thumbs in small circles. I can tell he's hesitant to talk to me, so I reach up and run my fingers through his perfectly groomed beard. "It's okay. Whenever you're ready."

His somber eyes stare at mine, and when he's ready, he takes a deep breath before speaking. "I told you once my parents died. That the McDermotts took me in as their own."

"Yes…"

"But you never asked me how they died."

It's not a question but a statement. "I know better than

anyone how it feels to lose your parents. What it's like to relive that day over and over again every time you are forced to talk about it. It chips away at your soul. So, no, I didn't ask you to tell me what happened, and I won't ask you to."

He stops rubbing my thigh with his thumb and moves both hands to my waist. Gripping me tightly, he lifts me off the counter and sets me on his lap so I'm straddling him. As soon as I'm settled on top of him, he plants a fierce kiss on my lips. I get lost in the way his mouth feels against mine. It's not just a normal kiss. It feels like he's pouring everything he has into this moment between us, like each passing second is giving him the courage to tell me a story that pains him to his core. Finn gently pulls my bottom lip between his teeth, and I moan at the sensation. Taking the opportunity, he slides his tongue into my mouth and caresses mine in smooth strokes. It's a slow and sensual kiss but filled with passion nonetheless.

I don't rush him or move to take things any further. I let him remain in control. I know that's what he needs. A few more minutes pass before Finn gently lifts his mouth from mine. Cupping my face in his hands, he gives me one last chaste kiss before whispering, "Thank you."

"Whenever you're ready," I say, repeating my words from earlier. He gives me the slightest smile, and I swear it's one of the most beautiful things I've ever seen. With his hands back on my waist, I rest my palms on his forearms and, like he did to me earlier, begin stroking them with my thumbs, silently giving him the courage to speak.

"My father's name was Cian. He was a strong man. Never took any bullshit from anyone. I remember as a kid how terrified I was of him. Not because I thought he would ever hurt me in any way, but because I never wanted to disappoint him. He was always there for everyone and did whatever was asked of him. He was an amazing friend, husband, father, and leader. Everyone knew they could count on him, and he wouldn't disappoint them. From an early age, I remember thinking I wanted to be just like him. The person everyone could count on. To be a person people respected. To be the person who could…"

"Fix things," I finish the sentence for him. Wanting him to know that I already know the answer, to let him know he's exactly who he set out to be. He lets out a shaky breath before continuing.

"And my mother… she was… she was beautiful, Harper." I feel unshed tears fill my eyes at the look on his face, like his mother was the love of his life, as a mom should be to a young boy. "Her name was Roisin. It means 'little rose.'" He looks down at the intricate rose he has tattooed on his forearm. The one I'm still rubbing my thumb over. "She was like an angel walking this earth. I can still hear her voice clear as day in my dreams. As I get older, the memories of them have started to fade, but not her voice. I live for the days when she visits me in my dreams. To hear her sing folk music or tell me, 'Get some rest, my dear, and everything will be okay in the morning.'" A stray tear rolls down his cheek, but he doesn't try to wipe it away.

"My parents were best friends with the McDermotts. Before Ronan and I were born, they came to New York. Our syndicate back in Ireland wanted a stronger foothold in America, so they sent Liam and my dad here to take over. My dad was Liam's right-hand man. As you can see, they created an empire that's unmatched." I bristle at the mention of Liam's name but try not to let it show, wanting Finn to continue with his story.

"I was eight when they died… when they were murdered."

"Oh, Finn." My heart instantly breaks for him, for the boy who lost his parents at an age when no one should have to go without.

"Don't pity me. Please."

"Finn…" He's not looking at me now. Instead, his gaze is firmly planted in his lap. *That won't do.* "Finn… Love, look at me." His face snaps up at the pet name. "I don't pity you. I understand exactly how you feel, how it feels to have the two most important people in the world stolen from you. To have them taken away when you need them most. I don't pity you, Love. I empathize with you."

Hesitation is written all over his face. He's afraid to tell me what happened.

Does he think I can't take it?

"You can tell me… If you want to." I really want him to. I want to know him inside and out.

With a slight dip of his chin, I know he's going to continue. "The McDermotts and my parents had to go to Ireland to meet with some of our leaders there. The American syndicate had become more powerful than anyone could have imagined, more powerful than the one in Ireland. Because of this, Liam and my father took some of their most trusted men overseas to help clean things up with the original syndicate. Ronan, Mac, and I were just kids, so we stayed in New York with family friends while they were gone.

"They were there for only a few days when some of Declan's men heard they were trying to strengthen their foothold in Ireland. The last thing Declan Whelan wanted was for our syndicate to regain power there. He was finally more powerful than us, and he was terrified of losing that power… in their home country nonetheless." I tense in his lap, horrified by the direction this is heading. "He was desperate. He didn't want people to see him as weak. He wanted to stay in control. He wanted us to fear him. The McDermotts and my parents were on their way to dinner one night when they were ambushed walking down the street. Declan and his men captured my parents. He used them to threaten the McDermotts. To force them and the rest of our men back to America and not encroach on his territory in Ireland. Liam agreed to his terms. He said they would all leave Ireland without trying to regain control of Declan's territory. That should have been that, but it wasn't enough for Declan. He wanted everyone to know how powerful he was. How evil he was. When Liam, Emma, and the rest of our men returned to New York, I watched as Ronan and Mac hugged their parents while I waited for mine to get off the plane. They never did. Declan Whelan tortured my parents for five days before he killed them and destroyed their bodies. I was an orphan. I never even got to bury my parents."

Tears are streaming down my face now. My family, *my blood,* destroyed him. Those people, the ones that ripped apart a boy's life, are a part of me.

Oh, god! How can he even look at me?

"I'm so sorry," I sob as I bring my shaking hands to my face.

He pulls my wrists away before tipping my chin up with his finger. "Hey, don't you dare apologize."

"But he… I'm… he's my… how can you…" I don't even know what I'm saying. I tried. I tried so hard to be strong for him, but this is too much.

"You are *nothing* like him, Harper. Do you hear me? It

doesn't matter whose blood runs through your veins. It matters who you are in here." He lays his palm flat against my heaving chest. "You are Harper Hayes. You are a gorgeous, strong woman. You have a heart bigger than anyone I've ever met. A heart big enough for three complicated men." He pauses to give me a sweet smile. "You are so smart, so caring, and so loving. There is not an ounce of evil in that beautiful heart of yours. His actions do not define who you are."

"How can… how can you even look at me? How can you alone be with me?" I ask as I lean into his hand, still firmly placed on my heart.

"Because you, my sweet Angel, are made for me. Who you are is everything I'm not. You fill pieces of me I've been missing since I was eight. Because whether or not I was looking for you, you came into my life and shook the foundation I so carefully built. One that was made of nothing but 'could have been's.' Because you… you are *all* of my 'should be's.'"

I feel like Finn has just stolen the breath from my lungs. Here I should have been, comforting him over the family he lost, the one *mine* took from him. Instead, I'm falling apart while he tries to put me back together. But I guess that's who he is, isn't it? It's what he does. In the blink of an eye, Finn has made every worry disappear. We may not have all of life's answers, but when I'm with Finn, that doesn't matter. He centers me. I only hope I can do the same for him.

I lean my forehead against his, and before I can speak, he says, "Please don't pull away. Just because I am who I am and you are who you are doesn't mean there is anything wrong with us being together." I shake my head, but he still doesn't let me speak. "I got this"—he grabs my hand and places it against his tattoo—"in memory of them. But now, just as much as it reminds me of the one I've lost, it represents the one I've gained. *Family*. Ronan and Mac, they're my family. My brothers. Now, you are too. You're my family, Angel."

"Finn, Love. I'm not going anywhere. No matter what's happened or what's going to happen, I'll be here. You were meant to be in my life. All of you. You, Ronan, and Mac. Whatever we went through in our lives brought us here, to each other. We can't change it. All we can do is move forward together. As a family. Because that's what we *should be*. A family."

I know I'm crazy. I know this is all crazy. But it's because I know in my heart of hearts that this is where I'm supposed to be. Here. With them.

Fuck it. Let's be crazy.

"I think I might actually cry." Finn and I snap our heads to the familiar sound of Mac's voice, finding him and Ronan standing near the elevator. Logan and Tanner are nowhere to be found. Finn and I were so wrapped up in one another I didn't even hear them come home or our guards leave. I move to wiggle out of his lap, worried he might be embarrassed by what his brothers heard, but he holds me steady. Ronan slaps Mac in the chest. "Shut the fuck up. You aren't going to cry."

"No, really, look." He points at his eyes; sure as shit, they're filled with unshed tears.

"What the hell is wrong with you?" Ronan jabs at his brother.

"Shut up. That was beautiful. Don't give me shit just because I have emotions, and you're a robot."

"I am not a fucking robot. You're just an emotional baby."

"Jesus Christ," Finn grumbles in my ear, and I can't help but laugh at the two of them still bickering in the background. He leans in and whispers, "Thank you, Angel."

I look back at him and just stare for a moment, memorizing how at peace he looks now. Like telling me that story took a weight off of his shoulders. "Thank you, Love." I lean forward and give him a featherlight kiss.

"Go say hello." He gives me one last kiss on my nose before I climb off of him and head toward the still-bickering brothers.

"Hi, boys."

Ronan grabs me first as his eyes rake over my body. "Stole another one of our shirts, I see."

"Get used to it."

He leans his face down toward mine. "You'll get no complaints from me. You look sexy as fuck." Holding me tight, he wraps one arm around my waist and threads one hand through the hair on the back of my head. "Missed you, Baby. Have a fun night?"

My cheeks blush. "I'm sure you already know the answer to that."

His lips brush mine. "Hmmm… I love the sounds of your screams."

If I were wearing any panties, they'd be wet. I think Ronan could talk me through an orgasm, honestly. Dirty, dirty man. He chuckles before giving me a quick, yet hot, kiss.

Mac pulls me from his brother's arms. "Hey, Princess." His hands slide down my thighs, and he picks me up off the ground. My legs immediately wrap around his slender waist.

"Hey, you big marshmallow." I tease him as I wind my arms around the back of his head.

Ronan laughs next to us.

Mac snaps, "Ronan, I swear to god if you don't fuck off."

This only causes Ronan to laugh louder. "Ronan, stop teasing your brother," I say in Mac's defense, even though I'm trying to hold back my laugh because it is slightly funny. I really can't believe Mac was about to cry.

Actually, yes, I can. He's a teddy bear at heart.

"Yes, ma'am." Ronan winks at me before walking toward Finn, who is still shaking his head in his chair.

"My hero." Mac beams down at me like I saved him from the boogie man.

"You two are ridiculous. Hold on"—I look at his hair, then behind me at Ronan's—"why is your hair wet?"

"We had to stop at Kings to shower."

"Have some hot woman's perfume all over you?" I ask, only slightly joking.

Mac quickly answers, "No, Harper. Just the blood of our enemies."

I wait for the "just kidding," but it never comes. "Wait, you're serious?"

He kisses my forehead. "We'll talk to you guys about it later. There are more important things to take care of." I tighten my legs around his waist, ready for him to make good on the promise he whispered in my ear this morning, but much to my disappointment, he doesn't move toward his bedroom. Instead, he sniffs in the air. "Harper, please tell me I smell burgers."

I smile. "Yeah, I made you guys lunch. They're on a plate in the microwave. They should still be warm."

He gives me a deep kiss, causing me to moan deep in my chest. Once he pulls his lips from mine, he yells to Ronan in the kitchen, who's already assembling one on his plate, "Ronan, she made fucking burgers! Burgers!" I don't get what's so impressive about burgers, but as long as they're happy.

"I know, you fucking dumbass!"

Mac lets the insult slide off his back and looks down at me. "I think you might be the love of my life."

Ummm what?

He gives me one big loud smooch before dropping me to my feet and speed walks toward the kitchen like he didn't basically just tell me he loves me.

"Baby, you didn't make dessert, did you?" Ronan asks with a mouthful of burger while Mac and Finn assemble theirs.

"Uhhh, no? Was I supposed to?"

"Nope. We've got it covered." Ronan fistbumps Mac across the counter.

What is even happening right now?

36

Harper

After lunch, I spent almost the rest of the day in my room, popping out occasionally to get a glass of water or grab a quick dinner. The guys said they had some things to discuss and disappeared into Ronan's office. I know something is going on, considering the fact that Ronan and Mac slipped out of the apartment so early this morning only to return hours later freshly showered and in a different change of clothes. I doubt that Mac was kidding when he said he had to wash off the blood of his enemies. I don't know if it's because I'm too afraid to ask or if I trust the fact that they'll tell me what I need to know when they're ready, or a little bit of both, but I didn't question them and left them to their own devices.

I've rarely gotten time to myself since they brought me here all those weeks ago, and I'd be lying if I said I didn't miss it. As much as I love spending time with them, or interacting with customers at the bookstore, or making conversation I meet with people on the street, I find solace in myself. So, I spent the day taking a long bubble bath, painting my toes, and I'm currently curled up on the chaise that Mac picked out for me, chapters deep in a new book.

As I turn the page, I snuggle deeper into my spot, pulling the blanket further off my body, and continue reading my book. This one is different from my usual choice. I ordered a few new ones online and had them delivered to the desk downstairs. Usually, I'm all about the happy ever afters—the typical story. A handsome, grumpy man reluctantly falls in love with the beautiful, bubbly girl next door. They get married, buy a house with a white picket fence, get a dog, and have two-point-five kids. You know the one. However, considering my current position in life, I thought I'd give something else a try.

Dark romance it is.

Currently, the morally gray male character—actually scratch that, I think he really might be a psychopath—is chasing his "chosen" through the woods to fulfill her fantasy. While it isn't something I am necessarily interested in, I see the appeal. The idea of giving over every ounce of control to someone else. Of letting someone make your every dirty and forbidden wish come true. There's something so freeing about wanting what others consider taboo and not giving a damn about their judgment. As long as it's between two consenting adults, gets you weak in the knees, and makes your panties wet, who gives a fuck?!

Ha. Good one, Harp.

The more I read about him pinning her down and fucking her into the forest floor, the more I wiggle in my seat. There's a knock at my door, and I snap my book closed. Ah, perfect timing.

Ronan pushes open my door, immediately spotting the book on my lap. "Wutcha reading?" se asks in a very un-Ronan, sing-songy voice.

"A book…" I quirk my head at him, still standing in the doorway, meeting his trouble-making gaze head-on.

"Well, judging by the flush in your cheeks, I'd venture it's safe to say you were just getting to a good part?"

"I think that would be a safe assumption. Perfect timing for you, don't you think?" I slide my glasses up to the top of my head. I don't know why he's being so flirty, but I'm here for it.

"Actually"—he steps into my room, and to my surprise, Finn and Mac follow behind him—"we remembered something when we were sitting in my office."

I cross my arms over my chest. "Oh yeah, and what was that?"

"We never had dessert earlier." His tall frame is now towering over me, looking practically edible in a pair of suit pants and white shirt, sleeves rolled up to his elbows, and the top two buttons undone.

"I told you I didn't make anything for dessert."

He bends over me, placing his hands on the back of the chaise, caging me in. His usual smell of whiskey and smoke warms my chest. "And I told you…" grabbing a fistful of my blanket, he rips it off my body, revealing my silk pajamas. It's a lavender cami and short set, trimmed with white lace, and covers the absolute bare minimum, but it might be the softest thing I've ever put on my body. Mac got me five sets, each a different color. "We already know what we want."

Between the greedy looks in his eyes and the fact that all

three of them are in my room, I'm pretty sure I know exactly what he's thinking. Yet, I remain firmly seated in my spot, not ready to cave. "Any of you care to explain to me what happened to you two while you were gone this morning?" I look between them, but it's still Ronan who speaks.

"Later, Baby."

"Promise?" I ask. I don't want them to hide things from me. If I'm in this with them and them with me, then I want to be all in.

"We promise." Mac and Finn nod their heads in agreement behind him. "Right now, the only thing I can think about is being between those delicious fucking legs of yours."

Okay, my resolve is dwindling... *rapidly.* I uncross my arms as Ronan brazenly looks at my heaving chest, nipples hard under the silk of my top. "Oh, really?"

"Yes, really. And I think it's time we see how much you can take, Baby." He removes one hand from the back of the chaise and squeezes the top of my thigh. I look down and admire the juxtaposition of his hand on my body. The back of his strong hand is covered in ink down to his fingertips. It's a stark contrast against my pail and unmarked skin. His skin doesn't look like it belongs touching mine, yet it feels like it was always meant to be there. A firm squeeze draws my attention back to his face, which is almost touching mine. "Think you can take all three of us, Baby? Want to see what it's like to have us fill you? To have every hole dripping with our cum?"

Shit. I don't know if I can take it, but holy mother of god, do I want to try. Wide-eyed, I nod.

"Words, Baby."

"Yes. Yes, I want you. All of you."

A series of deep moans erupt through the room as Ronan stands and holds his hand out to me. I grab it and let him stand me between the three of them. "Arms up," Ronan instructs. Without hesitation, I raise both arms and let him pull the silk cami over my head. Finn drops to his knees behind me and slowly pulls down my shorts and underwear, dropping kisses down the backs of my thighs as he goes. Mac removes my glasses and threads his fingers through my hair, pulling my curls from the clip on the back of my head.

Finn stands behind me, his breath against my neck sends shivers down my spine. "Go lay on the bed, Angel."

I turn my head to face him, reach behind, and quickly run my fingers through his golden hair. "Yes… *sir.*" I almost utter the name I screamed for him last night but think better of it, wanting to keep that as something only he and I share. He gives me a knowing wink, "Good girl. *Go.*"

I crawl onto my bed, lay on my back, and rest my head against the pillows, ensuring I can still see what the three of them are doing at the foot of the bed. I don't try to cover my body as the three of them stand there, looking over every inch of my naked flesh. Because as much as it might unnerve some, having three men who look like they belong in a Giorgio Armani cologne commercial, I see it in their eyes. The way they want to devour me, run their hands over every inch of me, worship me from the inside out. They give me the confidence to just *be.* So instead, I watch every woman's fantasy unfold before my eyes. All at once, the three of them begin removing their shirts, each still in the same clothes they had on this morning: Ronan in his suit and shirt, Mac in jeans and a black T-shirt, and Finn in his white V-neck and gray sweatpants. *It's like the female gaze on crack.* Their shirts hit the floor one by one, and I begin wiggling in anticipation.

The three of them are so different from one another yet so alike. Their bodies each riddled with perfectly sculpted muscle from years of being the most feared men in the city. "Like what you see, Princess?"

"Is that even a question?" *Because, boy, do I ever.* I run my eyes up and down their bodies. Each time I look at any of them, it takes my breath away, not even lying. But seeing the three of them together like this, it's otherworldly. Like a perfectly choreographed dance Ronan unbuttons and lowers his dress pants, followed by Finn's sweats, and my eyes drift to Mac as he drops his jeans. As per usual, he's not wearing any underwear. I let myself drink up the sight before me. A trail of dark hair runs from his navel down to his cock, already hard. I swallow the saliva pooling in my mouth as he smirks at me. Finn and Ronan follow my gaze, chuckling when they find Mac completely naked, practically eye fucking me. Much to my pleasure, they follow suit and drop their briefs.

Holy shit.

The four of us go completely still. Basking in the sexual tension that fills the room as I lie there waiting for their instruction. If there's one thing my guys have taught me about my sexuality it's that I get off on being completely submissive. I want them to own me. I want to be their good girl. Finally, as usual, Ronan takes control of the room and crawls onto the bed until he hovers over me, arms caging me in again. His eyes are dark with desire. I let out a shaky breath, wetness gathering between my legs, growing thirstier for them by the second. Ronan's nostrils flare, and, as if he can't wait a second longer, he begins devouring me with his mouth. His hands roam the entirety of my body, going from stroking me softly one moment to squeezing me fiercely the next. I can't keep up. Every change of pace causes me to whimper with need.

Sitting up straight, and back on his heels, he gently wraps his hand around my ankle, lifts my leg in the air, and kisses the inside of my calf.

"Fuck, Baby," Ronan growls once his mouth works up my leg, reaching the apex of my thighs. "I can smell how wet you are."

The moment his tongue swipes between my folds, I lift my hips in the air, desperately trying to gain more friction. Ronan places a firm hand on my stomach and wraps the other around my thigh, holding me in place. "My greedy girl." He gives my pussy another slow stroke with his tongue. "You taste so fucking delicious, Baby."

It's then that I hear Mac and Finn groan in appreciation behind him. I lift my head from its propped-up position on the pillow to find them slowly fisting their cocks, precum glistening at the tips. I drop my head back to the pillow and whimper. Ronan begins stroking at my clit with his tongue, using powerful, quick strokes, just how I like it. In seconds I can feel the familiar warmth building in my core. He knows how to play my body like a damn fiddle. A tattooed hand slowly moves up my abdomen until it hits my breast. Palming it, Ronan gives it a hard squeeze. Hard enough that I'm sure I'll be able to see his fingerprints in the morning, but that's what I love about Ronan. He pushes my body to its limits, allowing me to take the drops of pain and turn it into a sea of pleasure. I can't get enough. I thread my fingers through his dark curls and give them a firm tug. "*Yes,* Baby," he mumbles against my sex, so I pull harder. A groan slips out of his mouth, and it's one of the sexiest sounds I've ever heard. A rush of wetness pools between my legs, knowing I have this effect on him. Ronan bares his teeth against my clit and bites down.

"Ahhh! Ronan!"

"There's my girl. Let go for me. I want this pussy to soak my face." I tip my head further into the pillow, arching my back and rocking my hips against his face. The familiar tickle of his scruff against my thighs as he laps at the sensitive bud with his tongue is enough to bring me to the edge. I can feel it; the need to come is right there. Every muscle in my body is as tight as a spring, ready to release. But it's not enough. I need more. *"Ronan..."* I whine. "More. I need *more.*"

He lifts his head, and his baby-blues lock onto my face, hooded and filled with desire. "I know what you need, Baby." The hand that was squeezing my breast moves up to my throat as his opposite hand releases my thigh. It's then that I feel two large fingers slide into my pussy. He curls them at just the right angle, and the second he brushes them against my most sensitive spot, stars start to fill my vision. He doesn't let up, his tongue and fingers working in perfect rhythm as his hand tightens around my neck. I hold off letting go, just for a few seconds, because I know what awaits me if I do. Ronan chuckles against my throbbing cunt, and as if he's reading my mind, he squeezes harder. *There it is.* The edges of my vision blur as fogginess fills my head, and I feel my thighs tighten around Ronan's head. I fall over the edge as an intense orgasm takes over my entire being. My screams fill the room, likely drowning out the guys' moans. My body trembles and shakes on the bed. Ronan doesn't move from his spot until he laps up every ounce of my release.

Once I've come down enough to control my body, Ronan sits back on his haunches and licks his lips, not letting a drop go to waste. A severe expression takes over his face as he crowds back over me on all fours. I feel his hard cock brush up against my stomach as he slightly lowers himself so he's just above my face. "We're just getting started, Baby. Do you remember what to say?"

I don't have to ask what he means. "Yes," I respond, still feeling breathless.

"Let me hear it. I need to be sure you know it."

"Bubbles."

"Good girl. They know it." He nods toward Finn and Mac, who are anxiously standing at the foot of the bed. "If you want to stop anytime, that's all you need to say. No questions asked."

"O-Okay." I will myself to slowly move my head up and down.

Holy fuck. This is real. This is happening. I don't know if I'm terrified or beyond turned on or both. Probably both.

Focus, Harp!

"Hands above your head, beautiful. Finn's next. Don't move until he tells you. You know how he is." Ronan gives me a wink, then he's gone, sprawling out on the chaise by the window.

I'm going to have to get that cleaned one of these days.

I suck in a sharp breath when I feel a hand lightly graze up my leg on the opposite side of the bed. I roll my head over to look at Finn as he lets his hand wander up the rest of my body until he reaches my cheek, only touching me with the tips of his fingers. Even though Ronan just made me see through time and space, Finn's light touch is enough to make me want more. I'm always wanting *more*. More of them in every way possible.

"Watching you come apart for them is unlike anything I've ever seen, Angel. You're a damn work of art."

"Love…"

"I can't wait to unravel you," he practically growls down at me, sounding delightfully sinister. This man has an effect on me, unlike anything I've ever experienced.

Mac feels familiar, like my soul was always meant to find his. I know, without a doubt, that I can count on him to give me exactly what I need. He is my comfort and my peace. In a way, Ronan almost feels like the other half of me, the half I didn't even know I was missing. The half of me that wants to swim in the pain that life has to offer instead of drowning in it. He tests me every day, and I find myself wanting to rip his head off more often than not, but that's what I love about him. He doesn't shy away from me. He doesn't treat me like a fragile flower. Ronan makes me strong. And Finn… Finn belongs to the part of me that I've kept hidden from the world, and I to him. The deep dark corners of our desires, the ones we *need* to be truly happy but are afraid to bring to the light, are kept safe by one another. When I'm with Finn, I dance in the dark.

"*Finn…*" His name sounds like a prayer on my lips.

"I know, sweet Angel. I know." He's still standing above me, staring down at me with those whiskey-colored eyes. I could drown in them if he'd let me. "Do you trust me?"

"You know I do," I answer without hesitation. A look of longing passes over his face at my answer, as if he didn't know this already. I wouldn't have let him do what we did last night if I didn't trust him. I wouldn't still be here in this penthouse if I didn't trust them. It's then that it occurs to me… I need to let them know that, regardless of all of the uncertainties that hang over our heads and despite my fears, I'm as in this as they seem to be. "I trust all of you with my life." Ronan and Mac each let out a harsh breath, and suddenly it feels like the mood in the room has shifted, like something has slotted into place.

"Sit up for me, Angel." I give him a confused look and quickly dart my gaze over to Ronan, still sprawled on the velvet chaise.

"Don't look at me, Baby. I may own that ass when it's just you and me, but right now, he calls the shots." He nods toward Finn, who turns the corners of his lips up in return before turning back to me with a serious stare. I do as instructed, drawing my knees up and wrapping my arms around them to hold me steady, still a little shaky from Ronan feasting on my pussy like it was his last fucking meal.

Bending down, Finn begins adjusting the pillows and sits behind me, leaning his upper body against the headboard. "Scoot back for me, Harper." I inch my body backward, so I'm sitting against him, my back to his chest, with his legs outstretched on either side of me. "Wrap your arms around my neck. Don't move them unless I say so. Got it?"

Hesitantly, I interlock my fingers behind his neck as he rests his head on my right shoulder. I feel his hot breath dance across my neck. I'm about to ask what he's doing when he wraps his legs around mine, pulling them further apart. I move to bring them back together, testing his hold, to find that I'm clearly not going anywhere. I look at Mac, who's standing still as a statue at the end of the bed, his chest heaving as he studies my position in Finn's arms. My chest is pushed forward due to my arms being wrapped around Finn's neck, my nipples tight in anticipation, and I know he can see every inch of my pussy, swollen and wet from Ronan's mouth.

"I wanted to taste that sweet pussy just like Ronan did," Finn whispers hungrily in my ear. "But then I remembered how much you liked being tied to my bed last night. How much you liked being under my control."

"Yes, Love."

"Fucking hell, I love hearing that name roll off your lips." I feel his erection twist against my back, and I know he's telling the truth. "Then I thought, I'd love to see what she feels like struggling in my arms instead." I let out the faintest whimper, but I know he can hear me. "You love this, don't you? Me holding you down, not able to move a fucking inch?" I nod in response. "Words, Harper. I need to hear you say it... always."

"Yes. Yes, I love it."

Finn's hands slowly move up and down my body, only brushing my skin with his fingertips like he was before, leaving a trail of goosebumps in their wake. "I want to feel every second of your pleasure while I watch Mac feast on that fucking cunt." He brings one hand up to the side of my face and shoves the pad of his thumb into my mouth. I instinctively close my lips around it and suck. "Then when he's done, we're going to fill every fucking hole, and you'll take it like the whore you are. Won't you?"

Ronan lets out a low chuckle on the other side of the room, but it's not him who I'm focused on now. My eyes remain glued to my gray-eyed gentle giant at the end of the bed, the one with a mix of emotions playing across his face. If I couldn't see it on his face, I could see it clear as day by looking at his throbbing cock, which is gripped tightly in his palm. I watch as a bead of precum drips off the head and falls to the floor. He wants this as much as Finn does, as much as we all do. But there's also worry. I know it's because of how Finn is holding me down, how he's talking to me. Mac has been rough with me before, but it's nothing compared to how Ronan treats me and certainly nothing compared to the man behind me who still has his thumb shoved in my mouth. But that's okay. That's not who Mac is and not what I want from him. What he and I share is perfect, but that's also not the scene Finn is laying out for us right now, and I'll be damned if I don't want this to happen.

With a pinched expression, Mac stands there and stares at me. I know he's waiting for my permission. Waiting for me to tell him I'm okay. So, I open my mouth slightly and push Finn's thumb out with my tongue. I look at Mac and give him the most heartfelt look I can. "Yes," I nod, answering Finn's question. In the span of a few seconds, Mac reads the expression on my face, and I watch his body relax in front of me.

Mac gives his cock one more slow stroke before he crawls onto the bed until his face is right in front of mine. Finn drops his hand from my face, and Mac's finds its place. With a gentle stroke of his thumb on my cheek, he whispers, "You are so beautiful, Princess." I can't help the sting I suddenly feel behind my eyes. Then Mac's mouth is on mine. His tongue licks against my lips, and I let him in willingly. I want to run my hands along his muscular back, but I don't dare move them from behind Finn's head. Instead, I rake them through his thick blond hair. Finn groans against my neck in response as I sink further into Mac's kiss. Mac pulls away from my mouth and begins trailing kisses across my jaw, down the other side of my neck, and across my collarbone. He takes my breasts in his hands before leaning in and sucking a tight bud into his mouth. Mac switches his attention back and forth between each breast as I writhe beneath him, still in Finn's firm grip as he nips along my neck. Once Mac has had his fill of my breasts, he slides down the bed, peppering kisses along my stomach and hips as he goes. When his face reaches my pussy he leans down and inhales deeply, letting out a pained groan. "Do you have any idea how much I want you every second of every day?" The other two groan in agreement.

"Yes," I moan, looking down at him. "Because that's how much I want you." He licks through the slit of my pussy, and I tilt my head back to rest against Finn's chest. Mac parts me with his fingers and circles his tongue around my clit. "You taste so fucking good."

"Doesn't she, brother?" Ronan chirps.

Mac sucks and nips at my clit, flicking his tongue back and forth at just the right speed. Much like his brother did minutes ago, he slides two fingers inside me, finding my G-spot within seconds. "Holy shit." I can feel my legs instinctively fight against Finn's hold, trying to wrap around Mac's head, but he doesn't let me move an inch.

"That's it, Angel. Take everything he gives you." Finn's praise spurs me on. Mac doesn't let up, fucking me with his fingers and licking my clit like it's his fucking job.

Holy hell, can these men eat pussy. What have I been missing my whole life?

I lift my head from Finn's chest and look down at him, only to find him staring back up at me. I can't look away, he's fucking beautiful. "Mac…"

"Mo grá," he groans against my clit. He starts moving his fingers faster, and I can feel the familiar pressure building, ready to be released. Finn pinches each of my nipples hard between his fingers as Mac sucks my clit further into his mouth, and suddenly it's all too much. My back bows in Finn's hold, hips thrusting up into Mac's face as I come. Mac kisses my thighs, bringing me down gently in only a way that he knows how. He kisses back up my body and slants his mouth over mine, allowing me to taste my release on his lips. I move to unlock my fingers from behind Finn's head, and he gives my nipple a hard pinch.

"Don't you fucking move, Angel. We're not done with you yet."

"That was one of the hottest things I've ever seen," Ronan says as he climbs onto the side of the bed.

Mac gives me a quick kiss before turning his head toward his brother. "See what you've been missing out on, Brother? Watching her unravel is fucking unreal. Too bad you spent so much time sulking around like a jackass."

"Don't you fucking start."

I smile as I listen to them bicker once again. Finn groans in my ear, quiet enough for only me to hear, "I swear the two of them are a couple of fucking teenagers sometimes." I let out a soft giggle and feel him smile against my ear. "Hey!" Finn snaps at the two of them. Mac looks up at him from his spot between my legs and gives Finn a cheeky grin. "Sorry, boss."

I can practically feel Finn roll his eyes as he moves past Mac's smart comment. "Spin around for me, Angel. Keep your hands behind my neck." Mac climbs out from between my legs and lays on the opposite side of us as Ronan. I spin around and straddle Finn's hips, letting my wet pussy rub against his cock. "*Shit.*" He closes his eyes and lets his head fall back against the headboard as I feel him firmly grip my ass with both hands. After a few seconds, he tilts his head forward and dips his chin in Ronan's direction. Ronan climbs up from the bed to retrieve something from on top of my dresser by the door. The bed dips behind me a moment later as I hear the familiar pop of a bottle opening. "What do you say we show Ronan what he's been missing out on?"

"Y-yes—*Oh!*" The second the word "yes" leaves my mouth, Finn lifts me up by his grip on my ass and impales me on his cock. Once I'm fully seated, he holds me still, holding me with one hand on my hip and wrapping my curls around the other. He pulls my head back with his tight grip on my hair. "Stay still for us."

I feel a cold drip of lube land on the top of my ass before it slides down over my hole, followed by Ronan's fingers massaging the cold liquid over my opening. After rubbing his fingers back and forth a few times, I feel him slowly insert the tip of his finger inside me. I hiss at the intrusion and rock my hips backward. "What did I just say, Harper? Do. Not. Move." Finn pulls my hair hard enough I'm sure I'll feel an ache on my scalp tomorrow. However, judging by how this night is going, my whole body will be sore in the morning.

In the best way possible.

I still my hips as Ronan shoves his finger further inside of me. "You want more, Baby?" I nod against Finn's tight hold on my hair.

"Words. Harper." Mac snaps from beside us. The harsh tone of his voice makes me moan in response. *I knew it was in there somewhere.*

"Yes. More, please. *More.*" There will never be a time when I don't want more. Always, always, more.

"That's our good girl," Mac praises, and I think I could come on the spot. Ronan works another finger into my ass, stretching me.

"Holy fuck. You like that, Angel? I can feel your tight cunt choking my dick whenever he moves his fingers."

"Of course she likes it. She was fucking made for us."

The fact that they're talking about me like I'm not even here should bother me, but it doesn't.

It really fucking doesn't.

"You better get a move on, Brother." Mac sits up on his knees next to us and strokes his hand down my spine. I feel my pussy clench tighter around Finn at his touch. "One of them is about to break, and judging by the look on his face, my money's on Finn."

Finn moves his head to look around me at Ronan. "Hurry. The. Fuck. Up." I watch as a bead of sweat drops down Finn's chest, and I know he's holding on by a thread. So, just to be a pain in the ass, I clench around him again. His eyes dart to me in warning, and I smile.

Ronan laughs before leaning forward to whisper in my ear, fingers still buried deep in my ass. "Anything you want to say before we get started, Baby?"

He's giving me a chance to say the word, but I won't. I need this to happen more than I need air. Once we do this, there's no going back. *Ever.* And as terrifying as that is, I'm so fucking ready for it. "Nope." I say with a pop of the "p." "Nothing to say."

"Didn't figure there would be."

37

Mac

Hell, she was fucking made for this.

I know that sounds degrading to say a woman was made to take the three dicks at once, but it's not. *Because she was.* She was made for the three of us, and we were made for her. She handles us like the fucking queen she is.

How she hasn't had men throwing themselves at her, I will never know. None of that matters anymore, though. She's here, and she has us. No one will ever fucking touch her again.

I was worried I couldn't handle watching her with Ronan and Finn together. I know they won't be able to tuck it away just because I'm around, and I wouldn't want them to. But that's not how I am with her. I love treating her like the princess that she is and would never want to do anything to hurt her. So, when I watched Ronan and Finn punish her body or talk to her that way, it worried me just as much as it turned me on. Then I heard Finn call her a whore, and my protective instincts rose to the surface. I was ready to run across the room and punch my best friend in the fucking face. But all it took was one look. One look from Harper and I knew that it was what she wanted. She loved it. And knowing that it's what she wanted was enough to get me on board. Just because I can't give that to her doesn't mean she shouldn't have it. What she and I have right now is more than enough. Maybe one day I can give that to her but not now. Not when I can barely control my demons on my own.

I watch with bated breath as my brother pulls his fingers out of her and spreads lube along his dick. Harper's whole body tightens in anticipation, and Finn lets out a low groan. "You need to relax, Angel." His grip on her hip tightens. I know what he must be feeling. Her tight pussy is choking the life out of him, and they haven't even started moving yet. Ronan lines up at her back entrance. He pushes in ever so slightly and stops, a pinched expression across his face as he takes in a deep breath through his nose. I stroke my hand up and down her spine once more, trying to get her body to relax.

"Let him in, Harper. It'll only hurt for a minute, and then it'll feel so good. Remember?"

She looks up at me with hooded eyes, and I know she's remembering that night at Kings. She nods. "I remember."

Ronan slides in a little further. "Oh!" She tilts her head back and closes her eyes. I clench my fist at my side as I watch her, trying to reign in what little self-control I have left. "There you go. You're doing so well, Princess." Her eyes open, and she looks at me again as a small tear falls down her cheek. My eyes follow it as it trails down her neck and over her breast. I look back up at her shimmering green eyes, and suddenly I feel a deep ache in my chest. An intense feeling, unlike anything I've ever felt, blooms inside of me. A feeling that took root the moment I laid eyes on her. One that has been slowly growing every minute of every day. A feeling that I only hope to experience once in this life. *With her.*

A person might think that it's fucked up to fall for someone entirely while his brother and best friend are deep inside of her, but I don't fucking care. She has never looked more beautiful. Right now, at this moment, she has become ours *entirely.*

Mo grá... *my love.*

I hold it in, though. I can't tell her now. While it's true that I will always look back on this night as the night I fell in love with Harper Hayes, I refuse to say it to her when she has two other dicks inside of her. I'm fucked up, but I'm not that fucked up. But I know what I *can* do. I wanted to wait, I wanted to have my turn to be buried inside of her pussy, but I can't wait another minute. I need to be inside of her in any way I can.

Fuck it.

Ronan must finally be all the way inside. I can see her trembling beneath him. "You were fucking made for this, Baby."

"My thoughts exactly, Brother."

"You guys need to move. Please. *Please move.*" She's begging now, and it's fucking music to my ears.

Finn and Ronan begin working in and out of her in perfect rhythm. I watch as her entire body relaxes in their hold, letting the two of them take complete control of her pleasure. I shuffle closer to her on my knees, fisting my dick in my hand. I'm not sure I've ever been this hard in my life. Finn looks at me and must read my mind. He pulls Harper's hair so her face turns toward my dick. "I said we'd fill all of those pretty holes, Angel. You still have one left."

Harper's eyes watch as I work my cock, squeezing out a bead of precum, ready for her to lick. A loud smack fills the room, followed by a whimper from Harper. Ronan's hand gently massages the spot on her ass he just slapped before raining down another. "Suck his dick, Baby. Now."

Harper sticks out her tongue and slowly, *so fucking slowly,* licks the bead of cum off. *"Mo grá..."* I moan. Her eyes dart up to my face. She doesn't know what that means, but she will soon.

Another slap rings out. I give Ronan a stern glare, worried he's hurting her, but he just smiles at me as she whimpers. Finn warns, "Don't make us fucking tell you again, Angel. Be a good little slut and suck. Mac's. Dick."

Following his lead, I push the head of my cock against her lips. She opens her mouth and willingly takes me to the back of her throat. The second I'm seated all the way inside her mouth Finn and Ronan resume thrusting in and out of her. It's the prettiest fucking site I've ever seen. Me down her throat, Ronan filling her ass, and Finn fucking her sweet pussy.

Ronan adjusts his stance behind her, changing their angle slightly. Harper moans around my cock, and I know they've found it. Finn releases her hip and brings the hand up to her throat as she continues to move up and down on my cock. He squeezes her throat tighter, and she lets out another low moan. The vibrations cause my balls to tighten, and the last ounce of willpower I was holding onto goes out the window. I grab the sides of her face in my hands. "If it's too much, just unlatch your hands from behind Finn and tap my thigh." I shoot Finn a warning look, silently telling him not to punish her if she does so. He dips his chin in agreement. She nods around my cock, and I let it all go. I fuck her mouth with purpose. I feel the head brush up against the back of her throat and still my thrusts, holding there as she swallows around me. "Fuck yes, Princess. Choke on my dick."

"You take our dicks like you were born to, Baby."

"Our good fucking girl." Finn snarls.

Ronan reaches around her with one hand and begins rubbing fast circles against her clit. Harper mewls against me, but I don't stop. I want to feel her come with my dick buried inside her mouth.

"That's it, Baby. Come for us."

Harper's body tightens, and Finn slides his out of her pussy as Ronan rapidly rubs her clit. A rush of fluid sprays out of her and soaks Finn and the sheets beneath him. Harper screams around my dick as she comes.

Holy fucking hell.

"Fuck, Baby. Did you—did you just squirt?"

"Yeah, she fucking did," Finn answers proudly. "Give us one more, Harper. Milk our fucking dicks. I want you to take every ounce of our cum."

She pops her mouth off of me, tears running down her face, completely spent. "I can't. I can't. I can't."

I wipe away a few tears with the pads of my thumbs. "Yes, you can, Princess. One more."

She nods up at me before wrapping her pink lips around my cock. She hollows out her cheeks and swallows around me before I start fucking her mouth again. Ronan slowly pulls out of her ass, leaving just the head in, before slamming inside her with everything he has. He pounds into her in fast, hard strokes, rocking her up and down Finn's dick. Harper starts moaning louder around my cock, and it does me in. I can't hold off anymore. "Fuck! Harper, I'm going to come." When she doesn't let up, I thrust into her mouth, one, two, three more times, and spill my cum down her throat. She swallows every last drop.

"Harper," Ronan groans from behind her. She pulls her mouth off of me, and her screams fill the room. "Yes! Yes! Yes! Don't stop. Keep going."

I reach between them to swat Ronan's hand away and start playing with her clit, knowing it will give her what she needs. Ronan follows me, stilling inside of her as he comes. *"Baby..."*

I don't stop rubbing her as Ronan pulls out of her ass, but I do watch as his cum leaks out of her hole down toward her pussy where Finn is still thrusting in and out of her at a rapid pace. "You look so fucking hot with my brother's cum leaking out of you, Baby."

"I want you fucking full of us." I can hear it in his voice. Finn's right there. I pinch her clit between my fingers.

"Holy fuck!" she screams as she throws her head back, arms still wrapped around Finn's neck, her hair firmly wrapped around his fist. "I-I-I..." She can't finish her sentence as her orgasm takes over her body. I pull my hand out from between them.

"Fuck, yes!" Finn follows, spilling inside of her. "That's right, Harper. Take my cum like a good fucking whore." Harper buries her face into his neck, crying out as her body shakes violently on top of him. Her orgasm seems to go on and on, wreaking havoc on my Princess. It's fucking beautiful.

When she finally stops shaking, she relaxes in Finn's arms.

Her arms have slid down and are resting against his chest, his hand raking through her curls instead of fisting it as he peppers kisses on top of her head. A stark contrast to how he was just seconds ago, but I know that's all because of her. I lay on the bed next to them and just stare. I stare at how beautiful she is; it's practically sinful. I stare at the content and at peace look on my best friend's face. I stare at my brother staring at her from the other side of the bed. It's just perfect—all of it.

Then Ronan's smart-ass voice fills the room. "You guys are telling me this is what I've been missing out on?"

"You were too busy being an asshole," Harper sassily bites back. But I can see the smile take over her face as she turns to face him. He loves her attitude. Ronan leans forward and kisses her deeply as she lies in Finn's arms.

"Never again, Baby. Never again."

"Well, maybe sometimes. You're hot when you're angry."

"Lucky for you, Princess, that's how he is ninety percent of the time."

Ronan puts his hand to his chest and gives me a deeply offended look, but he knows I'm only kidding. It's more like seventy percent. I watch as he gives Harper a wink before climbing off the bed. "I'll go get us some water."

"Put some shorts on!" I yell after him, "I don't need to stare at your ass!"

"Not a fucking chance, Brother!" he yells back as he makes his way down the hall. Harper climbs off the bed and makes her way into the bathroom.

"You want me to draw you a bath, Angel?" Finn asks, already back to making sure she's okay and has everything she needs. Not that he ever really stopped, I realize.

She spins around to look at him, a dazzling smile covering

her face. "No, Love. I'm okay. I'm just going to shower quick and crawl into bed. I'm exhausted now."

"Alright, Angel. Mac and I will change the sheets." I watch a different shade of pink spreads across her chest and cheeks but choose not to comment on it. There's nothing to be embarrassed about. If I could watch her squirt every day for the rest of my life, I'd be a happy fucking man.

"Will you guys… will you stay here with me?" Finn and I look at one another in confusion, then back at her. "I mean, you don't have to if you don't want to. I'm sure you'd rather sleep in your own rooms. Don't worry about it." She waves her hands in our direction, trying to dismiss what she just said. I'll have none of that.

"Mo grá…" I say sternly. "Of course, we're staying in here. We wouldn't want to be anywhere else."

Her green eyes brighten. "Oh! Okay, well, I'm just gonna go…" She hikes a thumb over her shoulder before spinning around and closing herself into the bathroom.

I turn to face Finn and raise a brow. "Love?"

He rubs the back of his neck. "Yeah, I guess so." He and I get to work pulling the wet sheets from the bed. "We are so done for, aren't we?"

Laughing, I answer, "So fucking done, man."

Ronan walks back in with glasses of water, and we finish changing the sheets, ignoring that none of us have clothes on and Harper isn't even in the room. A few minutes later, she comes out of the bathroom, and we all get settled on the bed. Harper in the middle, Ronan and Finn on either side of her, and me curled up between her legs, head resting on her stomach. When I asked her if she wanted me to move, worried I was crushing her, she sweetly said, "No, Honey.

You're perfect." Fuck, if that name didn't do something to me.

One by one, the three of them doze. As their soft snores fill the room, I drift off to sleep with the sound of Harper's heart beating in my ear.

* * *

It's a little after nine the next morning when Ronan and I roll out of bed. I don't think I've gotten that good of a night's sleep in a long time. More often than not, I find myself waking up throughout the night or not being able to sleep at all. Nightmares of the blood I've spilled tend to keep me awake. Not last night. Last night, curled up against Harper, I didn't wake up once. For a moment, I thought sharing a bed with Ronan and Finn would be weird, but all of it just felt… right. Like we were all right where we were supposed to be. However, if we are going to make that a habit, we're definitely going to have to get a bigger bed.

Ronan and I decided to let Finn and Harper sleep a little longer, mainly because he and I knew we still had a few things to discuss, and we didn't want the two of them feeling like they *had* to weigh in on a decision about our parents.

When we got home yesterday, we spent most of the afternoon filling Finn in on what Ronan and I found out from Max. After brainstorming a few possible reasons why on earth our mother would be working against us, we decided to call it a day. Realizing we were just grasping at straws. We have no answers, and we're just guessing at this point. We still haven't even heard back from Ronan's contact in Ireland.

All of us are growing restless. The best solution to get the answers we needed would be to just talk to Mum directly.

She's nothing like our father. *Nothing.* She spent our whole lives caring for us and trying to shield us as best she could from the evil things he had done, but she couldn't hide everything. She had her own battles to fight. While I know he never laid a hand on her in front of us, that doesn't mean there weren't other things happening behind closed doors. I'd like to think he wasn't that kind of person. Unfortunately, I know better.

So, this morning, Ronan and I decided we would give her a call. We learned from one of her bodyguards that she should be on her way to the salon this morning and that Dad would be nowhere near her.

I open the oven and slide in the soda bread I quickly whipped up. A recipe our mother passed down to us after her mother passed it down to her. It's a simple dish but one that fills my heart and my stomach all the same. Once the bread is in the oven, I take a cup of coffee off the counter that Ronan poured. I'm immediately hit with the smell of whiskey. I look up at him from over the brim of my mug. "That kind of morning? Thought you'd for sure be in a better mood after last night."

A soft smile pulls at the corners of my brother's mouth. "We're Irish, Mac. There's never a bad time for whiskey in your coffee." He takes a long, dramatic drink. "And I'm never in a good mood." I snort into my cup.

"So… what do you think?" I ask him hesitantly.

"There's no way she's in on it, Mac… whatever *it* is." I nod my head in agreement. "I mean… this is our fucking mother. The same woman who sang to us and laid in our bed until we fell asleep. The same woman who begged our father to take Finn in when he had no one. She doesn't have an evil bone in her body. I'd be willing to bet she knows nothing about the deal between dear ole Dad and Delcan. There's no way she would willingly put an innocent woman in harm's way like that. Let alone the daughter of two people she cared for."

I agree with my brother completely, but ask, "Then why was she in contact with Max? Why was she telling him to steal our shipments?"

"I really don't know. Your guess is as good as mine. The only way we'll know for sure is if we talk to her." He takes another long sip of his coffee. Taking a deep breath, he looks at me dead in the eyes. "But I do know that she's going to be furious the second we insinuate she has anything other than good intentions."

"Ronan." I hold my hand up. "Let me talk to her. You have a hot head, and we both know you will say something to piss her off."

"I'll mind my tongue. I don't want you to worry about this. I'll talk to her."

"No, Ronan," I bite out. "This won't be on you."

"Yes, Brother, it will be. You've been through enough in this life when it comes to one parent. The last thing I will do is put this weight on your shoulders. Let me do this." I open my mouth to argue, but he stops me. "Don't even bother arguing. My mind is made up on this." Just like that, I know it's done. He's speaking not only as my brother but as the mafia leader. I know my place. "Let's give Mum a call, shall we?"

I remain on my side of the kitchen as Ronan pulls out his phone and video chats our mother, angling the phone so I'm out of the screen, but I can still see. After the third ring, her smiling face fills the screen. "Ronan! My sweet boy. To what do I owe this pleasure?"

"Morning, Mum." Ronan offers her a genuine smile. One he reserves for only a select few. "How are you today?"

"I'm good, just on my way to the salon. I've been so busy helping your father lately that I haven't had much time to myself." Ronan quickly looks at me before looking back at the phone. "What are you boys up to today? How's Harper doing? I'm sure she's going crazy stuck in that apartment with you three brutes all day. You boys better be treating that sweet girl well!"

"Oh, she's managing just fine," Ronan says smugly. I force myself not to let out a laugh.

"I know your father is trying his hardest to get to the bottom of everything with Declan so she can return to her life. The poor girl must be terrified. I can't imagine what she's going through."

There it is. At this moment, I have the answer I needed. The concern in her voice is genuine. We've all spent years learning how to read people, we're not as good as Finn, but we can still tell a lie from a mile away. And unless our mother has suddenly become a super spy who masters in deception, there isn't a hint of a lie in her words. But I know he needs to ask her outright. We need to understand why she was in contact with Max. We need to be sure.

I know Ronan is thinking the same thing I am as he lets out a heavy sigh. "Mum, I need to ask you something. You're going to be upset, but I need you to promise you'll tell me the truth. Okay?"

"Sweet boy, you're worrying me. What's going on?"

"How do you know Max?"

I see her brows pinch in confusion. "You know Max?"

"Yeah, Mum. We know Max."

"Your father has had me working with him the last few months. We've been intercepting shipments Declan Whelan has been sending over. Your father told me he's been trying to gain footing here in New York. Sneaky bastard. It wasn't enough to make us leave Ireland. Now he's trying to take this home from us too."

"Mum... those were our shipments. You've been stealing from us."

"What do you mean? I would never steal from you. Not from my own sons. I wouldn't make you appear weak like that." Ronan pauses a moment, waiting for her to put the rest of the pieces together. Sadness flashes across her face instantly. "Ronan... is that why I haven't heard from Max? Did you kill him?" Her voice is angry now, but my brother does his best to keep a level head.

"Yes. I killed him," he says matter-of-factly.

"Ronan!"

"I didn't have a choice, Mum. He and his crew were stealing from us, and I can't let that shit stand. Not from anyone."

"Why was your father having me steal from you? I don't understand. None of this makes any sense!" I watch as a tear rolls down our sweet mother's face. She's hurt that she hurt us, and I know it.

Ronan doesn't answer her. We don't have a good answer for her yet; the less she knows, the better. "I need to ask you something else, okay?" She nods into the camera. "Are you safe with him? With Dad?"

She inhales a shaky breath, and I immediately feel the bile rising in my throat. "It's complicated, Ronan. He's my husband. I'd be nowhere without him."

"Mum…" Ronan bites angrily, but I can tell he's still trying to control his temper. "Answer the damn question."

"It's never been this bad. He's always had a temper, but since he's stepped back as leader, it's gotten so much worse. It's like since he can't take out his anger on his enemies, he takes it out on me instead. I didn't want to say anything or put more pressure on you. I know you boys have your plates full, and the last thing I want to be is a burden."

That's fucking it. I can't take it anymore. I stand behind my brother as our mother lets out a pained sob. "Mum, you are not a burden. *Ever.* We will protect you with everything we have. Even against *him.* If he has ever laid a hand on you, even once, it's one time too many."

"I don't want you boys to do something you'll regret. I can handle your father."

"I will regret nothing! He is no father of mine! He has made my life a living hell, and now he's trying to tarnish everyone I love. I will not stand for it any longer." I can feel the rage boiling inside me, but I can't control it.

Ronan looks up at me, not missing that I said, "Everyone I love." I shoot him a look, now is not the time to get into it.

"Cormac…" Our mother sobs.

"No, Mum. He has gone to fucking far. He's done."

Ronan takes over, sensing I'm about to spiral. "Here's what's going to happen, Mum. You're going to go to your appointment as planned. Once you're done, you will go home and pack a few travel bags. If he is there, just tell him you decided to go on a last-minute spa trip."

"Ronan, I can't."

"Yes, you can. I will send one of my drivers to pick you up

with a set of instructions. You need to make sure you follow them to the letter. You're going to go stay with my friend, Pascal, in France until we get this all figured out. Okay?"

Pascal is a frequent VIP flier at Kings and one of our older customers. Though, his gray hairs don't stop him from having a way with the ladies. I swear that man gets more pussy in a year than the three of us have had in our lives combined. We've become close friends with him since we opened Kings, and the best part is our father has no idea who he is or that he even exists. When he's not visiting New York, he lives in Saint-Jean-de-Luz along the southern coast of France. He's the type of friend who wouldn't think twice when it comes to helping his friends. As a ruthless businessman, he's no stranger to people trying to take from him. He knows what it takes to protect what he loves.

"Ronan! I can't stay with some man I've never met in another country! This is insane!"

"No. What's insane is that man has been putting his hands on you for years. What's insane is that he's been intentionally trying to sabotage his own children. What's insane is he's planning on using the woman we love"—he outstretches his hand and points down the hall—"as a living breathing bargaining chip! FOR WHAT?! For some false sense of fucking power. After everything he's done. To you, to me, to him…" His finger now points at me. "He has to be stopped, Mum. I will stop him. *We* will stop him."

"I'm so so sorry, Ronan."

"Do not apologize for him. Just promise me you'll do as I say, and don't say a word to him besides what I've told you to."

She's hysterically sobbing now. I wish I could reach through the phone and hold her while she sits in the back of that car and falls apart. What I can do is keep her safe. I can protect her from him now.

"Mum…" I whisper. Her sad eyes meet mine. "Promise?"

"I–I promise." She sniffles as she pulls a handkerchief out of her Berkin.

"It will all be okay," he reassures her. "I have to call Pascal and tell him you're coming. He will take good care of you and keep you safe. I love you, Mum."

"I love you, sweet boy." Ronan hands the phone to me and grabs mine off the counter before quickly heading to his office to call Pascal. Knowing he'll be there to keep her safe, hidden away from our father's reach, feels like a small weight lifted from my shoulders, but in its place is the knowledge that our mother has been suffering all these years, and we did nothing to help her.

"I'm so sorry we didn't protect you. We should have known." I shake my head, willing tears not to fall, but it's a useless battle. She watches as they begin to drop down my cheeks. Damn me and my fucking feelings.

"Hush now. This is not your fault. It's not your brother's, and it's not Finn's. You were just boys."

"We're not boys anymore. We're men. Men that should have known better. Men that should have been keeping you safe."

"He only let you see what he wanted to, sweetie, and I was too afraid to say or do anything about it. This is not on you. Do not punish yourself for this too."

Do not punish yourself for this, too.

I've never voiced my struggles to her, but like any amazing mother, she just knows. She knows of the demons I fight because of the man he turned me into. I don't fight it anymore as I let an unexpected sob tear through me. I allow myself to feel *everything*. Mum sits on the other end of the phone, not moving from her car as she watches me fall apart. I don't know how much time has gone by. Seconds. Minutes. Hours. But once I feel like I can't cry anymore, I will myself to look back at the screen. "You, my son, are more than what he has made you to be. You are sweet, caring, and kind. You are the kind of man who feels with the intensity of a thousand suns, and it makes you who you are. And who you are is a person I am so incredibly proud of. Don't let your father or anyone else make you feel like who you are isn't enough. And don't *you* allow yourself to feel shame for protecting what's yours. Use what he's taught you to keep the ones you love safe. Be a force to be reckoned with. Do you understand me?"

This woman.

Here we are, turning her world upside down after everything she's already been through, and she's sitting here comforting me. Not unlike the woman down the hall. How did we get lucky enough to have not one but two of them in our lives? "I love you," is all I can say to her.

She gives me a soft smile that doesn't quite reach her ears. "I love you too, Sweetheart." Her smile grows a little wider. "I'm glad to see you boys have found a woman to love."

I don't admit it to her but I don't deny it either. "You don't think it's strange? All of us and her?"

"It's not unheard of in our world. I know several women who love more than one man. But even if I didn't, does she make you all happy, Sweetheart?"

"Yeah, Mum. She does."

"Then that's all that matters. Keep them all safe for me,

alright?"

All of them.

"I will, Mum."

"You boys will keep me updated every step of the way." It's not a question but a demand.

"Yes, ma'am."

"That's my boy."

She and I say our goodbyes, and I hang up the phone. I sit at the counter with my head in my hands until Ronan returns to the kitchen. I feel his hand grip my shoulder. "You okay?"

"Yeah, man. I'm alright. I'll be better when we figure out what the fuck we're gonna do."

"After I got off the phone with Pascal, who's ecstatic to have the company of a beautiful woman, by the way." He rolls his eyes in annoyance, and I laugh. "I sent out a message to my contact saying we need to talk to him asap. We should hear from him by the end of the day."

"Alright, good."

"I can't fucking believe this shit," Ronan huffs in exasperation.

"I can. Liam McDermott is a piece of human garbage, and I can't wait to rid the world of him."

"Brother. I—"

I abruptly stand from my chair. "No, Ronan. After everything he's put me through, after everything he's done, I will not feel a single ounce of remorse when I kill him. And *I will be* the one to kill him. Give me this, please. *Please?*" His eyes, ones that mirror my own, scan my face, looking for any hint of hesitation as tears fill my eyes yet again. He won't find any, only rage and conviction.

"Okay, Mac. You have my word."

I hear the soft sound of footsteps coming down the hall and quickly wipe my face. Ronan steps back and gives me a slight nod, assuring me I look okay. I spin to face Harper and Finn as they walk into the kitchen. Her beautiful smile instantly brightening the room. I swear it's like she's fucking magic. I don't know how she does it, but just seeing her centers me.

Fuck, I love her.

In a few long strides, I'm in front of her, wrapping my arms around her body and burying my face in her neck. I feel her smile against the side of my face as she strokes the back of my head. "Well, good morning to you too."

Standing up straight, I smile down at her, a real and genuine smile. "Good morning, Princess." I drop my head and give her a quick kiss.

"What is that heavenly smell?"

"I made us some breakfast. Ever had soda bread?"

She shakes her head. "No, but if it tastes as good as it smells, I can't wait."

"It should just be a few more minutes. Come on. Ronan will pour you a cup of coffee."

"I'm assuming there's a special ingredient in this coffee?" she asks as she licks her lip, probably tasting the whiskey from my own.

"You'd be correct."

"Perfect." She stands on her tiptoes and presses her lips once more against mine. This time I hold her still, kissing her harder, cherishing the feeling of having her in my arms. She's safe here.

Harper breaks the kiss first, and I see the flush in her cheeks. It takes everything in me not to drag her back down the hallway, but I know she needs to eat. "Go on." I nod in

Ronan's direction. Giving me a soft smile, she walks toward my brother, and I hear her giggle as he picks her up and sets her on the counter.

"You alright, man?" Finn asks from his spot behind where Harper just was.

"Better now." I mean that too. It's not like the mere sight of her solved any of our problems, but she made them feel a little less heavy. Like, with her around, we can do anything.

"What happened?"

"We called Mum."

Finn raises his brow. "And?"

"We were right. She had no idea what our father was up to. He's been using her this whole time." I hesitate to tell Finn the truth. I know he's spent much of his life looking up to our father, the hero who took a boy in when he had nothing. I know this has been difficult for him.

"Just tell me, Mac."

"He's been hurting her, Finn. I'm not sure how long or exactly what it entailed, we didn't ask her to go into detail. But she said it's been worse ever since he retired. She's afraid of him, and that's reason enough."

"Fucking hell."

"I'm sorry, man. I know this is hard on you. You've already lost both your parents, and now—"

"Fuck that. Your mother is a damn saint; I would protect her with my life. Even against him. What he's done to you, what he plans on doing to Harper… he's not the man I thought he was. He's not the man I looked up to. I'm sorry I didn't see it sooner. I'm with you guys. All the way. No matter what."

I clap him on the shoulder. There's nothing else that needs to be said. "Come on. I'll have Ronan pour some coffee in your whiskey."

After we fill Harper in on the updates about our mother and I pull the soda bread out of the oven, the four of us sit in the kitchen, Harper still perched cross-legged on the island where Ronan sat her, laughing and smiling as we eat breakfast. For a while, everything feels normal. Like the world isn't falling apart around us. I often catch myself, or Ronan and Finn, just staring at her. Admiring everything that she is. As conversation floats through the apartment, I wonder if this is when my life truly changes. If this is the point in my life where I will think, there was either before Harper or after Harper. The thought only intensifies my feelings for her.

Our bubble bursts in an instant as the sound of Ronan's phone ringing fills the apartment, an unknown number on the screen. "It's Patrick."

38

Ronan

"It's Patrick."

The three of them sit up straight, ready to hear what he has to say. Usually, I would take this kind of call in the seclusion of my office, prepared to deal with whatever fallout lies ahead on my own. But not today. Today I'll take this call in front of my family. The four of us are prepared to take on the world together.

I hit accept, quickly put it on speaker, and set the phone on the counter. I feel Harper's hand rub across my shoulder blades from her spot on the counter, silently comforting and calming me as best she can.

"Patrick." I greet him.

"Ronan. Sorry it took me a while to get in contact with you. I had to be sure nothing would get back to Declan. But from the sounds of your last message, it sounded urgent, so I'll cut right to the chase." The four of us share quick glances at one another, waiting for him to confirm what we already know.

"Your father has made a deal with Delcan."

"Yes, we already know this."

"No. I don't think you do."

"What's that supposed to mean?" I bite out. Anxious for him to get to the fucking point.

"In exchange for handing over the woman—"

"Harper," I correct him, growing rapidly more annoyed.

"Yes, Harper. In exchange for handing over Harper, Whelan has agreed to not only back off your syndicate in New York and pay your father the reward but also help your father regain control of your territory and push you lads out."

"What?"

"If I had to guess, the only reason Declan would have agreed to such a deal is because he recognizes the power the three of you have. He was never afraid of your father, and until you took control, your father was easy enough to push around. If I were a betting man, I'd wager that Declan will sit back while Liam takes care of you three, only to take care of Liam himself once he rises to power. It's a win-win for Liam either way. You boys will be gone, he will be able to get rid of Declan, and he will look like the all-powerful leader that took over the McDermott empire, all the while eliminating any other possible heir to his throne. It's not a bad plan, honestly, except for one thing."

"And what's that?" Mac asks.

"Well hello, Cormac. I'm assuming Finn is there as well?"

"Get on with it, Patrick."

"We want Declan gone."

"Why?" Harper asks before widening her eyes and covering her mouth with both hands. I reach out and squeeze her thigh, giving her a reassuring smile, letting her know that it's okay she spoke.

A soft chuckle comes from the line, but he picks the smart road and chooses not to acknowledge her. I'd hate to kill someone who's just trying to help us. "Because this bullshit has gone on long enough. He has spent years exacting his version of revenge on the McDermott syndicate. Ever since he murdered Freya and Aidan after your mother gave them a safe haven from him—" a pained expression takes over Harper's face before she shoves it down—"he has made it his life mission to fuck with you all in every way possible. Not only that but he's gone off the deep end since he found out about Harper. He has chosen to neglect all of his other duties and has wasted countless men and resources to fulfill his own fucking vendetta. Our organization has grown weak; everyone sees it except him and his few remaining disciples."

"How do we know we can trust you?" I ask the question everyone else is thinking.

"Because, Brother, you and I are the same. We want what's best for families and our organizations, and right now, he's destroying mine."

"Who's to say that you won't just come after us as soon as our father and Liam are out of the picture?"

"I have no ulterior motive here besides eliminating Declan. I have been basically running the syndicate for the last year. All that crazy bastard does is hide away in his office with his cronies and make plans against you and yours. He has hardly a single clue what's going on besides that. I'm doing the best I can, but without him out of the picture, our rivals in Ireland will continue to step all over me. They know I only hold so much authority. Furthermore, I don't give a flying fuck what you do about your father, nor do I care about Harper.

Harper…"

"Yes…" I grind my molars over the fact that he's speaking directly to her now but hold myself back and let her speak for herself. My baby is stronger than we think.

"Do you want anything to do with the Whelan syndicate? Do you want to come to Ireland and take over? If you do, tell me right now, and I will do everything I can to ensure you are successful. I will step back and let the rightful heir take over."

"No," She answers without hesitation. "I don't want any of it. I want to stay here, in New York. I want to stay with them."

I can't see him, but I can practically feel his entire body relax over the phone. In that moment, I believe him, and looking at Mac and Finn, I can see that they do too. No evil man would sound so relieved by the answer Harper just gave him. He was willing to give it all up if that's what she wanted. "So what do we do now?" I ask him. "There's no way we can get to him in Ireland. Our family hasn't been allowed to step foot in the damn country since he murdered the Donovans. He needs to come here."

"I actually have a plan for that."

The four of us listen to Patrick explain how he will get Declan and his men to come to New York, but first, we need to take out our father. With him out of the picture, Patrick will convince Declan that he needs to be the one to come to New York and deal with Harper. Patrick will book all the necessary travel arrangements and give us detailed instructions about when and where Declan will be. Once we take out Declan's men, we will end him. Slowly and painfully. That bastard doesn't deserve a quick death, not after all of the pain he has caused my family.

"Are you sure you all can handle Liam? He is your father. I know what that kind of vengeance can do to a man." The worry in his voice leads me to believe he knows from personal experience. Maybe if circumstances were different, I would take the time to ask him, but not right now. Right now I need to focus on the three people sitting in this room.

I open my mouth to answer, but Mac beats me to it. "We've already discussed it. Don't worry. We'll get it done." I watch as Harper stares at my brother, worry filling her eyes.

Right there with you, Baby.

I know I promised Mac I'd let him be the one to do it, and I'll stick to my word. But I'd be lying if I said I wasn't terrified. Not over what it will be like to watch my father die… nah, I could give two fucks about that. After everything he's done, I'd put a bullet in his brain without thinking twice. Blood or not. He's no longer my family. Not sure he ever really was. He was just a man in charge. What I am terrified about is the effect it'll have on Mac. I've spent years trying to get him to realize that his monsters are part of him. Just because he resents the killer inside of him doesn't mean he doesn't need it. The man wears his emotions on his sleeve. It's what we love about him. However, whether he will admit it or not, his bloodlust is one of those emotions. When he lets that monster take over and puts an end to the man we call father, the man that turned him into what Mac hates most about himself, what will happen? Will Mac finally be at peace, or will he need to find a new outlet for all the rage he's afraid to let out?

"Alright, then, boys. I'll let you know when I have a plan in motion."

"Before you go," authority coats my voice now. Letting

Patrick know that just because we asked for his help doesn't mean I'm someone he should fuck with. "If I even hear a whiff of you going back on your word, I'll fly to that godforsaken country and end you myself, banishment be damned. I have eyes and ears everywhere. Are we clear?"

The asshole has the balls to snicker on the other end of the line, but the few seconds of silence that follows proves he knows how serious I am. "Right back at ya, boyo." He hangs up, and the line goes dead.

The four of us sit silently for a few minutes, each individually trying to take in everything Patrick just told us. Finally, I look at Harper. "What do you think?"

She looks genuinely stunned that I'm even asking her. *Shit, she's fucking cute.* Pointing to her chest she asks, "Me?"

"Yes, you." I smile.

"Why are you asking me?"

"Because, Baby. I'm sure I can speak for all of us when I say we want to know your opinion. This is just as much about you as it is about us."

Mac and Finn nod their heads in agreement from their chairs beside me. She looks between the three of us, rapidly blinking those big green eyes before she hesitantly speaks. "I believe him. I think he's telling us the truth."

"I agree. He wasn't lying," Finn says from the other end of the counter. I don't know how he does it, but the guy can smell a lie a mile away. He's a walking, talking lie detector. So, if he and Harper say Patrick isn't lying, then he's not lying.

Once we clean up breakfast, well once Finn cleans up breakfast, the four of us draw up a plan. Deciding it's in everyone's best interest to act on taking out Laim sooner rather than later. Truthfully, I think it's because we're all afraid, well, everyone except Mac, that if we stew on it any longer, we'll start to second-guess our decisions. That's the way this life is, though, I suppose. There's no time to second-guess anything. If you take too long to come to a decision, it could very well cost you your life.

Protect the ones you love at all costs and show no remorse.

Mum called us a few times throughout the day. The more I thought about I,t I didn't want to risk just hearing from her via text message. Anyone could have taken her phone and pretended to be her. She let us know when she was on her way back to the house, when she was leaving for the airport, and when she was about to take off. I'll rest easier when I know she's landed and is safely hidden away at Pascal's.

Our father... you know what, *no, fuck that.* Liam, being the self-righteous prick that he is, made finding him tonight entirely too easy. The dickhead gives Mum access to his calendar because he's too old and stubborn to figure out how to use it on his own. Before she boarded the plane, I was sure to ask her for the login information. Come to find out, he's set to have a meeting down at the docks tonight, likely trying to figure out what happened with Max and his goons.

He'll never find them. They're currently fish food at the bottom of the Hudson.

The city is dark now, just after eleven. Mac, Finn, and I are getting ready to leave as we want to arrive before his meeting at twelve. We called the dock workers two hours ago and strongly suggested that they not be anywhere near there for the next twenty-four hours. They've already looked the other way toward Liam's antics and are lucky I haven't snapped their necks as punishment. When I told them as much, they were more than happy to oblige my request for the evening.

The three of us made sure to dress in our usual attire. That way, when Liam saw us, he might just think we were there by happy coincidence and not bolt.

We're waiting in Harper's room for her to come out of the bathroom as she gets ready for bed, so we can say our goodbyes before we head out. I look up from my spot on the end of the bed when I hear her open the bathroom door, only to find her wearing jeans, a black shirt, converse shoes, and a flannel tied around her waist. Her messy curls are piled in a bun on top of her head.

I bolt up from the bed. "No. No fucking way. Absolutely not. You're staying here."

She levels me with her most menacing glare, or at least she attempts to. Hands on her hips, she says, "Now just hold on a minute—"

"No, Harper. You are not going. End of discussion."

"Excuse me, but you are not the end all be all."

"Right now, yes, I fucking am!"

Finn steps up behind me. "Ronan…"

I don't even let him get another word out. My rage and protective instincts are soaring to an all-time high. "SHE. ISN'T. GOING!"

Absolute fury takes over Harper's face, and I know I'm about to get chewed a new asshole, but I don't care. I will not bend on this. It isn't safe out there. She's safe here. I *need* her to be safe.

I feel Mac on the opposite side of me now, hand firmly placed on my shoulder. I've never been more thankful for the two men next to me. I would never lay a hand on Harper in any way that wasn't welcome. I'd never harm a hair on her gorgeous head. They know that, and she knows that. But they, like me, would do whatever it takes to protect her, even from me.

"Brother," Mac warns.

I nod and take a deep breath, trying to calm my temper before speaking to her again. Hanging my head, fists clenched at my side I mutter low enough so only they can hear. "I know. I know."

I pick up my head only to find Harper's face right in front of mine. Gone is any trace of anger and in its place, understanding, and compassion. She cups my face in her hands, gently stroking my cheeks with each thumb. I take another shaky breath and let myself get lost in her for a moment, taking in every freckle, every stray curl, her long dark eyelashes, her perfect green eyes as they stare up at me, silently pleading me to listen to what she has to say. I reach up with both hands and grip her wrists, stroking them with my thumbs in the same rhythm she is my cheeks.

"Ronan, Baby, listen to me." *Baby. Fuck, that kills me.* I feel Mac's hand drop from my shoulder. "You all keep trying to pull me out of the darkness. You're trying to keep me away from it. I know it's because you're trying to keep me safe, but I don't want it. I don't want to live in the light because the darkness is where you are. It's where your life is, where all your dreams and desires lie. It's where I feel safe—not locked up in some penthouse. Safe is when I'm with you. All of you. Don't keep me out of the dark. This is my life, too, and it's where I belong. Let me in. Let me be your light. Keep me safe. *Give me everything.*"

I shake my head, trying to will away the sting behind my eyes. I don't fucking cry. *Ever.* Harper stands on her tiptoes, and I drop my head so my forehead rests against hers. "Let me in, Baby."

Fuck. She has me, and she fucking knows it. I could never say no to that. I tightly squeeze her wrists. "I just want you to be safe. If anything happened to you… Fuck, Harper. I don't think I could bear it."

"I'll be okay. You'll keep me safe. Finn will keep me safe. Mac will keep me safe."

"We can't ask her to stay behind, Brother. If she says she can handle it, we have to trust her."

"We'll have eyes on her the entire time, man," Finn voices, agreeing with Mac.

"Promise me you will stay in the car. Do not get out under any circumstances. I don't want him to know you're there. Promise me that, and you can come."

"I promise, Ronan."

I draw in a deep breath. No matter how much I want to, we don't have time to argue about this anymore. "Alright." I kiss her forehead lightly. "Let's go."

39

Ronan

Forty-five minutes later, the guys and I are standing against a building near the dock, tucked away from the flickering lamp post a few feet away. We wanted to make sure that Liam and his guards got out and away from the vehicle before we made ourselves known. Fog rolls off the river as the sound of chain link fences rattle in the wind. The entire scene is pretty fucking apt if you ask me. I parked my black Lexus LX down the way, Harper still inside as promised, and Finn's Audi Q2 is parked behind it. They're just far enough out of sight that if you weren't looking, you wouldn't even know they were there, but close enough that we can all get to Harper in under a minute if necessary.

"Are you both sure about this?" Finn asks, staring blankly into the Hudson as he leans against the brick building next to Mac.

Mac and I nod in agreement. "Yeah, we're sure. You don't have to stay if you don't want to, man. We'd understand if—"

Finn cuts him off. "Don't even start. I'm with you guys all the way."

No one else says anything until we hear tires crunching against the gravel. "Here we fucking go." Mac stands up straight next to me.

"Nobody moves until they get out of the car and walk toward the building." We watch Liam's guards exit the black Cadillac first, taking a quick look around them, scanning for any threats. Once they feel like they've done their due diligence, they nod at one another and move to open the back door. *Idiots.*

Like the mafia don he thinks he still is, Liam steps out of the SUV in a black suit, complete with a black trench, coat smoking a fucking cigar. He looks like he belongs in the show *Peaky Blinders* for Christ's sake. "What a fucking asshole," Mac scoffs, more than likely thinking the same thing as me.

"Alright." I shove off the wall and start moving out of the shadows as the three men make their way in our direction, quickly glancing at my Lexus to make sure no one is near Harper. Mac and Finn follow close behind.

As the guards see us step into the light, they immediately step in front of Liam and draw their weapons. I play it cool… for now. "Whoa, boys. It's just us." The second they see my face, they drop their guns, giving me an apologetic look. Not that it matters. They'll be dead in a few minutes anyway.

"What are you three doing down here?" Liam asks, already on edge.

"Hey, Pop. No 'Hi, how are ya?'"

"Cut the shit, Ronan. What's going on?"

"I actually had to talk to you about a few things and didn't want to do it over the phone. Mum said you had a meeting to attend tonight, so I figured this is where you'd be."

I watch as he clenches his jaw, assumingly pissed that Mum would give us that information. "Where's Harper? Shouldn't you be watching her like I fucking asked you to?"

I clench my fists, willing myself not to snap his neck right here and now for speaking her name. I can practically feel the same rage rolling off Finn and Mac behind me. I just hope they can keep their cool. "She's back at the apartment. We have two guards watching her at all times. Don't worry about it."

"Alright then."

"Walk with me?" I nod toward one of the docks. Liam steps to the side, gesturing his arm out, waiting for me to lead the way. I walk toward him, stepping around his guards. After a few moments, Mac and Finn follow behind, far enough away, so I can't hear what's happening behind me. Neither can Liam. His guards take that as their queue to step back, just like I hoped they would, falling behind Mac and Finn as we all begin walking out onto the long dock.

"What did you need to talk to me about that was so urgent? I only have a few minutes before my meeting."

There is no more fucking meeting but whatever. "I think I figured out who has been stealing our shipments, but I wanted to run it past you first."

His step falters. If you didn't know him like I do, you wouldn't catch it, but I do, and I did. "Oh yeah?"

"Yeah. I got the word out about a fake shipment that was supposed to arrive the other morning. Had some men camp out here and wait for whoever showed up. Got our hands on three of them. Mac and I interrogated them in the warehouse just over there, actually."

If he's getting nervous, he doesn't let on. He probably thinks I'm too fucking naive to assume he had anything to do with it. Jokes on you, asshole. "You get anything good out of them?"

Real damn good.

"Yeah, one of their names was Max. Never figured out who the other two were. Killed 'em before they had a chance to talk." I watch as he swallows hard at the mention of Max's name. *There it is.* "Max said he was just following his boss's orders. Knew nothing about who exactly he was stealing from or why."

Liam stops midstride, taking a long puff of his cigar as he looks into the distance. Not once does he bother to look over his shoulder to check on his men. *Big mistake.* "He tell you who his boss is?"

"Nope. Said he never even met them. Only talked to them over the phone. You know what I find strange though?"

"Hmmm?" Another puff of smoke permeates the air around me as I smile to myself. "Said the person he talked to was a woman." The cigar stills halfway to his mouth. I slowly reach for the gun in my waistband. "That she sounded just like me but with a thicker accent. Only one person that fits that description comes to mind."

He whirls around in search of his men only to find their lifeless bodies back at the end of the dock and Mac and Finn about five feet behind us. My brother grins, raises his hand, and wiggles his fingers, waving at our pathetic excuse for a father. "Too slow, Pop."

Liam quickly drops the cigar and moves to reach inside his jacket, but I'm faster. I press my gun to his temple and chamber a round. "What the fuck do you think you're doing, boy?" He's practically foaming at the mouth already, and we've only just begun.

"What am I doing? The question is, what have you been doing?" Slowly, he spins his head around to face me head-on. I don't remove my weapon; instead, I slide the barrel from his temple to the middle of his forehead.

"I am your father!"

"You are no father of ours!" Mac shouts as he makes his way toward us, pulling up the sleeves of his black Henley to his elbows, stopping once he's behind Liam. Finn follows behind him, coming to stand next to the man he once idolized. The three of us are caging him in now, there's no way out. Judging by the look in his eyes, he knows it.

"You wouldn't do this to me. Your mother would never forgive you."

I let out a dark laugh. "You see. That's where you're wrong. Mum is currently on a plane to the other side of the world." His mouth drops open in shock. "We've already spoken to her. She told us all about the work she's been doing for you, making her think she was stealing shipments from Declan Whelan and not her own children. But that's not all she told us."

"She told us *everything*," Mac says, leaning down to whisper in Liam's ear. I watch in enjoyment as his soulless eyes widen. "You put your hands on her. *On our mother.*"

"You can't take her away from me. She's mine."

"Wrong again. She's not yours. Not anymore. She's safe from you, and you'll never see her again."

"You don't know what you're talking about."

"No? Then why don't you explain it to us. I want to know why you ever gave up control to me, and us, if you weren't ready."

Nothing he says will matter anyway. He's as good as dead. But I want to hear the asshole admit everything. We deserve answers.

"I never wanted to step back. But it was clear I was losing respect. Everyone thought I was some old-timer who didn't know what he was talking about. Someone who couldn't keep up. Do you know what that's like?" His voice raises at the last sentence, but I don't let it get to me. Neither does Mac or Finn. We're not scared of him anymore. "What it's like to be feared and respected by everyone you meet to suddenly be treated like some sort of fucking imbecile? They thought you three could do better, so I decided to prove them all wrong. You couldn't make that easy for me though, could you?"

"Us succeeding wasn't enough for you? We were exactly what you turned us into. We did everything you asked of us. We were good sons." I can hear the sadness in my brother's voice, and it's like a knife to my fucking chest.

"Please," Liam scoffs. "The three of you are a fucking embarrassment. You're too soft, too weak. You would have run this syndicate into the ground. Everything I've worked for, everything I've handed you on a silver fucking platter, would have gone down the drain! For Christ's sake, I've been stealing from you for months, and you had no fucking idea. You're a goddamn disgrace!"

"A disgrace?!" My voice now matches his. "We are who we are because of you! Even after everything you did to us, to him!" I point over his shoulder at my brother, who is practically shaking with rage.

"The only thing I did to the two of you was try to turn you into men I could be proud of. The only reason I agreed to give Emma children was to carry on the McDermott name.

I have never been so fucking disappointed. What a waste of my damn time. You and you're fucking mother." All the masks he's been carefully donning all these years are now crumbling at his feet. In their place is the man he really is—a manipulative and cruel monster.

A heartless and empty laugh leaves my mouth as I press the barrel harder against his head. "You think you're a big man now, do ya, son? Finally grow a set of balls now that you're getting some good pussy? Must be a real slut if she's with all three of you."

For the first time since this exchange began, Finn speaks up. "How did you know?"

"What do you mean how did I know? I told Ronan about my deal with Declan. It was written all over his pathetic face. After I left, I had my driver sit outside the building until you three returned from Kings. I saw her hanging all over the two of you, looking like the whore she is. Maybe I should have just kept Harper for myself."

I draw my hand back and slam the gun across his face, splitting his nose wide open. "Don't you say her fucking name."

He licks blood off his lower lip as it spills out of his nose, a satisfied look on his face knowing he got a rise out of me. I press the barrel of my gun against his forehead again, hard enough that it pushes him against Mac, who wraps his arms around his neck in a chokehold. He doesn't apply enough pressure to knock him out but squeezes just hard enough to cut off some of his air supply. Liam reaches up to pull at Mac's forearms, but it's no use. Mac's strength is next level. He should know. He built the killer behind him.

"So what was the plan then, Pop? You were just going to get

Declan to help you run us out of town and regain control?"

"You're the one who's wrong now, *son*." I don't miss the way he hisses out that last word. "I wasn't going to just run you out of town. I was going to take you out. Couldn't risk you coming back." That's exactly what Mac and I needed to hear. We meant nothing to him from the moment we entered this world, and he will mean nothing to us as he leaves it. But there's one more person here who needs closure, one more son whose life has changed because of this man's bullshit. It might be hard to hear, but Finn deserves to know.

"So it was all a lie, then? Our entire lives? What about him? Why take in another child when you didn't even want the two you had in the first place?" Liam moves his stare over to Finn, looking him up and down in disgust. I don't dare take my eyes off Liam, but I see it out of the corner of my eye. Finn's shoulders dropping ever so slightly, an imperceptible drop of his head. The man who has done everything in his power to seek the approval of a father he wishes he had. The man who had a life taken from him, only to be tricked into another.

"Your mother felt so guilty for what happened to Cian and Roisin. She used to say that the minute she saw Finn's face when we landed back in New York, she knew he belonged to her. I saw something else. When you found out what happened to your parents, I saw darkness take over your eyes. There was a power there. It was something these two never had. They had everything handed to them, but not you. You were a kid who would do whatever it took to belong somewhere, to not feel alone. It was a win-win either way. The world saw a doting father who took in a lonely orphan, and I gained someone else to do my bidding. I saw a tool to be used, nothing more."

I can't help it, I look over to Finn, my brother, and watch as a tear spills over his bottom lid and down his cheek, too stunned to even stop it.

That's it. We've heard enough. Reaching inside his coat pocket, I pull his handgun out of his holster. Dropping it, I nod over his shoulder at Mac. I promised I would let him have this, and I'm a man of my word. I have nothing left to say to this piece of shit. He doesn't deserve to hear how we'll be better men than he ever was. He doesn't deserve to hear how Mum will live a long and happy life without him. He doesn't deserve to hear how we will make Harper a part of our family. He doesn't deserve to hear how much I hate the man he's become. Because to hate him would mean I feel for him, and he doesn't deserve the satisfaction.

Slowly, Mac releases his grip on Liam's neck, and for a moment, I look at him in confusion, but as I see him raise his hands, I read his plan clear as day. I should have known Mac wouldn't want to use a gun for this. He wants to feel Liam's death beneath his hands. Just as relief washes over Liam's face, Mac leans down to whisper a final time, "Loscadh is dó ort."

The second he deciphers Mac's curse, his eyes widen, but it's too late. Mac snaps our father's neck in a millisecond, and he drops to the wood dock like a pile of rocks.

It's fucking done.

I'm relieved as I watch Mac's entire body relax almost instantly and look at Finn, only to find him still as a statue. *Shit.*

"We have to move guys." Mac's looking at Finn now too, no doubt as worried about him as I am. I planned to take Harper and meet Tanner and Logan back at the apartment. I don't want her out here longer than she needs to be. Mac and Finn would stay behind and take care of the bodies. We would call Mum once we dealt with Declan and knew she and Harper would be safe. However, the longer I stand here and look at Finn, I'm not so sure it's a good idea to have him help Mac. "Finn…" He doesn't even look at me, still staring at Liam's lifeless body. "Brother." I clap him on the shoulder, and his eyes dart up to me. His entire demeanor changes at once, and he's the calm and collected Finn we know. "You good?"

"Yeah. Yeah, I'm good."

"You sure? Because I can stay with Mac, you can take Harper back." Even though I really hope he doesn't. I'm itching to have my eyes on her and in my arms again. Literally, I can feel my skin breaking out in hives.

"No." He shakes his head like he's shaking himself out of a trance. "No. I'm good. Stick to the plan." He sheds his suit jacket, setting it on the wooden bench nearby, and begins rolling up his sleeves.

"Go, Ronan. Get Harper back. We'll clean up this and meet you guys back there."

As much as I want to get back to Harper, leaving them here feels wrong. "Go, Brother. We're good. I'd love nothing more than to throw this asshole into the river, and captain OCD over here thrives on cleaning up crime scenes." Finn and I both scoff at Mac, albeit half-hearted. I offer him a thankful smile, though, doing his best to lighten an extremely heavy situation.

"Alright. Keep me posted, and call me if you need anything."

"Got it." They both answer in unison.

I make my way back to the car. The second I open the door and climb in the seat, Harper's arms are around my neck. Her vanilla scent wrapping around me like a warm blanket. "Are you guys okay? I was so worried. Once you walked out onto the dock, I couldn't see anything. I wanted to come out so bad, but you told me to stay in the car. I didn't get out, Ronan. I stayed in the car." I feel a few stray drops of water against my neck. I rub my hand up and down her back, trying to calm her breathing.

"We're as good as can be expected. He's gone."

"I stayed in the car, Ronan."

"Shhh. I know, Baby. You did so good." She pulls her head from my neck and takes my face in her hands. Her mouth slants over mine, and she gives me a deep kiss. "We're okay, Baby. We're okay." I mumble against her lips. Her mouth lifts from mine, and her misty eyes look over my body, reassuring herself that I'm in one piece. "Let's get out of here, okay?"

"Are you sure Mac and Finn are okay? I feel like we should stay here and help them."

"No, Baby. The best place for you to be right now is back at the apartment, and we don't want to be anywhere near all of that. They have it under control."

Harper scrunches up her nose and sniffles. Shit, she has no idea how beautiful she really is. I have to stop myself from pulling her into the backseat and sinking into her soft and slow. Not being able to help myself entirely, I give the tip of her nose a quick kiss.

"Alright," she says, "let's go home."

Home.

40

Finn

It took Mac and I all of two hours to dismember three bodies, dispose of them, and get rid of any trace that we were ever here. There are no cameras anywhere down here so only some good old-fashioned cleaning was necessary. Which I didn't mind. It allowed me to get lost in my thoughts for a while.

Mac's over by the warehouse, burning the rags we used to clean up everything in a barrel. I walk back up the dock toward the bench where I left my jacket. Sitting down on it, I drop my head into my hands. I can feel myself spiraling. For as long as I can remember, I've felt like nothing but a burden. Just the orphan child that someone took in because they felt like they had to. The traumatized child that lost his parents to a monster. The tagalong. The extra kid that nobody ever looked at twice. Poor, lonely Finn. It's why I've always tried so hard to be perfect. If I was who Liam wanted me to be, if I did exactly as he asked, if I cleaned up the messes that other people made, I would be indispensable. I would matter. It's why I've always fought so hard to control myself. If my emotions got in the way, I'd get sloppy. I couldn't afford sloppy.

Then Harper came along.

Ever since I saw her that day in the bookstore, the thundering voices in my ear, screaming at me to always be perfect, were drowned out by her sweet voice, her smell, and her gorgeous green eyes. They were still there but ringing at a low hum, barely noticeable unless I focused on them. Now they're back, and I feel myself losing control. That one sentence from the man I idolized for years repeatedly rings through my head.

I saw a tool to be used, nothing more.

I tug at my hair in my hands, trying to recenter myself. *Nothing.* I roll my sleeves down, attach the buttons at the cuffs, throw my jacket back on, and wipe off the scuff of dirt on my knee. *Still nothing.* Closing my eyes, I imagine the feel of Harper's hand on my face, running her thumb across my cheekbone, staring at me as I try to count the freckles on her cheeks, but it's not enough. *Fucking nothing.*

I can feel the panic clawing at my chest as I drop my face back onto my hands. The voices in my head drowning out everything else as they get louder and louder.

You're just the extra.

You have no one that loves you.

You're weak.

You could disappear, and nobody would fucking care.

You're nothing but a burden.

I don't hear him walk up to me, but I feel his hand on my back as he silently sits beside me on the bench. "Talk to me, Brother."

"I'm not your brother," I mumble into my hands.

"Yes, you are, Finn. Just because we don't share the same blood doesn't make you any less of a brother to me than Ronan. Hell, I usually like you better than him anyway." I know Mac's joking, trying to diffuse the tension. Any other time I might offer him a smile, but not today.

Dropping my hands from my face, I continue to hang my head. "How are you so okay, and I'm the one sitting here falling apart? He was your dad, for fuck's sake."

"He stopped being my dad years ago. That man has been the bane of my existence for as long as I can remember. I haven't felt anything besides hate for him in a long time. The second I felt his neck snap beneath my hands, I felt like a free man. But I know that's not how it is for you." I can feel his eyes boring holes into the side of my face, but I can't bring myself to look at him. I don't want him to see how weak I am. "He was the man who took you in. He gave you a home when you had nothing. You looked up to him. I didn't want to take that away from you when you already lost so much."

I turn my face to look at him now, expecting to find pity. Instead, I see only understanding. "I wish I would have seen who he really was sooner. I wish I could have helped you… Helped Emma. You guys didn't deserve that, and I was too blind to see it."

He shakes his head. "Don't man. We have enough things in our past holding us back, don't let something *he* did add to it. What happened between him and I are my demons to fight, not yours."

Mac moves from the bench and stands in front of me, holding out his hand. I grab it with my opposite hand and let him pull me up. Still firmly gripping my hand, he wraps his other arm around my shoulders, hugging me. I'm a little bit taller than him, but right now, he feels much larger than me. I stand stunned for a split second. We're not the type of men that hug, but as the seconds tick by, I relax into his embrace. "Listen to me," he commands in my ear. "You are not a burden, Finn. I know you tried hard to be a perfect man for him, to fit into our family. But you didn't need to then, and you don't need to now. We want you here. Not because of what we can get out of you but because you are our brother. End of. *You're our brother, and we love you.*" His last words are barely a whisper but ring the loudest through my head.

I take a deep breath as I let them sink in. I know a part of me will always have to fight this battle, just like having my parents taken from me, but I know Mac's telling the truth. I know he and Ronan are my brothers, and I know they love me. I love them. And Harper… *fuck, Harper.* I've never felt like I belonged somewhere more than when she's in my arms. If there's one thing I'm sure of in this world, it's that they are meant to be my family. I love them. I—I love her.

Just admitting that to myself steals my breath away. I need to tell her. I need to tell her tonight. I've had enough love stolen from me to know it's not something I should waste. I'm not an emotional man, but for her, I would scream it from the fucking rooftops. For her, I would do *anything.*

I pull back from Mac's embrace, instantly wishing we were back at the apartment. Giving his hand a firm squeeze, I softly smile. "I love you guys, too. Thank you." I'm not entirely sure what I'm saying thank you for, whether for comforting me in this moment or always treating me like I belong. But it doesn't matter. He knows, and now, I do too.

"Don't mention it, man." He gives me a light shove.

"Seriously, don't. Tell Ronan I hugged you, and your ass is fucking grass." This time I laugh at his joke.

"Alright." I button the front of my jacket. "Let's go home."

Mac and I start walking down the dock toward his Audi when my phone rings in my pocket. Assuming it's Ronan checking in on us *again,* I pull it out and answer without looking. "I just texted you twenty minutes ago. We're still fine and on our way back."

"Hello, Finn." The deep timber on the other end of the line stops me in my tracks, causing the hair on the back of my neck to stand on end. Mac looks at me in concern. I hold my hand up at him and put the phone on speaker. "Who is this? How did you get this number?" All of us have secure phones. Our numbers aren't available to anyone unless we give them away. Harper's now too.

"I'm hurt, Finn, really. As someone who altered the course of your life so drastically, I would have figured you'd recognize my voice." Mac's brows pinch in confusion, mirroring mine. "I got your number from a friend of yours. Logan, is it?"

Mac and I look at each other in panic at the mention of Logan's name. He points to the Audi, and we barrel toward it. Mac starts it and speeds away in seconds as he pulls out his phone to call Ronan. "Who the fuck are you?"

"Knew your parents a long time ago. Was such a shame I had to kill them."

"Declan." I can feel my hand tighten around my phone, gripping it to the point it might shatter in my hands. I look over as Mac frantically tries Ronan's phone again as he weaves through the city streets toward the apartment.

"The one and only. I'm going to get right to it. I'm assuming you don't have much time. I know you have to get home to see my granddaughter."

"You'll never fucking touch her." My carefully disguised temper is now raging like an inferno.

"You see, that's where you're wrong. No matter where you go, no matter where you hide, no matter what you do… I will get her. I have my ways."

"You mean like Liam McDermott? Joke's on you, asshole. We figured that one out. His body is currently in pieces at the bottom of a river."

A heavy sigh fills the car, along with Mac's heavy breathing. "That's unfortunate, but no matter. He was just a small pawn and is easily replaceable. If I'm honest, I wasn't relying on him too much."

When Ronan doesn't answer a third time, Mac's hand slams down on the steering wheel before calling Tanner. It doesn't even pay to call Harper. When she's asleep, it's like waking the dead. Once the phone rings out, Mac drops his onto his lap and looks at me shaking his head. Desperation and sadness fill his eyes. Terror runs through me, and I fight the urge to vomit as bile crawls up my throat. Mac quickly refocuses on the road as he flies through the city streets, trying to return to the apartment as quickly as possible. But with New York traffic, we're easily still thirty minutes away.

That's too long.

Declan's voice cuts through the car like a gunshot. What he says next is enough to shatter my already fragile heart into a million pieces. "Tell me, boy. How does Harper like her new security detail?"

41

Ronan

Harper fell asleep shortly after we got home. As soon as we entered the apartment, I greeted Logan and Tanner, who had met us here, put her in the shower, and tucked her into my bed. As much as I wanted to spend hours inside her, I could see exhaustion all over her face. She needed the rest. We're used to these things, but our sweet girl isn't. I knew she would be worried about us, but I didn't realize how much. I'd be lying if I said it didn't make the sadist in me a little happy.

Once Harper was asleep, I crawled into bed next to her and caught up on some work on my laptop, not wanting to go to sleep until Mac and Finn were back. Finn texted a few minutes ago, letting me know they were just finishing up and would leave shortly. I really thought that the events of the last five hours would have more of an effect on me, but surprisingly, I'm relatively unaffected. I'm sure that speaks more to my level of sanity than anything, but I don't give a fuck. We did what needed to be done to keep our family safe, and I will never apologize for that. Now all that's left to do is deal with the asshole that's after our girl.

I'll send a message out to Patrick in the morning letting him know that our end of the plan is done so he can start up on his. I'm sure he'll be shocked at how quickly we got that taken care of.

I begin answering an email and realize I need some paperwork I left in my office. Before sliding out from under the covers, I lean down and softly kiss Harper's forehead, and she wiggles deeper into the mattress. "I just have to run to my office quick, Baby. I'll be right back."

"Hmmm. Okay. Love you."

"Baby? Did you just…" She doesn't hear me, already back to softly snoring. Meanwhile, I'm completely frozen.

Did she just say she loved me?

Holy shit.

Harper Hayes just told me she loved me.

Holy. Shit.

I want to grab her shoulders and shake her awake. I want to say it back over and over and over again. I knew I loved her the night Finn and Mac took her to the club. The night she and I stopped fighting how we felt about one another. I've never felt for a woman what I feel for her. I'm not an easy man to love. None of us are. I push and argue with her every step of the way. But what I love most about her is that she pushes back. She fights back. As someone who wasn't meant to be part of this life, someone who is so caring and kind, she holds her own against me when others would back down. She doesn't bend. She doesn't break.

I let her sleep, though. I'll tell her in the morning when I know she'll hear my every word.

Softly, I slide out from under the covers and leave my room, quietly closing the door behind me. As I walk down the hall, I notice I don't see Tanner or Logan anywhere. *That's strange.* I walk through the kitchen toward my office when I step in something wet.

"What the—"

My body runs cold as I look down to find Tanner dead on the floor, blood pouring from a cut across his throat.

Not wasting another second, I turn to run back toward Harper. As I reach the mouth of the hallway, I see Logan standing against the wall. I couldn't see him there when I came from the other direction. I don't react fast enough, and his fist moves toward my face. Between the blow and my feet slick from Tanner's blood, I fall back on my ass. Before I have a chance to get my bearings, Logan towers over me. "Sorry, man. Boss's orders."

It all seems to happen in slow motion. I watch as he rears his arm back, hand wrapped around the barrel of his gun, only to bring it forward and slam the handle across my face.

It only takes a split second for darkness to take over, but as it does, the only thing I see is a pair of forest-green eyes staring back at me.

Harper, Baby.

* * *

Harper

Holy shit!

I sit up straight in bed, realizing I just told Ronan I loved him and went back to sleep! I slap my palm to my forehead. "Harp, you idiot."

That is *not* how I wanted to do that, but in my comatose stupor, it just slipped out. Maybe he didn't hear me? No, no. He definitely heard me. Ronan misses nothing. "Stupid, stupid, stupid." I hit my forehead with my hand at each word.

There's no taking it back now, but I can go to him and look him in the eyes as I say it. Flinging the covers off of me, I move toward Ronan's dresser and throw on one of his shirts, making sure it covers enough that Tanner and Logan don't get a free show. I notice the pile of rings he took off before bed on top of the dresser. I pick up one of my favorites, a silver signet ring with an "M" on it that he always wears on his pinky, and slide it onto my pointer finger. I smile down at it, a reminder of the men I have fallen so hard for. I mindlessly spin it around with my thumb as I head toward the door.

As I reach for the handle, it swings open toward me. "Logan? Is everything okay?" They usually stay in the main living area and *never* come into the rooms, especially without permission.

I watch as he reaches into his inside jacket pocket and pulls out a syringe full of liquid. Immediately, I back up toward the bathroom, wanting to lock myself inside. Logan is quicker than me, though, and as I spin around to get away from him, he's already on me. His arm wraps around my chest, holding me tight to him, my back to his front. I don't have time to beg or plead as he shoves the needle into my neck. My vision begins to blur in seconds, and I feel my body go weak in his arms. I hear Ronan's phone ring from the bedside table, Mac's picture filling the screen, but I can't get my legs to move in its direction. If I could only reach it… If I could just talk to Mac, he could save me.

It's wishful thinking. I can't move.

Logan scoops me up in his arms and carries me toward the elevator. The last thing I see before darkness takes over is Ronan's lifeless body lying on the floor.

"Baby…"

TO BE CONTINUED…

Acknowledgments

There are so many people I want to thank, I honestly don't even know where to start. Dangerously Safe is my first novel, and I never thought I would actually be able to finish it. There have been so many ups and downs in my adult life, and I have continuously struggled to find my passion. To find that *thing* that sets my soul on fire. This book, writing these characters, was that thing. Any thank you's I write in here will never be enough, but I am certainly going to try.

First, to anyone who reads this book. I cannot thank you enough. Like any author, the thought of releasing this to the public was absolutely terrifying, but the thought of it having the effect on you that some of my favorite books have had on me made it worth it. Writing is hard… really fucking hard. There were times when I wondered what the hell I was doing or if this was all a gigantic waste of my time. But I fell in love with the story, and I fell in love with the characters. My love for them and my drive to find my place in this world pushed me through. My only hope is that you love them as much as I do.

I poured my soul into this book, and there has been no greater joy. I hope you come out of this feeling like you experienced it right along with me. I appreciate all of you for taking this journey with me.

Next are the two people who worked through this book

with me from start to finish. Without them, I'm not sure I would have ever had the courage to finish it. They were the first to read it and talked with me *endlessly* about the characters and plots, answered my questions, and offered advice. They never once judged the dirty inner workings of my brain, and for them, I am forever grateful.

Samantha. You're my sister and my very best friend. We have walked through this life hand in hand, and I couldn't have done any of it without you. You have always been my number one fan, no matter what, and have shown me a love I could never experience from another. I can't wait to continue laughing until we cry for the rest of this life and into the next (and share endless amounts of *New Girl* Tiktoks). Thank you, thank you, thank you.

Emily. My sister from another mister. Using the word friend doesn't even feel like an accurate description. You have a piece of my soul, and I truly don't know where I would be in this life without you. No matter where life takes either of us, how long we go without talking, or the new friends that we make… you are always a constant. I know I can go to you for anything without judgment, and that is a gift I will cherish forever.

I love you both more than I could ever put into words. I don't know what I did in this life to deserve people like the two of you, but I'll never take it for granted. Dangerously Safe would not be what it is if it weren't for the both of you.

To my love. You are my person. Now, forever, and always. I know I've said it a million times, but I'll say it a million more. Thank you for everything you do for our family. We wouldn't have the life that we do without you. You work hard to support us every single day and have given me the opportunity to chase my dreams. I can say that, without a doubt, without you by my side, I don't know where or who I would be today. You pick me up every time I fall and chase away all of my self-doubt (that's a full-time job in itself;). I could fill up page after page with what you mean to me, but this book is long enough already. So for now, I'll just say... I love you.

To Mom and Dad. I hope you didn't read a single word after this page (or hear about its contents), but if you do... I'm so sorry. But, uhhhh... Thanks for making me:)

For everyone else... Thank you.

About the Author

S.R. Clark is an indie author who lives in West Virginia with her husband, toddler, and hound dog. She writes reverse harem/dark romance books. She has a soft spot for characters who live unapologetically for themselves and who will lay down their lives for the ones they love. When she's not writing, she loves getting lost in a good book, cooking/baking, and exploring with her family.

Also by S.R. Clark

Dangerously Kept

After finally allowing herself to love again, Harper wakes up miles away from the men that have kept her safe, and in the hands of those determined to destroy her from the inside out. Unsure of whether or not she can rely on Ronan, Mac, and Finn to save her, Harper must find the strength to free herself.

But if she does, how is she meant to face what comes next?

With a world of unknowns hanging in the balance, Ronan, Mac, and Finn know two things for certain. They are willing to burn the world down around them to get her back, and just as they own her heart, she owns theirs.

They just need to figure out how to keep her.

The Prices We Pay

As CEO of Vittori Enterprises, Luca Vittori has made his fair share of enemies both in the corporate world and in less... legal business. But with the help of his teammates, best friends and family—Enzo, Dante, and Sebastian—no one has been a worthy opponent. That is, until they're forced to hire a new employee in the tempting form of Josephine Jenkins. The four of them rapidly have to decide whether or not their feelings for Josephine and one another are worth the risk.

Will love destroy everything they've built, or will it make it stronger?

Josephine Jenkins is a woman who truly marches to the beat of her own drum. After running from memories better left buried, Joe made a life for herself in New York City. She finally had the life she always wanted for herself. Everything was perfect... until she took a job at Vittori Enterprises. Upon her arrival she quickly learns the four men who captured her attention have more going on behind closed doors than they lead on, and if she isn't careful, they could be the end of the life she so carefully crafted.

Is falling for them worth the price she'll have to pay in the end?

Strong Side

Clayton Aldrich is everything I'm not, and everything I despise. He's rich, never had to work for anything a day in his perfect life, is the pretty boy on campus, and is always doing everything he can to get under my skin. But when we're forced to become partners I have no choice but to set my predisposed feelings for him aside. However, as the season progresses, two things become abundantly clear. There's more to Clay than meets the eye, and my feelings for him don't appear to be so black and white.

My entire life has been mapped out for me since the day I was born. Major in business, dedicate every moment of spare time to volleyball, win the Olympics, and when the time comes, take over my father's company. And the only part of that plan that didn't make my skin crawl was playing the sport I loved. Rockwell Campos, the infuriatingly cynical man I feel an inexplicable draw toward whenever he's near, thinks he has me all figured out. But, when we unexpectedly become partners our senior year, Rocky shows me there's more to life than sacrificing who you are and who you want to be in order to be part of a family. Sometimes the families we find are stronger than the ones born in blood.

The two of us may share the same goal, but the question remains... is our strong side, strong enough?